SWORD OF HONOUR

Also by David Kirk:

Child of Vengeance

SWORD OF HONOUR

DAVID KIRK

SIMON & SCHUSTER

London · New York · Sydney · Toronto · New Delhi

A CBS COMPANY

First published in Great Britain by Simon & Schuster UK Ltd, 2015
A CBS COMPANY

1 3 5 7 9 10 8 6 4 2

Simon & Schuster UK Ltd
1st Floor
222 Gray's Inn Road
London WC1X 8HB

www.simonandschuster.co.uk

Simon & Schuster Australia, Sydney
Simon & Schuster India, New Delhi

A CIP catalogue record for this book is available from the British Library

HB ISBN: 978-1-47110-244-8
TPB ISBN: 978-1-47110-245-5
EBOOK ISBN: 978-1-47110-247-9

Typeset by Hewer Text UK Ltd, Edinburgh
Printed and bound in Great Britain by CPI Group (UK) Ltd, Croydon, CR0 4YY

For Rona,
As much as a book of this sort can be for her.

'Do not mindlessly follow the way and customs of the world.'

Fifteenth precept of *Dokkodo* (*The Way of Walking Alone*)
Musashi Miyamoto, 1645

Colour was everything, colour was all.

The Forger of Souls looked up into the night sky and saw only the vast blackness, the white of stars and the grey of the shadows upon the autumn moon. The night was still and endless, and amongst it all he thought himself invisible where he sat upon the hillside.

This was good; he needed this blackness. It was a canvas to contrast against.

'O Forger of Souls,' came a voice, 'I believe the temperature to be adequate.'

The Forger turned and saw the dull red outline of his apprentice, lit by what burnt behind him in the small hut. The drapes and the doors of the building were cast open, and the roar of the furnace within could be heard.

'Good,' said the Forger. 'Let us go, boy.'

The Forger was an old man, and rose stiffly. He had a name of course, which his wife and his sons and daughters knew. But to everyone else he was only the Forger; what else could they call him without insult? The apprentice in turn was thirty-four years old, but in their art was still fit only to be called 'boy'. This the apprentice knew, and did not disagree with.

The pair of them went to the hut and slid in, quickly closing the doors behind them and then pulling down the heavy velvet drape, sealing them in darkness within darkness save for that which burnt. As he turned inwards towards the furnace the Forger had to shield his eyes against the light for some time, feeling the familiar heat against the back of his hand, which had long ago been scoured of any hair.

A pair of boys – actual boys, voices unbroken – worked a huge standing bellows, using the entirety of their bodies to force it through its wheezing motion, air heaving constant into a small pile of coals the flames of which burnt just shy of blue. From underneath this pile the blackened handle of a perfectly straight rod of metal was clasped in a long, heavy pair of tongs. A trough of water stood nearby.

Wordlessly the Forger took an iron poker and began to concentrate the coals along the centre line, underneath which the rod lay, and he snarled at the boys to quicken the bellows. They were sweating and exhausted, having worked for near an hour already, but now they flung their weight with renewed determination. Their eyes shimmered with youthful awe; they could hardly believe that they had been chosen by the Forger to be a part of this.

The apprentice, who many years ago had worn the same expression as he had worked the bellows, took the pair of tongs in his hands and stood braced and ready. He and the Forger had worked on the rod for near two months already. They had taken the ingots of tamahagane steel that looked like no more than ossified turds, had heated and hammered them and then assembled them like a mosaic into one long line segregated by which pieces the Forger deemed would yield hard metal and those that would yield soft. More hammering, more heat, forcing the steel together, and then the resultant rod they had flattened and folded nine times.

That was the science and labour of it; what came tonight was the art.

The Forger needed the eye of a painter now, for the metal rod needed to be heated to the exact temperature, and the only way to judge this was by the colour it glowed. He had heard some men describe this desired shade as that of the rising sun, others as burnished gold or persimmon peel. The Forger could not say with any clarity what colour he knew to be correct because he was not a man of words, but over the course of decades he had come to know it fundamentally.

He nodded at his apprentice, and the man pulled the rod outwards from the furnace and held it at arm's length up against the perfect blackness at the back of the hut. The rod glowed cerise through the ashen murk of the clay slurry with which it had been coated. The Forger shook his head, and so back in it went. The Forger tossed more coals on, rifled through those already burning, sparking them into greater flame, and shouted at the two boys for more air. Their little bodies bounced, bruises forming on their shoulders, and the flames roared and roared until the Forger saw in them the purple-blue of the kakitsubata iris that flowered on the slopes in the early summer.

Twice more the rod was withdrawn and examined, and twice more it went back in. The third time it was so very close, so very near that the Forger took the tongs from his apprentice and began to move the rod back and forth underneath the coals himself, twisting it from side to side where he knew it needed to be heated just that little bit more and then . . .

He hauled it out and offered it up to the darkness, frail old arms quivering with the weight. Vivid orange leading into glorious yellow rife with shimmering albescence – the rod sang rightness. It was time, and so the Forger swivelled on his heels and plunged the rod into the water.

Steam rose, and through the tongs he could feel the pull of the metal warping. The rod squealed, bucked first forwards and then back as hard and soft metal fought against each other, and then finally settled into a long and elegant curve, and thus the great transubstantiation was complete.

A sword was born.

When dawn had come they had scraped the clay from the cooled metal, and the four of them knelt covered in soot and ash and their hair in sweated disarray as the Forger held the unsharpened blade upwards to the rising sun.

There was no religion here, not for this sword just quite yet. It was simple veneration and pride; the heavens were the heavens and men were men, and yet, of all the millions and millions of creatures upon this plane, it was men alone who had looked into the long dark chaos of the earth and sought to understand it, to improve it, to perfect it.

The Forger held the immutable symbol of this fact skywards, and all bathed in the light.

PART I

Wake

Late in the year, Fifth Year of the Era of Keicho

Chapter One

Hear it! Proclaim it!

The sundered realm is made anew, the shattered gem whole once more! Upon the dales of Sekigahara east of the Great Lake Biwa a tower of thirty thousand heads stands in testament!

The Armies of the East are triumphant! Proclaim it!

Take it to the ashen slopes of the sleeping volcanoes spread beneath the amber sunsets of Kyushu, call it to the birds there as they flock south so they too may bear it forth across the waves! Carry it northwards, to the very tips of frigid Michinoku and the shores of alien Yezo, scream it so that the bearded Ainu hear it clustered in their frozen holes!

All of Japan! Hear it!

Oh, the very land beneath our feet hums that we should live in such a time! A Shogunate dawns once more, the progenitor of order, the bestower of benevolent peace, the way of things restored to how they ought to be! Serenity in the heavens, joy upon the earth!

Hail his militant grace the most noble Lord Ieyasu Tokugawa! Hail his imperial and undying majesty the Son of Heaven!

Swords at his sides, armour heavy upon him, onwards Bennosuke Shinmen walked in solitude. He had left battle behind him, left all behind him.

A glancing blow from an unseen weapon had split his scalp, and the clotted wound now throbbed in time with the beat of his heart. The white of his left eye had turned crimson. The flesh upon his legs was scraped raw by the pinching of his greaves, knees and ankles calcified as he clambered over bush and trunk and waded through scrubland.

But he was alive. That alone was important, he knew now. He smiled as he suffered. Sekigahara, his enlightenment.

What things he had endured that day. Rout and defeat and the slaughter of those men that he had called comrade for two years. The army he fought for was vanquished, the powers that army served laid low. But it was not a defeat for him – not for himself, not for *he* as an individual. He had fled the battle and yet no words like coward nor any sense of shame at all occurred to him because he knew that he had not left in base terror but rather because his eyes had finally been opened.

He had seen hundreds of samurai killed, thousands, and in their bleak end spread before him he had realized the futility of servitude to callous Lords that sought nothing more than selfish power. Thousands of men bringing their own meaningless deaths down upon themselves through the act of choosing to follow these Lords, choosing to obey them, and, even more than that, thinking such things glorious and proper. This, the Way of the samurai.

Not for him, no longer.

This Bennosuke had sworn to himself in the midst of the carnage, and he swore it to himself again now a thousand times over; all Lords, all thought of service or deference to them, he had left behind him to die alongside all those that thought such things righteous. The revelation was profound.

He walked through wilderness headed for nowhere, but such was his rapture that he did not care. *He* was choosing to go – he alone. Bennosuke hauled himself up slopes, pulling at roots and creeping vines where he could. The gold leaves of autumn sighed deep around his feet. Hours passed. Gradually the pain from the wound on his head grew worse. His vision began to blur and eventually he vomited.

Clouds were gathering above, threatening a great rain. He looked up at them in the dimming light, but they did not seem to him foreboding. They were there, as he was here; neither had any right over the other.

With no energy to go further, he simply sat and watched as they darkened and burst, and as he felt the drops fall upon his brow he did not run for shelter. The rain grew heavy and it washed the blood from him, washed the filth from him, and he held open his mouth and let it fill with the water, and nothing he could remember had tasted so real, so immediate.

A rare moment then that men meditated many hours seeking; a sense of perfect attunement.

Dark now, full night, only the sound of the rain falling through the half-bared branches, landing heavy and fat on the metal and wood and leather of his cuirass and spaulders. He sank onto his back, nestled himself into a cleft in the earth half covered by a fallen trunk in which leaves had gathered and now formed a soft bed for him. As he sheltered there, lying in wonderful solitude, it occurred to him then that this was a good place for Bennosuke Shinmen to die.

Bennosuke Shinmen had wanted to be a samurai above all else, after all. Like breath clearing from a mirror, the name to which he had been born now clarified its stark obsolescence.

No, what he had done was choose to live, and in that choice redefined himself. Choice mattered. There was a name that he had used, that until now he had worn only as disguise. But it seemed to him natural to *become* this name now because, ultimately, it was he who had chosen it for himself.

Musashi Miyamoto.

It felt good. It felt right.

In the darkness, Musashi smiled.

Sleep came soon, one that he knew he would wake from, and for that time all was well.

But how quickly the world imposed itself back upon him.

He was drawn back into consciousness by the sound of a man howling in rage and despair. The blackness was entire, the stars and the moon stolen by the clouds. Only the screaming and the sounds of the rain told Musashi that he had woken at all.

Musashi listened for some time. There were no words in the man's wailing, just a racked and torturous lament that had no end. Whoever it was did not sound far away, doubtless oblivious of the presence of any other, such was the dark. Musashi felt the chill of the rain now, his limbs numbed. He tried to rise. His hands groped blind and his feet found uneven purchase, a mess of leaves and roots and mud beneath.

'Hello?' he called.

The howling stopped immediately. Musashi peered towards its source but it was hopeless. He could not discern his hands before his face, let alone some distant figure amidst the trees.

After a few heartbeats he called out again, and this time the man answered tentatively, 'Who is it that skulks out there?'

'I am not skulking,' said Musashi, and thought for some time about what to say next. The voice waited in guarded silence.

Eventually, Musashi said, 'I was at the battle.'

'Were you?'

'I was.'

'Are you alone?'

'I am. Are you?'

'I am.'

They were both of them hesitant to offer any more. Was there a harder thing to trust than an unseen voice in the night? Yet the pain in the man's voice had been too real, and so Musashi put aside his own suspicion.

'My name is Musashi Miyamoto,' he said, and how natural it seemed. 'I fought for the western coalition.'

'As did I,' said the man after a moment.

'What is your name?'

'That matters not now,' said the man. 'What Lord do you serve?'

'That matters not.'

'No. It doesn't, does it? It's all of it destroyed.'

The rain spattered off Musashi's armour, a cold rhythm on the metal. 'Where are you? Shall I come to you?'

'I am here.'

'Keep talking, I'll find you.'

'And speak of what?'

'Of what you will.'

Musashi began to try to move towards the voice. Against his face he felt bare branches and he stumbled and slipped over unseen obstacles. His longsword at his waist caught against something, twisted him.

'You'll not find me in this dark, and I do not ask you to,' came the man's voice. 'I ask only of you to bear witness to something.'

'To what?'

'I hereby pledge my soul against the Lord Kobayakawa. It was his betrayal that doomed us to defeat. He, the insidious thief that stole our dignity from us, that son of a whore, that son of a . . .' The voice cracked in rage, and was silent. When it spoke again it was leveller: 'For these reasons I protest his existence to all creation and pray for his damnation to the myriad hells. My ghost shall haunt him mercilessly until it has its rightful vengeance.'

'Ghost?' said Musashi, hands closing on something slick, wet moss upon a bough, perhaps. 'Why would you speak of ghosts? You live yet. Are you wounded?'

'No.'

'Then why do you speak of ghosts?'

'Only one thing remains left undone,' said the voice.

Seppuku. Self-immolation. Emblem of the Way.

Nausea returned to Musashi's empty stomach. 'Do not do that,' he said.

'It is all that remains.'

'It is not.'

'Why should I live? All is gone. Now, I am no more than the stink of smoke after arson.'

'No!' said Musashi. 'No, you are not.'

'If you would like, I in turn shall hear any final vows you should care to make.'

'Do not perform seppuku!' said Musashi. 'Wait for me, I'll—'

He forced himself through the blackness. He slipped and fell, felt the stomach of his armour smash onto something hard like rock. Though he was shielded, the shock of it still hurt. He hauled himself to his feet once more.

'No seppuku for me,' said the voice. 'I have not the implements to observe the ritual properly. I shall settle for opening my throat. It feels as though I am already in oblivion in this darkness.'

'You can't,' said Musashi. 'You mustn't.'

'I am of the Way. What else is there to do?'

Musashi's body contorted itself around the sightless realm. For all his effort the voice did not sound any closer. The wound on his head was throbbing once more, the pain searing, stealing words from him: 'Don't. Don't do it. Don't!'

'What are you, some deceptive spirit? A tengu haunting me and leading me from truth? No. That cannot be. Tengu are old and wily. You have the voice of a child.'

'I'm sixteen. I'm a man.'

'Indeed,' said the voice, and it laughed cruelly. 'How is it you think you stand in a position to advise me? I am twice your age, boy.'

'I understand enough,' called Musashi. 'My father committed seppuku at command of his Lord. He thought he would save his honour, but he was betrayed and died disgraced instead. If he had chosen to live, he could have . . . No. Why wonder? He didn't. He chose to annihilate himself.'

'What was your father's crime?'

'None, he performed it on account of . . .' *Me*. 'He performed it, and now all men speak ill of him. His name was Munisai Shinmen.'

'I have heard of him.'

'And what have you heard?'

'That he died a coward.'

'He was not. I swear to you this. The agony he endured with that sword in his stomach . . . Yet, because he is dead, he cannot contest this, and that agony was for nothing. No. Stupidity was his only crime. This is what you are assenting to. Do not do it.'

'You do not sound as though you honour your father.'

The hate that surfaced as he thought of Munisai was familiar, but could not be spoken. 'I avenged him,' Musashi said. 'Just this day I killed the man responsible. After years. The clan Nakata, you know them?'

'The burgundy men. Sworn to the Ukita.'

'Yes. The heir. Hayato – I cut his head from him after the battle. I had the chance to kill him two years before but it would have cost me my life. But I did not, and I hated myself for living. But I lived, I chose to live and I will live, and in that I have everything I need.' He felt exhausted, Musashi, felt hollow, but sudden energy came as he thought of what had inspired him. 'The battle! Were you not at the battle earlier? Did you not see those thousands of bodies? Why should you aspire to be that? A corpse is not godly.'

The voice was not swayed: 'So you will seek to shirk your honour.'

'What honour?' called Musashi, voice breaking with the effort and the pain. 'The honour of a . . . The Way, the Way of death, that honour? No! It is an act of stupidity! The greatest stupidity! Nothing less than that! Nothing more! Seppuku, a-a-a mist, a black mist, that some spirit had blown into the minds of men! What is the point of birth at all if your ultimate act is to negate yourself, all you have done, all you might do? My father, ended by it! Thousands, millions, who knows how many? Ended! Think of all they could have achieved instead of casting everything aside! Choosing to cast everything aside! Bad enough that a Lord would demand it, worse still that someone would choose to give it! You have a mind of your own, do not let it be broken over ancient words and codes only to find the same worthless nothingness as all that went before you!'

He found himself shuddering, from what he could not tell, cold or exhaustion or the pulsing throbbing wound that seemed to be digging into the centre of his skull, the wound that flared fierce with each word spoken; but when the samurai spoke next it was as though Musashi had said nothing at all: 'So you will not die this day?'

'No,' said Musashi. 'No I will not. I choose to live.'

'What do you intend, then, with this precious life of yours?'

Musashi had not considered this. 'I shall return home.'

'You can bear that?' the man laughed. 'To see your mother? To see your father? To see your wife and your sons and your friends and the men who rake your garden, see the hatred in their eyes when they learn that you live after such calamity?'

'Why would they hate me?'

'Because it is proper to hate those who linger after all is lost. No – not I. I cannot return home. I refuse to be hated.'

'What if they're wrong?'

'They're not wrong.'

'But you know them to be wrong. You said it yourself – the defeat was the fault of the clan Kobayakawa.'

The rain fell relentlessly, splitting the silence between them.

'That matters not,' said the voice eventually. 'Still they will hate.'

'But you know the truth.'

'What does that matter? A pearl that but a single person can see is no pearl at all.'

'That's . . .' said Musashi, and how his head throbbed and how he wanted to vomit. But still the blackness overwhelming, still his hands formless and powerless, and the words he needed now equally invisible to him.

'I have said all that is needed to be said,' said the voice. 'May my spirit find its vengeance.'

'Don't!' said Musashi.

Above the rain he thought he heard a sound that was equally as wet: a hiss that settled into a gurgle that settled into nothing. Musashi called to the man but received no reply, and eventually he accepted that he was gone. He felt his way to the floor, sat down amidst the mulch and felt the ache of his entire body.

'Why?' he called.

The world gave him no answer.

'Why?' he called again.

Around Musashi was a void, broad and seamless and the extents of it unknowable, and in this expanse his voice was frail and lonely, but he was not deterred. He asked his question again and again, rain sputtering from his lips, as though he were demanding the darkness to account itself to him.

The rain fell on.

Chapter Two

Kyoto

Upon the wall a yellowed scroll was hung, its ancient paper surrounded by a textile field of black thread patterned over rivermoss green. The brushstrokes of characters etiolated through centuries formed words still adhered, still adored:

The sword gives life. The sword gives death.

Beneath the scroll the newly forged longsword was arrayed naked, free of all trappings of guard and grip and pommel.

The tang remained dark and unpolished, indistinguishable almost from the black silk on which it rested, whilst the curve of the blade itself had been meticulously worked to assume the colour of calm water beneath a clouded noon sky.

Across that serene shade the reflection of the Shinto priest in his ochre robes warped as he paced his way around the sword in a slow circle, chanting long and deep. He swept a flail of paper folded into sacred lightning bolts over the unadorned weapon as he went, quick little motions, hands swift, voice sedulous. The Forger of Souls and the others there knelt and listened as formally as they would at a funeral, at a seppuku, and, though the words of the priest were so undulating and archaic that no man there save the priest himself could understand what it was exactly he intoned, they all understood that it was holy and sacred and so they listened faithfully, watched as he placed the flail down and began to scatter handfuls of salt around instead, still singing his incomprehensible hymn. It wound its way on until eventually the priest ceased abruptly, cast himself to the ground and placed his brow on the floor towards the sword.

Now the blade was purified, evil spirits banished, fit to be wielded without fear of malevolent possession.

The priest rose and retreated. The Forger of Souls moved forward on his knees, agony in his old joints yet his face entirely level, and took up the blade. He placed his gnarled right hand bare upon the dark of the tang, but with his left he took the blade in a folded length of hemp to avoid sullying it. He bore it aloft with ritual slowness, the cutting edge held towards himself to prevent veiled threat or insult to any other. He brought the steel close to his eyes and inspected it minutely. This examination was no more than appearance, as symbolic to the ritual as the salt. He had checked the sword countless times already since that dawn when he had held it skywards and would have not proclaimed it ready if the slightest hint of any imperfection lingered.

Duly, the Forger passed the sword on to the Polisher of Souls with ceremonial diligence, the pair of them bowing and raising the blade above their heads as they exchanged it. The Polisher then examined the blade with equal care not to level the edge or the point of the weapon at anyone else. It was he who had sharpened the weapon to its utmost keenness, he who over two weeks had taken the forge-darkened steel and made it shine with his vast collections of whetstones and buffstones and oils.

The Polisher saw something amiss, and from a small box withdrew tiny fragments of stone like ochre eggshell. These he placed on his thumb and, with the smallest of movements, rubbed them back and forth to fix a marring only his eye could see. He took a piece of cloth with oil upon it, wiped his fingerprints clean and then nodded, satisfied.

On the blade went, swaddled and passed like a holy babe to the Balancer of Souls and the Encaser of Souls, and though they did not work upon the steel itself they were just as vital in making it a sword proper. The Balancer made the collar, which sat between guard and cutting edge, copper-coated in etched gold, crucial both for weighting the sword so that it might cut true and for holding the blade suspended in the scabbard free of dulling contact with the wood. The Encaser in turn made that scabbard out of magnolia wood, as well as the accoutrements of the grip, the pommel and the guard, and, though they were all artists, he was the most artistic, his the realm of lacquer and embossing and carving.

The pair of them dressed the sword, collared it, pinned guard and grip and pommel to the steel with bamboo pegs, then slid the length of it into the scabbard. Thus the sword was placed back upon the stand and the silk, complete.

Forger, Polisher, Balancer and Encaser each produced their personal stone seal, dipped it in red ink, and the Recorder of Souls passed them his work. Yesterday he had made a rubbing of the sword, and then, freehanded, had shaded the grain and the pattern of the blade itself with impeccable detail. The drawing would be added to the annals of all the many weapons this smithy had produced, and one by one all the masters stamped their personal approval upon the paper.

A final bow from each of them, long and low and reverent, and then up to rest their weight upon their calves once more.

'It is done,' said the Forger of Souls.

'It is remarkable,' said Tadanari Kozei.

Tadanari was kneeling in impeccable formality. He was a samurai and almost entirely bald, the last vestige of hair he had clinging around the nape of his neck in a stubborn scrub. He had a sombre face, round and hard, a neatly trimmed grey-flecked beard that added weight to his jaw.

He was a master of the sword school of Yoshioka. He had brought a dozen men with him who knelt behind him in ranks, each as skilled as he was at hiding awe and respect behind the impenetrable masks of his face.

'May I, O Forger of Souls?' Tadanari asked.

The Forger nodded. Tadanari shuffled forward on his knees slowly, each increment of progress carefully measured, and then he bowed to the sword and spoke the proper words: 'Humbly I receive this privilege.'

Eyes still upon the floor, Tadanari took the sword and raised it above his head before he allowed himself to look upon it. He appreciated its weight in the palms of his hands, and then drew forth the blade from the scabbard. Mindful as the masters had been in which direction he let the edge and the point fall, he rested the flat of the sword on the back of his left forearm and the silk of his jacket there. Tadanari turned to the door open to the light of day and raised the sword as though it were an arquebus, sighting his eye down the flat of the blade.

He took a breath.

Slowly he began to twist it back and forth in the light, and now the true beauty and craftsmanship of the sword revealed itself. The texture of the grain of the metal laid bare, the layers where it had been folded writ in lines and motes that flashed in silver instants. The sweeping temper line of the hard cutting edge, a milky white sash set against the darker, softer metal of the flat, running in an undulating line like an erratic wave breaking along a lethal coast from base to point of the blade.

Flawless.

The breath that he had taken caught in Tadanari's throat. What he had paid for this sword could have bought a street full of houses, but he knew then that he was the one who had struck a scandalous bargain. What he held here was a thing for ages, for all the centuries yet to be.

'Come,' he said to his son. 'See.'

Ujinari was set at the head of the Yoshioka men. He pressed his brow to the ground and then advanced on his knees. That autumn he was in his seventeenth year, and had a longer, thinner face than his father, a slighter, taller build. Ujinari took the blade from Tadanari, spoke the same deferential words, looked at it in the light in an identical manner. His breath, however, escaped him, low and long and admiring.

'Your opinion?' asked Tadanari.

'I have held nothing more wonderful,' said Ujinari.

'It is not I you should be saying such to.'

Ujinari carefully placed the sword back on the stand and then turned and bowed low to the Forger and the other masters alongside him: 'Truly you are men of worth. I thank you for letting me witness all you have shown me this day. I could never hope to make something so beautiful.'

'Everything we do was taught to us, as we teach it in turn,' said the Forger. 'All it takes is the willingness to learn.'

'And decades of dedication,' said Tadanari.

The Forger bowed benevolently at the compliment.

Ujinari did not notice. He was staring at the sword wistfully. 'I believe you shall be the envy of all Kyoto with this at your side, Father.'

The bald samurai turned his head and pronounced sternly, 'An old man needs a sword that fine like a hag needs a cradle. The sword is yours.'

Awe unfurled behind Ujinari's eyes as he turned to stare at Tadanari, and then he lowered his brow to the floor. He held the bow for a long time before he spoke.

'I cannot begin to thank you,' he breathed.

Tadanari's face did not change in the slightest. He was the gift-giver, and he could neither express joy, for that would imply arrogant pride in his own magnanimity, nor feign some casualness or whimsy, for that would disparage the gift.

The boys who worked at the forge rolled up reed mats and stood them on their ends in the dusty yard outside, and

Ujinari set to testing the blade. He cut smoothly, his form long-studied and his arms able, passing the steel on the diagonal through the mats. The other men of the Yoshioka watched on, called encouragement or congratulation, marvelled to one another at the beauty of the sword.

Tadanari was sitting on a stool outside of the glare of the noon sun. Free of the solemn ritual of the hall, he was smiling openly as he watched his son's ability. It was he that had dictated the mood for them all, and even though he was jovial it did not mean that those beneath him were freed of any protocol. The lesser samurai there merely had to assume the protocols of joviality, the practised ways of expressing it, all that the collective might reassure itself that it was indeed in a time of ease. They slouched upon stairs, they sat cross-legged in the dust, they stood with thumbs in belts, but they were not relaxed.

The samurai standing closest to Tadanari jerked his chin at the sword Ujinari wielded.

'Master,' the man said, and he shuffled his shoulders and scuffed his feet as he sought some fresh-considered posture of what was accepted as casual, 'unless I see it wrong, the engraving there upon the flat of the blade – that is the sword of Saint Fudo, no?'

The carving he spoke of lay on one side only just above the golden collar and ran half the length of the blade. A sword within a sword, but no samurai weapon this. An ancient sword, a foreign sword, a single-handed weapon straight and double-edged.

What he asked was not a genuine question, of course, and Tadanari knew this. There was no real chance of an error in identification, not with an icon as strong as that. It was merely spoken because it offered the chance for Tadanari to say, 'Keen eyes as always.'

This compliment in turn allowed another, returned and magnified: 'As I thought. Houken. The Cutter of Delusions. A wise choice, master, yes, but of course you in your wisdom would choose well. Provident.'

Mutually flattered, the two of them took to nodding in satisfaction at different tempos as Ujinari continued to cut.

'The Cutter of Delusions,' repeated the samurai, because something further needed to be said.

'That which purges the fallible man of the snares of the mortal dimension.'

'A strong meaning.'

'The great Saint judges us all.'

'Of course. Your grandsons will hold that sword and see that mark, and know the same.'

'My great-great-grandsons.'

They spoke as though in platitudes and smiled and nodded on, and yet inside Tadanari a well-hidden resonance hummed. He allowed himself a momentary fantasy, saw some distant descendent in place of Ujinari, and, though this conjured man might not know Tadanari as anything more than a name scrawled upon some yellowed sheaf of genealogy, he would be armed, be samurai on Tadanari's account, and that was everything.

This the deeper satisfaction. But he did not allow himself to wallow in the conceit of centuries yet to be. Saint Fudo laughed at those who did so. Instead, Tadanari sat back and watched Ujinari for who he was, what he was, and this was fine enough.

They, all of them there. His men. His school. He did not bear the name and was not the dynastic head, but that man Naokata Yoshioka was his finest friend, and he served as the foremost teacher. Over their kimonos each of the Yoshioka samurai wore a jacket of silk dyed in the same peculiar colour. In the shade of the halls within, the garments had seemed a muted brown, but here outside in the light the peaks of folds became a vivid green. A unique dual tone, emblematic of the school, which no person could describe better than as the colour of tea.

It unified them, and yet even so one man wearing this shade sat separate. He kept a practised silence, and simply mimicked the expressions of the others as though he were not apart from them. The boys of the forge peered at him from around the corners of walls, fascinated at his oddity. The samurai's skin was in tone somewhere between honey and persimmon wood. His eyes were almost the colour of moss, the brown frail and tinted. Both were the opposite of what they should have been: pale skin, black gaze.

'The Foreigner, the Foreigner,' the boys named him in their whispers, and the samurai elected not to hear them.

Tadanari saw the boys in their furtive gawping, and saw the dark-skinned man ignoring them. It put him in mind of other duties he had to attend to, and his interest in the spectacle of his son and everything he represented waned. His face grew serious and he adjusted himself upon the stool, assumed a more formal posture, and then he beckoned the dark-skinned man over.

The samurai heeded the command, bowed, knelt beside his superior's stool on one knee. 'Master Kozei.'

'Sir Akiyama,' said Tadanari, 'I have duty for you.'

'I await your command.'

Tadanari did not look at Akiyama whilst he spoke, uttered his words quietly, not wanting to distract attention. 'Word has come from the east. The turmoil there has been resolved. The Tokugawa have triumphed.'

'I had heard rumour already.'

'Distant Edo must be rejoicing. The Lord Tokugawa, I suppose, will come here soon to swear fealty to the Son of Heaven. Kyoto will be as it will be, and there is much promise for our school in the coming years. Yet here and now, in particular we have received a missive from Sir Ando.'

He was interrupted by a rising murmur of excitement amongst the watching samurai: in swift, graceful movements Ujinari cut one, two, three slivers of a mat away, lessening it by finger lengths at a time with strikes so clean that the unbraced mat did not move or topple. He passed the blade through a fourth time, and the watchers held their breaths and then sighed as the mat teetered, rolled on its rim and fell. Nevertheless, there was applause. Three such blows was a feat, four exceptional, five rare, six the most that any one of them there had seen.

'Sir Ando was present at the decisive battle,' said Tadanari, who had cut those six slivers a decade previously. 'He has given us a name to add to the list: Musashi Miyamoto.'

'I have not heard of him.'

'Neither have I. Of no renown that I can tell.'

'His crime?'

'Insults to the school, offered before the watching armies of the nation. Thousands of witnesses.'

'What words did he speak?'

'Sir Ando did not elaborate upon their specific nature. There was much glory earned by our adepts present at the battle, and attesting to these feats occupied the majority of his writing. But Sir Ando is not a trivial man and I trust his judgement, and the list is the list. Therefore I wish for you to find this Miyamoto, and claim his head in the name of the school.'

He spoke evenly and Akiyama listened in the same manner. There was no need for either of them to feel or feign affront at distant slurs any more than the foot needed to pull away when the hand touched fire. Neither was there a need for debate on their response, for it was only killing. Such a thing as this was not unusual. A school possessing the esteem the Yoshioka held could not exist without creating those who envied, who belittled, who detracted, and each of these grudges, when discovered, in turn birthed a grudge in the Yoshioka also.

A rock falls into a pond, a splash occurs, the waters settle as they were before. This, a simple matter of balance. This, the Way.

In the unshaded yard Ujinari's sword caught the light in its motion and the steel flashed brilliantly. Akiyama looked at the earth, smoothed the folds of his tea-coloured jacket over his thigh. A question that he had waited for months to ask welled within him.

'Master Kozei,' the pale-eyed man ventured, 'I am informed that the Lord of Aki province is seeking to take on a member of our school as swordmaster.'

'This is so.'

The sword held up, aligned, hopeful.

Tadanari said, 'It has been decided that Sir Kosogawa shall be serving in that appointment.'

Down the blade came, dashed all before it.

Akiyama nodded. His pale eyes took in the dust at his feet, his face entirely neutral. 'Sir Kosogawa is a worthy man and able in our techniques. He shall uphold the name of the school faithfully.'

'Doubtless.'

'I will leave at once, Master.'

'Do not return until you have avenged our honour, or can offer proof that some other fate has claimed this man,' said Tadanari, dismissing him with a nod of his head.

Akiyama pressed his brow to the floor and then rose. He slid his longsword into his belt of broad cloth and strode off. In the frame of the gateway he turned and bowed to his fellow swordsmen.

Not one man commented on his departure.

PART II

Foreigners

Spring, Eighth Year of the Era of Keicho

Two Years and a Winter Since Sekigahara

Chapter Three

'It's the eyetooth. The canine.'

'Nnn.'

'I can feel it. It's loose. Can move it with my tongue.'

'Nnn.'

'Musashi, are you listening?'

'Yes.'

'You don't look it. Your eyes are far.'

'Tired, is all. Hungry.'

'I can't think about the hunger. I can't think about sleep. This tooth, the pain . . . Weeks now, rotting. The gum is bleeding, it's all I can taste. I can't bear it.'

'So what am I to do about it?'

'I need you to pull it out.'

'How am I to do that? I have no . . . What tools do you even require to pull a tooth?'

'It's loose. Use your fingers.'

'I can't grip a tooth. Too slick. Too small.'

'You have to.'

'Just bear it.'

'I can't. Please.'

'There's nothing I can do.'

'Look at me. Look. Is the entire side of my face not swollen?'

'It is swollen.'

'And listen to me – I can't even speak properly. The agony of moving my jaw . . . Is my voice not marred?'

'It is altered.'

'And you intend to leave me this way?'

'There's nothing I can do.'

'Please, Musashi. Try, at least.'

'Try what?'

'Try something! Please. I can't bear it. This pain, it'll drive me to madness if I have to endure it any longer.'

'Nnn.'

'It'll madden me, like a dog with its paw in a snare. You wish to make a dog of me?'

'Are we not as dogs already?'

There was silence for some time.

'Maybe you could . . . Instead of pulling, could you not knock it out?'

'That'll hurt you, Jiro.'

'I already hurt.'

'What, you wish me to punch you?'

'No. It doesn't need . . . Something precise. Hard and quick.'

'A rock?'

'Why not the pommel of your shortsword?'

'Would it work?'

'It's metal, is it not?'

Jiro stood up and crossed over to Musashi. His feet stirred the pallid ashes of their pitiful spent fire. They were in a copse of trees. He lay down and put his head upon the earth, tenderly pulled back his lip to show Musashi the tooth.

'Do you see?' he said. 'Just give it one hard crack, and then out it comes. It'll work.'

Musashi looked at the tooth. It was yellowed and the gum around it was excrescent and decayed. Jiro's breath stank of the rot. Musashi picked up his shortsword. The pommel was a squared cap of iron that had started to rust at one edge.

'You are certain?' he asked.

'Do it. Quick.'

Jiro closed his eyes and braced himself. Musashi put a hand upon the man's chest. Tentatively he lined up the pommel to the gum.

'Certain?'

'Do it!'

Musashi struck. The butt of this once treasured and immaculate heirloom met the abscess. Jiro cried out. Musashi had to hit twice more before the tooth squirmed free of the gum.

Jiro's swelling went down quickly, a half-day if even that. His face returned to its normal gaunt rictus. He was a small man with eyes that in this privation seemed to bulge from their sockets. He had served in the army of the Lord Mitsunari, and had fled Sekigahara with a longbow strapped across his back and a spent quiver at his waist.

The longbow served him still. They made arrows for it by sharpening sticks, the shafts primitive and unfletched. He would spend his mornings at a shallow creek near to where they were sheltered, loosing into the gently flowing waters at the small forms of fish. He was a talented and well-honed archer, had once been able to hit an unfurled fan five times out of five at two hundred paces, and even with the crude arrows and the emaciating of his arms he read the water's warping to spear their sustenance.

In the long empty hours whilst Jiro fished, when he was not foraging for firewood or seeking mushrooms or berries or edible mosses where they could be found, Musashi busied himself in labour. He spent a week carving the emerald bark from trunks of bamboo into long, carefully measured strips. Then he began weaving them together. He had seen many such wicker screens and baskets in his life, and he had thought long about their construction from those memories, and he saw no reason why he too could not make one.

The green square matrix he produced was large enough for both him and Jiro to sit under, and they were cheered when this kept the gentle rain from them for a day, and then winds came for the first time and blew it into pieces.

Musashi looked at the strips of bark caught amidst the boughs of nearby trees flapping like gay streamers, and he fell into a foul temper. He set about kicking at clods of earth and throwing stones at nothing.

'How long are we to hide for?' he demanded of Jiro.

'They'll never forgive us,' said Jiro. 'We'll never be forgiven.'

'I don't need their forgiveness! I don't want it.'

'Do you think that Koresada thought that after six, seven hours upon that crucifix?'

That silenced Musashi. Yet the pair of them had been forced together so long it was as though they were bound by some umbilical, and emotion passed back and forth between them as wind. Jiro was angry now.

'We but two and they how many?' he spat. 'Pebbles before a mountain.'

'And what our crime?' said Musashi.

'The twist of fate that casts us such, makes of us the punished for another's failure.'

'The Lord Kobayakawa.'

'The Lord Tokugawa.'

'The Way.'

'Lay low the mountain, bring down the sky!' shouted Jiro. 'Call the seas to account! Line up the wind and the spirits of the earth and let each one of them stare me straight in the eye as they condemn me!'

He was ranting now, and Musashi saw the joy of the release of it in his eyes.

'Bring forth fresh clothes that I might spend a day without scratching at the rashes that plague me! Bring out my bed that I might sleep without a crooked back! Bring out my wife if she lives yet, and let me know that tender softness that she once gave me!'

The thought of her broke his anger. The rant collapsed upon itself, and Jiro's shoulders slumped.

'But we remain pebbles, and what our choice? To live as nothing, or to become nothing.' He plucked one of the bamboo strips from the ground, and wrapped the sodden length around his palm, his wrist. 'Ah, the scales, they tip further each and every day.'

Musashi looked at Jiro for a long time.

'You and I, we both chose to live,' he said.

'Did we?' Jiro said, staring at nothing. 'Did we?'

Whether they had ever actually spoken such vows aloud to one another, Musashi could not remember. That they yet continued to breathe was their only testament to it.

He could barely recall first meeting Jiro. In the wake of Sekigahara, a fortnight after it, maybe more, he had stumbled upon their camp, the boundaries of which he had not even spotted it was such a meagre thing. Only a few traversable paths through the wilderness perhaps, all those fleeing the battle channelled along them, and at Musashi's arrival not one of the men there had seemed surprised. There were five of them then, and they had looked at him with no more alarm than if he were a passing shadow cast by an errant sun.

Caught in a perpetual stupor, mired in a haze of shame and despair.

Their helmets now hung inverted from a bough of a tree to catch rainwater. There for a year or more, mosses grown over the cords where they were wrapped around the wood. Though rust had barely beset the iron they all seemed ancient and worthless things. One had belonged to Koresada, who had tried to steal a fisherman's net. One had belonged to Uesugi, who was caught by chance upon the roads by a band of Tokugawa samurai. One had belonged to the man from Tosa, who had never revealed to any of them his name, who had seldom spoke beyond grunts and stared constantly with wide and harrowed eyes, and who had borne the sickness that claimed him with a resigned acceptance, lain there shivering until he was still.

One, the grandest, the finest, had belonged to the Lord Hayato Nakata.

The Lord had been a rich man, one of the wealthiest in the nation. The bowl of the helmet was inlaid with beautiful carvings of mystical phoenixes, blighted now, and the panels of the neck and cheek guards were bound with burgundy and silver threads that had lost their lustre and were beginning to rot. Affixed to the brow was the great symmetrical frond of a golden crest. The metal was impermeable to marring and shone bright still, and yet it hung there alongside common ores with equal disregard.

What worth gold, when none would trade with you?

Musashi sat gnawing on a stalk of grass to try to alleviate his hunger, and as he did so he stared at the inverted golden crest. Memories took him. He *let* the memories take him. It was all he had. It was Hayato who had sabotaged Musashi's father's seppuku, led to his being so thoroughly and agonizingly disgraced. Young, desperate to become samurai, mind filled with the poison of the Way, Musashi had set out on a quest of vengeance. A quest of years, which had led all the way to Sekigahara, where at last he had held Hayato to account and had taken from the Lord more than his helmet.

On the course of that vengeance Musashi had spent great stretches in wilderness much like he was now in, enduring starvation far worse than this. He had been a child then and had not yet learnt what Jiro and the others had taught him, the basic methods of survival, of lighting fires, of finding sustenance, of hunting and fishing. Even so, he had not felt the hardship, or the ache of it, if that was the word, as he did now.

Pursuing something like vengeance, or indeed anything, granted one a horizon to focus upon. To judge progress towards. Here, all there was was an emptiness and it was this that wounded the most, a great crushing pressure that never relented. A recurrent despair, the mind caught gyring around the same agonies it could do nought but confront, because what else was there to occupy it?

Musashi chewed and chewed on the bitter grass, and he stared at Hayato's helmet, and in his chest he felt something grow larger, bloat an incremental sliver in the same manner as whatever this thing was had done each and every time his eyes had lingered on the golden crest over these past months. Something almost like longing, or envy for what had been.

Jiro sat alongside him rocking on his posterior, arms wrapped around his shins and his chin on his knees. His mind looped through his own familiar obsessions.

'Is it us they hate?' he said.

Musashi had heard him talk before and he knew exactly who it was who would despise Jiro. Two daughters, a wife, a mother, his father gloriously dead but his father's father alive yet. Hideously alive, a mutilated survivor, legless, Jiro's grandfather had terrorized him through his youth, carrying his torso around on his hands, constantly vigilant. Any time Jiro would waver or stray from his dedication to the Way, the man would thrust his naked, mangled stumps at the boy as proof of what was demanded of him, of them all, and, when he exposed his lessening, always there had been fierce pride in his eyes.

That proper old samurai would never forgive, nor permit any other to forgive, Jiro for the audacity of surviving his Lord, and this he feared more than the tortures of those named enemy. This, why they were exiled here.

'Us,' said Jiro again, shaking his head, chin glancing off his knees. '*Us* – you and I. Musashi Miyamoto and Jirokyuro Hori. We're not the ones they hate. It can't be. We're . . . What difference, individual difference did you and I make at Sekigahara? We two amidst thousands? Yet our army lost, and so we two must bear the shame. To be hated. What if our army had won? We would be loved, and yet we would have had the exact same effect upon the victory. Would have had . . . what we had before. But magnified. And what would we have done to earn it? Nothing. No. No. It is as though we . . . As though human beings are . . . buckets or, or, or . . . vessels.'

He pointed up at the helmets where they hung, filled with water.

'That's us, there. There's simply a hate in the world, and a love, and it just needs to be poured,' said Jiro, and he sort of laughed to himself and mimicked tipping a kettle. 'We two – us, you and I – we are incidental.'

This was a new conclusion he had reached, and Musashi watched the man with interest. 'You think so?'

'It seems so,' said Jiro. 'But . . . How did this come to be? Creatures do not have this prejudice. Is it innate in men, this? Or is it something that was created?'

Musashi thought about his answer for some time. 'My uncle taught me men were innately good. Born without any prejudice. No. It's the Way. It's the Way that makes men think as this. Twists them thusly. Must be. Deep within all there is an honesty.'

'Uncle?' said Jiro. 'You've never spoken of him before.'

He hadn't. Why today he should speak he did not know, but he found that he wanted to. 'His name was Dorinbo,' said Musashi. 'A monk.'

'Buddhist or Shinto?'

'Shinto.'

'Shinto?' said Jiro. 'Never much paid attention to the priest of my vale. The celestial spear dipping into the chaotic seas, wild Susano'o abroad in the heavens making it thunder . . . It all washed over me.'

'I know it well,' said Musashi. 'I helped my uncle with the ceremonies. Told the stories, read the prayers. He raised me.

My father was absent, serving his Lord. My uncle taught me . . . everything. How to read and write . . . All of it. He wanted me to become his apprentice and follow him down the holy path but I . . .' He took a breath and thought how to express it best. 'I chose the sword.'

'And the sword led you here,' said Jiro.

Musashi did not hear him. Now, thinking of Dorinbo, he felt warmth in his heart and he was driven to speak further, if just to remember, if just to recall: 'He was a healer. Talented. People would come from afar to be treated by him. None were turned away. Lepers, the mutilated . . . Not all could be cured but he would try equally. There were wounds, festering wounds that smelt so bad I ran from the room in disgust, but he would stay and lay his hands upon those vile rotting limbs with tenderness. His hands . . . His ability that he had learnt for himself, and he put his hands on filth all to try to alleviate it. And he asked for nothing. And there are children in the village where I was born that stand upright this day because of him. Made it to adulthood because of him. He did things of worth, and, and . . .'

His voice faded away. He could speak no further.

Jiro had noticed the change in Musashi. Rare that any kindness seeped into their voices. 'He sounds a fine man,' he said. 'One that would not hate.'

Musashi did not reply. His eyes were distant now. Jiro watched him for some time. A sparrow alighted on the rim of Hayato's helmet and bobbed its beak to the water and then threw its head back to drink.

'Perhaps he is different,' said Jiro. 'Not as my kin would be.'

Again the sparrow drank, again, again, again.

'Why is it you do not return to him?' Jiro pressed. 'Do you think he is the sort of man that would hate you for what you are, for what you've done?'

'How could I return to him like . . .' snapped Musashi, and he tugged at the rags he wore and glared at Jiro for an instant. But it all hurt to say and it hurt to think of, a wet heat behind the eyes. It could not last. Musashi's face softened and he let the rags fall from his hand. Jiro turned away, embarrassed.

The silence resumed. The sparrow had fled to the skies at the sudden outburst. Musashi put the stalk of grass in his mouth once more and ground it between his teeth.

His eyes returned to the golden crest.

A fortnight after he had been defanged, Jiro returned from bowfishing despondent and empty-handed save for his longbow. He sat down by the bracken fire Musashi had made and laid the stave of the weapon across his lap. He stared at nothing for a long while, probing the hollow of his gum with his tongue.

'Bowstring snapped,' he said eventually.

'It had to, some time,' said Musashi.

'It was the last one I had,' he said. 'The last one. What are we to do?'

'There's plenty of mushrooms here,' said Musashi, and he waved a hand at the trees, which were rife with stairs of fungi. 'We'll make do.'

'No!' shouted Jiro. 'No! I refuse to subsist. I will forego rice, I will forego tea, but . . . I must have fish. A man must have fish.'

He repeated these words several times, his voice racked with the desperate emotion of the long-deprived, and yet his distress was a matter of more than simple food. What was an archer without a bow? His eyes roved in furious rotations and his fingers wrung themselves around the bow's stave.

'There's a town a half-day's walk eastwards,' he said. 'I'll go there. There must be a bowyer there.'

'We don't need a bowyer,' said Musashi. 'Perhaps we can make a string ourselves.'

'Out of what?'

'I don't know . . . Hair. Some vine or grass we can find . . . The very first men who made bows, in the time before bowyers, they must have had exactly what we have here before us now. Surely we can find some substitute or . . .'

'A string as sturdy as your wicker kite, no doubt,' said Jiro blackly.

'What in the myriad hells do you intend by that?'

Jiro met Musashi's eyes for a moment and the two of them swelled with imminent conflict. But before it could manifest the small man relented, looked at the ground with a sigh.

'I apologize,' he said. 'An unnecessary insult to a friend, born of my disquiet. I will head into town.'

'You can't,' said Musashi. 'Remember Koresada.'

'I'm not like . . . I'm no thief . . . I'll . . .'

Jiro rose to his feet. He laid his longbow aside and walked over to where the helmets were hung. He placed his hands around the golden frond of Hayato's helmet, and began trying to wrench it off. It was loose, the joints rusted, and he yanked it again and again. Musashi placed a hand on his shoulder, tried to place his body between the man and what he sought.

'How do you think it will look,' he said, 'you arriving in town two years starved and clutching a golden samurai crest? What conclusion do you think they'll reach?'

'I'll trade, they'll trade, they'll listen. Let me go.'

'No.'

'I must have a bow. I must have fish. I must, I must, I must . . .'

'Are you mad?'

'Let me go!' shouted Jiro, and he snapped the crest loose and stood back with it in his hands. Musashi looked at him, and in his anger his first instinct was to strike at the man that he might force some wits into his head. He hesitated, though, because it was Jiro, and yet Jiro saw the intent in him and his eyes tightened in response, and he made to stride around Musashi and leave their camp.

Musashi yelled at him to halt, half-pleading, half-commanding, and Jiro shouted back a half-insult and began to half-run. Musashi grabbed him by the scruff of his clothing and tried to haul him close, and Jiro swung around and attempted to pry himself free, and like this they began to struggle, began to dance around each other, snarling and spitting, a golden crest in their hands and a wilderness around them.

Bigger, stronger, Musashi drew Jiro in close, and he tried to restrain him without choking or wrenching at joints as he had been taught, instead wrapped his arms around the man's chest and tried to pin his arms to his sides, but still Jiro fought, kicked, butted with his head. Musashi growled and brought his friend over his waist, threw him to the ground and fell with him, and there simply kept his hold upon the man, let him struggle as he would until hopefully he would see sense.

'Let me go!' Jiro pleaded, trying to look over his shoulder and meet Musashi's eye. 'I must have fish!' And on and on he repeated this until he was actually weeping, tears streaming from his eyes. He spoke of fish but it was more than that, everything bared in this piteous, pathetic moment, everything mourned, and Musashi understood this, and the fact that someone older than he could be so thoroughly broken made him want to weep also.

Thus they lay until Jiro's struggles subsided. Musashi's grip lessened. Jiro assured him that he was calm, and, when Musashi chose to believe him and released him entirely, he calmly went to sit with his back against a tree. There he sat cradling Hayato's crest, staring dumbly at his own distorted reflection barely visible upon its surface for some time.

Then he looked up at Musashi, smiled, and tossed the crest away as though it were nothing.

They ate nought but boiled mushrooms that night in silence, and the next morning, when Musashi awoke, Jiro and the crest were gone.

His longbow and his swords remained.

Musashi knew what this meant, yet he spent the morning lying to himself that the man was only twenty heartbeats away from reappearing in the camp, and perhaps for a while such was his desire for this to be so that he even believed it. But he knew that ultimately he had no choice but to go and search for Jiro, if only to confirm. Guardedly, he brought both his and Jiro's weapons with him and at the very edge of the town, on the wooded slope of the hill that led down to the paddy fields, he hid the four swords and the bow between the roots of a great dead oak tree.

Musashi traversed the narrow paths that bisected the dry paddies and entered the town, trying the best he could to be inconspicuous. He wore a peasant's straw sandals, a decrepit old kimono and a rough jacket of hemp. These things by themselves would attract no attention. Yet he had a full head of hair that hung loose to his chin, where peasants tended to keep theirs cropped close; his emaciated flesh was pale and dirty; and in this gauntness he stood a head taller than most.

He was wary for any staring at him, but not a single eye followed him, for the town was silent and empty. He walked along the main thoroughfare, through all the things that had long since been relegated to memories – the smell of rice cooking, the curls of incense that warded insects and kept away stench, colours beyond pallid tones of earth, silk-threaded cushions, soft tatami mats, roofs, walls – and found not a single person.

They were all gathered on the moor on the far side of the town, an expanse of rutted brush bordered by pine trees. Musashi joined the back of the crowd, and looked over their heads. At the fore of them all, he saw Jiro.

Jiro was kneeling, bound by the wrists to a stake that had been driven into the ground behind him, his arms pinioned up in odd contortion. They had bled him to death by a score of deep cuts across his body and his back, and to make a fool of him they had cut his nose and his ears off.

A samurai, swords at his side and a spear in his hands, stood nearby. The steward of the town, perhaps. An executioner from the hamlet of the corpsehandlers, his work completed, had been exiled some distance away, where he knelt with his bloody hands upon his thighs and his eyes upon the floor. Some swordless higherborn, the headman of the town or the minister whose jurisdiction it fell under or some other titled authority, was pronouncing final judgement.

'Look, then, you all upon this enemy of civilization, and see justice enacted in the name of his most noble Lord Natsuka,' said the minister, and then he realized his mistake of habit and corrected himself quickly: 'The justice of the most noble Lord Tokugawa, may he reign ten thousand years hale and serene. In his authority, I hereby rule that the corpse of this degenerate shall stand for a week upon this moor that all passing on the road might heed its warning.' He fumbled at his belt, and brought up a velvet bag noosed by a leather cord. 'Where is the upstanding artisan known as Nobutsura?'

From the crowd a man stepped forward. He was a hardy-looking fellow with hair cropped so short he all but resembled a monk, and he dropped to his knees and pressed his brow to the ground. 'Here, most honourable one.'

'Rise,' said the minister, and the artisan did so. The minister pressed the bag into Nobutsura's hands. 'Here, your reward. One shu of gold. Let every man and woman know that bounties persist upon the wretched and vile masterless that served the vanquished coalition, and vigilance is a virtue upon which all the heavens shine.'

The artisan murmured his thanks, dropped into a bow again and then returned to the crowd. The minister or whoever he was had pronounced all he wished to pronounce. He gave a formal farewell, bade the populace be about their business, and then he retired to the box of his lacquered palanquin. A dozen men bore the cabin aloft on its yoke, and the townspeople dropped to their knees in salute as it departed.

The palanquin's pace was ponderously slow, the six men who held the leading yoke walking backwards so that they might keep their eyes respectfully on the charge they bore aloft. The box of it was big enough for two, and Musashi, kneeling on the very edge of the crowd, heard the sound of a woman's laughter as it passed.

The congregation dispersed to return to the town in grim silence, save for Nobutsura, who was rattling his bounty in its pouch in satisfaction. The corpsehandler vanished unnoticed by any. The samurai steward remained by Jiro, stood guard to ensure that none tampered with the corpse.

Musashi retreated to sit under the eaves of the wall of a smithy's yard at the edge of the moor. He sat with his back against the stone foundations, rested his hands between his legs, sat there suddenly exhausted with the fatigue of years. He stared at Jiro, desecrated and destroyed. He stared at the samurai, upright and immutable.

The man held a spear, wore two swords at his side. He seemed proud to be doing his duty, topknot immaculately oiled, silks upon his shoulders. At his sternum his jacket was joined by a tasselled soft cord ended in teased white horsehair. Frail accoutrement no doubt tied and cleaned by servants' hands.

Musashi stared at the samurai. Musashi stared at Jiro.

Musashi marked the difference between himself and the samurai. The samurai's nails well filed, Musashi's blackened. The samurai's belly full and contented, and Musashi's lean with lack and want. One of them a torturous murderer, and the other an exile. Had that man been at Sekigahara also? What for him these two years?

He stared for a long time, able to do no more, no less.

A gate on the walls opened beside him. The smith came out, a man with a head like a rock. He was clutching his hand, burnt on a poker, and cursing to himself. He too cast his eyes over the spectacle on the moor, and then he became aware of Musashi.

'No,' the smith said, rounding on him. 'No, no, no. Away with you. No vagrants here.'

Musashi stared up at him.

'Away with you!' snarled the smith, slashed his hand towards that same vague distance to which he and Jiro had been condemned. 'Away!'

Musashi rose to his feet. The smith's eyes were level with his chin.

'You just watched?' he said.

The smith took a step back. Musashi followed.

'Let them torture a man to death, for no crime at all?'

The smith's mouth flapped.

'Just watched,' said Musashi, and two years welled and he drew his hand back and slapped the man across his face.

The smith yelped. Musashi slapped him again, again. Each blow considered and meant, realizing something. An inked brush flitting across fine paper, forming the outline of a long-envisioned image.

The samurai saw the violence, abandoned his guard of Jiro and came over shouting some command. Musashi saw the man in his peripheral, and he saw this man too for everything he was, his arms, his legs, the authority he carried, the authority he assumed, the authority Musashi also had assumed and hidden from these past two years, and it was stark and clear now.

The samurai did not expect Musashi to move with the speed or ability he did, thought him some drunk and rowdy malingerer. He barely managed to move the spear before Musashi had placed both hands on its shaft and wrenched it around. Musashi drove the samurai backwards and forced him up against the wall, pushed the spear shaft up against his throat.

'Was it you who cut his ears away?' Musashi hissed into his face. 'Was it you who cut his back and bled him dry?'

The samurai struggled but Musashi was taller and stronger and did not allow the spear's pressure to relent, forced it onwards, began to truly choke the man. Eyes bulged and spittle flew, and Musashi began to strike at the man without releasing him, began to drive his knees into the samurai's belly and his brow into the samurai's nose again and again, and each blow was born of two years of agony and indignity.

The samurai managed to wriggle out from beneath the throttling press of the spear, but Musashi continued to hit at him, and the man collapsed to the floor and Musashi kicked and stamped at him until he was no more than a cowering ball. Seething, he stepped back, looked at what he had wrought. He looked around and found that walls still stood and that the sky was still blue.

Why stop here, when the outrage spiralled ever outwards?

'Where's the one who betrayed Jiro?' Musashi demanded of the smith, who had watched him beat the samurai in cowed incomprehension and fear. 'The one who claimed the bounty?'

The smith stammered something, pointed towards town. Musashi commanded him to lead with a jerk of his chin. The smith staggered off. Before he followed, Musashi wrestled the samurai's swords from his belt, carried them both clutched in one hand and retained the spear in the other.

Through the streets they went. Musashi's blood was running warm, his teeth clenched, eyes wide with a furious focus. Two years of nothing, when each day was formless and endless and asked the question of why it was even endured, and here and now the opposite, carried as a pulse, as a facet, as a thing of pure purpose, a thing that could achieve something, anything.

The smith gestured to a storefront and fell to his knees in the dust like a supplicant pleading for mercy. Musashi threw the spear and the swords to the ground, parted the navy half-curtain that hung across the entrance and strode in. It was a bowyer's. Three long unstrung staves were hung upon the walls.

Nobutsura knelt upon tatami mats, varnishing a fourth. He turned and looked up into Musashi's face.

'All he wanted was a bowstring,' said Musashi.

Nobutsura began to say something, but Musashi stepped forward and kicked over the table of his tools. He hauled down the rack of bow staves from the wall. Nobutsura scrambled backwards on his arse and the heels of his hands. Musashi stamped on him, once, twice, then he picked up one of the fallen staves and began to strike at him. It was long and thin and flexible and lashed like a whip.

'Turned him over to that torture, for what?' he spat. 'To keep yourself in rice for a month?'

Nobutsura tried to rise at his feet, grabbing at a chest of drawers to pull himself up. His hands yanked them open, spilled their contents out onto floor, and there the golden crest that had once sat above Hayato Nakata's eyes tumbled out. It fell at Musashi's feet, and he looked down at it for a moment, and all within him flared hotter, and he looked at Nobutsura through a veil of perfect loathing.

The bowyer fled out onto the street, whimpering and pleading. Musashi followed, slashing at his arms and his arse with the bow. A crowd had gathered now and they drew back in shock at the sight. Musashi threw the bow at Nobutsura, and then he bent down to retrieve the spear and the swords. The bowyer began to retreat, not running but rather caught in a great confusion, alternating moment by moment between begging Musashi for mercy and crying out for the steward who could not hear him, he lying beaten and senseless against the blacksmith's walls.

Musashi advanced after him steadily, watching him, observing each and every little thing he hated about the man, cataloguing them like piles of coals stacked before a furnace. He pursued him until they came to the river that bisected the town.

The bowyer stopped on the banks.

'Keep going,' said Musashi.

Nobutsura turned and looked down at the river. 'But—'

'Get in the water.'

Nobutsura hesitated.

'Get in the damned water!' shouted Musashi, and he pointed with the tip of the spear.

It was not a death sentence. The river was not deep and the current mild. Nobutsura jumped from the banks and stood looking up at Musashi. He commanded him to wade out into the centre, and there the bowyer stood with the waters up to his sternum. Musashi threw both scabbarded swords at him, and the weapons vanished beneath the surface, and still he was not sated.

The outrage spiralled ever outwards: 'Where's the bastard in the palanquin?'

He could have demanded anything and been granted it at that moment, so shocked were the witnesses at his rampage. He was led over the arch of a bridge that crossed the river, spear clutched in both hands, and the anger did not subside. He did not want it to. This all some wild improvisation on its behalf. He did not know why he had sent the man into the waters. He did not know why he had thrown the swords in after him. All he knew was that this had to be, that he could make this be, and he was carried and shielded, and how far could this take him? How far could he go?

Ahead were the white plaster walls of a rich estate. The gates were oak and iron, studded and imposing. How many the men that had stood supplicant here, believed themselves supplicant? Musashi hauled on the handle but the gates would not open, locked or barred. He pounded on the gate, kicked at it, pried at it with the head of the spear. It held firm. Inside he heard roused voices.

The walls were not high. He abandoned attempting to open the gates and instead threw the spear over the tiled eaves and then hauled himself over afterwards. There was a neat garden of grass that ringed a pond, and he saw that the minister and a woman half his age in a peach-coloured kimono had been sitting eating rice cakes beneath the shade of a wicker screen.

A romantic little hideaway that Musashi had breached, and now the old man stared aghast, his pointed grey beard wavering.

'You, that ordered such torture on another,' Musashi said to him.

The woven screen the pair of them had sheltered beneath was curved and beautiful, would no doubt stand up to anything shy of a gale, and Musashi saw this and snarled in his envy and his rage and picked it up and hurled it against the wall. The minister was not a samurai, had no swords to go for, and so he just stared. Musashi kicked the platter of rice cakes at him.

'You can eat, after seeing that? After causing that to be? Choke on them!'

The doors of the fine foreroom of the house were wide open to the fair weather. Musashi saw a styled copper kettle whorled with patterns, a plaster orb of the limbless saint Daruma and his benevolent scowl, the paper walls painted with a triptych view of Kyoto. Neat and beautiful things, gorgeous things, and what law was it that said such things should stand when in their shadow lay mutilation? He could not bear their existence suddenly, and he grabbed the minister and hauled him inside and sent him hurtling through the walls. Paper split, wood splintered, Kyoto was annihilated.

He heard the sound of footfall, saw motion in the corner of his eye. The woman charged and threw herself at Musashi, dedicated as a samurai, perhaps even born samurai herself. She had a knife clutched in both hands and its edge cut across his forearm as he raised it to block. He hissed in pain and grabbed at her wrists, wrestled the knife away from her, and then he pushed her against a beam. She was much lighter than he was, and she bounced off the hard wood and fell to her knees and did not rise. He looked down at her. She looked up at him.

He remembered the sound of a woman's laughter from the palanquin.

He spat at her, and then he went and picked the old man from out of the wreckage of the walls. The minister was moaning feebly, his body jarred. Musashi wrenched his arm behind his back and bent him double. He was helpless, and Musashi looked to the woman.

'Do you see?' he snarled at her, and to himself as well. 'Do you see?'

He forced the old man outside. In the garden, a servant was staring at the wreckage of the wicker screen in complete surprise. When Musashi emerged the young man turned and whimpered, dropped the shovel he had been holding and fled.

One more tool. One more implement. Musashi picked the shovel up and entwined the old man's arms around it, wrapped them around the wooden shaft. He cried out in pain, and Musashi forced him onwards. He unbarred the gates and walked back towards the town.

'Please,' the old man began to plead. 'Don't kill me. Don't kill me.'

They crossed over the bridge. The bowyer Nobutsura was hauling himself out of the river up onto the banks.

'Get back in the river!' shouted Musashi at him.

The bowyer gaped.

'Get back in there right now or I swear to the heavens I will gut you!'

He obeyed.

The minister was moaning, 'Where are you taking me? What are you doing?'

Musashi forced them through the town, until they were back at the moor once more. The beaten steward remained slumped against the wall of the smithy, face bloodied. A gaggle of concerned apprentices were crouched nearby, fearful to approach him. The man could barely discern his own hands before his face, let alone rise to stop Musashi.

The minister moaned when he recognized where they were, and again when he saw Jiro's corpse. Musashi released him, pushed him towards the body. The man stumbled, then rose as straight as he could. He looked at what the torturer had wrought, then at Musashi.

'Cut him down, take up the body,' said Musashi.

The minister stood there. He was repulsed and disgusted, and nor did he want to bear the shame of acting as a lowly corpsehandler would. Yet he feared Musashi more, and so he untied the lashes and with great difficulty bore the ruined remains of Jiro up across his shoulders.

'Walk,' said Musashi.

There was no destination. He simply made the minister march back and forth across the moor until he collapsed beneath Jiro's weight, exhausted. Then he threw the shovel at the man's feet.

'Dig,' he said.

'What do you mean?' panted the minister.

'Dig,' said Musashi.

The man shuddered in a half-moan. 'I'll pay for the corpse's cremation, if that is what you wish. A proper cremation, at the temple—'

'Dig!'

The minister rose and thrust the head of the shovel into the earth. Musashi watched as he worked. He realized he was bleeding, examined the knife-slash across his forearm. It was not deep. He demanded the minister's jacket, and when the man relinquished it he tore it into silken bandages.

It took time to dig a grave. A crowd drew near. It was late in the afternoon by the time the hole was dug to Musashi's satisfaction. It was thigh-deep and Jiro's body fitted neatly within it lengthways. He looked at the minister setting the corpse in the grave. The man made to get out of the hole.

Musashi stopped him with the head of the shovel at his clavicle.

The old man looked up at him, quivering, smeared with dirt. His hands, unused to labour, were bleeding from the palms. This man, this pathetic man, was the power he had rejected at Sekigahara. He was all Lords, all samurai, the Way. For two years Musashi had consented simply to hide from all this, agreed to a life apart, but now he looked and saw this man and his authority anew. Saw that it could be confronted. That it *ought* to be confronted.

The anger told him this, made it truth, and how far could this take him? How far could he go?

'Kneel,' he said.

'You cannot be serious,' said the minister, sweating, hands bloody from the labour. 'This is a crime of great magnitude. Reconsider. Do you know the power of my most noble Lord?'

'Is your Lord here?' asked Musashi. 'Let him draw forth his own sword and lay me low. Let he himself give me evidence of his power.'

The minister had no answer.

'Kneel,' said Musashi.

The minister did so, legs astride Jiro's chest. Musashi took up the shovel and filled the grave around him, buried him up to the neck until only his head remained above the earth. Musashi looked down at him and saw him for what he was. He placed his foot square upon the man's crown and kept it there for some time.

'I am going to go,' he told the minister. 'When I am gone, command these people watching to dig you free. See if they will. See how much true authority you hold over them.'

He took his foot off. The minister's head wriggled helplessly. He looked like a maggot issuing forth from a wound. Like a yellowed tooth in a rotting gum. Musashi raised his eyes to the watching crowd.

'My name is Musashi Miyamoto,' he said to them. 'I will hide no more. Musashi Miyamoto! Thrall to no man!'

It felt right to say. It felt as though it had to be said. The crowd heeded him in silence. He looked at them, he looked at the minister, he looked at what he had achieved. The anger had given him this.

How much further could it take him? How much further could he go?

Musashi did not even know the name of the town, but when he left it he had declared a war upon all the world.

Chapter Four

Nagayoshi Akiyama climbed down from his saddle.

He rode a white horse, a steady creature bred not for war, nor racing, but for its stamina and constancy of temper. He hitched the reins to a post, and then drew his longsword in its scabbard, from where it was hung amidst his bags of travel. He slid it into the wide silken belt around his waist, and then took a moment to right his clothes from where they had been pulled on the ride. He wore greaves that clung tight to his shins, patterned trousers that bloomed out like paper lanterns over his thighs, and on his shoulders his jacket the colour of tea.

With fastidious hands he checked his hair the best he could. He had shaved his crown and oiled his locks up into a topknot before a mirror in the morning, and from what he could tell the ride had not sullied his efforts.

He was outside a small compound, low walls of thin wooden planking greyed with age. Above the modest gate was hung a sign, varnished cedar with engraved characters painted black:

Sakakibara School of the Way

Akiyama set his shoulders, put his thumbs to his belt in proper masculine posture, and then strode a measured pace. He rapped upon the door, and it was opened all but immediately. He was expected.

The master of the school was an old man, gaunt of face. He and a few younger adepts awaited Akiyama, and, as always, as they first beheld Akiyama and his red skin and his mossy eyes, there came that jarring little instant. An instant Akiyama had long learnt immaculate hair styling or propriety of dress could not overcome, and yet, each and every time, he persevered, shaved and combed and oiled and hoped anew and simultaneously loathed himself for it.

To be polite was to wear a face of serene unreadability, to put up a barrier so that you might not trouble another with selfish want or emotion. Yet behind this barrier for Akiyama there was always another. A certain tension that did not yield, carried over as the polite words were spoken as they should be spoken and the protocols were observed as they ought to be observed.

He ignored it as he had learnt to ignore it and humbly he introduced himself with precision as Nagayoshi Akiyama, of the school of Yoshioka, of the realm of Tajima and of the bloodline Tachibana.

The master Sakakibara pushed his brow to the ground. 'It is an honour to receive an adept of the esteemed school of Yoshioka.'

'It is I who am honoured by a reception I am unworthy of,' said Akiyama formally. 'I am in your debt. It was with great interest and gratitude that I received your missive.'

'I trust it came not too late? Your initial request came some time before, but, regrettably, with things of this sort, one cannot offer assistance until, by chance, one is in a position to do so.'

'I assure you, our school's interest in Musashi Miyamoto endures.'

Sakakibara smiled with his mouth.

They knelt on soft tatami mats in the small tearoom that overlooked the garden of ordered and raked sand. Patterns of Zen abounded. One of the adepts had set about making tea for them. He stoked the hearth pit in the centre of the room and set a kettle of water heating. Akiyama watched him. The man fumbled and struggled, worked only with his left hand, for his right forearm was set in a splint.

Given what he had read in Sakakibara's missive, it was fairly easy to deduce why the man was wounded so, and not wishing to confront the man with his humiliation Akiyama elected to wait in silence. He and the master sat, offering neither assistance nor comment as the splinted man ladled the readied water into pewter dishes. Akiyama swirled the liquid, watched the green tea powder diffuse into the clear.

In silence the three samurai drank.

It was only when the splinted man left them to remove the kettle and the cups did Akiyama feel it polite to broach the subject of Miyamoto once more.

'Tall and wild, lean and slender, no topknot,' said Sakakibara, and his face darkened as he spoke. 'On his face were scars, many scars sprent like a constellation of the stars. Pox in his childhood, perhaps. He stank, stank beyond incense. Stank like the masterless.'

'And he came with sword drawn?' asked Akiyama.

'No,' said Sakakibara. 'But he came in aggression, I . . .' He hesitated, struggled for words. He did not want to present himself or his students as incapable, but he was avowed to honesty and furthermore he had already weighed the potential disgrace against the worth of aiding the Yoshioka, and so he spoke on with a reluctant candour. 'There was a confrontation on the southerly road. One of my students, an earnest young man named Yoshisada, encountered Miyamoto there. Yoshisada has taken to reclusion in his shame in the days since, and so I have not discerned the truth of that particular incident, but they arrived at our school with Miyamoto's arm around Yoshisada's throat, and Yoshisada stripped of his swords.'

Akiyama nodded evenly. 'A rare misfortune.'

'I need to emphasize to you the size of Miyamoto,' said Sakakibara. 'You must understand, wrestling technique can only overcome—'

'I do not cast aspersions upon the brave Sir Yoshisada's ability.'

'As you should not.' Sakakibara nodded. 'He is a diligent practitioner of all the martial studies, as are all my—'

'Let us concern ourselves with Miyamoto only.'

'Of course. Of course.'

'Miyamoto arrives here maddened . . . ?'

'Maddened as I have ever seen. He seemed as a monk when they work themselves up into a frenzy, feel the breath of old Saint Fudo blowing through them, that sort of look in his eyes.'

'Why is it you and your adepts did not cut Miyamoto down where he stood?'

'I will not suffer the ghosts of rotten men haunting my dojo.'

The answer sounded false, and Akiyama simply cast his pale gaze upon the master until the man was unavoidably reminded of what he was sworn to.

'Miyamoto issued a challenge of wooden swords,' admitted Sakakibara.

Thus challenged, one could not refuse. Drawing steel on wood was a tacit admission of inferiority.

'How many men of yours did he overcome?' asked Akiyama.

The old master was now deeply ruing his vow of truthfulness. 'Three, ultimately. Yet bear in mind that he fought with brute strength unrestrained, whereas my students were tempered with the grace of civility. One might as well swing a dirk at a bear.'

Akiyama's brow furrowed. 'Miyamoto carries steel swords?'

'He does.'

'But even so, and even though he was as maddened as you say, he did not give himself over to bloodlust?'

'He did not.'

Akiyama looked to the garden. Grey sands and grey rocks, and on them fallen petals of cherry blossom. Sweet detritus of the nascent year that danced in swathes of the breeze.

'What was Miyamoto's purpose in even coming here?' he said.

'Who knows how a frenzied heart beats?' said the old master, and he cast a hand to nowhere. 'He was spouting slanderous things. Shouting his name. Urging us to cast down the Way as he snapped bones. Saying all Lords were worthless. Saying he had come on our behalf. Things of this sort.'

'Indeed.'

Sakakibara saw the expression upon his guest's face. 'You seem surprised by all this.'

'I have hunted men of Miyamoto's ilk before,' said the

pale-eyed samurai. 'When they abandon the Way, ultimately they either turn to cowardice or become wanton. However, it sounds as though he has retained a code.'

'There is no code outside the true code.'

Akiyama nodded slowly. 'Indeed.'

There was little else for Akiyama to say. Sakakibara spoke on effusively for some time, obliquely implicating a hope this boon might lead to the start of cordial relations between the two schools. Akiyama could make no promises on behalf of men horizons away. He thanked the old master for his hospitality, wished the wounded a quick recuperation, and then set out upon his horse once more.

Akiyama often wrote poems he knew none but himself would ever read. The summer before, inspired by the sweet sound of cicadas, he had written what he considered his finest verse:

Unseen for a decade's slumber;
Emerged from blackened earth but to sing.
The song as fleet as the golden moon.
Summer's equilibrium.

Miyamoto put him in mind of a cicada. Two years dormant, and now burst forth in sudden desperate struggle and unrelenting noise. The incident at the school, before that burying a man up to his neck and leaving him . . . On and on and on.

Akiyama was surprised to even be here. He had never harboured much hope of finding Miyamoto, even from the very moment he was issued the command. A name and nothing more to hunt amidst the hordes of the defeated coalition that had flooded the country? A name was easy to shed.

After six months' initial cursory search he had been certain Miyamoto was either dead or irrevocably vanished. This, however, did not mean that Akiyama could return to Kyoto and the school: after so short a time it would seem he was derelict in his effort. He could not say, for example, that he had ridden to either end of the country in that span, which would be the very least of what was expected of him. He reasoned that eighteen months or thereabouts would stand as sufficient proof of dedication and tenacity to duty, which consequently Akiyama knew meant he would have had to sacrifice twice that or it would have been taken as unspoken proof of what all believed was innate in him.

How could the Foreigner possibly understand basic Japanese ethics, after all?

Two years, then, lingering nowhere, achieving nothing, and he had known this, had accepted it, had resigned himself to the waste of this plus a further year also. His life was a series of cycles that spun upon the same bitter truth, around again and again. This rotation, it had been Sir Kosogawa who was rewarded in his stead. This rotation, it was Musashi Miyamoto he hunted. Sir Kosogawa, seven years his junior and now swordmaster in Aki. Miyamoto the ninth man of no meaning he would kill. Never a champion that he could fell in the name of the school. Always the vermin and the outlaws, which he would extinguish in furtive anonymity.

All this Akiyama knew, and what galled him most was his own complicity.

Now that he had emerged, Miyamoto was the easiest man to track that Akiyama had ever hunted. Contacts of the school and those he himself had cultured over previous hunts awaited in each town or at the waypoints upon the road trading rumour for coin. Others simply coincidental witnesses of a man of great stature and flecked with pox scars, sullen innkeepers or shaven-headed priests or peasants thigh-deep in paddy silt, and slowly he was pointed across realms and mountain trails.

The high summer found Akiyama in the province of Kaga, speaking to the captain of a garrison. A stern man who had been chosen to act as a second in the seppuku of a serial scapegrace, Ogawa. They had erected a palisade of silk out upon a meadow, and Ogawa was writing his death poem when Miyamoto had cut his way through the brocade. Burst in and disrupted the ceremony, beseeched Ogawa to forsake his honour and live.

'The knave has proclaimed himself against the dignity of the Way previously,' said Akiyama, nodding pensively.

'Well, he mentioned nothing of that sort here,' said the captain. 'His true anger, if you must know, was directed at Ogawa himself when he protested Miyamoto's interruption.'

A confrontation had ensued thereafter, the resolution of which was unclear; the captain claimed to have cut Miyamoto down, but he could provide no proof of this. Akiyama did not challenge his assertion, but a woman with a baby slung across her back who lived at the edge of town said she had seen Miyamoto heading westwards at twilight.

The woman also told him Ogawa fulfilled the ritual the following day.

Through the wilderness outside of the sight of others, Akiyama rode with his hair unbound and unoiled. It hung in shaggy locks that turned a deep red when they were caught in the sun – curled and knotted in the manner of his horse's mane, not the straight black hair of men, of samurai.

Horsehair, a boy had called him in his childhood, a cat-eyed, horse-haired freak. They had duly got into a fight until the other boy's father had hauled them apart by the scruffs of their necks and then dragged his son off. Akiyama had followed them, wiping blood from his nose as he hid around a corner and listened.

'Don't fight with him, not that one,' the father was saying. 'You don't know what he's going to do. Leave him be. He could bite you or gouge your eyes out. You want that? Just leave him. Beat somebody else.'

Akiyama had delighted in this. As all children did, he had thought being feared was the epitome of manliness and adulthood. But time passed and with the contemplation of adolescence he saw that he had never been singled out and bullied as other aberrant children were, the stupid or the fat or the cowardly, and he realized this fear was not fear at all. It was merely an enmity perfectly devoid of all emotion, and the warrior he imagined himself was in fact a no more than a scarecrow; he was there, apart.

The root of all this went back to Korea.

A diplomat for the long-abolished Ashikaga Shogunate, Akiyama's father had served as an envoy to the royal court on the mainland. He had served for a half-dozen years there, until things fell apart completely due to escalating skirmishes between the two countries on the seas, and all ties had been severed. His father was granted a grudging escort back to his homeland, and when he arrived on the docks of Osaka the Japanese wife of the Japanese father was pregnant.

Oh, what scandal!

The first time Akiyama was aware of it, he was perhaps seven or eight. Raised voices in the night had woken him, and, confused, he had crept through the halls to where his parents were entertaining a handful of other men and women for the evening. Things had gone sour; from the shadows he saw his father as he had never done so before, utterly furious, standing and pointing at a man who remained sitting cross-legged on the floor. Akiyama's mother was on her knees, clasping at her husband's waist, trying to still his hands and calm him.

The skin of both of them was ivory, their hair straight and dark.

'In my own house you question my wife?' his father was shouting. 'She is as faithful to me as any man could hope for. I trust her, but you! You think you can imply such vile things knowing what? Knowing nothing! Nothing, you fool!'

'Please sit down, my dear, please,' Akiyama's mother was saying gently. 'This is embarrassing. Oh, won't you please calm yourself?'

'I merely stated the fact that the boy looks—' said the accused man stubbornly.

'Again! Again!' spat his father. 'Have you no mind? You cur!'

There was a silence then, the words exhausted. Akiyama's father seethed, shoulders juddering, until his wife took one of his hands in both of hers and brought his fingers to her lips. He looked down at her, saw the sadness in her eyes, and that pacified him. The man sat down and took up the bowl he had been eating from. No one moved as he stared at what lay in his hands for a long while, and then he spoke:

'You will eat my food, you will sleep in my bed, and then tomorrow you shall leave. If I hear of you saying anything the like of which you have uttered this night once more, you shall find me far less civil.'

That was the end of it. No one had noticed Akiyama in the darkness outside the room. He had returned to bed, not quite understanding what he had seen. It was one of those little incidents that reveal themselves fully in time, age and understanding decoding what the innocent has witnessed.

He had summoned the courage to ask his father only when he was a young man with his first peach-down moustache worn vaingloriously proud upon his lip. As Akiyama sat on the raised porch and listened, his father had paced back and forth in their little rock garden, not caring that he dashed the finely raked sand beneath his feet. The man had been both dreading and expecting the conversation.

'Koreans don't look like . . .' *you*, he neglected to say. 'They're like . . .' *us*. 'Except that they have . . . squarer jaws and eyes. You'd understand if you'd met them. And they're not savages, whatever men say. They're decent, kind, intelligent. They could have sent my head home in a box, your mother's, too, but . . . But, your mother couldn't have . . . My father's grandfather was said to be dark of face, and . . . I'm sure your mother's family must also . . . She couldn't have – do you understand?'

'I do, Father,' said Akiyama, quite neutrally.

'Yes. "Father". Exactly,' he said, rounding on him. 'You are my son. My son, and her son.'

Akiyama had nodded, and though he had seen the worry in his eyes and wondered about it at the time, again with the passing of more years he came to realize that this was merely the fear that all men harboured about their wives. He decided eventually that he believed him.

There was only one other person who could have told him the truth, but what son could possibly ask that of his mother? The two of them were intertwined, his odd looks and the fact that his parents had been outside, that he himself had been conceived outside. He often wondered, if he had been spared one 'contaminant', would he be treated as he was? If he looked as others did, would people have cared for the gossip of the geography of his birth? If he had been born to land-locked stoic retainers but still had these eyes, would people have dismissed his appearance for what it was – no more than the whim of fate?

It was not that Akiyama felt open excitement the closer he drew to Miyamoto. He knew the ultimate utter futility of his mission, and yet it was impossible not to feel some sense of anticipation welling just as he had all the times before. Perhaps it was on some level beneath his human consciousness, a natural instinct that could be neither quelled nor ignored. He kicked his horse faster, he forwent meals, he rode through the night.

He an eager servant of those who would not recognize him, who he knew would not recognize him, both quivering with the secret hope that maybe, finally, this would be the head that bought him welcome amidst his peers and despondent with the certain knowledge that it would not.

A woodsman with an axe across his shoulder told Akiyama that he had seen a man matching Miyamoto's description upon the road the day before, passing in the opposite direction to him. Looked as though he was heading to the nearby town, the woodsman thought, and that upon a fine steed like Akiyama's he'd be there within the morning. Akiyama thanked him with a few coins from the school and spurred his horse onwards.

He was hopeful of finding another witness or two within in the town, and yet immediately he knew that he had come across something far more substantial. He found panic, he found clamour, women fretting and men mustering, gathering what lower tools might suffice as weapons: hammers and sickles and shovels and clubs. Akiyama was reminded of the aftermath of earthquakes – everybody wanting to help or to assure themselves that all was well, and yet nobody knowing quite what to do.

'What has occurred here?' he demanded of the first person he drew close to, a young man consoling what must have been his equally young wife with one hand and a charred poker clutched in the other.

'A masterless,' said the man. 'He attacked the steward and—'

'Tall?' barked Akiyama, and then he tried to contain the rush, clutched his reins tighter. 'The masterless – was he tall? Full head of hair? Scars on his face?'

'Yes! Odd-looking devil.'

'Where is he? Which way did he flee?'

'They've got him trapped in the mill down by the river, last I heard.'

Akiyama's horse was attuned to his mood. It reared beneath him eagerly as he asked for direction, and as soon as it was given the pair of them were off.

He saw the wheel of the mill first, a great wooden thing set into the broad, fast-flowing river. It was attached to a plain and utilitarian structure that overhung the waters on a raised platform. The roof was thatched, the wood grey and square, and the wheel turned slowly, the paddles of it painted green with algae.

The doorway was cast open, what lay within dark.

There were two samurai standing watch over it at a cautious distance, huddling behind a wagon of straw that was half empty and hitched to nothing. A gaggle of perhaps ten of the boldest lowerborn also stood nearby, keeping a fearful vigil. There was a nervousness in the air, in their poise and manner, as though they had cornered a tiger in its lair.

Akiyama headed straight for the samurai, and the two men saw him coming. Perhaps right then any unknown would be regarded as a potential threat, but rather than prepare to fight him the pair of them seem rattled. They watched him guardedly as he dismounted, and neither one of them bowed more than a sliver, lest they let their panicky eyes wander from him for more than a moment.

They made their tense introductions, and then Akiyama jerked his chin at the mill. 'Musashi Miyamoto? Is he in there?'

What must have been the senior of the two turned to the other, and Akiyama realized this man was clutching a wrist with the other hand, pain upon his face. 'Was that what he called himself?'

'I believe so,' said the wounded man.

'Good,' said Akiyama.

'You know this vagrant?' asked the senior samurai.

'I have come for his head in the name of the school of Yoshioka.'

The two samurai heard Yoshioka and looked at him anew. Stared at the colour of tea more than at the colour of his skin, as they had been previously. Akiyama let them. He stood examining the mill.

'How many are in there with him?' he asked.

'Himself alone.'

This seemed odd. 'Why is it then that the two of you tarry out here?'

Neither one of them could either answer or bear to meet his eyes. Akiyama swallowed his irritation.

'We sent a man on horseback to the garrison eastwards,' said the senior man obstinately. 'We'll have thirty samurai here before sunfall.'

'A full cadre of swordbearers in addition to those levied here already,' said Akiyama blackly. 'A proportionate response indeed. That is, of course, provided the wretch doesn't find an escape before then. I am to assume there is only the one avenue of entry into the building?'

The wounded samurai spoke: 'There's a trapdoor down onto the river, hidden beneath the mill itself, and he'd have to swim, but if he searched thoroughly . . .'

'Or simply had enough time,' said Akiyama.

The two samurai looked sheepishly to the distance.

'It's dark in there, he'll not . . .' the senior muttered.

Akiyama ignored him, turned to examine the mill again, made a closer tactical assessment of it. It was a large building, but it had to be braced to take the strain of the wheel and the mill. Therefore there were many beams, which meant space would likely be confined in there. Violence would be close, and that was not something he relished, for he was a swordsman and he needed clear arcs of attack from every angle to practise his art.

He scratched at his chin, pondered. He was reminded of Saito, twelve years prior, the second man he had been tasked to hunt for the crime of drunkenly shouting public profanities at an icon of the Buddha whilst clad in the colour of tea.

Desperate, the shamed adept had taken refuge in an old dilapidated estate, and for much the same reasons Akiyama had been reticent to enter.

Akiyama had found a direct solution then, and it presented itself here also.

'This time of year . . . I assume there is straw or hay set to dry in there?' he asked the senior samurai.

The man nodded. 'Bales of it.'

'Then have you considered smoking him out?'

The senior looked at Akiyama as though he had just demanded his wife for the night. 'Absolutely forbidden,' he said. 'That's the winter feed for my most noble Lord's cavalry.'

Akiyama grunted his displeasure. He stood there for some time, considered other options. The wheel continued to turn, the river continued to flow. There was no sign of any motion from within. Every moment that they delayed was another moment Miyamoto might find his freedom, if he had not done so already.

The thought of this gnawed at him until he could wait no longer. The two samurai and the lowerborn watched as he strode forward. Akiyama placed himself twenty paces from the door, and there he spread his legs, set his hands upon his hips. The door was wide enough for one man only to pass through at a time, and even at this proximity still the gloom inside was such that it was impossible to say who, if anyone, lurked there.

'Musashi Miyamoto,' he called inside, waited.

There was no response.

'I am Nagayoshi Akiyama, of the bloodline Tachibana, of the school of Yoshioka. I have come to claim your head.'

Akiyama thought perhaps that he heard the sound of wood creaking, saw a shadow move upon a shadow. 'Yoshioka?' came a voice.

'Of the ward of Imadegawa, foremost school and pride of Kyoto.'

'I've no feud with you,' said Miyamoto. 'I've never even encountered one of your men before.'

'You offered insult at Sekigahara.'

'I did no such thing.'

'Regardless, your head has been demanded.'

'Indeed.'

There might have been, just about audible, a snort of laughter. Akiyama watched the door for ten heartbeats before he spoke again.

'I call you out to duel,' he said, imploring with an imperious gesture of his hand. 'Come, face me honourably beneath the sun.'

Now there was no doubt about the laughter: 'So you and your men out there can swarm me?'

'I stand alone.'

'I'll not run out there to be cut down by however many await.'

'There's fifteen of us!' called the senior samurai.

'So there are fewer than ten,' said Miyamoto to Akiyama, amused. 'Even so, even so . . . I am not in love with death. I think I shall remain here. But, if you're so eager for my head, why don't you come in here? All of you, why not? One after the other.'

The threat hung in the air, and it was a valid one. Akiyama decided to try his luck.

'Suppose I rain down fire upon you?' he called. 'A lot of hay in there. It will burn quickly.'

'As you will,' said Miyamoto. 'But I think as many bales as I see gathered here have been set aside for a reason, no?'

The man had his wits about him. Frustrated by this,

Akiyama stood rolling his tongue across the inside of his teeth. He waited for forty heartbeats longer before he admitted the futility of waiting. Evidently, Miyamoto was not be goaded or tricked, which left him with only one recourse.

He went back to the two samurai and his horse. He took his tea-coloured jacket off and hung it from the pommel of his saddle, and then began rolling the sleeves of his kimono up and binding them under his armpits with a length of soft tasselled cord, freeing his arms for unrestrained motion.

'Tell me of the interior,' he instructed the watching samurai as he tied the knots. 'Have I room to use my longsword?'

'I do not know your style,' said the senior man.

'Would it be possible to wield *your* longsword in there?' said Akiyama, beginning to detest these fools.

And, of course, neither one of them answered.

'The short it is, then,' said Akiyama. He slid the unneeded longsword in its scabbard from his belt and replaced it within his saddlebags, then withdrew his short. The steel of the blade was oiled and polished and gleamed in the light. 'Anything else I ought to know?' he asked. 'How much straw exactly is in there? Other materials? How impeded will I be in my ability to move?'

'It will be narrow,' said the wounded samurai. 'I do not think you will have chance to manoeuvre around him. You will be facing him directly.'

'And how large is he exactly?'

'He will have reach over you, certainly,' said the leader, and then his voice softened: 'See sense – just wait an hour. Our men will be here then. They'll have lances with them, and—'

'Or the outlaw will have fled.'

That was all he would say. Akiyama rolled his shoulders,

worked flexibility into them. His torso was crisscrossed and braced by the cord. He felt taut, balanced. He turned to the mill and strode over without looking back. He was pensive, for he knew that he was more proficient with his long that with his short, but then he reasoned that in there a man as big as Miyamoto reputedly was would be even more constrained. He made his strategies, took a breath, and then committed himself.

He stepped up onto the wooden platform the mill was set upon and approached the door. He stopped two paces shy of it, peered in. He could see nothing. Braced, prepared to strike at anything immediately, he broached the threshold.

Nothing attacked.

He stood there in the frame of the door, let his eyes adjust to the gloom within. He saw straw piled all around, the heavy blunted forms of blackened beams that were roughly hewn and shaped, and before him the great mechanism of the mill and all its gears hung still and disconnected from the wheel outside. There was no trapdoor that he could spy from here beneath it.

Neither could he spy Miyamoto himself.

Holding his shortsword out before him in a low defensive guard, he ventured slowly in. Murky stacks of baled hay abounded, and each of them could hide a man behind it easily. He held his breath, listened for Miyamoto's. The beams were tight as a cage, constricting, concealing. He thought he heard something, turned, and then in his peripheral he sensed movement.

From above.

It confused him and he turned, and he looked, and he saw an open loft, a second floor that he had not been warned about, and there were bales of hay stacked there too, and one of these bales tipped now, crashed down upon him. It was larger than he was, but Akiyama was quick and writhed mostly out of the way, was not crushed under it but rather knocked from his feet, and he lost grip of his sword.

Immediately, he struggled to right himself. There was further movement from above. Miyamoto jumped down and landed roughly, scrambled over the burst bale of hay and threw himself on top of Akiyama before he could recover his shortsword. He was huge, barrelled Akiyama onto his back as easily as he would have done a child, wrestled to sit on top of him with his legs astride his chest. Akiyama struggled beneath his weight, reached up to try to gouge at the man's eyes, but Miyamoto simply began pounding his fist down into his defenceless face, again, again, and the blows stunned Akiyama, and then he felt Miyamoto shift the position of his body, come closer, press his forearm down fiercely upon his throat.

The pressure, the terrible pressure, he was dead, Akiyama knew. Miyamoto would choke the life from him and he was too small, too feeble, too dazed to resist. Lights in his vision, an oddly disembodied feeling, and he felt as though his spirit was leaving him through the sockets of his eyes like smoke along flues. Tongue fat as a bloated fish left to rot upon the shore. Couldn't even see his killer's face in the darkness, and, and, and . . .

Miyamoto relented.

Akiyama sucked air through the sliver of his throat Miyamoto allowed, forearm still held there, pinning him where he was but not with intent to kill, not any longer.

'Why are you here?' Miyamoto hissed down into his face. 'You come on their behalf? On account of some school? Why aren't you as you? By yourself, for yourself?'

Then he was up, gone. He ran for the door and out. Released, Akiyama scrambled across the floor, recovered his shortsword and, still spluttering and heaving for breath, tried to rise and follow the vagrant. His left leg gave out under him and he fell, and he realized the knee had been wrenched around in the struggle, that it was in fact in agony. Frantically, he hopped across to the frame of the door and fell against it, held himself up, looked out.

Miyamoto was running and the lowerborn had scattered at his emergence exactly as before a charging boar, and the two useless samurai were simply watching as the masterless fled. Akiyama spat a low curse at their incompetence, and then he slid to the floor, sat with his back against the frame. No point going for the horse to try to give chase. If he could not stand he could not wield a sword.

He felt the throbbing of his knee and of his throat and of his face, and consented for now to Miyamoto's escape.

Chapter Five

That summer it was all about definitions.

The youth that had defined itself and thus left childhood behind, and believed fervently that the same could be done to the world as a whole, that chaos could be mapped, that a million different forces and elements could be arrayed and ordered like wicker woven into a screen.

The definition of bruises. To look at them, to prod them, to feel their ache. Musashi would sit squeezing at his purpled forearms or probing at his cut lips. The pain gave him energy, gave him proof that he was a thing of substance, could be touched and in turn touch. In turn alter, on the path that he had set for himself, that had been set.

Food tasted better when he could scrounge it. Water tasted better mixed with his own blood. More vital, more imminent. Everything like this, that summer. Exhilarations felt higher, despair banished entirely. It was in the simple act of brazenly wearing swords once more. It was in taking the hand that would cast him down and turning it back upon itself, feeling the ligaments beneath the flesh wrenching. It was in overwhelming some pompous fool sent from the capital and throttling him amidst lowly hay, and even more than that in granting the samurai mercy.

Ultimately, it was about honesty. Musashi knew himself to be honest, innately – that he was honest as he was now in his defiance, not as he had been before, hiding away, assenting. Honest to himself, to the heart that beat within his chest and the mind that throbbed with raging thought behind his eyes. They, all of them, were dishonest, twisted away from how they ought to be by adhering to their ancient codes and dogmas. Denying themselves, denying the world all it *could* be.

He woke of a night for no obvious reason that he could discern. No noise, no movement, no primal sense of fear. He was in the hills, sleeping rough in a copse of trees where soft mosses abounded. He held himself still for some time in the darkness, suspicious of why it was he had woken. The early summer air was pleasant, warm, the perfect temperature. His consciousness was not fogged in the slightest; he was awake, entirely awake.

It was as though he were simply meant to rise now, as though he were being summoned. That there was something he had to witness.

Musashi rose in thrall to this strange inkling. The sky through the branches above was afire with stars, and behind them the heavens were split by that vast celestial cloud that billowed like an instant of smoke frozen entirely still. He parted a swathe of boughs and looked down into the valley spread below, and there he saw what he knew immediately he was meant to see.

The moon was full and red and lucent and it hung above a

benighted lake, and upon those black waters its reflection shimmered immaculately.

He stared, captivated, for a long time. Took it all in. Never did he think the moon could seem so vivid a colour. Never did he think it could be so beautiful. All existence seemed to hold its breath along with him, as though it were afraid to disrupt this image. Two red orbs perfectly apart, lights in the void, and Musashi looked at them, and soon enough he realized what it was he was beholding.

Here he saw himself, what he had become. They, the Way, all of it, they were the scarlet moon, and he was the reflection cast upon the surface of the lake. Before, hiding with Jiro and the others, he had simply been the black waters. Now he was a separate body of an equal boundary, of an equal shade, of an equal magnitude, one created by the other and yet never meeting, always apart. And was this not fine? Was this not the heavens blessing him?

He sat down in his solitude and continued to stare and felt a stirring in his heart.

How far could this take him? How far could he go?

Peaceful vigils, though, were things for the night, momentary breaths between great lungfuls of hatred, and in the light of day what things there were to hate. Topknots and swords and hubris, but most of all seppuku. Seppuku, the mark of ultimate acquiescence. Sometimes he imagined himself on his knees, actually performing the act, and he envisioned his own intestines in his hands as he had seen his father's intestines, and the questions and the anger this begat in him were so hot they were blinding.

He first learnt of the seppuku of a man named Sanshiro

Okita from a notice carved in wood hung up in a coastal village. The ritual was to be performed in a fortnight in a town Musashi knew to be leagues away, having passed through it some time before, and he looked at this message deeper, looked at it for what it truly was. The loathsome *culture* of it. The expertly carved cedar, the complex letters, the poetic respect afforded to the brutal act in the language, but most of all the galling anticipation sent out wide across the land as though this were a thing of worth and beauty – all of it amounting to what?

What better thing to oppose? Nothing so definite, so clear ahead of him, and so he doubled back upon himself, went back the way he had come. The pomp, the ceremony, the spectacle grew and grew, the seppuku also boldly proclaimed in each hamlet as he drew closer, and, after biding his time in the hills surrounding the town, on the day of the ritual Musashi witnessed an actual herald crying out the act upon the streets as though it were a joyous thing.

None could ignore it. None were permitted to ignore it. This was good, this was fine. None would ignore his opposition to it also.

A red summer moon reflected on a benighted lake.

The seppuku was to be performed in a dojo, and, when he saw the dark bulk of the hall surrounded by a white palisade, Musashi was reminded of his father's suicide. He too had extinguished himself in such a place. The memory gave him cause to shudder, and the eerie sensation lingered as he approached the hall. The streets were quieted. No lowerborn would be permitted to witness such a thing. Conversely, no doubt the hall would be packed with samurai, all but lusting to see with the lewd eyes of voyeurs.

Musashi smelt incense in the air as he approached, saw

curls of it drifting out between the top of the palisade and the overhanging eaves of the tiled roof. On the earth around the hall handfuls of salt had been scattered. From within there was silence. No death poems being read aloud, no faint utterances of contained agony, no blood spattering on callous dark wood. He had been careful to come with the sun to his fore, that his shadow would not be cast upon the palisade as he drew near, and he unsheathed his longsword on the steps leading up to the hall without any sound of alarm from within.

He hesitated for a moment, thought of all he opposed, let that harden him, and then he was committed. He ran up, slashed his sword through the silken palisade and barrelled inside.

There were samurai within, but fewer than he expected, and not one of them was wearing white, the colour of the dead. They were sitting on stools, clad in rough vestments, and though they were surprised by his sudden entry they were not startled, not outraged, recoiled momentarily and then recovered as one might at the crack of fireworks. Fearful of the bang, yet eager to see the subsequent beauty.

One man alone was standing.

'Musashi Miyamoto,' this samurai said, and he slid his longsword out of his scabbard.

Immediately, Musashi recognized him – it was the Yoshioka swordsman he had evaded those weeks ago. He remembered peering through the cracks of the mill's walls, studying the man thoroughly as he stood waiting in bold challenge. Here he was again, his odd-coloured jacket that shimmered brown-green, his weird skin, his cat eyes.

His sword in his hand.

There was to be no seppuku here. He looked at the Yoshioka

samurai – Akamatsu? Akitani? – and knew implicitly from the set of his face that this man would not be argued down to some test of pride with wooden swords, that Musashi's head alone would satisfy him, and that furthermore the others watching would permit nothing less. A dozen of them, armed and prepared, and no chance for him to stand alone against such numbers.

The Yoshioka samurai stepped towards Musashi, his eyes grave. Musashi snarled, upended a brazier of incense and sent the iron frame tumbling towards the samurai, scattering coals and sands and embers that hissed and burnt and smoked, and then he turned and ran from the hall. He heard the outcry behind him, the cries of cowardice and the commands to halt, but he did not listen.

He chose to live. Always would he choose to live.

He ran back towards the hills beyond the edge of town and the safety of the forests upon them. He was a fine runner, honed from youth, and he had no doubts about his ability to outpace the men. He worried, though, about leaving some incriminating trail a tracker could follow through the wilderness, and so as he ran he turned and looked over his shoulder, that he might see if he was leaving footprints in the dust of the streets.

He saw instead that the Yoshioka samurai was chasing after him on a horse.

It was a white steed and its mane was long and shaggy and the hair flew wildly as its rider kicked it into a gallop. Musashi began to sprint, a stupid, instinctive response as though he might outrun the creature, and it seemed the samurai was upon him immediately. Yet, though he had his longsword bared in his right hand, the Yoshioka samurai made no attempt to ride Musashi down or to strike at him from the saddle as he passed. Instead he guided the creature in as wide a berth as he could around the young swordsman, and then halted perhaps twenty paces ahead.

The horse snorted and kicked at the ground, agitated, and the Yoshioka samurai stared at Musashi grimly and kept the point of his sword levelled at him. Musashi stared back. He did not know what was happening. Then the samurai swung one leg over the horse's flank and began to dismount.

The man expected him to stop and duel in full propriety.

Musashi could have laughed. Stupid form of honour, their honour, and he turned and ran back in the opposite direction. The Yoshioka samurai shouted a curse at him, grabbed at the reins and began to haul himself up onto his horse once again, but before he could give chase Musashi ducked around the side of a building. The passage was narrow, walls close, and he hoped it was too tight for the horse to follow directly. He had no idea where he was headed.

At the mouth of the passage one of the samurai from the dojo appeared. He raised his sword, and Musashi raised his. He had no intention of stopping, of being stopped. Musashi swung as wildly as he could, led with the blunted reverse of his blade, and simply smashed it into the samurai's weapon with all the force he could muster. There was a fierce crack and the samurai's sword was knocked askance, but the man managed to keep his grip on his weapon. He recovered, kept his eyes solely on Musashi's blade, began to manoeuvre his body and raise his own sword to parry any reverse blow, and, with the samurai's focus directed so entirely, Musashi kicked the man so hard between the legs it lifted him partly off the ground.

He connected with his shin and he felt it all crushing against the bone of his leg, and the first the samurai knew of the unsighted blow was the pain, and then he was on the floor, writhing, gasping in that ultimate male agony, and Musashi left him behind. Stupid as the Yoshioka man. Fighting was fighting, more than swords. He looked around, saw no horse, kept running.

Ahead he spied a torii gate, vermilion red and standing four times the height of a man. Holy ground, a Shinto shrine, a walled compound. As he ran beneath it he heard a scream of rage that told him he had been sighted, and, as he turned to shut the far more humble iron and oak door that lay beyond the torii gate, he saw them coming, the samurai and the Yoshioka man on his horse all charging in a mad rush.

He slammed the door shut, and then he pulled the wooden beam across to bar it. The door was heavy, thick, it would not be breached by anything short of a cannon. Musashi stood back, lungs heaving, and heard the clamour outside as the samurai arrived. There was the pounding of fists, shouted threats, the sound of hoof-fall cantering back and forth.

'Miyamoto!' called the Yoshioka samurai, the sound of his voice moving with the sound of those hooves. 'Come out and face me!'

Musashi ignored him, ignored all of them. He stood looking at the walls of the compound, gauging their worth. They were not imposingly high. He supposed if he jumped he might grab the top, and that meant the shorter samurai outside could certainly do so if they raised one of their number upwards on their shoulders. Or if they went and found a ladder in the town.

Or if they leapt from the saddle of a horse.

The walls were vulnerable, suddenly of no worth at all, and he felt a panic begin to form. The samurai continued to pound upon the door, but the number of blows was beginning to lessen, and they too must be peering up at the walls, they too realizing what Musashi had realized. From behind him came the priest of the temple, striding over with his mauve robes flowing

'What is going on here?' he demanded of Musashi. 'What is this madness?'

Musashi silenced him with a slash of his hand. The priest obeyed out of sheer confusion.

'Make no attempt to enter here,' Musashi called over the walls to the samurai outside. 'My blade is at the throat of the priest. If any of you try to scale the walls, I swear that I will kill him.'

There was a fierce outrage. 'Dog! Cur!' they shouted, and more insults besides, and then they silenced themselves, a tense, worried hush stealing over them. One of them spoke up after a moment: 'Seigan, wise Seigan? Are you harmed? Do you yet live?'

The priest looked at Musashi. His momentary confusion had passed, and now he was stern, unafraid, cynical. Musashi's eyes narrowed.

'Must I actually raise my blade?' he hissed.

The priest sighed in irritation. 'I am fine,' he called over the walls. 'The wretch has not harmed me. Heed his words. I wish for no violence here.'

There was a further roar, further threats and vows, and Musashi shouted over all of them.

'Leave this place now!' he commanded. 'Away from the walls!'

'If the priest is defiled the slightest, Miyamoto,' one of them called, 'you will be flayed and crucified. I promise you this.'

'Then do not test my resolve!'

Reluctantly, the samurai retreated. Musashi pressed his eye to the seam above the hinges of the gate, checked to ensure they were not merely feigning. Yet he could see no trickery – the lot of them were going, including the Yoshioka samurai on his horse. The concern in their voices for the priest had sounded genuine, something beyond mere protocol and respect for the holy, and this pleased Musashi. That meant they would be less callous, less likely to try to force a resolution.

But that simply left him trapped here. He had bought himself time with the ruse, but not escape.

The priest Seigan stood watching: 'What is it you intend now? They will surround this compound, you know.'

'I promise that I will not harm you,' said Musashi. He sheathed his longsword.

'It is not myself I am worried for.'

Hours passed.

Musashi scoured every sliver of the temple grounds. The shrine was modest, larger than the one of his home village, but far from grand. The gong that hung above the altar was dented, scabbed green with age. There was a hovel where the priest lived his ascetic life. Opposite in the easterly corner was a pond where placid carp mouthed nothing at him, and a spring of water that had been channelled so that it turned a little wheel. The grass was short and lush and emerald.

There were no further exits or entrances that he could find, concealed or otherwise.

The priest sat on the steps of the shrine with his hands on his thighs and his back straight. He watched Musashi cautiously, but it seemed he was not prone to panicking. A man of austere countenance, and the longer he stared the more Musashi began to feel a sense of being judged. Eventually, when no avenue of flight revealed itself after the fourth time of inspection, he relented and went and spoke to the man.

'You must help me,' Musashi said.

The priest shook his head. 'I refuse to aid an outlaw.'

'Please,' said Musashi, his voice low. 'I cannot die here.'

The priest looked at him for a long moment, looked at him deeply, and then his eyebrows moved the slightest amount. He rose to his feet. Musashi watched as he went over to his hovel and went inside. When he emerged he had in his hands two peaches. He tossed one to Musashi. Then he sat down where he had been before, and began to peel his own fruit with his thumb.

Musashi looked at the man in disbelief. The priest did not look back. His concentration in the peeling was either entire, or a pointed dismissal. The peach in Musashi's hand was half green, unripe, and, since there was nothing else he could see to do, he took a bite, skin and all. The flesh had little flavour. It sat poorly in Musashi's stomach, and soon he regretted eating at all.

Time crawled on like a tightening noose, and the shadows began to grow, distend, and so too his wariness. There came a noise, an innocuous single knock, and Musashi leapt into startled action, convinced the samurai were trying to scale the walls. He screamed at them not knowing if they were truly there, repeated his threats, and though he received no response nor saw no enemy emerge it took the longest time before he could admit that they were not near.

Twilight fell, and still he had conjured no escape. The sky was a serene shade of lavender and bats were in the air.

Over the wall came the calm voice of the Yoshioka samurai.

'Miyamoto,' he called, 'it is I, Nagayoshi Akiyama.'

Musashi gave him no response. But the samurai was determined and steady, and he persisted in his communication until Musashi could deny him no longer. He went and stuck his eye to the seam of the gate once more, and saw that the man had come alone, was standing not ten paces away in his jacket that seemed brown in the fading light.

'Away with you, Nagayoshi Akiyama,' said Musashi, 'lest you want this priest's death to stain your conscience.'

Akiyama was not deterred. 'You cannot stay in there for ever,' he said. 'Come out. Behave as a man and let us settle what must be with dignity before the light departs.'

There was something in his voice that surprised Musashi. There was no hatred. There was almost a sadness, a resignation, as though there were no personal desire in him to kill. Musashi stepped back from the gate, stared at the constellation of the iron studs upon its surface, thought of how he might respond.

Above his head two bats passed spiralling frantically around each other, hissing at the limit of human hearing, and whether they were at war or in some mad dance of courtship he could not tell.

'Why is it you have come?' Musashi asked eventually. The simplest question. The most potent.

'I told you before,' said Akiyama. 'Insults at Sekigahara.'

'No,' said Musashi. 'Tell me why *you* have chosen to come and kill on your school's behalf? Don't you understand if a man asks you to do something for him he is weak? Don't you understand if he is incapable he is unworthy of your service?'

There was silence that stretched on long enough that Musashi began to wonder with a burgeoning confusion if his words were not being contemplated. A span of time alive with a potential he had not expected.

Who was this Akiyama? In truth he was surprised to have encountered him again. He had assumed after being shamed and humbled in the mill that the samurai's pride would have consumed him. But here he was, uncaring of any accrued dishonour in being bested by what the Way considered a subhuman, imploring Musashi to fight as though he were an equal. A man who had not run him down mercilessly when he had the chance.

A man, Musashi realized for the first time just then, who must have constructed the supposed seppuku that afternoon as a lure for him and no other, and the complete specificity of this and what this implied Akiyama knew about him set him reeling.

He stood there considering all this, wishing he could see the man's face clearly that he might better gauge his supposed assassin, and then he thought he heard Akiyama sigh, a sad sigh, and subsequently the Yoshioka samurai spoke.

'Nevertheless,' Akiyama said, 'your head has been demanded.'

The statement quashed all, the gate was a gate once more and boundaries were boundaries. 'Away with you!' Musashi snarled. 'Away!'

The pale-eyed samurai did not obey. He stood there continuing to beseech Musashi sporadically without any reply until it was undeniably night. Then, at some point Musashi could not be certain, Akiyama retreated into the darkness, and was gone. Only then in turn did Musashi abandon the gate, returned to sit on the steps of the shrine beside the priest.

Seigan had busied himself lighting oil lanterns, and by their frail light Musashi sat with his longsword resting between his thighs. He was unsettled, one heel bouncing nervously off the earth. Even though Akiyama was gone he felt as though the man watched him yet.

He *was* being watched. The priest Seigan had turned his eyes to him.

The stern gaze grounded Musashi, focused his thoughts.

'Wise one, hear me fairly, without prejudice,' he said to the priest, as honestly as he could. 'I do not want to die, and neither do I want to kill. But these men will not release me, and I fear before dawn they will attempt to storm the grounds. Do you wish for that to occur?'

The priest did not respond.

'Do you want to see these fine grounds sullied with blood?'

The thought did not seem to bother him.

'Innocent blood – I swear to you that I am innocent. My only crime is living, in wanting others to live. This the reason they would flay my skin from me.'

Silence.

'Do you really want for our ghosts to haunt you through all the years to come?'

Something passed across the priest's sombre face. Only a sliver, the slightest twitch of a muscle beneath one of his eyes, but Musashi saw this, saw the opening.

'Please, I beg of you,' he said, his voice lower now, beseeching. 'Is there any way out of here you have kept hidden from me?'

'No,' said Seigan.

'Then surely,' said Musashi, 'there must be something else you can think of. Anything. Please.'

The priest was reluctant, so reluctant, but he weighed the potential scenarios before him against one another and made a decision. He rose to his feet, took a lantern in his hand and went to the rear side of the shrine. There, with some effort, he pulled a loose plank aside and revealed a space beneath the hollow wooden dais the shrine was set upon.

'In there,' said Seigan. 'You can hide. I'll open the gate, let the samurai in, tell them you knocked me on my head and when I awoke you were gone. That you've probably snuck off away into the night. When they're truly gone, then you can make good your flight.'

It occurred to Musashi, when he was nestled down in the darkness and Seigan was lowering the plank over him, that he was placing his faith entirely in this man. The priest could very well board him up in here and go and rouse the samurai outside and deliver him like that. But he looked up at the man's shaven head, at his impassive features, and he felt no sense of threat.

For a moment, it was not Seigan he saw.

Seigan in turn saw the way Musashi was looking at him, and he hesitated for a moment before he lowered the plank entirely. He spoke with curt distaste:

'Consider the path you walk.'

And that was all, and again it was not entirely he alone that spoke. The priest reset the plank and the light was stolen from Musashi, and in the complete blackness, down amidst the rocky earth and the caresses of cobwebs and the smell of damp sawdust, Musashi lay there listening to the muffled cries from outside, thinking of the holy.

* * *

How it would go, how he had envisioned it countless times over in the years since Sekigahara, is that Dorinbo would be standing at the altar of the shrine of Miyamoto. Standing beneath the burnished disc of the gong hung on high and the carved gaze of Amaterasu, the wood of it bright and new, and his uncle would turn and he would take in the boy that had left and the man that was now before him and then he would come to him as though he sought not to disrupt a spectre.

'Bennosuke,' he would breathe.

'Musashi now, Uncle.'

'Musashi, Musashi!'

Dorinbo would accept this instantly and laugh then with his eyes quivering and wet. His uncle's eyes so very visible because they were eye to eye here, perfectly level as men, although Musashi had not encountered one of equal height to him since his early adolescence. Dorinbo, though, of course, would be so, deserved to be so, then and now continuous. And he would clap Musashi on the arms, a warm and honest gesture like that, and the monk would say, 'You live! You live!'

'I do. Through it all I came, Uncle. It is over now. I understand. It is better to live.'

'You have forsaken the Way?'

'Yes.'

'You understand! You see!'

'I do.'

'And you will follow me now?'

Musashi would not answer that, or could not.

'But you live,' said Dorinbo, still smiling but less exultant, his expression altering. Something behind his eyes burning less bright, something liquid subliming, 'You live.'

'I live.'

'You live.'

Repetition robbed it of its status as a word, and it became just a sound in which its emptiness was revealed.

'Live.'

'Live.'

Dorinbo would be amongst the sick and the maimed, of course, those he had dedicated his life to helping. Those with the twisted bodies and the festering wounds, those that Dorinbo had tended with selfless love. They stood around him like a bodyguard, looking at Musashi through eyes missing or misted with cataracts or weeping with rheum.

'Here are the things that I have done, that I have bettered, that stand in testament to me,' said his uncle.

'I live' was all Musashi could say, but he could not bring himself to speak it aloud, and yet Dorinbo heard it nonetheless and Musashi's silent voice had the cadence of a child.

'You come to me and you live,' said his uncle, and his smile now was sad and pitying.

'I live,' said Musashi, and through the mended horde he looked into the eyes of his uncle, who was much taller than he now, and there was no pride in them as there ought to be.

'You live, Bennosuke.'

'I am Musashi.'

'Can you name a thing of worth that stands in testament to that name?'

Outside there were many lanterns now that roved back and forth clutched in hands, light seeping through the cracks of the planking, and the night was rent with furious cries and the heavy thud of footsteps on the wood above him, and this went on for some time but never did Musashi feel as though he would be discovered. He was immune, cocooned away by the thoughts of higher things that temporarily burdened him.

For a moment a form of perspective struck him. He saw the segregated triumphs of this year for what they amounted to, felt the hard, sharp forms of rocks beneath him, and he wondered if, somewhere out there, there was not a grander path he might walk with these same furious steps, if only it might reveal itself.

Thusly the hours passed, and he drifted into some semblance of sleep thinking of Dorinbo, and yet, when he was awakened just before the dawn by Seigan prising the plank free once more, all doubt was dismissed. There was only the flight to focus upon, another achievable challenge, and he thanked the priest, who did not bid him farewell, and then he was away, out of the town, running between the paddy fields that erupted with the cries of frogs, and then up into the forests of the hills and safe once more.

Chapter Six

The rainy season was coming, skies greying in the day but not yet the deep charcoal colour they would become, and through the night the first waters fell. Akiyama sat huddled in a damp stable listening to the drone of it spattering on the thatched roof above. His horse was nearby and there was a humid taste of straw and dung in the air, lining his mouth.

A feeble bracken fire burnt before him, and he stared at it sightlessly.

He struggled to understand how it was Miyamoto had managed to escape him at that temple. The lure had been sound, pitifully easy to construct. The dojo had belonged to a school who were awed by the colour of tea, had gratefully loaned him the use of their hall. They had even paid for the proclamations of the false seppuku to go out across their realm, so eager and excited were they that they might witness the fabled Yoshioka technique with their own eyes.

But Miyamoto had done what he had done, had chosen to run and to take the priest captive, and Akiyama had marched around that temple compound a score of times or more and verified its entirety, had posted men at its every corner, and still somehow Miyamoto had eluded him, slipping through the lot of them in the night.

Perhaps the outlaw had the ability to simply vanish as entirely and as suddenly as he had emerged.

That boded poorly. He doubted he would see Miyamoto again. Akiyama knew he could not use the same bait to try to draw him close a second time, and if the wretch had half the wits he seemed to possess Miyamoto would abandon his other wild assaults and keep his head down and his mouth shut in whatever nest he conspired to find. The chance to claim his head had almost certainly escaped Akiyama, and here he sat staring at the fire, contemplating the dilemma of whether to persevere in blind hope in his hunt or to admit defeat and return to the capital and the school.

That night, such was his mood that he rued the utter pointlessness of either.

It was always ever thus. For all the malicious rumour that delighted in telling of his cuckolding by a barbarian, Akiyama's father had remained a man of wealth and influence. He paid for his son to be enrolled in the school of Yoshioka at the age of thirteen. Surely the colour of tea upon his shoulders would override the colour of his skin.

Akiyama was admitted, and soon found himself last in line, on the edge of the crowd, his work never praised or scorned regardless of how much or how little effort he put in. Patronized or tolerated or endured, never trusted or confided in. That very particular shade of courteous detestation that defined his life from then to now.

Young and hopeful, he had taken this as a challenge. Surely he could make them respect him, to make them want him.

Nothing worthwhile was ever given freely, and what did samurai respect more than the ways of the sword? He threw himself into his studies of the blade and of the countenance of the warrior, staying in the dojo long after others had left, practising the strokes and hardening his body.

Nights he spent in solitude listening to the distant merriment of others, wanting to join them but never quite having the courage to invite himself. Busying himself instead with duty or pastiches of it, scaling and gutting fish for tomorrow's breakfast or polishing the lacquer upon his scabbard, which was already so pure he could all but use it as a mirror, so that if others should stumble upon him he could offer this as an excuse for his absence. A lie that was easier for both parties to accept.

The sword came to him naturally, his forearms strong and his balance uncanny. The Yoshioka had their rigid method, their style, and this he took in quickly. Yet he hungered for more, and so he took to reading tracts of rival philosophies, hoping that maybe if he incorporated fresh techniques it might earn him recognition. That he might better their cause. In a dojo hall filled with a dozen men mimicking the master's moves down to the smallest muscles of the hands and feet, thus Akiyama began assuming different stances, balancing his body in new manners, holding his sword at the opposite angles to others as they all prepared to strike the same blow. This was a taboo, and why he did this at first he did not know. Indeed, he even expected retribution, but received none.

The master didn't comment on his aberration. Neither did the other novices. Of course the Foreigner would have a hybrid style. It was only to be expected.

When he realized this his attitude changed. He became more obnoxiously errant, deliberately so, part of him even wanting to be chastised or punished; at least if they had to forbid him something, they would have to recognize him as an individual. But he was permitted to stray over the course of years and so his method of the sword became a mongrel version of his own devising, and yet, despite its oddity and their determination to render him a nonentity, his raw ability was impossible not to notice.

So, what to do with him? The school found a solution. Whilst those around him were rewarded with emissary status or embedded in fiefdoms to serve honourably under Lords the length of the nation, Akiyama was sent to eradicate the debased. The low men – never the high men, the champions whose heads would garner esteem – who either offered insult to the school in some way, or those of the school that disgraced its name. Akiyama became a negator, a nullifier, the school's void that it sent after other such voids to consume them, to reduce a double aberration into a single.

Years of his life given over to these meaningless quests, Miyamoto, the heretic Saito, the covetous Murakami, all of them, eight heads that he had brought to the masters in Kyoto, eight heads he had presented convinced that each would be the last. His sole reward however each time was no more than the lingering, his continuing to live as the penumbra of them all, until the wheel would inevitably turn again and everything repeated itself.

And he knew this, understood this tacitly, knew that whether he had succeeded in killing Miyamoto or not would have had the exact same effect upon the course of his life. Yet here he sat, feeling a failure, wanting to please them yet just in case, just in case. A slave to this compulsion that governed him. This lifelong resolution to strive to belong to something that did not want him, that he *knew* did not want him.

What was this urge that haunted his heart?

Did the leeches sucking upon the legs of paddy-field oxen long to be absorbed up into the whole of the creature too?

Of course he persevered.

He was too stubborn to relent, or too timid to confront the truth, and so he went on as he had gone before, resigned himself to sacrifice the exact same span of time that he had been prepared to before Miyamoto had buried that man up to his neck in the spring that year. Next spring he would return to Kyoto. Next spring somehow things would be all all right; somehow his diligent but futile pursuit would be recognized. Next spring full of all potential, as all the previous springs of his life had been, and how he hated himself for thinking this, and how some other part of him persisted to believe it.

He went about as a shell of a man, sent his missives, rode his horse, and then, some two months after his last and presumably final encounter with the man he hunted, to Akiyama's complete surprise, he received word of Miyamoto once more.

Akiyama read the message over several times. No doubt that it was Miyamoto, a confrontation with local samurai, a grand act of destruction, and his name shouted over and over. He could scarcely believe it. What was Miyamoto doing? Why would anyone persist in shouting his own name when he knew he was being hunted, and hunted by the school of Yoshioka no less?

What sort of man was he?

Akiyama asked himself these questions as he traversed the land blighted by the direst rainy season in living memory.

People spoke of the heavens suffering a flood and the excess being cast out by the gods to come falling down upon them. Rivers burst. A landslide that swept the road ahead away entirely waylaid him for days, and how frustrating those hours were when he was impeded so. He felt like a moth bouncing off a paper door at night, trying to get at the candle within, again, again, and his eagerness surprised even himself.

Eventually he reached the town where the incident occurred. He approached the site he was pointed towards by the witnesses, sheltering beneath a waxed paper umbrella. Rain fell warm as sweat, so heavy that the earth was hidden in a mist of vapour. The light was muted by clouds and it could be anywhere between noon and twilight.

Out of the gloom ahead coalesced the wreckage of a tree.

Akiyama moved to stand before it. It lay like some massacred dragon, its long and slender trunk split and collapsed upon itself, the splintered inner wood vivid and pale against the grey bark. It had been shaped over the course of years so that when it stood the trunk had looped out and then back over itself unnaturally. So unnatural that it had needed bamboo tripods to support its queer balance.

Miyamoto had cut these tripods down, and caused the tree to destroy itself.

Akiyama stood there for some time. The churning water puddled on the earth came up to his ankles and on its surface leaves floated chaotically, caught between sinking under the downpour and rising again, and on and on, patterns woven around his feet. He told himself that he was feeling pity for the spirit of the tree, to have lived so long only to find this ignominious end, and pity for all the men who had spent so many years carefully shaping it in vain. It was an appalling act.

And yet it captivated him.

What compulsion drove Miyamoto? The tree had been brought down some fortnight previously, which meant that it was perhaps a month and a half after the miraculous flight from the temple, and Akiyama wondered how Miyamoto's heart had beaten in that span of time. Had it welled and welled, this desire for confrontation, until Miyamoto could contain it no more? Until it overrode his senses?

Was he too stricken with an urge, an urge as absurd as his own?

Akiyama thought of Miyamoto, and thought of a wild boar charging, or imagined one, for he was city-born and had never seen such a creature. Then he recalled a dog he had seen once when he had been a child. It had been digging in the streets, its claws scrabbling frantically in the dust, digging neither to reach somewhere nor to uncover something. Merely digging, digging and digging, waging war upon the earth day after day in the same spot for no other reason than that it *had* to, slobber on its maw and its eyes rimmed white.

The rain did not relent, and would not do so for a week yet.

Akiyama circled the ruins of the tree slowly, as though viewing it from a different angle might reveal to him what he sought.

Those who had witnessed the debacle had told him that Miyamoto had shouted something as he cut the tripods and set the tree to its ruin.

What he had shouted was, 'Something that cannot stand for itself should not stand!'

This was what held Akiyama's fascination.

Common vandals destroyed for nothing more than the thrill of destruction, and yet, perverse though it was, it seemed that there was some consistent purpose to Miyamoto's actions. Enemy of the Way, he pronounced himself. But which was he truly, thoughtless or thoughtful? Governed by reason or slave to mad impulse? Here a man who so thoroughly lusted to provoke that it could not be contained, even apparently supplanted any sense of self-preservation, and yet at the same time it appeared a tempered form of bloodlust that held him enchanted, if such a thing could exist.

Maddened enough to charge into a dojo and yet not giving himself entirely over to blind carnage, retaining enough sense to flee when he saw the odds against him. A man who held a sword to the throats of priests, and yet spared Akiyama's own life when he was entirely at his mercy.

Was there something higher here?

Or lower.

Deeper.

There, an empathy the pale-eyed samurai felt a sense of guilt for. What was it like not to care? How did it feel to have a complete disregard for the concerns and wills of others, to possess a complete faith in oneself as Miyamoto seemed to? The fierce courage, if courage was the correct word, of taking your sword and cutting as you saw fit, because you yourself willed it and believed it to be right?

Akiyama looked at the ruined tree.

A final tripod yet stood, supporting the base of the trunk.

He stared at this for a long time. Then he set his umbrella down. He did not close it, and it floated inverted on the surface of the muddy water, drifted languidly away. He did not feel the rain on his brow.

Tentatively, he drew his longsword.

He stood there, contemplating the blow he might strike. Whether he should even strike it.

His jacket had become sodden in a moment. The silk of it hung over his arms as dark and clinging as seaweed as he raised his sword above his head, aligned the cut.

Akiyama levelled his spirit, managed his anticipation, and then he struck.

Steel split the bamboo cleanly.

The tripod fell away, but the trunk remained standing. Its roots were set well enough into the earth to support its surviving weight.

Whatever Akiyama had expected to feel, or thought he might feel, or had longed to feel, he had not felt. He stood looking at the tree for some time. He became aware of eyes peering out at him, sheltered under eaves. Familiar expressions. Suddenly he felt foolish, realized what it was he had done. He sheathed his sword and hardened his face and assumed his false mantle of one who belonged once more.

Rain had pooled in his upturned umbrella, had sunk it. He picked it up and shook it empty, resumed his shelter under it. He walked off, and the people of the town watched him go until the haze of the weather swallowed him.

In his mind the words remained: 'Something that cannot stand for itself, should not stand.'

Chapter Seven

Harvest time, and the dried fields were alive with rhythmic song as the rice crop was joyfully gathered in by the peasants, and Akiyama had Musashi caught upon the plains.

Musashi did not understand how the Yoshioka man had found him, but he had, and he had been running for a half-day already. Not straight sprinting from the horse, not making that mistake again, but rather taking cover, ducking into ditches or burying himself beneath the piles of stalks and husks that lay discarded at the edges of fields, looping back upon himself, waiting, biding his time, hoping that Akiyama would follow some false signal of his passage, but the samurai was skilled in tracking and judged the situation correctly again and again.

He longed for the hills and the forests, and they were there within his sight. But between that safety and behind him lay nothing but flat paddy fields segmented by raised pathways between them. One could all but see clear to the coast, and a lone figure navigating between the bands of peasants would stand out so obviously aberrant. Musashi was crouched down behind one of the raised pathways, and with as little of his head as he dared expose, he was watching Akiyama. The samurai was far – if Musashi raised his smallest finger at arm's length he could blot him out with but the very last bone of it – but he was on his accursed horse, and such was the distance to the hills yet that, if he attempted a dash for them and was sighted, he could not be sure the creature would not outrun him.

This was the most distance he had managed to put between them yet. This was the closest he had come to escaping. His heart was beating as fast as though the man were close enough to touch, the muscles of his legs shivering. He fought to overcome. If he was to get away, he needed calmness. It would be about timing and cunning, not raw physicality.

Thus Musashi waited, watched, hidden. He saw the tiny figure of Akiyama stop on his horse. The samurai was at a crossroads of the pathways, and he remained there looking in all directions for some time. Patient and vigilant, he understood the strategy that would come into play here as well as Musashi.

Eventually, something caught Akiyama's attention at an opposite angle. The samurai turned on his horse, and led the creature away at a trot with his back almost entirely to Musashi.

His chance was here and his first desperate instinct was to simply run. He did not. He kept as low to the ground as he could, and he advanced towards the hills, looking over his shoulder at Akiyama, hoping the pathways would shield him from his hunter. The paths came up to his thighs only, and he had to be at least partly exposed, but he had chosen a compromise between speed and concealment. Writhing on his belly like a serpent would take much too long.

His luck held. Akiyama continued in the way he was going. Musashi managed to cross three fields in his crouching gait, and the hills drew ever nearer. In the field ahead there were peasants working. There were maybe sixty of them, squatting down with sickles in hand, and they were so occupied in their work that they had not spotted him approaching. He hesitated for a moment, wondering if he should avoid them entirely, and when he looked over his shoulder next he saw that Akiyama was now looking towards him.

Musashi's immediate instinct was to throw himself to the ground or simply to flee. So strong this desire, so innate, that he felt it almost as a spasm, yet he resisted, held himself still. Akiyama was too far to identify him, too far to be certain, and the samurai was not moving. Give him any evidence of who you are, and he will come. No, what Musashi forced himself to do was to turn his back on the Yoshioka samurai entirely, and calmly walk towards the band of peasants as though he were one of their number who had perhaps ducked aside to urinate.

The sheer will it took not to look back. Each step seemingly of no distance at all. Halfway to the peasants he realized his swords were at his side. Distant proof of who he was to Akiyama, and fearful to the lowerborn. Slowly, as inconspicuously as he could, he slid them out of his belt one by one and tried to hide them in the folds of his kimono. The short fitted well but the long was scantly concealed, the point of its scabbard rattling between his thighs and its pommel under his chin, but at least they were to his fore. Akiyama, looking from behind, would not see them.

The peasants were singing still, a call and response between the men and the women. Musashi did not know the words, but the melody seemed familiar, perhaps sung in the village of his childhood also. He came to edge of them and squatted down into a crouch, grasped a handful of rice stalks and drew them close as though he too were harvesting the grain. Here he allowed himself a covert look over his shoulder. Akiyama was still looking, but it was hard to tell if he had drawn closer.

Musashi hid his longsword down in a furrow, and he shuffled his shoulders in vague time to the song. Tried to belong. For a time it worked. But Akiyama was definitely coming towards them, the samurai perhaps but three, maybe four fields over, and more and more curious glances were being cast Musashi's way by the peasants. The man nearest to him rose to stand. He had stripped his plant bare, meant to move on to the next one, and innocently he turned around stretching the strain of squatting out of his knees. As he did so he happened to look down into the furrow and saw Musashi's longsword.

He stepped back immediately, looked between the weapon and its owner. The peasant had a sickle in his hand, but he used this only to shield a woman next to him, perhaps his wife. Musashi hissed at him that he meant no harm, for them all to carry on as they had been, but a panic was rippling outwards now and all were turning to him. Half were drawing back in apprehension, half saw the swords and thought him samurai and dropped to their knees, and he was left alone in a widening gap like a rock amidst a field of grass blown by the wind.

Musashi turned.

Akiyama saw him for who he was, and kicked his horse into a gallop.

Cursing, he grabbed his longsword from where it lay and sprinted for the hills. Nowhere else to hide but there. He kicked his way through the stalks of rice in their neat rows, vaulted over the raised pathways when they came, and through the wind in his ears he could hear Akiyama bellowing something behind him. Didn't care for what he said, could guess at its exact extent, just kept running. There was a cleft between the hills, a gorge of sorts, and he ran for this, hoping that it might afford a gentler ascent.

There was a bamboo grove at the foot of the slopes and he danced through the emerald trunks, tried to disrupt as little as he could. No horse could follow him through here, and maybe it might mask his trail. Beyond the bamboo, higher up the slope, he found gnarled pine trees and straight tall cedars and thick, entangling bracken everywhere. Knowing that Akiyama would not be far behind he lunged and thrust his way upwards as far as he dared, felt his legs cut and shred on old dead wood, and then threw himself down into the first viable cleft in the earth he saw.

He lay there trying to hold his breath. After a moment he reconsidered, pulled whatever lichen and branches and leaves lay close by on top of him, and then he kept still. He looked down into the gorge, through the trees, through the bamboo. Akiyama rode up on his horse. Close enough that Musashi could see the clasp that bound his topknot. The going was dense and he was forced to stop. His horse circled about itself again and again, and the samurai calmed the animal until it was still.

Then he simply looked about, and listened.

There was silence, or what seemed like it. Musashi's hands grew tight on his scabbard, longsword clutched before him on the ground with both fists. Hadn't had time to reset it in his belt, could not do so now. Somewhere on the slope opposite a pine cone fell, rattled its way to the ground. Akiyama turned instantly, peered up at where it had fallen until he had ascertained it was nothing of interest. The samurai was astute, honed. Musashi knew he would make far more noise trying to push through the undergrowth that abounded. He dared not move.

He was caught here for the moment.

For the first time Musashi could recall, Akiyama seemed to grow impatient. His hand began to rattle against the pommel of his saddle, and then he called out. 'Miyamoto,' he said, 'reveal yourself. Face me.'

He addressed either slope of the gorge, head turning from one to the other, and Musashi watched him and remained motionless, silent.

'I know you are here, somewhere. Reveal yourself! I will not slay you running through the woods, caught and cramped by branches. I offer you the chance to step out here into the open, sword in hand, and face what must be with dignity.'

Wind blew and leaves scattered across the gorge.

'What is this?' cried Akiyama, and the first hint of anger entered his voice. 'Again and again you venture out into society solely in pursuit of violence, but when I offer fair combat you refuse? Is your heart crazed?'

Musashi bit down on the knuckle of his thumb.

'Very well,' said Akiyama to the silent forest all around him. 'At your leisure, then. I have my duty, and my duty holds me here. I await you.'

He dismounted from his horse, took a bamboo flask from his saddlebags and took a long drink of whatever liquid was inside.

Musashi watched him, and how dry was his own throat, how empty his stomach.

* * *

The Yoshioka samurai did not relent. He stayed close to his horse through the hours until night fell and he was finally stolen from Musashi's vision by the dark. Only then did Musashi dare to move. Akiyama would hear him, of course, but he would not be able to spot, to pursue. This, the only recourse available to him. Hopefully he could put some distance, any distance between them through the night, and that was better than waiting pinned where we was, hoping futilely that Akiyama might have grown bored by the dawn and departed.

There was no chance of that, Musashi knew. He had studied the man's face well, seen the determination there.

Musashi began to rise. His body had grown cold as the earth against which it had been huddled, and after being held in tense contortion for such a long time his muscles ached. He brushed the debris he had hidden beneath from his back, and then made to head along the route he had plotted in the light. It was up and to his side, what appeared the least impeded path from his poor vantage, but whether he found it or not he could not tell. Dead branches cracked beneath his feet, his knees and hands grazed against trees, and each noise seemed to resonate in the quiet of the night.

He heard noise behind and below him also. Akiyama, perhaps, knowing he was on the move, probing his own blind path.

Progress was impossible to judge. He did not think he was moving far. The slope seemed to shift beneath him. One time his foot did not find purchase where he expected it, and he fell forwards. He cried out in shock, a yelp stolen by the impact of something blunt and hard on his chest, and he lay there listening, ruing the clamour. When he had purged himself of the stupid, instinctive notion that Akiyama was swooping in immediately upon the sound, he rose, entirely disorientated. He chose a direction, and on he stubbornly pushed through the night.

Where was his scarlet moon to light his path, to assure him all was well?

With every further graze, every twist of his ankle, every moment he was caught perilously balanced between two footholds he could not discern, he began to curse Akiyama silently. Began to hate him, his persistence through this entire year. He was a thrall to the Way, perhaps its perfect embodiment even. Nothing to him but duty. Nothing to him but killing. He questioned why it was he was running. Why not oblige what the samurai demanded, fight him with steel? End it?

Every time he asked himself these things, he forced himself to think of how Dorinbo would answer.

But it was difficult to remain faithful when all about you was blackness and exertion. He could not tell if time passed quickly or slowly, but eventually the sky began to lighten in the east. All assumed tinges of blues, and he could see the forms of trees around him now. Saw that there were not many above him, that the forest seemed to end abruptly, that he had put most of the hill behind him. Sighted, he advanced quickly, and soon he achieved the crest. He looked down upon the opposite side, and found the hill entirely bared. Nothing but churned mud and earth before him.

A landslide must have occurred here, back in the rainy season.

He could have laughed. A path, a clear path here laid for him and him alone. Gleefully he extracted himself from the last of the undergrowth, and he ran. Didn't care for how much his legs hurt, how many times they had been cut, he skittered down the slope all but dancing in mad release, and the earth was soft and obliging, and in a matter of moments his descent had matched the distance of his arduous ascent, surpassed it, and he was at the foot of the hill, and he was gone. Ran unimpeded through spacious meadows, unseen, unknown, ran until his heart and his lungs could bear no more and he assured himself he was free of all pursuers, and there he found a spot to hide amidst soft grasses, and the sun was rising in the sky and all was warm, and like that he closed his eyes and slept.

When he awoke it was afternoon. The sun had apexed and the sky was pale. He peeled back his clothing, torn and thick with ochre clay from the hill, and examined his legs, counted the scrapes and cuts upon them. He had seen a leper once, and so many were his lesions that he was reminded of that blighted flesh, but none of the wounds were deep. Superficial grazes. He washed the dried blood away in a pond, splashed his face, and then from another spot drank until he was sated.

His escape from Akiyama had robbed him of any idea where he was. There was no mark of man around. He decided to head for high ground, that he might spy some road or hamlet, or failing that the coast. Looking around, he saw a bared slope some distance away, the grasses upon it short and tough and strawlike. Seemed the best compromise between vantage and ease of ascent, and he headed towards it.

Halfway up its slopes, with the sun now beginning to set and the sky turning golden, the wind blowing constant, something flickered in his peripheral vision. He turned and looked down, and there he saw, once again, Akiyama on his horse.

Musashi simply stared down for a moment in utter

disbelief. At how he had managed to find him, at the fact the man *persisted* in even attempting to find him. Stared and felt his lip curl, and the Yoshioka samurai saw that Musashi had seen him, and now he kicked his horse into an open gallop, began to ascend the hill, and Musashi turned and ran.

He never really got going. There was nowhere to hide on this bared slope, and more than that the anger took him, the incredulity. He was cursing as he stopped, and he turned back to Akiyama, drew his longsword and spread his arms wide, waited. Akiyama did not come straight for him, but rather took his steed in a cautious berth to the gentle crest of the ridge and then came at Musashi from above.

'Here!' Musashi screamed at him. 'Fine! Come as you will, you son of a whore!'

Akiyama did not charge. He cantered up and stopped some twenty paces shy. There he dismounted and slid his long-sword from where it was hung upon his saddle. His jacket was a fine hybrid colour in the light, rich, gorgeous, and his eyes matched the shade of the grass at his horse's feet.

'Musashi Miyamoto,' he said as he approached, 'I am of the school—'

'I know why you are here,' said Musashi. 'Spare me the pomp. If you want my head, out your sword and to my throat, and not a word more.'

Akiyama did not draw his sword, though. He stood there looking at Musashi, straight at him, and in his eyes was what appeared to be curiosity. Musashi glared back, but the man would not be provoked. The longer he looked, the more the set of his own shoulders lessened, and eventually he lowered his longsword to his side. There they stood for some time, around them the last heat of autumn.

Slowly, their eyes were drawn to the landscape below them.

They saw the plains stretching away, and in every dry and empty field all remnant husk and haulm of the rice harvest had been knotted and stacked like cenotaphs and set alight. The sky was golden now, and rising into that great expanse were a hundred tendrils of smoke.

'There,' said Musashi. 'Can you not see?'

Akiyama did not answer. The wind blew on.

'That is how it needs to be,' said Musashi, and he felt a shudder as he spoke, as he realized that what was manifested here was as vibrant and as piercing as a scarlet moon. 'Can you not see? There, it's right there. *There!* See it – a necessary and complete destruction. All those husks, a million of them, a million worthless things eradicated and the ash of them buried in the earth to fertilize. The fields cleared and revitalized and what follows is a new growth, bounteous, and bounteous entirely because it is free of all that came before. Can you not see?'

Akiyama looked, but he said nothing.

'It is that simple,' said Musashi.

'Something that cannot stand for itself,' said Akiyama hesitantly, 'should not stand?'

'Yes!' said Musashi excitedly. 'Who was it that told you that?'

The samurai had a strange reaction to those words. It almost seemed as though there had been hope in his eyes prior to their being spoken, or longing, but that in hearing them this nascent emotion was slaughtered. That Musashi had slaughtered it, and now there was a personal disappointment that radiated from him.

The man's face hardened and he made himself deaf. The strange moment and whatever it might have held had passed, and now he put his focus upon what he had come here to achieve. With ceremonial slowness and eyes never leaving those of Musashi, the samurai took a tasselled cord and wrapped it over his shoulders and under his arms, binding the sleeves of his jacket back and freeing his arms for movement. With equal care and precision he drew his longsword, blade bright in the warm light, and lowered it one-handed into a neutral position by his side with the tip resting a finger's breadth above the ground.

Musashi watched him. The mad overriding urge to fight had passed. But he was caught here, and his sword was in his hand, and the horse was there, and he could not outrun that.

At his stillness, Akiyama put his free hand to his waist, and produced another length of tasselled cord, which he tossed to Musashi. Musashi caught it and, not having any choice, nodded his thanks and then bound his own sleeves up as Akiyama had done. The man made no move to attack as he did so, even with Musashi's sword temporarily scabbarded once again, waiting with perfect formality. Then, with bare arms turning to gooseflesh, Musashi drew his longsword once more, dropped into a fighting stance and held the weapon before himself.

Musashi nodded. Akiyama nodded.

They began.

Chapter Eight

Immediately, Musashi was unsettled. Akiyama sank into a stance he had never seen before, turning his body so that his left shoulder faced towards Musashi with his legs spread in a wide crouch. His sword he held at his hip with the blade trailing behind his body, hidden almost and leaving the length of him seemingly open and vulnerable.

Not knowing what else to do, Musashi chose a neutral, defensive posture: facing straight towards Akiyama, shoulders broad, left foot braced perpendicular behind the right, sword in both hands out before him with the pommel pointing at his navel, the length of the blade marking the distance between them.

The great wait, then, both of them staring each other in the eye, judging. It was said that masters of the sword could see a man's spirit, his *ki,* flowing out of him and from this discern weaknesses in his soul and technique. Musashi saw only a man a head smaller than he and utterly unafraid.

How long it took to start these duels, to summon the courage to step into the lethal range of the sword. To charge into battle was one thing, clad in iron and leather and wood and plunging into a chaos of chance and a maelstrom of sudden foe, but here two men with a definite enemy before them wearing only silk and rags and skin and flesh and muscle. That against steel, the fear innate in every mote of the body. Even for veterans like Akiyama a quailing, as though arms and legs and chest and head were creatures separate from the heart, each individually terrified of the risk.

A sickly feeling in Musashi's muscles, his upper arms, the bottom of his thighs, hardening as if the blood within was congealing.

The earth soft beneath his soles, feet digging in, affixing himself.

The columns of smoke rising.

The feel of the grip upon his palms, ridges of the twisted cloth, ring finger and little finger tight, thumb, fore and middle loose, cradling.

The eternal seething of the wind.

The sun inert, the chill, the chill . . .

Akiyama lunged forward, and the path of his sword was concealed almost entirely by his body. Musashi saw it loop over the man's head at the very last moment, where he had been expecting a low attack. Hands moved autovigilant, raised his own sword and caught the blade not flat but glancing. The two edges ran down each other hissing until the handguards of both swords met with a crack.

In they both followed, in tight, shoulder to shoulder, Akiyama and Musashi, knuckles rubbing against one another, the points of their blades waving over each other's back. Immediately Musashi attempted to make it a matter of strength, barging forward, trying to unbalance the man.

Akiyama simply rode the push, sliding backwards whilst maintaining his posture perfectly. Feet gouging trails in the earth. Like a pan of water shaken, fluid and then still as it was before. Twice more Musashi tried before he admitted the futility.

There they stood, locked, the guards of their swords as close as though they had been fused together in some forge. No growling or fighting or tussle, weapons resting light, simply checking the other. Musashi turned his blade and rolled the edge of it towards Akiyama with his foe's sword as the fulcrum, once, twice, meeting the flesh of Akiyama's biceps on the second try. A thin red line of blood appeared, the cut a mere razor kiss. Akiyama gave no sign of pain or worry. He knew that he could not be grievously wounded here.

Therein lay the predicament: close like this they could not be hurt, but if they yielded and retreated each would have to pass back through the cutting arc of the opponent. Where before they had to step in, now they had to summon the courage to step out. They circled on tense feet, blades entwined, Akiyama's oiled bright and Musashi's dulled and worn.

Akiyama was superb. Musashi felt fear, real fear, the wooden sword victories he had notched this year hollow and worthless now. He had no conception of how he had managed to counter the man's opening attack, and now he could not unsettle him with his strength and his size.

It was Akiyama who made the first move outwards, withdrawing his sword slightly, taking the tiniest step back. Musashi consented, and in stuttering slivers they began to separate. Feet barely leaving the ground, never crossing, left behind right, always braced. Blades in constant contact, but the point of that contact slowly moving up the length of each. Twisting, each man turning his wrists, trying to keep his sword on top and watchful of a sudden thrust from the other, bit by bit until the points were circling around and around each other like swallow's tails, and then . . .

Freedom of space, and the same challenge as before.

Akiyama resumed his original stance, the sword concealed behind him once more. His face was serene, his mouth thin, his eyes unwavering. The perfect swordsman, no hint given at all to his intentions. In turn Musashi's mouth hung open, he unaware of it, his eyes roving, seeking, his sword now held horizontal at his waist, ultra-defensive, a turtle crawling into its shell.

Perhaps invited by that stance, or emboldened by the knowledge of his superiority, Akiyama did not wait long to attack once more. His second strike came without warning, and this time the blade sliced from the side, seeking to cleave him at the waist. Again Musashi managed to parry, but before the blades had even met, Akiyama was moving into his next action: rolling his body around the fulcrum of the swords, pirouetting as though the block was entirely expected, and making to strike at Musashi's exposed back.

This time brute strength and speed did save him. Musashi threw himself backwards before Akiyama's blade could start its slashing arc, barrelling into the man whilst his sword was still rising over his shoulder and knocking him off balance. The pair of them scrambled to right themselves, clods of dirt flying, and then they whipped around to face one another once more.

Closer now, each sensing it, fear fading as they knew that into this they were inextricably caught and that it was nearing its end. Most duels ending in one move; all ending in under five. Breathing heavily, Musashi saw the man and saw his killer, and the liberating anger came, the warmth, the fatalistic warmth. If he was dead then he was dead, and there was no point defending a corpse, and what mad joy in that.

Musashi raised his sword above his head, pommel facing his enemy, the most aggressive stance he knew. Committed to one tremendous downwards blow, stomach and chest bared provocatively. Akiyama saw the change in him, and changed in turn. He rose out of his crouch, brought his sword to rest at shoulder height so that the blunt back of it rested along his collar bone with the point towards Musashi.

Twitching, each daring the other to go. Musashi towering, Akiyama poised. Breath heaving, blood racing. All things balanced. Mind unfettered, seeing all: unorthodox stances, where Akiyama's true ability came from perhaps. Unorthodoxy. Musashi grasped at this, clutched it with wild and final passion.

He stepped forward, arms beginning to bring the sword over his head.

Akiyama's feet parting as he kicked off to lunge, sword whipping around, aiming upwards, seeking to sever those arms before they could bring the sword over, clever, pre-emptive.

Duped.

Musashi's body checking the strike, jumping backwards instead, both feet leaving the earth, sword still high above.

Akiyama's sword slashing across where those arms should have been.

Musashi twisting his body in the air, seeing the blade of his enemy arcing before him, slicing nothing. Landing, body sideways, immediately putting all his weight on his front foot.

Akiyama turning his sword, reacting, desperate, bringing it up to put the length of it between them, seeking to skewer Musashi's onrushing heart.

Too short.

One hand only on his sword, long arm stretching out to its utmost extent, Musashi reached over the guard and smashed his sword downwards. All strength, all weight, body tipping forward, everything behind the blow, battering Akiyama's arms aside as it went.

The point of Musashi's sword raking downwards, downwards, deep and cleaving, the proper cry of striking, a great *ssssssssa!* erupting uncontainable from his lips.

Akiyama didn't scream. He gave one low gasped grunt, fell to his knees, and then tried to stand once more but staggered away drunkenly. His sword fell from his hands, and then he pawed feebly at his chest and collapsed onto his back.

Musashi was perfectly still, longsword held out by his side where the fullness of the blow had taken it. In him, though, the great joy of victory erupted, and everything seemed to hum as though his spirit had been struck like a bell. These were the moments he was made for, that no wooden sword duel could compare to. He tried to keep the grin from his face, knowing that such delight was shameful. But it was there, this marvellous wellbeing, this pride . . .

One-handed! One-handed! No one could cut a man with a sword in one hand! That was what they said, that was what they had said for centuries, what they were certain of. Another delusion of theirs that he had shattered, another profound victory.

He wanted to scream and shout and dance, but he contained himself; rotated his sword in his single hand, saw the blood there, made himself look. He took deep breaths, thought of calm and dignity. Slowly he rose out of his combat stance, and with one final inhalation forced the primal triumph from him, leaving him only with a deep, human satisfaction.

The smoke rose. The wind blew. The world went on. He turned to look at Akiyama where he lay.

The man was not dead. Slowly Musashi walked over to him, and looked down. So clean was the cut it seemed as if Akiyama was barely wounded, a thin dark line across his chest where the blood was soaking into the brownish material of his clothing from beneath.

It occurred to Musashi then that perhaps this was why the samurai had taken the old Chinese swords, the heavy, short, double-edged weapons that were used for battering through armour as much as cutting, and refined and refined them over centuries into what the longsword was now – a slender single-edged thing of grace designed purely for splitting and slicing.

Wounds so clean they were no more than a line drawn across a man, and the billows of a kimono masked this only further. The elegance of mortality, easy to believe that it was painless, that dying for a Lord or a school was nothing. The long calligraphy strokes of a death cult writ upon the bodies of men.

Strokes that he here upon this hill had written.

Musashi forced himself to see, because he longed to be a good man, and because he thought a good man would want to understand what he had wrought. With the point of his sword he peeled Akiyama's torn clothing back, and saw.

When Akiyama breathed in it went *heeeeeeeeeee.*

When Akiyama breathed out it went *ngu ngu ngu.*

And when Akiyama started laughing, it gurgled forth from both his mouth and from his wound in a bubbling choke.

Chapter Nine

Kyoto

The cadastre was unfurled, spread across the hard darkwood flooring of Goemon Inoue's personal chambers, and every morning he, the captain of Kyoto, would stand and look down across his supposed city spread before him in the exact same manner as one who prodded a burn to see if it yet hurt.

See it then: the ten-thousand-year city, the millennial city rendered in black ink on white paper. Encircled by the peaks of thirty-six mountains, nestled between the river Katsura in the west and the river Kamo in the east, and, from river to river and from north to south, Goemon saw the familiar recreated rigid angles of the great moat that had been built by the Regent Toyotomi that marked the boundary of the city proper, saw the dozens of bridges broaching it, saw the myriad gates that led inward. In the north-east of the city he saw the abode of the Son of Heaven, in the south-west the grounds set aside for the castle of his most noble Lord Tokugawa, and in between these poles like a geometric pattern on butterfly wings he saw the interlocking of all the streets, blocks upon blocks thriving and vital, the estates of distant absent Lords and hovels reliant upon alms all marked and recorded here, dens of sin and peaks of virtue, the markets of great guilds of rice and silk and salt and oil surrounded by backstreets and alleyways and all the deep cunning a city could hold; as long and as broad as the outstretched arms of two men, this cadastre, ruthlessly detailed with minutiae of ownership and conflict and still so lacking.

Here a hundred thousand homes according to some, and a population in constant flux with travellers and merchants and warriors and Lords and scoundrels all coming and going, and within that number and the number of the residents how many schemes, how many plots? Mouth dry, body slick with sweat, he stood and looked down upon it as he always did, and wished for nothing more than an arrowhead of cavalry simply to plough through it all.

But there were no horses here.

Goemon rolled the cadastre up and placed it back in the neat lacquered chest from which it came, and then began to prepare himself to actually walk upon those streets. He chose to wear three underkimonos. Two of them were padded and added the appearance of weight to his midsection, intended to draw the eye away from his shoulders and make him seem solid, implacably balanced. Over these came the outer kimono of dark silk, which hung to his ankles, and over the skirts of this he wore wide stiffly pleated hakama trousers. Both were bound tight around his stomach with a broad belt he tied himself.

Finally, his jacket. This was of wide billowing sleeves and the hem of it hung to his midthigh. The silk it was made of was dyed a rich, deep black. On either breast, on either arm, and in the centre of his back the crest of his Lord was sewn in white. Three inwardly facing hollyhock leaves, broad and pointed, encircled by a ring. The crest of the Tokugawa.

It still jarred his eye to see that aberrant symbol upon himself, jarred him in the manner of cold bringing forth white paths of scar.

He spent a few moments debating whether or not to wear his helmet of office. It was of steel painted black and circular in shape, a disc with a hammered indentation in the centre to accommodate the crown of his head. The crest of the Tokugawa was inlaid at its fore in bronze. Militant and imposing, which was not in itself undesirable, and yet his duties today were civic. He decided it was better to remind the city of his authority rather than his face, and tied the cords of the helmet beneath his chin.

A longer debate was whether or not to ride in a palanquin. Nobility and men of the highest office rode in palanquins. It would imply him high and worthy and a man to be listened to, and convey the majesty of the clan. But was it majesty that the clan wanted him to convey? Kyoto was the Son of Heaven's city, and no person or thing within it could compare, or even suggest itself comparable, to that indisputable grace. He fretted, caught, and then went with what was most familiar to him. He left the garrison with a bodyguard of eight men and travelled the streets on foot. Better to show his swords, the two things in this city in which he had unwavering faith, than the reed curtain of a lacquered box.

Goemon went first to the Chaya guild of salt, two great warehouses that stood in a walled compound in the south of the city. The men there bowed to him. He reminded them of their duty to pay their taxes punctually and honestly. He went to the Kiyomizu temple on the slopes of Mount Higashi. There it was Goemon who bowed to the high priest in his purple robes, and assured the holy man that his seat on the Son of Heaven's council was safe and that the ascendant Lord Tokugawa had no intention of interfering with the council itself.

He followed his list of appointments diligently. His men carried the standard of the Tokugawa in lieu of the palanquin, here the crest black on a white field, an icon that had seldom been seen in Kyoto until this year. Goemon was aware of the way the people stared at it balefully, of how they murmured of the delicate hollyhock flower suddenly thriving in the city as fierce as the stubborn yutzu vine.

His face, however, he set in perfect sternness.

He arrived at the school of Yoshioka at least a full hour late, and Goemon was well aware of this as he and his men walked down Imadegawa avenue. He saw a member of the school standing waiting in front of the gates, a bald samurai clad in their curious brown-green silk. The man must have stood there for the entire delay, yet Goemon did not increase his pace. He decided neither could he apologize: he was the clan and the clan held the power.

The Yoshioka man sank to his knees at Goemon's approach. 'Most honourable Captain of the most noble clan Tokugawa,' he said in the elaborate courtly tongue, 'it is the humble honour of Tadanari Kozei to welcome the most honourable Sir Inoue to the Yoshioka school of the sword.'

'Rise,' said Goemon.

Tadanari obeyed. He bowed and let Goemon enter. In the yard of their compound a cadre of adepts were waiting to bark a salute to the triumphant Lord Tokugawa. They were swordsmen, who merited respect, but their numbers and their power paled to that of the Tokugawa. Acknowledging them fully would imply equality, perhaps, and after a moment's hesitation Goemon gave only a stiff nod to their assembly.

The master Kozei showed him around the school, the barracks, the gardens, and lastly the dojo. Goemon took it all in impatiently, having been subjected to a half-dozen similarly circuitous and supercilious tours of buildings he held little interest in already that day.

'Are you not taking me to the head of your school?' he said, curt as he thought appropriate. 'Where is Sir Yoshioka? Does he think himself above the most noble Lord Tokugawa?'

'The most honourable Naokata Yoshioka regrettably lies stricken with a grave malady, and is unable to receive the privilege of the most honourable Captain Inoue's presence. Humbly, Tadanari Kozei serves in the most honourable Sir Yoshioka's absence.'

'Very well,' said Goemon, and then thought it would be best here to add a kindness: 'I will pray for Sir Yoshioka's health.'

Tadanari bowed in gratitude. His eyes were black and the lids of his eyes were as still as though they were carved of wax.

The master led him to a forehall, where they waited for a meal to be brought to them. They knelt opposite each other in the formal position, thighs rested on calves and the pressure of the entire body's weight wrenching constant at the knees. Neither one of them revealed his discomfort; this had to be endured for the sake of manners. They looked both at and through each other in silence. Goemon would have guessed Tadanari's age to be fifteen, perhaps even twenty years greater than his own, the bald man appearing to be in the waning years of his fifties. Yet the samurai retained a dignified presence about himself, a hardness in the shoulders, a bearded jaw that brooked no argument.

The longer he looked at the master of the Yoshioka, the less Goemon wanted to look. He found himself, if not intimidated, then at least keenly feeling the disparity in their ages. The man seemed ensconced here, and not just solely in this room. He gave out a sense of ownership, of possession.

Goemon's eyes fell elsewhere. At Tadanari's belt he saw netsuke beads clasping the thongs of the pouches that hung from his waist, beautiful things carved out of either ivory or some pale wood that held a sculpted edge as fine as bone. He recognized the form of an ogreish being sitting cross-legged with a halo of fire rising from over his shoulders, a lash clutched in one hand and a foreign, double-edged sword clutched in the other.

'Saint Fudo.' He nodded. 'You have an affinity for the saint of swordsmen.'

Tadanari mimicked the nod. 'It is he who has an affinity for all of us, most honourable Sir Inoue.'

That was all they spoke, were permitted by etiquette to speak, until the food was brought in. The meal was of yuba, rolled skins of tofu dipped in soy sauce and wasabi. Goemon offered his polite thanks and began to eat, slurping the skins quickly. Halfway through his platter, he became aware Tadanari and his lesser men that had joined them were savouring each mouthful, considering the flavour. The food must be some delicacy of the city, he realized. Yet he could not admit the mistake clad as he was in Tokugawa livery, and so he fought the blush and forced himself to eat at exactly the same speed he had done before.

When he was done he set his chopsticks down as though he was entirely without guilt, and placed his hands upon his thighs.

'My thanks,' he said, and he spoke with great care to twist his accent into that of Kyoto. 'It was most delicious. To business, then.'

'Of course,' said Tadanari. His own plate remained half full but he gave gestures and servile staff came and began to clear the cutlery and dishes away. 'It was with great delight that this most humble school received the request of the most honourable Captain Inoue for an audience. If you will permit the audacity, the most humble Tadanari Kozei foresaw the intent of such a meeting.'

'Wonderful,' said Goemon. 'Then it shall not take you long to accumulate a registry of your numbers. I assume each man carries two swords, and that is fine and well, but my most noble Lord would also have of you a tally of all additional swords your school possesses in its armoury. Bows also, polearms, guns if you have them.'

This was clearly not what Tadanari had anticipated. The bald samurai paused for a moment, finding words, his eyes wandering to the floor but his face remaining still. The request had jarred him enough, in fact, that when he spoke next he had abandoned the courtly tongue.

'Most honourable Captain,' he said, 'I would question the need for the Yoshioka school submitting a catalogue of our arms to your most noble Lord. We are the foremost of the martial schools in the capital. During the conquest and ascension of your most noble Lord, members of our school served faithfully as swordmasters under his gracious and just command, and other Lords sworn to his wise rule. Does that not speak of our trustworthiness?'

'As I understand it, many of you served under false Lords of the traitor coalition also.'

'We are faithful, I assure you,' Tadanari said. 'Adepts of our style serve many Lords, this is true, but we ourselves harbour no affiliation to their political stance.'

'I was at Sekigahara,' said Goemon. He had meant it to sound imposing, or as a hint that he himself was a blooded warrior that Tadanari should not take lightly, but it came out even to his own ears as a shallow boast.

Tadanari bowed in respect regardless. 'I assure you, Captain, our sole interest is the sword and the beauty of its wielding. We infallibly and willingly serve the rightful government. Indeed, that was what I had assumed your visit here was in regards to.'

'How do you mean?'

Tadanari gestured to the adept attendant at the door. He slid it open, and a third man came in bearing a lacquered tube with great reverence. This man placed the tube upon the floor, bowed to it, and then shuffled backwards on his knees out of the room once more. Tadanari then bowed to the tube, unscrewed its lid and very gently brought forth a scroll within.

He unrolled it with great care and laid it on the tatami mats before Goemon. The writing upon it was very ornate and it was stamped and sealed in gold leaf.

'As you can see,' said Tadanari, 'the school of Yoshioka are the incumbent swordmasters to the Shogunate. I had assumed your most noble Lord Tokugawa had sent you this day that we could continue to render faithful service to your master.'

'My most noble Lord has not been awarded the Shogunate yet,' said Goemon.

'It is, however, imminent,' said Tadanari.

Goemon did not deny this. He read the entirety of the proclamation. He read it again, feeling the eyes of the Yoshioka upon him. The proclamation of office was worrying. It concerned an authority the true power of which he did not quite understand, and neither its relation to his Lord. He waited for as long as he could, until he squeezed out an attempt at command.

'As I see it, this appoints your school swordmasters to the Ashikaga Shogunate,' he said. 'They have not held power for half a century. This has no relevance.'

'If you would examine it closer, no mention of the fallen Ashikaga is made,' said Tadanari. 'Thus we are sworn to the Shogunate itself, regardless of which bloodline holds that mantle, and will be honoured and humbled to fulfil our duty to the most noble clan of the Tokugawa.'

Goemon said nothing.

'This is a proclamation ordained by the Son of Heaven himself,' said Tadanari.

It was. In desperation, Goemon chose the safety of acting affronted.

'It is true,' he said, 'that my most noble Lord is indeed seeking to appoint a swordmaster and is considering which school he shall adopt as patron. If attaining this appointment holds the interest of your spirit, it might be prudent for you to send the head of your school to Edo to demonstrate the virtues of your style. I believe the masters of the Yagyu and the Itto are attendant already, others on their way.'

'Honourable Captain,' said Tadanari, 'this . . . If I may be so forthright, the school of Yoshioka should not be made to parade itself in some lowly audition. The position is ours by right. We have immutable precedent.'

'Do you?'

Goemon said it obnoxiously innocently, too obnoxiously, and he saw the anger flare in the depths of Tadanari's eyes. But the man was decades practised at civility and had fine composure. 'Very well,' he said, perfectly courteously. 'I am certain that this shall all be clarified in Edo. We will send an emissary to your court, and when he presents this proclamation I am sure rightness will prevail.'

'Emissary?' said Goemon, committed to his path. 'The head of your school shall suffice.'

'As I have informed you, Captain, the most honourable Naokata Yoshioka is currently suffering from a sickness. He is unable to rise from his bed and so—'

'If you think anything less than the head of your school will suffice for the head of the nation, then you are entitled to do so. Edo awaits.'

'Edo awaits,' repeated Tadanari.

That ended their meeting. There were other platitudes, but nothing further of substance was stated. Goemon worried about the course of it that night as he sat drinking in solitude in the hard berth of his chambers. Soon his mind wandered to distant places. He thought of his wife, now married to another man, and then of his sons and his daughters, who now carried that man's name, and, lastly, as his conscious mind faded and sleep imposed itself upon him, he heard once more the pack of his hounds that he had left behind howling at his departure.

Chapter Ten

The first snows of winter were falling. The trees of the woodland were a wilderness of barren dark limbs punctuated by errant clouds of the proud jade needles of pine trees. Musashi hauled upon the reins of the horse, and the beast followed after him along the trail. Both their breaths were steaming.

Ahead, enveloped almost by the wild, lay an old dilapidated house. Its beams were blackened with age but the thatch on the roof remained whole. Musashi watched it cautiously for some time. It was still and silent. He looped the horse's reins over a bough and then walked forward to explore inside.

It was a small structure, perhaps belonging to some long-departed woodsman. The door of it was lying on the ground, the desiccated husks of shed cicada skins mustered on its planking. He could see holes rotted through the walls, and the thatch was fetid with rotten dampness. He was about to step inside when he heard the sound of feet behind him.

He turned. There was a young girl swathed in frayed clothes much too big for her, she no more than eight or nine years old. Her surprise was equal to his. She froze for a moment, saw his size and his swords, and then she ran. Instead of fleeing, however, she skittered past Musashi and vanished inside the house.

Musashi could hear her whispering, hear her panicked breaths. Tentatively, he followed after her. In the shadows of the single room, he saw the girl bending at the shoulder of another person sitting against the walls. Their form was indistinct, a mess of blankets and long hair.

'A man, a samurai,' the girl was whispering to this adult, and then she saw Musashi entering and shouted at him, 'Leave us alone!'

'I mean you no harm,' he said.

'Then leave us!'

'I cannot,' he said. 'I need shelter.'

The adult spoke now. It was a woman, her voice low and accented. 'Then go to town. Town close.'

'They will not have me.'

Musashi stood in the doorway. The woman did not rise, did not move at all. The girl seemed caught between wanting to hide behind her and wanting to shield her from Musashi. With great care, Musashi pulled the swords from his belt still in their scabbards and laid them on the ground between them. The girl whispered what he was doing into the woman's ear.

'I mean you no harm,' he said, stepping back from his weapons. 'I thought this house was abandoned. I am sorry for intruding. Is this your house?'

'No,' said the woman.

'But you live here?'

They did not answer.

'I need shelter,' said Musashi. 'I am in great need – the

snows are here and I cannot spend the night outside. I do not wish to force you out. There is space enough for us all.'

Still they were scared of him. He pointed at the hearth pit in the centre of the room. Within its square depression there were old leaves and translucent snakeskins and hardened nuggets of rabbit dung, but no fresh ashes.

'Does either of you know how to light fires?' he said. 'It will be cold, and colder still in the weeks to come. I know how to light fires. I would share this heat with you.'

'Why your great need of this house?' the woman said.

Musashi beckoned the girl outside. She left the woman behind and followed him at a cautious distance. He showed her the horse, and the pitiful litter the creature had been pulling. He had constructed it himself out of saddlebags and belts and fallen boughs, and strapped tight to it lay the delirious form of Akiyama.

'He is in a grave state,' Musashi told the girl. 'Another night in the wild might kill him.'

Akiyama murmured something. His eyes were closed and his red skin was pallid and sweating. The girl watched him, and then she disappeared inside once more to tell the woman.

The snows continued to fall through the night. The flue was clotted and the smoke from the fire Musashi made curled thick around them to billow out of the door. He had stoked the fire well, and had covered Akiyama in as many covers and blankets as he could spare, but still the man's brow felt cold. He sat cross-legged by his assassin's side, helpless and watching.

Outside, the ground was already covered in snow. It had come weeks early and boded for a long season.

The woman sat against the wall, guarded yet. She held the

girl between her legs protectively, wrapped her arms over her shoulders. It was clear that she was blinded; she would not raise her face to Musashi, hidden always by the long tresses of her hair, and the girl patiently explained everything that was happening to her.

Over the past few hours the girl, for her part, had decided in that way of children that something that was not immediately dangerous could be trusted. She sat looking at Musashi and his swords in open curiosity.

'Why are they so dirty?' she asked.

She spoke of the sorry state of the scabbards, the lacquer chipped and scratched, of the rusted pommel and guards, and of the shortsword's grip, which had rotted clean away and which Musashi had replaced with a leather cord lashed and helixed over the wooden handle.

'Hard to keep them clean,' he said, and shrugged. 'I keep the blades sharp and tended. That's all that matters, as far as a sword goes.'

'But they look so ugly.'

The woman pinched the girl's shoulder in warning. The girl spoke to her: 'But you can't see how ugly they are.'

'Yae,' the woman said in a low voice.

The girl sighed and obeyed.

'Your name's Yae?' asked Musashi.

'Yes,' she said. 'What's your name?'

'Musashi.'

Yae squeezed the woman's hands. 'She's Ameku.' The name was odd-sounding, and Yae saw this on Musashi's face. 'She's from Ryukyu.'

'Never met a Ryukyuan before,' said Musashi.

Ameku tutted. 'No snows on Ryukyu.'

'It's hot there, she says,' said Yae. 'Ryukyu is just small islands, in the middle of the south sea. They don't even speak our language there. Sometimes Ameku speaks it to me, and it sounds like yarr-rarrr-rarrr a-baa-baaa-baaa.'

Ameku muttered an irritated string of something foreign.

'See?' said Yae, proudly.

In the morning Musashi melted snow in a pan to wash Akiyama's wounds. He peeled the samurai's blankets back and revealed his body bandaged in scavenged hemp rags, and these he peeled away also. There were two lacerations, one across Akiyama's left clavicle and a second that split the right side of his stomach from sternum to outer thigh. Caused by the same blow, Akiyama's body perhaps twisting so that the blade glanced off the ribcage and spared it its ruin.

Ameku turned her head away at the smell. Yae peered in morbid fascination at the suppuration Musashi washed tenderly away.

'His wounds are festering,' Musashi said. 'He's been like this for near a fortnight. The poultices he needs, they cost money. Would you please watch over him in my stead? I will head into town and see if I cannot chop firewood for someone, or . . .'

Over the next two days he ventured into the nearby town, where he was greeted with a muted hostility. He was masterless and the masterless could not be trusted. Yet it was a small, rural hamlet far from the castle of their realm and they had no steward to look to for protection and none amongst the populace possessed swords. They could not force Musashi away, and, though they would not suffer him to shelter within the boundaries of their settlement, they soon realized they had no real choice but to reluctantly submit to his helpful impositions. Under their suspicious and scornful gazes, swallowing his temper at their prejudice for the sake of Akiyama, he chopped wood, he hefted straw barrels, he scaled, gutted and salted river fish.

Those first few nights they sat more or less in silence, the blinded woman, the swordsman on the verge of death, the girl and Musashi. Ameku was wary of him, and she seemed to have coaxed the girl into caution also; Yae would look at him, smile, but not speak.

Musashi found himself uncomfortable in their presence, and he wondered over this. He recounted his isolated childhood, his years wandering on the path of foolish vengeance, his service in the army of the Lord Ukita and then his exile with Jiro and the others, and he realized that over the nineteen years of his life he had decapitated more men than he had had conversations with women.

He found the backs of his arms itching, and that he was compelled to busy himself with trite labour, or checking needlessly on Akiyama's unaltered condition, or fidgeting with the pommels of his swords rather than simply sit there in the silence, acknowledging the discomfort. Yet it was not the pair of them he blamed but rather himself, and why this was he could not say.

On the third morning of their lodging together, Ameku rose and spoke to him directly for the first time.

'I can use loom,' she announced, 'make tatami mat. Take me to town. Someone must have a loom there. Perhaps I can weave. Get money.'

'You would help?' asked Musashi.

'You make fire for us.' She shrugged.

They left Yae to tend to Akiyama and to keep the fire stoked over the hours they would be gone. Musashi and Ameku walked a slow pace, the blind woman stumbling over the snow. She started by holding onto his shoulder for guidance, but the trail grew so narrow she fell in behind him and took to clutching the scabbard of his longsword where it jutted backwards from his waist.

'How is it a blinded woman knows how to weave?' Musashi asked over his shoulder.

'Worked at a place . . .' she said. 'Buddha people? Monks? Where monks that care for blind, for . . . people with bodies that are not good. Cannot hear, no legs. Those things, at that place, they taught me to use the loom. The monks sell the mats, buy food. On and on. Eight years.'

'You came to Japan eight years ago?'

'Nine.'

'Why did you leave the care of the monks?'

'It was the war, after the big war. The Lord of the province was killed, or dead, or killed himself, and after him – nothing. The Tokugawa came slow. No law for a year. Many men, they think the monks are rich. One night they come, and they killed the monks but there was no gold for them, only me and Yae and the others, the no legs, the weak minds. All of us, cast out to the world. Dead now, most of them, probably.'

It was not a shocking tale. Musashi had heard of many similar incidents. Ameku in turn spoke of it plainly and seemed to feel no pity for herself. He turned to guide the woman over an uneven hump of land, walked backwards and held both of her hands in his. 'Yae is your daughter?' he asked.

'No. No husband for me. Like a cat, I found her. Met her three years before, she also came to the monks. No one care for her. Mother, father, I don't know.' She sighed, and her throat was hoarse with a weariness of years. 'A fine world, no? Blind woman is all that care for child, and child is all that care for blind.'

'And why is it you left Ryukyu?'

'Why is it you heal the man that try to kill you?' she said sharply.

He did not answer. They walked on in silence.

The people of the town were even less enthused at his bringing a marred foreigner, and yet they could not protest. They had a threshing mill that was stilled after harvest, filled only with piles of grasses drying into straw, and on one of its walls lay a loom. It was a big contraption of interlocking levers, operated with both the feet and the hands. Musashi watched Ameku as she manipulated the machine, hooked reeds with sightless fingers and swayed her body in time to the pressing of the pedals. She was not fast, not even really proficient, but she could do it.

He found that admirable.

*

It was sound that called Akiyama back, dragged him through the dreams he did not see, the slurried images that coalesced into nothing. He had known pain and cold, and on his lips were the tastes of salt and copper, and as far as he could recall this was his entire existence. How long this had been he did not know, could not know, for he was barely aware that he possessed physical form.

Yet something about this noise . . . It bound spirit to flesh once more, it gave raw sensation personal relevance. He stirred, and suddenly he remembered that he had a head that could stir, the back of it resting on what felt like a throbbing floor.

He listened to the noise. It was singing, he realized, a

lulling, beautiful voice, a woman's voice. A woman singing in a way no woman had ever sung for him before. A lullaby or something like it, its sweetness such that it bestowed consciousness rather than stole it. The melody lilting, the singer shifting through octaves in single phrases, swapping from a low, sultry quaver that guided the song to sudden high peaks of passion that crested and then fell, and her voice fell with it, fell like the paths of birds to some warm sea cast a persimmon orange in the dying of the sun.

A song of wistful remorse, or secret hope, or old agonies, or all these things and more; and he listened, Akiyama, wanted to understand and to feel these emotions, because to do so was a human thing. Wounded though it was, his body retained its form; he was human, remained human, and his mind was at last ready to agree with that once more. He was not dead, he would not die. All that remained was that final clarifying calibration between his spirit and his body.

He willed for the song to grant him such, to guide him home, and he tried to listen to the words, to glean some higher understanding. His lips quivered without his knowledge like a babe suckling at nothing. But, though he listened and listened, he could not parse a single recognizable sentence from the beautiful miasma. There were words there, definite words, but he could not understand them. It taunted him, denied what he sought so fundamentally at that moment, and he realized then that in fact he must be in a form of hell.

Personally crafted for himself: he now condemned to live as an actual Foreigner.

That could not be. He rejected the idea, fought against it, and suddenly he had sight. He was in a room he saw, darkened, lit by some crackling fire glowing in a hearth pit close by. He was covered in blankets and his breath was misting up in the air above him. He twisted his head, and over the pit through the smoke he saw a girl he did not know, and a woman with her back to him. It was she who was singing. Her shoulders rose and fell. Long hair, perfectly straight and black like his mother's had been, like his own was not, lustrous, and he longed to touch it. But the space between them was abyssal, and he could not move and he was denied, and in his despair he looked elsewhere and then he saw his murderer Miyamoto.

It jarred him for a moment, stunned him entirely.

Except it could not be Miyamoto. It was not he. He was different. The young swordsman was swaddled in rags against the cold, sitting up against the wall of the hovel. He too was looking at the woman, and his face was entirely changed. No anger, as Akiyama remembered facing down upon that hillside. None of the hatred, the hostility. Miyamoto's eyes glistened in the firelight, and in them was some composite emotion Akiyama could not describe. A humbled longing, it seemed. He too was enthralled by the song, or perhaps enchanted by the singer, and perhaps he too wished to reach across that gap as Akiyama had wanted, that he might take up the essence of the song and cram it into the space of his heart so that something significant might resonate there, and, like Akiyama, he too knew that he could not.

Eventually Miyamoto became aware of Akiyama looking at him. He turned and looked back. Something began to change on his face, and Akiyama tried to sit up.

A brilliant albescence claimed him.

He awoke next to the feeling of liquid upon his lips. A bamboo cup was pressed to his mouth and its hard, rough rim knocked against his teeth. There was water in it, tepid and delicious, and suddenly he had no desire greater than simply to drink.

'I told you, I told you,' the girl was saying. 'He was talking this afternoon, calling out for someone.'

She was not speaking to him and Akiyama did not care. He drank until he was sated, no more than a few sips that somehow felt like rivers ending themselves into him, and then he looked up beyond the cup to find that it was Miyamoto who was holding the vessel to his mouth.

The singing had stopped. Miyamoto knelt back. The pale-eyed samurai looked up at him for a long time. Miyamoto looked back. The water had given Akiyama strength enough to talk.

'I would not have been able to find you, had you not insisted upon shouting your name,' he said. 'Shouting your name as though it meant something.'

It took all the vigour he had left. His head fell back, and he was nothing once more.

Consciousness returned to him in greater and greater stretches over the next days, like the waxing of the moon. The fact that he was entirely vulnerable panicked him at first, and he felt a prisoner in his own body. He watched them all with the apprehension of the paralysed, his pale eyes, entirely rimmed white as they rolled in their sockets, following them about.

Yet they seemed to bear him no malice, and Akiyama studied them and quickly learnt the pattern. Miyamoto would leave in the morning with the woman Ameku, and the pair of them would not return until the evening, always with food and sometimes with a fresh poultice when it was needed. The girl Yae was left to tend to him. Without either of the adults there she seemed to find Akiyama fearsome, and he would not see her for hours at a time. Then she would dash in and pile fresh wood into the hearth, or force water down his throat, and then she would go again.

He did not blame her. His wound was nothing he would choose to be around, either. He struggled to view his injuries when Miyamoto tended to them, pushed his chin into his neck, but all he could see was a vague ugly cleft and a sense of something white and gummed within. It made him shudder to think that this was how it appeared in a state of healing, that weeks before it might have somehow been more unpleasant to behold.

Akiyama thus abided long hours of solitude, lying with his jaw shivering or feeling the beads of sweat pool in the hollow of his philtrum. There was nought else for him but introspection.

On the wall was hung his jacket. The colour of tea was stained by his blood. He would stare so long that the patterns of the stain would swim and coalesce before his feverous eyes. He wondered if any in the school of Yoshioka thought of him, contemplated or sympathized with this potential suffering of his. He wondered if his name was spoken at all, if his absence was even noted.

He knew the answer.

His strength returned gradually. Of a dawn, Akiyama managed to roll himself onto his side and wriggle across the floor so that he might see outside through a hole rotted clean through the wooden walls. The exertion was agony, but he saw light that was sharp and pure and reflected by snow, and he could feel the cold of it in his lungs. Outside he saw Miyamoto, practising the methods of the sword before he left for the day's labours. Akiyama watched him both critically and enviously, examining what fundaments made up Miyamoto's style and wishing that he himself could move so once more.

To his surprise he saw Miyamoto begin swinging the long-sword one-handed. That was the extraordinary manoeuvre that had killed him, or would have killed him, and yet to see Miyamoto repeating it here it seemed a barely realized thing. There was a curiosity in the tall man's gait, a tentativeness in his movements as though he were slowly working out the balance and the combination of the muscles as he repeated the motion over and over again.

It set Akiyama to thinking of their duel over the lonely hours in solitude that day. He ran through the stages of the fight over and over, and he was surprised anew by his loss each time. Who was this man of no renown who did things that ought to be impossible, cut as he should not be able to cut? More surprising to him was that, the more he considered it, he found in truth he bore Miyamoto no hatred for cutting him down. The colour of tea hung above him on the wall, and Akiyama stared at it and realized somehow that innately he felt this fate was inevitable. Miyamoto's arm – his single arm! – was incidental in its part.

When he accepted this, Akiyama's guardedness began to fade. He took instead to studying Miyamoto not as a captor or a tormentor, but rather for who he was. He saw a young man who carried himself in relative silence, and gave his hours over to tending another nominally his enemy. The questions he had asked himself about Miyamoto's nature over the months of the hunt resurfaced.

'Why is it you cut down trees?' Akiyama asked him one evening.

Miyamoto gave him an odd look. 'I am no woodsman,' he said.

Again he failed to remember, as he had failed to remember on that hillside before they duelled. A gesture that had fascinated Akiyama so, perhaps to him simply envisioned and enacted and then gone. He, free of the brooding contemplation that had guided Akiyama through the years and led him here.

Young.

On a subsequent day he asked Miyamoto his age. Miyamoto told him.

'Nineteen,' repeated Akiyama, and he laid his head back and closed his eyes. 'Cut down by a child.'

Ameku was a suspicious woman, particularly when Yae was present. Her distrust, however, did not seem to Akiyama to be levelled subjectively against him alone. She kept her hands upon the girl incessantly, brought her close, and Yae in turn would whisper to her all that she saw. He wondered blackly what words the child used to describe him and his wretched state.

'You're actually foreign?' he asked Ameku, when he learnt that she was from Ryukyu. 'You were born outside the nation?'

She grunted.

'But . . .' he said, 'your skin is so pale.'

She grunted again, thought him a fool. She did not understand the import of that to him, and nor did she seek to learn anything about him beyond whether he had died or lived yet.

His wounds healed slowly. Of an afternoon deep into the winter, on his fifth attempt he managed at last to rise to his feet for the first time in months and stumble to the frame of the door. The girl was nowhere to be found, but beyond the wandering lucent specks of exertion in his eyes he was surprised to see his horse amidst the snows outside. It was stripping a trunk of its bark, chewing noisily.

'You're fending for yourself?' he said, fondly.

The horse did not react to the sound of his voice. It had lost weight, ribs visible on its pale flanks. It was not tethered, wore no bridle or saddle, and yet it remained close. Akiyama smiled. The thought of loyalty warmed him through the day and into the night also. He lay sprawled straight-backed on a plank of wood set at a gentle angle, the pain too great for him yet to sit forward cross-legged. He had a steaming bowl of soy leaf broth in his hands, and the taste was good and the clay was hot upon his palms.

Ameku was combing Yae's hair with a whalebone comb, the one thing of any value she possessed, in silence. Miyamoto sat across the way preparing the poultice for Akiyama's wound, grinding herbs with the steel pommel of his shortsword upon a broad piece of flat shale he had scavenged from the woods.

The pale-eyed samurai watched him for some time.

'I am in your debt,' he said.

Miyamoto looked up for a moment. Then he clucked his tongue and took to rolling the sword harder.

'Fortunate for me that my killer should be so adept at healing,' said Akiyama.

'I am not your killer,' said Miyamoto.

'I know that,' said Akiyama. 'And I thank you for your mercy.'

Miyamoto grunted. Yae was looking at Akiyama, and for the first time there was no fear in her eyes. She was not, however, yet ready to return the smile he gave her.

'How is it one so young as you knows the ways of medicine?' asked Akiyama of Miyamoto.

The young swordsman's grinding stopped. He stared down at the sword, and after a moment he began to scrape the moist green-black salve from off the pommel. 'I had an uncle who taught me.'

'An uncle?'

'A monk of Amaterasu. A great healer. A man of worth. This, one of his remedies.'

'Then I am in his debt also.'

Miyamoto grunted again, and gave no further answer. He pushed the salve around with his finger as though he were checking it for consistency.

There was something in his demeanour that he tried to hide, and in search of further warmness, in hope of bringing it forth, Akiyama pried: 'If you revere him such, how is it you did not return to him after the War?'

Miyamoto did not respond as he expected. He seemed to grow flustered. 'He . . . he died,' he murmured eventually, spoken without much conviction in either tone or the young man's eyes. This wavering seemed only to gall him further, and his face hardened and he spoke in challenge: 'Why is it the Yoshioka sent you to take my head?'

The bracken branches squealed faintly as they burnt in the hearth, and the smell of pine was rife. Akiyama met his gaze. After a moment Miyamoto's eyes dropped, and the desire for confrontation departed.

'I told you before,' Akiyama told him. 'At the battle of Sekigahara you insulted our school.'

'And I told you before – you lie.'

'It is the truth.'

He held Miyamoto's gaze, and the look in his eyes must have convinced Miyamoto. 'Insulted?' the young man said, and now he seemed genuinely confused. He thought about it before he spoke again. 'Insulted – I insulted *you*, yourself, you?'

'I was not at the battle.'

'Then . . . ?'

'A man named Sir Ando witnessed your offence.'

'I never . . .' said Miyamoto, and again he seemed to think deeply. After a long while, he offered a hesitant nod. 'I recall now that I killed one of your men before the battle in a duel.'

Now it was Akiyama who was surprised. Miyamoto did not seem to be feigning his trouble recollecting. How was it that he could forget felling one of a school as renowned as the Yoshioka before near every samurai in the nation? Men earned swathes of land and status for less. What other things must he have witnessed that day that taking a Yoshioka head was relegated to an afterthought?

Miyamoto spoke on: 'He was wounded, your man, but the duel was of his urging. I killed him cleanly and offered no insult to his body after that I can recall.'

'You've killed a man?' asked Yae.

Akiyama ignored the girl. 'It is claimed you did.'

'And not one man can recall these words?'

'Perhaps Sir Ando can.'

'Regardless . . . For this, they sent you all this way, across all these years to claim my head?'

'They did.'

Miyamoto sucked air through his teeth. His eyes were unseeing for a moment. Then he shook his head and began tearing leaves from the stems of the various herbs he had collected and placing them on the slate ready for grinding. His fingers wrapped around his shortsword, and, with his shoulders hunched and his teeth clenched, began to work once more.

'Yoshioka,' he said, perhaps to none but himself, 'there in the heart of the nation . . . Of all things . . . All aspiring to become them . . . Be as them . . .'

Akiyama saw his mood and did not try to speak to him again that night. He sipped on his broth and watched as the pommel mulched all beneath it.

There were many more hours to fill that winter, long dark hours, and as his body mended Akiyama found returning alongside his health an energy he was not accustomed to.

'Nineteen, nineteen,' he said, and this was how it felt to speak, to be heard. 'At nineteen, what was I doing? A long time ago. I was an acolyte of the school. Four years in. Every spring, at the time of the cherry blossom, the school holds the annual assessments. Up at the Rendai moor, in the north of Kyoto. No cherry trees there, though, but this was before the Regent built his great wall and the moat, so you could see the river Katsura flowing past. The Yoshioka . . . We . . . The Yoshioka grade practically. One advances in rank through beating a superior twice in three bouts. Bamboo blades.'

Though the woman and the girl were present it was Miyamoto to whom he truly spoke, the swordsman, the one who might relate the keenest.

'At nineteen I beat every one of my contemporaries in consecutive victories. I was permitted to challenge a senior adept. Sir Mogami. He won the first, I the second and the third. The third was perfect. I stabbed him with the point of my sword in the hollow of the throat, struck clean, breached his guard as though it were not there.'

Here he gestured with his hands, mimed the lunge, rapped the fore- and middle finger of his right hand on the flesh beneath the knob of his throat.

'You understand the achievement of that, no? You, one of your skill, you too must have struck similar blows. The cleanest strike, the hardest point to attack. Were he wearing armour I'd have killed him still, and he did not strike me in return, his blow wasted upon the air. That I could have seen the manoeuvre with eyes not of my own, appreciate it from another angle. But I knew its worth. Felt it. Pride in the victory, pride I cannot describe it to you, I . . .'

His body shuddered with the memory, of the achievement that the long years of study had yielded up to him.

'But of course,' he said, 'all kept within. I bowed to Sir Mogami, and Sir Mogami bowed to me. One had to present oneself before the masters of the school, who were all sitting witnessing upon a dais. Sitting on stools like generals observing battle. There was the old dynastic head of the school, Naokata Yoshioka, and the master Tadanari Kozei. Both of them there, and I knelt before them, and I could hear the blood flow through my ears, such was my nervousness. I knew recognition was here, that moment for which I had strived imminent at last. After my bow, I looked up and they were both looking down at me. Faces of stone. Did not see me, acknowledged nothing further than my physical state of being.' He sniffed, and his eyes were bleak and distant. 'They killed me with those gazes.'

Yae was running the whalebone comb through Ameku's hair, and it stuck for a moment on a knot that her small fingers quickly found and parted.

'There was a third man there also, I remember,' said Akiyama. 'A visiting guest from some other school on Kyushu, too old for anything but frittering about in vacuous diplomacy. He was a, a . . .' – and these next words had waited decades to be spoken aloud – 'a drunken old sot, and his face was florid with sake. Him. What he did was, he began to clap at me. *At* me, not *for* me. Clapped as enthusiastically as he would have done for a child, and what he said was, "Isn't it astounding how you've managed to learn *our* ways so well?"'

Akiyama threw a fresh handful of branches into the hearth pit.

'Sir Mogami went to serve as swordmaster for the Lord of Tajima, and my reward was . . .'

His words trailed off.

'That is the Way,' said Miyamoto.

'Of which you claim to have freed yourself.'

Miyamoto nodded.

The depths of winter came and went. The snows began to melt. Akiyama's wounds ceased to weep, and formed scars. They were his first, or rather his first of any real size, and their hard pale ridges stood out brazen on his dark flesh. He realized how close it was he had come to death, of how much blood he had shed, of how he had wandered through the delirium of infection.

Of how he had been guided through.

Akiyama was holding his horse by the bridle as Miyamoto picked ticks from its haunches with a short knife. Yae was kicking clods of thawing ice around and laughing. It was then that the pale-eyed samurai asked the question that had hovered unspoken the winter long.

'Why is it you spared me?' he said.

Miyamoto thought about it some time, as though he too

had been pondering the answer over the months. 'Because after I cut you down,' he said, 'you lay there laughing on that hill. A bitter laugh as you died. I do not think I have seen anything more honest.'

'Honest,' repeated Akiyama. He thought about it, and could not disagree.

The horse clacked its teeth, shook its head. Akiyama patted it on the nose.

'And where now from here, you and I?' he asked.

'You owe me nothing,' said Miyamoto.

Akiyama looked at him.

'Nothing,' Miyamoto repeated.

'What are your intentions, then?'

Miyamoto rose and wiped the blood from the dagger on the sleeve of his jacket. 'I intend to head to Kyoto and force whoever it was that sent you to kill me to fight his own duels.' He patted the horse's neck, then looked his assassin in the eyes. 'The question is you, Nagayoshi Akiyama. Will you return, and hold those who ruled your life so callously to account?'

The spring sun shone in the heavens, lit up the new and emergent life so brilliantly.

PART III

The Colour of Tea

Summer. Ninth Year of the Era of Keicho

Seven years since the death of the Regent Hideyoshi Toyotomi

Approaching four years since Sekigahara

The first year of the imperially ordained Shogunate of the clan Tokugawa, may it last ten thousand more

Chapter Eleven

There were moments Goemon Inoue found when he felt not as himself, jarring slivers of some higher lucidity where he could simply see what lay before him as though from some distance away and behind his own eyes, see it all as the absurd circumstance of another. A black, mocking play put on by actors and he merely a spectator that had somehow ended up on the stage, surrounded and overwhelmed by it.

The heat of the humid high summer swirling, churning, trapped in the crowded forehall of the garrison of the Tokugawa, Goemon feeling sweat coursing from his brow, down the back of his neck, from the pits of his arms, stagnating on his stomach, his thighs, and yet for an instant suddenly he was cool, apart, feeling nothing. He saw the beseeching guild master who stood before him with perfect objectivity, and from that unknown void he temporarily inhabited Goemon wanted to laugh.

The guild master had umbrage in his eyes, honest umbrage, and he held himself as though he wore swords, or at the least as though he were adorned with some form of armour that the actual blades at Goemon Inoue's side could not penetrate. 'Captain, I demand of you to explain yourself to me. This is intolerable. Never before have taxes of this sort been levied. You demand what? A full third of our profits over that which we already pay? This is unheard of . . . I simply cannot believe that you would intend to . . .'

On he droned, on and on, such that it pulled Goemon back into his own flesh. Heat was felt and his pulse at his temples was felt and sweat salt was on his lips, and Goemon had to make a conscious effort to hide the disdain from his face. The guild master was a portly man with too much face for his skull, froglike almost, draped in fine silks in gaudy shades of chequered blue and flower-patterned burgundy, and he, this gold-hungry merchant, this lowerborn, stood brazenly speaking as though he had the authority of samurai.

Goemon raised a hand and silenced the man for a moment. 'As it has been explained to me,' he said, 'your guild profited exponentially selling rice to the campaigning armies during my most noble Lord's rightful conquest, grew several times your size. It seems only just that you should yield some of the bounty of what my most noble Lord enabled, does it not?'

The guild master bridled – the rage in him, the actual genuine indignation over such venial things! 'We offered our tribute of rice grain to the most noble Shogun and his armies as is our duty,' he said. 'All profit we made beyond that we made by selling fairly to those who needed it. It is beyond reproach for us to be expected to be raped of all our diligent labour's reward, and I wish to protest it formally!'

Very thinly, lips all but white, Goemon said, 'It is not my business to set the law, merely to enforce it. Pay what is due or face the consequences.'

'The Regent never saw fit to tax us such! This is without precedent!'

'It is the new order of things.'

The contemptible coin-grubber made to speak on, but Goemon simply turned away from him. There was no respite for him, however, and he merely found another seeking to petition him. Goemon's men, knowing their orders, had long since given up trying to enforce order on the mob that swarmed, and there was a constant thriving clamour for his attention.

A shaven-headed monk forced himself before the captain, and the man had come in his full formal black robes and his saffron sash that hung across one shoulder, even clutched a rosary wrapped around his fist.

'Your men, Captain, have desecrated holy grounds,' he said, the look of a flagellant in his eyes. 'Unpardonable. They knocked the northern wall of our temple down merely that they might have an easier route to transport the great blocks of stone to your master's castle-to-be.'

'I . . .' said Goemon, and he hesitated out of residual deference to the holy. 'I apologize on their behalf, but you must understand that for the sake of order upon the streets the construction is of the utmost imperative.'

The monk's face twisted in venomous zeal. 'Vain mortal constructs pale before the glory of the Teachings! Thou shalt right this offence, or thou and thy Lord will incur the wrath of the heavens!'

From the side a new man interjected. It was hard to gauge what status or rank he held because the man placed himself so close to Goemon. 'I have waited months Captain, and I wish to know what the ruling is upon the estates of the traitor

Lords up in the northern wards of the city. Four years they have stood empty, going to ruin. All I ask is that I be permitted to purchase, for a fair value—'

'Those are property of the Shogunate by right of triumph,' said Goemon. 'They are not to be bid upon like farmlands or—'

The monk hissed over him: 'Revered be the Regent, who understood the paths of harmony! Who clad in gold the capital city, who built for himself no intrusive palace but enshrined what ought to be enshrined!'

A fourth man now spoke: 'Truth there – in the Regent's time it was safe upon the roads. Captain, my caravan was waylaid upon the Tosando road by bandits east of the Biwa for the third time this year. The third time this year! What is being done about it?'

Goemon rolled his tongue across the insides of his teeth and prepared to answer, and yet all words were stolen from him by the one who lusted for the Lordly estates actually placing his hand upon the captain. The man wrapped his soft fingers around the lapels of Goemon's inner kimono and then proceeded to speak his piece, repeat his bland mercantile inanities, and such was his self-absorption the man did not even notice Goemon's entire frame become rigid with affront. Spoke blindly on as Goemon's jaw grew tight and his eyes went wide with fury.

This how they saw him, this how they all of them out there in the city saw him.

There came a banging and a gruff voice demanding silence. It was the Goat, Goemon's adjutant, thumping on the frame of the inner door with his fist. He was an older samurai, grey of beard and lamed of leg, and he used his longsword in its scabbard as an ersatz walking cane. He snarled at the crowd to relent and they obeyed and shrank back, and then in the silence he hobbled over to whisper in Goemon's ear after snapping out a curt bow.

'An incident developing, sir,' he said. 'Out in the street front. You are needed there more than you are here.'

With some relief, Goemon jerked his head and the pair of them left the forehall behind and set off through the garrison. It was a military building, close corridors with low ceilings to prevent the swinging of swords, everything dark wood, bereft of ornamentation and thick enough to stop spear-thrust, and also, at the back of every man's mind, heavy enough to crush should an earthquake come.

As they navigated the tight hallways the captain reset his clothing where it had been pulled out of order. He tried to level his spirit, clenched his fist around the handle of his sword that he might grant himself a measure of satisfaction. The Goat was attentive and perceptive, and noticed Goemon's disquiet.

'You should have the men impose some order on that lot, sir,' he said in a voice low enough that none but they would hear. 'Disgraceful impertinence.'

'What am I to do, Onodera?' said Goemon. 'You know the remit of my command.'

The Goat did, and he gave nothing but a vague grunt and a jerk of the chin onwards.

Outside the sun was fierce in a cloudless sky, fierce enough that the burnished heads of spears were hard to look at after the shade indoors. The yard was dusty and the samurai who crowded it were silent. They were waiting for Goemon with grim anticipation, and at his appearance they barked a salute and dropped to one knee. He gestured them up immediately. An odd atmosphere pervaded. The garrison was no moated castle and beyond the walls of its compound lay the common thoroughfares of the city. Silence reigned there also, when usually there was the bustle of commerce.

Through the mouth of the gate itself, Goemon found the cause: a group of men stood before the garrison in bold challenge. There were perhaps twenty of them clustered close together, and though they were all unkempt they were all obviously samurai: they wore kimonos rather than jerkins; those that were not wearing wide-brimmed straw hats wore their hair in topknots; and each met Goemon's gaze as an equal would.

Yet, for all this, not one of them wore a pair of swords at his side.

Goemon took this in with his face a picture of level sternness. He was standing between two great banners of the Tokugawa livery, white field and black emblem, both splayed taut on the right angle of their bamboo frames. He looked to either end of the street, where the lowerborn had clustered to watch on. Then he turned back to the group and spoke, careful as always to twist his voice into the Kyoto accent.

'I am Goemon Inoue, proud vassal of the most noble Shogun Tokugawa,' he said. 'I command in his name in the city of Kyoto. What is your intention here?'

One man strode forward from the group of men, his eyes squinting in the brightness. He struck a proud stance with his arms crossed, hands hidden up the sleeves of his jacket, but his voice was not aggressive.

'We have travelled far, Sir Inoue,' he said. 'We would ask that you hear us in the name of your Lord.'

'I shall do so.'

'We are all of us indebted to you,' said the man, and bowed not quite deep enough to be respectful. 'We have come on the cause of protest.'

'I would inform you, before you speak,' said Goemon, 'that my jurisdiction is limited to the city of Kyoto alone. Should you have a problem in your realm, Edo may be better able to settle your dispute.'

'We come not to dispute the minutiae of the law of the nation,' said the lead man. 'No, we come to protest a perversion of the proper way of things, and what better place than Kyoto for that?'

Samurai eyes peered out pensively through triangular arrow loops from within the garrison. Goemon said, 'I fear you have been a victim of some cruel circumstance.'

'That we have,' said the lead man, and from one of his sleeves he produced a folded, sealed sheaf of paper. 'Here, then – formal written protest at vile humiliation visited unjustly upon decent men.

'Our clan was neutral in the war in which your master Tokugawa claimed the Shogunate. We raised not a single weapon against your warriors, prayed not for your defeat, but even fed you, aided you, and guided you through the mountain passes of our realm. We were assured by your Lord Tokugawa that our fiefdom was inviolate, and, in the spirit of honour, in the code of fellow samurai, we believed in such promises.'

His voice was deep and carried well, drew in the distant crowd. He waved the sheaf of paper with one hand as he spoke, kept the other hand clasped upon his elbow. Goemon became aware of a faint smell of burning in the air, a chemical smell. The oil merchant up the street must have been burning in excess of his permit once again; yet another petty grievance he would be forced to address.

'But how long they lasted, these vows,' continued the swordless samurai. 'Fleeting things, soon forgotten like the gold of dawn, and come the spring this year: shameful betrayal! Our most noble Lord assented to the new way of things, gave no objection to your Lord's proclamation as Shogun last summer but rather paid loyal tribute, and what is his reward? He, commanded to seppuku! We, all of us, our swords confiscated! Such was our Lord's loyalty, he ordered us not to resist. But still he lies dead, and still we linger here.'

Goemon nodded his head. 'A sad case of affairs. But my most noble Lord has his considered reasons for every action, and it is not for me to explain nor question them. What now, of you? What now your intentions?'

'Stripped of purpose, stripped of meaning, we have decided that we do not wish to clutter the world any longer. We have come here to die, as samurai should.'

'Noble,' said Goemon.

'Here are our seventeen names and the seventeen seals of our families in testament. Take them. Record them. We wish to be known as true followers of the Way, and by our deaths prove our unyielding loyalty.'

'Of course.'

'We also with our deaths protest this obscene government, pray to all righteous spirits for the death of the devil-tyrant Tokugawa and ask that he face judgement for his shameful duplicity in the myriad hells.'

There was a long silence that followed. Goemon sighed sadly.

'That you had but held your tongue,' he said, 'yours is a

sympathetic story. I would have shown you mercy. I would have even lent you my own sword, that you could perform seppuku as it should be done. But no. Insults. Now what is left to us but—'

'Do you really think,' said the lead samurai, 'we would have come this far without a way to be the masters of our own end?'

He withdrew his other hand from under his sleeve, and the source of the chemical burning smell became apparent: two burning lengths of arquebus matchcord in his hand.

Behind him his men burst into action, tossing off their straw hats and shawls. Amongst their huddle they had been hiding two large casks, which they now revealed with a grim flourish. The swordless samurai dropped to their knees, their leader tossed their declaration towards Goemon, and then turned and headed back to his men.

As the samurai clutched their bodies tight to the barrels like leeches, the leader handed one matchcord to another man, and then, within a cold moment, Goemon knew what would follow.

From behind him one of his men began rushing forward out of sheer instinct, levelling his spear. Goemon grabbed the man by the belt and tried to haul him backwards. He struggled, but the captain was stronger, dragged him back towards the shelter of the walls of the garrison, screaming at all his men to do likewise, and then the matchcords were at the caskets and there was the punch of a roar beginning and—

Goemon became aware that he was horizontal, that he was in the dirt, and so he sat up, and he found the street was dusty and that the swordless samurai were gone, and also that it felt as if his teeth had shattered and that every bone in his ribcage had been forced inwards. There was no sound, though he could feel his throat moving spastically and knew he had to be making some kind of noise.

There were bits of things everywhere, cloth and meat, the great banners of the Tokugawa he had been standing between annihilated. The man he had tried to haul backwards was nearby, he on his hands and knees. His face was dirty or bloody or something, he didn't look good, and there was sound now, painful, coming in from Goemon's left ear like a lance of boiling water: wailing, the samurai on his hands and knees, he was wailing piteously.

Across the street a storefront collapsed in fitful stages, belching more dust into the air. And there behind the dust he saw smoke, the flickering of budding flame, and he tried to shout 'Fire!', tried to summon someone to deal with it before the buds of it bloomed blazing, and perhaps he did, perhaps he formed actual words but he could not be sure.

From above then he thought he felt rain, but he did not look up, looked instead at the ground, at the folded piece of paper containing the names of the seventeen obliterated samurai, and he saw that the rain that fell upon the paper was red, the smallest parts of their bodies that had risen the highest now falling, all the little gobs of gore and hair like warm sleet, and then Goemon was horizontal once more, felt it pattering on his face, caressing him into oblivion.

The Goat's ears howled with a piercing resonance. All was chaos, all was noise. Tiles slid from the shattered roof of the gatehouse, falling one by one arrhythmic, crashing, shattering. A Tokugawa samurai rushed outwards to help, obliviously, only for a tile to connect with his head. He collapsed amidst the debris and bodies, added to them.

Later, tend to him later.

The Goat sought his captain first and foremost, and he limped and staggered as he checked upon those sprawled out in the street. He found Goemon senseless, and he grabbed him beneath the arms and began dragging him inwards, struggling in his dazed senses and on his maimed leg.

Across the street in the wreckage of the buildings opposite he saw the flames now, rising fierce, erupting almost, consuming what had been a purveyor of grilled fish. Doubtless coals and hearths had been burning within prior, and yet the Goat gaped aghast at the how rapidly the fire progressed, and so many buildings next to it, behind it, whether damaged or pristine, they were all things of paper and wood, awaiting kindling . . .

A lowerborn ran up to the Goat, pulled on his shoulders as he pulled on Goemon's in turn, trying to draw his attention.

'Do something!' the man was shouting. 'The fire! Fire! Are you not in command? Are you not the Tokugawa? Do something!'

'What?' said the Goat. 'Do what? What can I do?'

The words were barely heard, but he saw the look of horror and helplessness on the man's face. Perhaps he owned one of the buildings. The lowerborn began to dance a pathetic fretting dance from one foot to the other, hands pulling at his hair as he beheld the blaze beginning to spread from building to building.

He was not alone in this, so many dozens of people just staring, tentative shouts going up for the volunteer firefighters of the ward to assemble, but how long for them to arrive, to organize? How many more buildings, more livelihoods would be turned to ash before then? The teeming despair, the dread, the fear, and, as it deepened, threatened to become abyssal suddenly there came a great heroic cry.

Teams of men were arriving now, running down the street in perfectly arrayed columns. They were not lower-born but samurai, and yet they came bearing the necessary tools for combating the fire: hooked ropes, ladders, saws, mallets. The Goat stared at them, these samurai not of the Tokugawa, watched as with perfect discipline these dozens of men set to work.

With no choice but to sacrifice the block the fire was burning on already, the samurai cast their hooked lines on the buildings of the street fronts opposite and began the frantic process of pulling down the structures before the fire could reach them, sawing and cutting and hammering where they had to, creating a firebreak that would isolate the blaze. So effortlessly skilled at it were they that it was as though they had had practice in it, surprising for men of the sword, and on they cut and dragged and hauled, tireless, throwing their entire bodies into the cause, they not panicking but confident, strong, shouting in unison as they worked.

It was infectious, and, though the flames and the heat rose and rose, the people of the city saw the fearlessness of these samurai and felt their own dread lessen. They began to cheer the swordsmen on, felt joy in their hearts as they knew these men, these familiar samurai, to be their protectors, their true benefactors. They and their school of the city and for the city, and though the air was rent with smoke their kimonos all shimmered in the shade that all of Kyoto knew and revered, shimmered the colour of tea.

The crowd cheered for them rhythmically: 'Yoshioka! Yoshioka! Yoshioka!' And the chant went on as the fire raged against, and then died in, its cage; and, as the ash blew and reddened eyes dried, the Goat recognized the bald samurai who had led the Yoshioka.

Tadanari Kozei, and through the smoke he was looking at the ruins of the Tokugawa garrison, and on his face was a wide smile of black satisfaction.

Chapter Twelve

The dawn was nascent as a cobalt smear in the eastern sky when Musashi felt eyes upon him. A primal instinct that pierced his slumber. He saw two brown orbs low to the ground, catching the light of the remnants of the fire that smouldered still. A canine form, and he thought it first a ranging wolf poising to strike, and started. The animal, though, skittered back at his sudden movement, and he realized it was in truth a famished dog.

Its hide was mottled tan, though great clumps of it were missing and the bare skin beneath revealed lean muscle and the shape of bones. One of its pointed ears had been torn away in some long-ago struggle.

An exile from nearby Kyoto, perhaps.

Wary, it did not approach, but neither did it flee. Musashi watched it for a long while. He realized the creature must be tantalized by the smell of the mushrooms he had boiled the night before. Some remained in the little cast-iron pot. He picked one of them up and held it out in the palm of his hand, offered it to the dog. The dog lowered its head and growled, distrustful.

Musashi smiled.

He tossed the mushroom towards it, and quickly the dog snapped it up. One by one he continued to throw the remaining vegetables, closer each time, drawing the dog in. Eventually it was close enough that he could reach out and touch it, and to his surprise the dog allowed this. Its fur was brittle, the missing ear a ridge of hardened scar. He stroked it, soothed it, and he felt right then a profound sympathy and kinship with the dog, saw himself in it.

Most men would prefer to think themselves the wolf, some fearsome master of the wilderness stalking the night the more pleasing and romantic image. But the truth was wolves were born wild. Dogs were bred to the leash, as Musashi had been born to the Way. He and the dog, the pair of them here had liberated themselves, earned this life of meagre subsistence and magnificent substance.

Toughened.

Pure.

Words of this sort, he told himself.

Across from him, over the fire, Ameku stirred. The woman rose to sit. He wondered if the blinded had some acuter form of hearing, if the dog's gentle panting had not somehow disturbed her.

'Here,' he said softly.

Her head turned slightly, but she asked no question. She understood what he meant – that it was he that was awake, and that Yae and Akiyama slept still. It was a laconic form of communication that had developed over the months together. She sat there rubbing and stretching the doze from herself in silence, not wanting to rouse the others. Musashi continued to watch her, scratching the dog on the hard scruff of its neck.

Always Ameku put the fire between them, so that he saw her mostly through some veil of smoke. Always she turned and hid her features with the long locks of her immaculately combed hair, so that he only ever saw her jaw, her lips, and nothing more. Her face remained a mystery to him. Never had he seen her blinded eyes.

The dog continued to pant, and her head twisted in query.

'What is here with you?' she asked.

'A dog.'

'A dog?'

He grunted.

'Dangerous?'

'He's an ugly old thing, but he seems friendly.'

Ameku said nothing.

'Do you like dogs?' he asked. 'Would you like to touch him?'

'No.'

The dog took the rejection evenly. Musashi continued to pet it. In the woods around them the insects of the summer pulsed and sang. They recognized no difference between the sun and the moon, the chirping crickets, the quavering suzu-mushi, the howling cicadas, offered their chorus relentlessly. Ameku fumbled around her until she found her bamboo flask. She pulled the stopper from it and drank from the stale water within.

'Today – Kyoto?' she asked.

'I believe so.'

'I want to sleep on bedding once more,' she said with blunt desire. 'You think, definitely, I can find work in the city?

'You can work a loom, and here . . . It is the capital. All things come from here, so too silk or tatami mats or . . . There must be great mills. There *are* great mills. Someone will take you on.'

'You are certain?'

'Yes.'

'But never have you seen Kyoto?'

'No.'

'Nnn,' she said, entirely dubious.

'There will be work awaiting you.'

He tried to put confidence in his voice. Whether she believed him or not he could not tell. It had taken some convincing to get her and Yae to accompany the swordsmen to the capital. He had told her all these things many times, and furthermore insisted that with two samurai with them they would walk safely upon the roads. This had proven true – only once had Musashi seen a hostile face peering out from the cover of the trees, and the man had seen both Akiyama's horse and the sheer size of Musashi and the look that he returned, and then had retreated. There would be others, given time, unarmed and vulnerable; banditry a game of patience.

The dog lay down on its side, warming its belly on what was left of the fire. Musashi nestled his fingers in the warm spaces between its ribs and let his hand rise and fall with the creature's contented breathing.

'Do you have dogs on Ryukyu?' he asked.

'Of course,' she said, and she said it as though it were absurd to be asked so. 'Cats too. Fish and birds and—'

'It was only an idle question.'

She smiled, not quite kindly. 'Do you think Ryukyu some . . . new world? All different?'

'Your songs, the way you sing . . . It is like nothing I have heard before.'

'Ah.'

'The words . . .' said Musashi. 'Do you think . . . Could you speak your language for me?'

'What would you have me say?'

'Does it matter? Can you not just . . . speak?'

'No.'

'I . . .' said Musashi, and he tried to think of some fine poetic utterance that he had heard across his life, '"Swift as the wind. Silent as the forest. Fierce as the fire. Implacable as the mountain."'

Her face twisted for a moment. Then she spoke. What she said was much longer than the phrase Musashi offered, and he wondered if it was simply a difficult translation or whether she was mocking him.

In the silence after, Akiyama's horse offered a great sigh as it slept on its feet.

'What was that you had me say?' she asked.

'Something I heard. Something my father taught me, about the way men ought to be.'

'You like the sound better in my tongue?'

Musashi did not answer.

'Well, now, what matters the most?' she asked. 'If I sang my song in your words, words you know and understand, would you like it more? The same? Or is the, the . . .' she said, struggled for a word, and then under her breath so as not to wake the others she hummed a wordless phrase of melody. 'That alone, which you like? That which enters your heart? The thing that has no meaning, the thing that you can give any meaning to?'

Musashi could not answer.

She smiled again. 'I will tell you this: I have known Japan. I have known Ryukyu. They are the same. Dogs are dogs, men are men, women are women. Words are different, but their meaning . . . ?' She circled a finger over her heart, tapped her chest. 'In there, the same. All as we are.'

The way she said it, the way she smiled – Musashi could not gauge the level, nor define the subject of her scorn, whether it was he himself she was toying with or whether she was earnestly trying to teach him something she found so risible she took bleak amusement in it. If only he could see her eyes, he might ascertain which it was.

'What of samurai?' he asked. 'The Way? Are these things also in Ryukyu?'

The blind woman sucked air through her teeth, thought about it. 'In Japan, you have much iron. In Ryukyu, little, so in Ryukyu there are few men that wear swords. In Japan, you Japanese . . . Some of you, swords the thing that you love. The star that you follow. This is true. But truly . . . do you think a small thing like a sword can shape a man? Change him?'

'If it is wielded dishonestly.'

'So you, Musashi, are honest?'

'I am,' he said.

Ameku said nothing further. Musashi sat looking at her with his hand upon the dog's flank. She was cynical, hardened by something, but what exactly had made her this way he could not begin to guess at. But he too had been hardened against all the wrongs of the world by his own circumstance, and, as the dawn fully broke above them both, he looked at her anew.

He began to wonder if he had not found in her one who felt as he did.

Akiyama slept in odd contortions to keep the weight of his body from pressing on the scars across his chest. He no longer had any need of bandages but the pain of the wounds remained, and a part of him wondered if it would ever truly subside. A host of old warriors he had encountered through his life moaning of the aches of decades-past battles paraded themselves through the pathways of his mind, and each time he dismissed them as no more than phantoms sent to drain his spirits.

When he awoke that morning he saw that Miyamoto had somehow befriended a dog through the night. It was a wretched-looking mongrel but it was placid enough, and it stayed with them through their mean breakfast of mushrooms and tough scraps of dried fish. Yae adored the creature immediately, and it sat there with its little lungs heaving as the heat of the day began to impose itself, ambivalent to her petting. Then, when it had assured itself that there was no more food, it shrugged itself free of the girl's arms and walked off without looking back.

Yae was upset at what she saw as a betrayal.

'Dogs are dogs,' he said to her. 'That's their nature. Immediacy. Have you ever seen a dog hauling on an old piece of rope? He fights and fights and he doesn't know why, but for those moments he has to fight entirely . . . Then he drops it, as though it never was.'

'So the dog didn't like me?'

'Oh, I have no doubt that it liked you entirely for the moments that you fed it.'

'But . . .' she said, sad and stubborn, 'the monks back at Nankodai, they told me a story about a dog that waited and waited and . . . I thought dogs were supposed to be loyal.'

'Well,' said Akiyama, 'loyalty is a thing of many facets, and . . .'

He did not finish. Defining loyalty had governed his thoughts these past months, and of the answer he was no longer certain.

It led him to a dark introspection, and deepened the anxiety he felt this morning. He found himself restless. For the first time since the day he had been cut down, he was compelled to pull his hair up into a topknot. The hair upon his once-shaven scalp had grown in fully and he had no oil with which to force his longer red locks straight and dark, but even though it was a poor approximation he nevertheless felt that it had to be done.

Miyamoto noticed him binding the queue of his hair and gave him a black look, but said nothing out loud.

This feeling had grown the closer they got to the capital, like a hailstone gathering ice amidst the clouds. It was one thing to make a decision in isolation, it was another to confront the consequences of it. Akiyama felt in some ways like a child, nervous, wanting to hide, to deny. He had left his bloodied and torn tea-coloured jacket to rot upon the walls of the hovel they had sheltered in, but now, suddenly, he wanted nothing more than to put it on once more, to smother himself in it, to let it cover his entire body and have the colour obscure his individual self.

His mind chose to fight this by fixating solely upon Kyoto.

It made of the city a portent of a kind, and Akiyama now found he desperately wanted to see it exactly as he had left it. If it had not changed, if it had retained its beauty and its splendour, if serenity still reigned, then he reasoned that he himself could be serene also. In judging himself against familiar things that he had judged himself against before, he might mark and understand the change in himself better. Yet a sort of dread in this . . . He was like a man waiting to be struck, braced for some pain and yet also simultaneously wanting to feel the pain so that it could be over and done with.

They readied themselves for travel. Yae gathered up her and Ameku's things and Miyamoto helped Akiyama stiffly up onto his horse. The pale-eyed samurai had ridden the entirety of their journey as the others walked. He was wounded but he felt hale enough to walk and had offered many times to alternate their time in the saddle, but Ameku had never ridden and was fearful of the height, Yae would not let any other lead Ameku, and Miyamoto had simply refused.

'Don't like horses' was all he had said. 'Bad memories.'

Instead Miyamoto held the horse's bridle as they walked, led the creature as Yae led Ameku. From the saddle Akiyama looked at the waystones on the sides of the road. They had travelled upon the Sannindo road, which ran from the western tip of Honshu to Kyoto broad and flat. Every half-*ri* a stone offered the distance to the capital. No other great city of the southern coast was afforded recognition upon them, not Osaka, not Himeji, not Okayama; only Kyoto nestled in the centre of the nation. Things only ever looked inwards.

They were close now and the road was busy. An irregular procession of irregular caste and fortune that approached on foot or on horseback or riding in palanquins. In the gutters that ran beside the roadway aspirant monks and destitute beggars beseeched for the same coin, voices pleading in desperation or murmuring steady prayer. People took tea in the shade of a roadside inn, kimono skirts and jerkin trousers hiked up and their bare feet set in a cool, running stream that had been channelled.

Akiyama marked a shrine that he remembered passing those years past, a little wooden structure set upon a plinth mimicking the form of a temple yet no larger than a clothes chest. Inside was a holy stone encircled by rope. He saw this and immediately thought of a rope around his throat, and so he took to thinking instead of the sights he would see in a matter of hours. What was it that defined Kyoto most to him? Was it the sight of the rising sun breaking over the eastern mountains, or fireworks loosed at night over the arch of the Nijo bridge? Was it the delicate smell of gathered summer hydrangeas or the overwhelming grease smoke of grilled river salmon cooked over red-hot coals? Was it the sound of the sigh of a crowd as a golden festival shrine was raised magnificently aloft, or of the great bells of the Gion temple tolling with low and resonant puissance, mourning the fleetness of existence?

Perhaps thoughts could be thought too loudly. Over his shoulder, Miyamoto asked, 'What is Kyoto like?'

And, for all his musing upon it, Akiyama found that he could answer no better than he could define the concept of loyalty. 'There is great beauty there,' he said. 'I cannot describe it as it deserves.'

'Is it as men say? The ten-thousand-year city? The capital of flowers?'

The pale-eyed samurai grunted evasively.

'How many people?' Miyamoto insisted.

'I don't know.'

'Is it . . .' said the young swordsman, and struggled for a word, 'populous?'

'What is your meaning?'

'I have walked the streets of other cities, and I have found the weight of people there channelled to feel as . . .' said Miyamoto, and he made a vague gesture with one hand, clutching at his throat and then banging a fist on his sternum. He looked up to see if Akiyama understood him, and all Akiyama could do was stare back in confusion.

'That is something I have never felt,' he said. 'You would do well to focus yourself upon the Yoshioka.'

Miyamoto's tone darkened. 'How many, their numbers?'

'I cannot say for certain. There are many adepts serving all across the country. I would expect at least fifty resident at the school, however.'

Miyamoto spat. 'That may be. But I only have feud with one.'

'The master Kozei is a talented swordsman. It was he who taught me. You cannot rush like a boar into conflict with him. If you seek—'

'Kozei?' said Miyamoto. 'I want the head.'

Akiyama adjusted himself in the saddle. After some moments, he said, 'Kozei was the one who ordered me to hunt you down.'

'But who is it – you told me – him of the bloodline, who carries the name?'

'Sir Seijuro reigns now that his father Sir Naokata has succumbed to his illness. He is young. Older than you, but young enough that he is likely under the sway of master Kozei still.'

'Seijuro Yoshioka,' said Miyamoto, fixated, tongue rolling out the words venomously. 'The Lord-King Yoshioka.'

They carried on in silence. The capital was imminent. They were sweating profusely, dark stains upon their worn and weathered clothes. The heat seemed to swell around them. Kyoto was inland, ringed by mountains that trapped the temperature and kept out wind, and the road ahead shimmered in a wet haze.

Other cities tended to coalesce gradually, outlying hamlets increasing in their density until the city was simply declared to start at some unseen boundary. For Kyoto proper, however, there was a firm demarcation. It had been both moated and walled by the will of the late Regent Toyotomi, vast amounts of earth packed hard and tight to stand at least five times the height of a man and the slope of them almost vertical. Gatehouse structures fifty paces long and three storeys high stood on top of the walls, and it was one of these buildings that Akiyama saw first, his first glimpse of his home in near four years.

The gatehouse was silhouetted against the bright sky and, set athwart the light, it was robbed of form, seemed vague and indistinct, and he found no comfort in it. He looked down instead, and from the vantage of his saddle he could see the moat before the walls. It was thirty paces wide, and Akiyama thought of its waters, remembered their deep jade-green colour, luscious, tauntingly so, as though the liquid might in fact be viscous enough to coat the body in, to wear as a second impermeably cool skin against the oppression of the summer.

But that was no more than a delusion, and there were other more tangible forms of oppression. A low bridge spanned the moat, barely above its surface, and Akiyama saw that before it a crowd of hundreds of people mobbed in sullen anger. Paper fans waved in vain, women hid beneath the shade of parasols, labourers in no more than loincloths and sandals sat with their arms around their knees, backs glistening. The lot of them were being prevented from crossing.

'This is very unusual,' he told Miyamoto. 'Not even during the War were the gates of Kyoto barred. The city is inviolate.'

Suspicious, he told Ameku and Yae to linger a distance away whilst he and the young swordsman went forward to investigate. At the mouth of the bridge they saw that a line of Tokugawa samurai were standing with spears, clad in full livery and conical iron helmets. Each one of them sweated piteously beneath the metal and the layers. Their leader was up on a dais, and he was shouting to the crowd, had shouted so long that his face was red and his voice was hoarse. He explained over and over, eyes bulging, that without specific permission entry to the city was barred owing to some calamitous incident he only alluded to, and the crowd seethed and murmured of explosion and fire and arson.

'The Tokugawa hold authority over the city now?' Akiyama said, and he was genuinely surprised by this development. 'How can they dare to assume that mantle? This is the realm of the Son of Heaven.'

He turned to Miyamoto, and found that the young man was not listening. His eyes were locked upon a samurai who was equally fixated upon him. The samurai wore a wide-brimmed straw hat that kept his face in shadow, stood with his arms crossed. He wore a kimono of fine black silk and a jacket of teal, and from the handles of his swords hung a long chain of Buddhist rosaries. He took in Miyamoto, blistered and gaunt, his hair pulled back into a wild tail, and made no attempt to mask his disdain.

'Kyoto is no place for the masterless,' the samurai said.

'This world is no place for the mastered,' said Miyamoto.

'What?' said the samurai, and he sneered. 'There are relics of the Teacher within that city. They shall not be sullied by the presence of a degenerate soul that persists in living beyond all dignity.'

'I am not here for temples.'

Akiyama interjected. 'Neither are we here to spread disharmony,' he said, and bowed to the samurai as politely as he could through his wounds and his seat upon the saddle.

'There is no conflict here. I humbly apologize for upsetting the tranquillity of your spirit such.'

'*You* have no cause to apologize,' said the samurai, eyes not leaving Miyamoto.

'And I do?' Miyamoto asked.

The man said nothing more. He simply persisted in staring, as though he were a warden. Miyamoto continued to stare back, matching the man in this contest. Akiyama felt the change as much as saw it. Something in the young swordsman hardened, something welled. A hatred in his eyes as he looked at this man and all he was. The samurai, and his beads of his rosary's lacquered ebony. The set of his jaw. The look in his eyes that outshone the shadow of his hat.

Miyamoto surged towards the samurai.

There was an outcry and the crowd drew back. Akiyama reached down and tried to take Miyamoto's shoulder, but he could only slow him. The samurai did not move, spread his legs into the balanced fighting stance. Put his hands to his longsword, left on the scabbard, right on the grip, waited for Miyamoto to enter his range of attack, and Miyamoto's hands were at his longsword also, and Akiyama snarled at him unheard, hauled at the scruff of his clothes and was nearly pulled from his saddle, a wrench of pain as his torso twisted, and there were five paces between them, four, and then Ameku silenced the crowd.

The woman gave a low hiss and spread her arms wide. Panicking, Yae had brought her close, yet even the girl drew back at the sound. Ameku's face was to the floor, and her hair obscured her features. She began to shudder and to sing in a low ululation, and the sheer alien sound of her words jarred and then began to terrify the crowd. Akiyama stared.

Miyamoto stared. Ameku continued, rhythmic and low, an aggressive conjuration. She brought her hands to her face and caught the tresses of her hair between her fingers. She sang into her palms as she slowly brought them upwards, and then in one savage gesture she snapped her head back and tossed her hair behind her, and revealed her eyes opened wide and staring at the samurai.

They were not the flawless orbs of some statue but marked and misted as though they were being consumed by chrysalis-thread, fogged of an ugly sick colour, and still she sang. Sang like a witch, like a ghoul, held her clawed hands out before her. Her in the throes of this dark foreign orison, its higher meaning unheeded, but in the primal gut of all those witnessing it a complete knowledge that she was pleading for some doom or malice conceived in outer places to manifest itself here and now.

'What is this hex?' quailed the samurai, clutching at his rosary. 'Is she a fox-demon?'

The Tokugawa samurai had seen the disturbance and they hurried over, twelve of them with twelve cruciform spears. Harried, choking on the heat, they were all of them in a foul mood and the points of their weapons were lowered eagerly at Musashi and the affronted samurai. Even they, however, were unsure how to treat Ameku still in her terrifying passion.

'Desist!' shouted their leader at her, for he did not know what else to do and it showed in his eyes. 'Desist!'

Yae pulled on Ameku's sleeve. Ameku let the note she was singing fade through a choking rattle into silence, but she kept her blighted eyes open and staring towards the samurai who had taken to murmuring the name of the Amida Buddha in warding. In the wake of the commotion, Akiyama's horse was panicked, bucking and whinnying beneath him as he spoke to the leader of the Tokugawa samurai.

'Good sir samurai,' he said, speaking quickly and deferentially, for he knew that crucifixes might await. 'You are vigil and just, but there is no crime here, only a restlessness caused by—'

The leader ignored him. 'Your names?' he demanded of the two swordsman.

'Eijun Yamanaka.'

'Musashi Miyamoto.'

'Eijun Yamanaka, Musashi Miyamoto,' said the leader, and Akiyama heard the tone of his voice and dread took him as he thought of the pronouncement to come. 'You are hereby formally ordered by the imperially ordained Shogunate of his most noble Lord Tokugawa to remove yourselves from before these walls immediately. Disperse in peace, in separate directions.'

Musashi was seething, Eijun unimpressed.

'We obey,' said Akiyama, and bowed in the saddle.

Quickly he took Miyamoto by the shoulder once more, and turned him away before the Tokugawa samurai might command a graver punishment. He did not know why the man was beholden to such leniency, but neither would he question it. Miyamoto jerked free of Akiyama's warding hand and strode off without looking back, and the crowd parted for him. Akiyama nodded at Yae, and the girl led Ameku through the cleared channel. The pale-eyed samurai then followed behind both of them on his horse. His instinct was to shield them, but it was unneeded. There was not a person there that would dare to provoke the foreign woman once more.

Akiyama turned to look over his shoulder only a single time. The samurai Eijun was still there. To his surprise, however, he found that Eijun was not looking vengefully at Miyamoto or fearfully at Ameku.

Instead, he was looking straight at him.

Akiyama returned the samurai's gaze for a moment, then righted himself in the saddle and left the crowd behind them. Miyamoto stalked on ahead without looking back, and when they were alone Ameku took to screaming at his back. She called him idiot, she called him fool, and then she began spitting long and vicious things in her own tongue. She seemed embarrassed more than anything, had pulled her hair across her face once more, and it appeared she had no intention of sparing Miyamoto for making her feel such.

Akiyama did not say anything. Seeing such raw, naked anger as this was unusual to him, and he wondered if in her land they had no concept of restraint. Then he wondered if this perhaps was not better, to simply expunge oneself of all emotion when it occurred rather than to accrue it until it combined with other furies, magnified them, all festering within until it simply could not be contained any longer.

He kept silent, though, let the pressure of his own inner turmoil bubble away at a constant.

'Why?' Ameku persisted in asking Miyamoto in stunted bursts, her anger robbing her of fluency in the language. 'Why do you make me . . . ? Why fight? Why do you want to fight? How many men there?'

At the fifth or sixth time of asking Miyamoto was finally provoked. He stopped and turned and stood with his lean frame hunched and coiled as though he might strike at anything, and as he spoke he looked solely at Ameku: 'Don't you understand?' he said. 'That is samurai. That is the Way. I told you. Men like that. That . . . hubris. Standing there assuming authority, as though he were on some righteous vigil. What authority? Authority he gave himself! I see it, I see men like that, and it is as though I am burnt. Burnt with something for which there is no balm. Do you not feel it? Knowing that what stands before you is wrong, entirely wrong.'

'Him . . . ? *He* is wrong?' asked Ameku.

'Yes!' spat Miyamoto, and he spat it with such hatred that Akiyama was moved to try to calm the situation.

'A samurai's first and ultimate enemy is always himself,' he said.

Miyamoto turned his gaze to Akiyama. 'I am no samurai,' he uttered.

It was all he needed to say, perhaps all he could say. He turned and left. Not one of the three of them he left behind him made to follow, watched him stride off away. They were by the banks of the river Katsura, broad and shallow, lush green grass soft and vital all around them. Akiyama's horse flicked its tail at the minute insects that clouded around it. He could think of nothing to say, and so he simply looked across the waters for a moment at the walls of the city on the far side, and they were dark and impenetrable and offered no comfort.

Ameku took a breath, and with that the tension slid out of her. She set her hair back over her shoulders, sniffed, and then jerked her head. Yae, who had been hiding behind her, led her onwards. In wordless consent they followed the path Miyamoto had taken. Akiyama flicked the reins and the horse matched their gentle pace.

'What . . . What is this?' Ameku said. 'Him . . . Can you believe?'

'It was quite a reaction,' said Akiyama.

'This morning, he was calm. Asked gentle things. Different. And now . . .'

She was not wrong. The change in Miyamoto was startling to Akiyama both in its scale and its immediate revelation. Secluded in the wild, tending to his wounds, Miyamoto had been placid and considered, a reticent speaker. Here, though, was the man he had hunted, the face he remembered facing down at the end of the sword, the outlaw who shouted his name and threatened priests and cut down trees to prove his point.

'This morning,' said Ameku, 'he told me he was honest. Well . . . which is it? Is this him as he truly is?'

Akiyama did not answer.

They went on in silence for a while. They passed a man thigh-deep in the waters casting out fishing nets, and he had snared already that day for on the banks a fat trout lay glistening in the sun. Akiyama realized this was the first time he was alone with the woman and the girl. He wondered without malice why it was they were even here. He himself thought it dubious that they should accompany the swordsmen given the ultimate purpose of their journey, but it was Miyamoto who had over the course of days insisted.

Why was this? If Miyamoto wanted witnesses to what he was attempting, the blinded were a poor choice.

Yet there were things that he wanted to ask, and his curiosity grew until it could not be contained. 'If I might ask of you a question, lady?' he dared to venture.

Ameku grunted.

He chose his words with care, and he asked with utmost honesty, 'Before, as you chanted . . . were you summoning the Christ?'

'Who?' she said.

'Aren't all foreigners Christian?'

'No!' she said, and a hint of her anger resurfaced. 'It is . . . old things, old words, old prayers I do not . . . It is a thing to stop storms, sea storms. I do not like to . . . But him,' she said, and waved to where she thought Miyamoto was. 'Because of him, I must.'

'A queller of tempests,' said Akiyama, mulling it over. 'The power of your voice belies your stature. For a woman of your size to chant in so grand a manner . . . You must have had some form of training, no?'

Yae looked up at Akiyama and gestured silently for him to cease his questions. The samurai did not wish to pry, and heeded her.

Some time later they found Miyamoto waiting for them. He was crouched down by the river's edge tossing pebbles into the water, and he seemed fascinated by the rings they cast out. Perhaps it had calmed him. His anger had lessened, or he had forced it tight within himself, but regardless he offered no apology for it.

'Where are we headed, then, if the city is denied us?' he called as they approached.

'There are two places as I see it,' said Akiyama. 'There are the slums of Maruta, which lie outside the walls of the city to the north-east. No man of the Yoshioka would risk the dishonour of being sighted in so lowly a place. Or there is Mount Hiei, a little beyond that. The monks will provide us sanctuary.'

'Which is your preference?'

'Hiei, though the walk is a little more arduous. My ancestral crypt lies upon its slopes, and in truth I worry for how it has been tended in my absence,' said Akiyama. Then he added, 'Maruta also has a certain odour at this time of year which I am not eager to experience.'

'Hiei, then. Show me the way.'

It was the late afternoon by the time they reached the foot of holy mount Hiei, where men had studied the Enlightened Teachings for a thousand years. There was nothing visually remarkable about it to distinguish it from the other nearby mountains, a low and forested slope with a blunted peak. They ascended its trails shaded by the boughs of the trees that surrounded them and watched by the time-ravaged faces of carvings of the manifold Buddhas. Salamanders striped black and white skittered before them, and above them fawn monkeys capered.

It was all calm and placid, a place of considered thought, yet Akiyama felt no contentment. He watched Miyamoto, and wondered what it was that boiled within his heart. For the first time he was acutely aware he had made the decision to follow a man near twenty years his junior. They should have been in the city now, perhaps standing as he had stood a hundred times before beneath the gates of the Hongan temple looking up at their inner roofs painted like lotus ponds, but Miyamoto's temper had spoilt that hope, and they walked as exiles yet. Hiei tonight, but where was the ultimate destination of their journey?

He sat feeling unsteady in his saddle with his faith wavering, and then at a curving of the path suddenly the trees cleared and they were afforded a view across the city of Kyoto lit by the golden haze of the setting sun opposite them in the west. A view so remarkable that it rose Akiyama up in his saddle. Immutable, enduring, beautiful. Unlike any other city in the nation, unlike any in this world for all he knew.

He looked and saw it all. The tiered majesty of the multitude of temple pagodas that reigned benevolent, their curved roofs set entirely symmetrical, beautiful spears that sat to catch the sun. The broad peaks of the Son of Heaven's palace that emerged from the high walls of his compound like celestial mountaintops through mist, crested with golden statues of peacocks and dragons and lions. The paddy fields that capped the city to the north and the south, there in case of siege, here shimmered and reflected and seemed to hold all between them with hands of light.

This was what he had wanted to see. If something like this was in the world, then the world could not be so foul. There was hope in him suddenly, hope as warm as the light they all bathed in, and he looked over at Miyamoto and found that hope grow. Gone was the fury. The young man was taken by wonder, and in that look Akiyama saw once more the higher thing he had believed in, had elected to heed.

He smiled and said to the young swordsman, 'Your mouth is flapping open like a carp's.'

'I don't think I've ever seen trees as tall as those,' Miyamoto said, pointing at the towers of the various pagodas. 'How is it that men can make such things?'

'In truth I do not know myself. Each houses a Bodhisattva's bones, or so I've heard.'

'The mathematics behind them . . .'

He stared on. Akiyama looked over the city fondly. No words were needed.

'I am tired,' Ameku said from behind them. 'Come. Move. Go. On. Up.'

Akiyama turned and saw the woman clutching Yae's hand. He realized the folly, and felt a great pity that Ameku was denied this experience, would have had to rely on the words of a child to sense anything at all. He nodded to the girl and made to kick his steed onwards up the path once more, when Miyamoto asked him a question.

'What's that in the west?' he said. 'Looks as though they are constructing something.'

Akiyama looked and saw there was a swathe of land that had been cleared and razed flat, like an ochre square cut out of the cityscape. A great cloud of birds were circling above it. 'I had heard before I departed that the Shogun was planning on erecting a castle in the city,' he said. His lip curled. 'What an ugly thing.'

Chapter Thirteen

Goemon stood and watched the crows circling above. They were a constant here at the emergent castle of the Shogun Tokugawa. Great mounds of shells of oysters and scallops and mussels were stacked high before the castle, the insides of them shimmering with pink-green-blue nacre, and the birds waited to swoop down and steal one hoping that some scrap of flesh yet lingered within.

The shells were a national tithe. They awaited burning, the ash of them a fundamental component of the mortar that would form the foundations of the castle. The mounds of them so many and so tall that the jokes ran of a fresh range of mountains sprouting in the city: Tokugawa's Fuji, ringed not by clouds but by carrion seekers.

Usually, boys circled in turn beneath the birds with long sticks daring the creatures to dive; they charged with the shells' protection, and usually the street rang with the shrieks of their struggle.

Today, though, silence.

The castle was only a year into its construction, no great spires or buttresses stood yet. The land had been cleared, the outer moat had been dug fifteen paces wide and the height of three men deep, and now the slow process of lining the walls of it with stone was under way. All had been progressing well, until today.

Goemon watched the crows for as long as he could. They were so enviously free, moving without effort, coasting, gliding. He wished that he could do such. Motion was agony to him. Standing was agony. The length of him hurt still from the force of the suicide blast, the flesh beneath his clothes mottled with ugly queer-coloured bruises. He rolled his jaw out of recent recuperating habit, felt his ears still popping like the sound of wood burning.

He sighed, and brought his eyes downwards, to what the crows now circled above waiting for a chance to feast upon nine severed heads raised up on spears.

Lowerborn men all, heads full of hair and all blood within drained upon the dust beneath, they were solemn totems of a desolate scene. Around them the wooden pulleys and cranes of construction were stilled. Bamboo scaffolds stood skeletal. There was that familiar, queer hush of death across the entire site.

'Tell me, then,' said Goemon, and through his damaged ears his own voice sounded distant, 'what happened here?'

He spoke to one of his own men, clad in Tokugawa black, kneeling in the dust at his feet. His helmet was discarded and the samurai's shaven scalp glistened with sweat, and blood was dried upon his hands and the sleeves of his clothes. The man held his gaze downwards as the etiquette of contrite submission demanded. The Goat stood by this man's shoulder, both hands on the pommel of his longsword grinding the point of it into the ground, ready to enforce any deviation from this.

'There was a disturbance, sir,' the samurai said.

'A disturbance?'

'A riot.'

'A riot.'

'Yes, sir.'

This was all he offered. Goemon looked at him until the man was compelled to speak again.

'The instigator . . . He assaulted one of the architects. The man was lowerborn, a drunkard, staggering on his feet. He's . . . up there,' said the samurai, meaning the row of heads. 'Third from the left.'

'Why is he up there?'

'When I accosted the man for assaulting the architect, he was . . . He spat in my face, and said, "Why don't you and all the other whores of Edo choke on your own shit?"'

The Goat grunted in mild affront.

'So you took his head?' asked Goemon.

'What else am I to do? I will not suffer . . .' said the samurai, and his voice trailed off.

'Why are there eight more beside him?' Goemon pressed. His voice was growing lower, so low in his throat that he found a fresh pain.

'When I took the instigator's head,' said the samurai, 'the gathered city folk reacted unfavourably. They have been gathering more and more recently. Malingerers. There was a rush of them, which I and my men had to quell. They were soon dispersed, and peace restored.'

'Peace,' said Goemon blackly. 'Doubtless now in a hundred homes whispers of barbarity and murder are spoken, but you – you talk to me of peace.'

'Captain.'

'Was it deliberate insubordination, or was the urge to countermand my order idiotic negligence on your part?'

'Captain.'

The Goat rapped the point of his scabbard on the ground and snapped, 'Answer!'

The samurai licked his lips, considered his words before speaking thinly. 'Am I to stand by and let drunks spit insult at me? Am I supposed to forego my honour?'

'Obedience is the highest form of honour,' said Goemon. 'And you were ordered not to draw blood within the city limits lest you have my explicit permission, let alone to slaughter a crowd.'

'Sedition,' said the samurai. 'You also commanded that any case of sedition found was warranting of immediate death. And tell me, is a man of low stature speaking thus to me, to us – is that not sedition?'

'Your judgement is marred.'

'Why? Why stay our swords? They are our most noble Lord's to control, this city is, and they should all be made to recognize this truth.'

The samurai in his anger chose to look up then, met Goemon's eyes in defiance, and the Goat cried out in rage. 'Yours is not the place to question!' the hard old man shouted, and he raised his sword and drove the point of the scabbard into the back of the man's head, forced his face downwards into deference once more.

The samurai seethed on his knees, but obeyed.

'Have there been any instances of this before?' asked Goemon.

'No, sir. Not openly.'

'Then why today?'

The samurai could offer no answer. Goemon thought about it. He looked over to the distant crowd of citizens. They were witnesses, all on their knees, marshalled by a cadre of samurai with spears. Some of them expected death. Others still glowered with residual fury. The captain limped over stiffly and looked them over.

Only one stood out to him. It was a woman wearing a fine kimono of peach patterned with clouds of pear green, sullied with dust now, and though her face was hidden to the floor her shoulders were shuddering with her silent weeping.

'You,' he said, 'stand.'

She obeyed, though she stood as frailly on her feet as Goemon did. She kept her head down and tried to hide her face and her tears with her hands.

'Why is it you weep?' he asked her.

She was terrified of Goemon, fearing some reprisal on top of her misery, and it stole all words from her. She simply pointed to the severed heads with a shaking hand.

Goemon looked. 'Your husband?' he asked.

She nodded.

'Which one?'

'Third . . .' She faltered. 'Third from the left. I tried to stop him, sir, I did, but ever since that day, ever since, ever since, he's been drinking and—'

'Murderous Edo bastards!' howled a hidden voice from outside of the crowd, and Goemon became aware that they were being watched by the city, marked by it. 'Leave her be!'

The Tokugawa samurai bridled at the insult and the vulnerable crowd at their feet shuddered, but the captain gestured at them for calm. The woman had fallen back to her knees, and he did not want to press her further. He had but one question left to ask: 'Why?'

'We lived in Shinmachi' was all she said.

Shinmachi, the ward opposite the garrison of the Tokugawa. The ward that had been burnt down in the fire a week previous.

Goemon said nothing further, left her to her weeping. She bore no bruises as he did from the incident, but her wounds were far more grievous. He turned and limped back towards the severed heads, the setting sun, the Goat and the samurai in the dust still dank with blood. The captain stood over the man he commanded and made his pronouncement:

'We shall pay for the cremations of these men,' he said. 'Your duty now is to liaise with their families to oversee the funerary rites. You will do so with our explicit apologies. These are my orders. Adhere to them exact.'

'I understand and obey, sir,' said the samurai, and pressed his head to the earth.

The Goat gave a curt gesture for the man to rise and be about his work, called to his back, 'Ensure you match the heads and the bodies correct. No further scandal here.'

Night fell. Goemon remained at the site of the castle until the moon was proud in the sky on pretence of securing the area and ensuring it was properly manned and guarded, but in truth the exertion of the day had drained all vigour from his battered body. Night and its curfew also offered a passage home bereft of witnesses, and when all seemed quiet the captain and his adjutant hobbled off together to return to the garrison. Their pace through the empty streets was slow. The Goat could see the effort even walking took from Goemon, each little movement stiff, his weight shunted from foot to foot.

'Good you're up, sir,' he said. 'Better to face the pain than wallow in thrall to it.'

'Indeed,' said Goemon, though there was no conviction in his voice. The Goat noticed his accent had slipped away from that of the proper tongue, reverted. A sort of sigh escaped the captain. 'So the city blames the clan Tokugawa for the fire?'

'That is apparent, sir.'

'We are as the hornet here, and now the hive of bees is stirring. Heads on spears will only anger them further. What tomorrow? A fresh riot? Agh, how do I . . . ?'

He never finished. For a long time he remained silent, the pulsing of insects all around. The heat unyielding even at night, the sweat drenching his topknot so that the hairs of it formed little points that curled downwards, met the skin of his shaven scalp, tickled, no, scratching constant: a tiger's claw atop his head. He looked around for something to distract him, even for a moment, found nothing. Here was still and silent, the mercantile wards desolate at night, the honest folk that worked and lived here homebound by dark and up with the dawn.

Honest? A vestigial word used only through habit, one ingrained from when the lowerborn to him were no more than things he passed on the way from the keep to the field of battle.

The things he had learnt. See all the stores pressed together, see the fronts of them only a pace or two or across. This, Goemon now knew, was because only the space the property took up on the actual street itself could be taxed, a theoretical infinite depth behind that space permissible. A devious little ploy, which he knew and the 'honest' craftsmen knew was immoral, and which he knew and they knew he could do nothing about because that was how it had always been, all these buildings here compacted slender and deep like rows of larcenous razor clams embedded in the sand.

Embedded in his throat, squeezing, pressing.

This just another facet of these streets that never seemed to end, through which he was doomed to prowl staring at the wooden lattices of the shutters over windows and doors, these like the bars of a cage not imprisoning him but instead keeping him – the captain, the supposed master and commander of this city – out. He could recite facts of ownership and land usage and special permissions all cadastre-precise, and all truly meaningless.

Without comment he handed the lantern he held off to the Goat and limped his way into the shadow of an alley. There he vomited, the arcing of his back and the convulsing of his body agony. Sweat fell from his brow, stars swam in his eyes, the tiger's claw rapped its knuckles on his scalp. He stood there bent double, a hand out upon a wall, stood there secreted and anonymous for as long as he dared.

Formal, very formal.

The year before last, a mansion blanketed with a finger's depth of snow within the myriad ramparts and moats of the grand castle at Edo.

Twenty of them, high-ranking retainers of the Tokugawa all, wearing leggings so long they trailed along the floor behind them, in which they could only shuffle or become entangled, hobbling them and preventing any sudden movement. The shoulders of their sleeveless overjackets stood out exaggerated, wired with bamboo so that the silhouette of their torso was an inverted, blunted triangle. So too their spines wired, vertebrae affixing upright as they settled to kneel in ranked and painful repose upon their calves.

They were made to wait. The walls around them were painted with mythical peacocks, the feathers of their tails gold leaf and vivid lapis blue, flowing wide, enveloping, embracing. This was the antechamber designated for receiving friends. There was an antechamber for neutral guests Goemon knew, adorned with the devils of judgement inviting the guests there to think upon any transgressions they might have, and one for enemies also – the largest, grandest hall, where each wall was dominated by a single huge tiger coiling to pounce, facing inwards and dwarfing whomsoever would be sitting between them.

With no given signal the door to the main chamber was slid silently open. Behind it was revealed the cadre of the most private guard of the clan kneeling in similar ranks, old men all, for true loyalty took decades to prove, but these samurai were neither enfeebled by their age nor divested of their longswords nor encumbered by effete robes.

And there, behind their fierce barrier, the Great Lord Ieyasu Tokugawa himself sat cross-legged upon a dais.

Goemon could barely see him. The antechamber where he and the others knelt was at a right angle to where the Lord faced and the corner of the wall obscured him. Not daring to turn his head, Goemon could only discern the far hand of his current master where it lay resting upon a knee covered in the black skirts of his stiffly pleated trousers.

'There are fine tidings,' said the Lord Tokugawa, his voice thinner and older than Goemon expected. 'In the spring I am to be proclaimed by his most holy Emperor formally as Shogun and the high protector of the nation.'

'May the reign last for ten thousand years!' barked one of the inner guards.

'Ten thousand years!' all the samurai shouted, and pressed their heads to the floor.

'I shall travel to Kyoto and receive the blessing of his undying majesty,' said Tokugawa when they had risen. 'And then I shall hopefully never return.

'I have no purpose lingering in Kyoto. None can rule Kyoto. Kyoto has never had a formal Lord for Kyoto is the Emperor's city. The Emperor cannot rule Kyoto because he is heaven-touched, and cannot understand the realities of this savage plane. Kyoto is as it is. To try to grasp it is to flail in the river with the tail of the eel slicking between your fingers.

'Hear then, this proclamation of mine: I vow unto thee, unto the skies and the heavens, that my first act as Shogun will be to make Edo the true capital of this nation.'

'May the moss grow thick upon the never-falling walls of Edo!' bellowed the guard.

Oblique, that. Goemon chose to shout, 'Forever Edo!', others 'Glorious strategy!', 'The walls shall never fall!', 'Moss!' Tokugawa let them fall silent. The words were not important. The vigour and obedience were.

The Lord continued: 'This proclamation, however, will never be announced outside the walls of this hall. Kyoto and the Son of Heaven cannot be seen to be lessened. But everything of worth – policy, trade, law – all will have their centres moved here where I and my scions can control them. I concede the hallowed beast its own cage, but therein lies the problem: Kyoto cannot *not* be my city.'

Utter silence, save for the crackling of wood where it burnt in braziers, keeping the winter out, and then a rustling, a choked cry. At the back of the Lord's hall a man stood with a hooded falcon upon his arm, the bird agitated for but a moment, the wings then stilled.

Did birds dream, Goemon thought, or was it simply attuned?

'How do you wish us to bring it in line, most noble Lord?' asked one of the men to Goemon's right. 'Shall we dispatch an army to occupy it? It shall be an honour to lead such a force in your name.'

'No,' said Tokugawa, and it was clear that he had expected that most obvious of answers. 'I forbid that – Kyoto must not burn on my account. Listen once more: Kyoto is a symbol. Repeat that.'

'Kyoto is a symbol,' said every man there.

'Good,' said Tokugawa. 'Understand this. It has its verification in history: a hundred and thirty-five years ago the Ashikaga Shogunate let the city be razed to the ground. Their inability to protect the capital lost them the respect of the entire country, and the war that followed did not stop until Sekigahara. Go find the Ashikaga dynasty now, I challenge you – rake through the pebbles and the ashes and see what you can summon.

'Now, I ask you to imagine how much worse that would be if, instead of simply being unable to prevent the capital from burning, the clan Tokugawa was seen to be the one that actively started the blaze? "Unite against the arsonist that dares to bring down the walls of heaven" is a strong rallying cry, is it not?'

'My most noble Lord,' ventured one of the men, 'how many enemies are left to rally? All are slain or humbled or enthralled.'

'You think only of the present. It is impossible for a man to kill all his enemies, and given time they will recover, or secret ones shall emerge. In the reign of my son, or in the reign of my grandson, if the beacon still shines will these dogs not hearken to it?

'You also think only of warriors. Know that Kyoto is a symbol to all, not just to those with swords. Temples pervade its streets, monasteries in the hills around it. Should I send spearmen to march through the city, inevitable obstinacy and outcry, and then inevitable damage and death. And, should these inevitably sullied things wear saffron robes or be carved with images of the Buddha, then we shall see true bedlam in every vale the length of the country. Angered monks rousing armies of peasants.

'You are all of you young men, and you do not remember it as it was. You perhaps think a renunciant is a samurai who reneges his courage, his will to fight, his ability with arms. You are wrong. A renunciant is a samurai who retains all that, and gains religious zeal. Throughout my youth I fought rebellions by these heaven-maddened men, and never do I wish to do so again. The Warlord Oda scoured Mount Hiei clean thirty years ago, ended the last major uprising, but even though he – foremost of all tacticians – led thirty thousand samurai he lost half of them, taking no more than ten thousand ordained warriors.

'Consider that. Take that as proof. Do we have the force to do this, here, today? Once, of course. Twice, yes. Ten times? Twenty times, with the daggers of the "enthralled" at our backs? Understand that this clan is at a very precarious moment. We have clambered at last to sit atop a mountain's peak only to find that the sky is full of spears. Wounds and grievances against the clan Tokugawa run deep already. We do not wish to deepen them. The truth is we are stretched thin, very thin.'

Dark, darkening further the black paint that was woven between the blue and gold of the peacock's feathers on the walls. Odd how something so beautiful could suddenly seem so throttling, for Goemon and every man in the antechamber knew where this was heading.

'Kyoto must not be free and it must not be shackled,' said their Lord, laying it clear before them. 'Bloodlessly, it must be brought into line. One of you is to receive the honour of this task. It is vital to the clan. I leave it up to you to decide who amongst you shall have the privilege, for you are all deeply, deeply trusted by this clan. Is the meaning of my words understood?'

'Yes, Lord!'

'Hail the Shogun Tokugawa!' came the cry from all of the inner guards.

'Hail the Shogun Tokugawa!' responded those in the antechamber, and then they bowed a final time. The hand of the great Lord Ieyasu Tokugawa gave a slight gesture, and the door slid closed without anything further.

Sealed away, the twenty men rose to kneel in silence. They were not the sons of clerks or diplomats: they were soldiers all. Bloodless was alien to them, and from the desperate battlefield they knew the feeling of doom well. It lingered heavy now. A fruitless venture that would likely yield at best their head displayed in shame on a spike, and at worst the ruination of the entire clan.

Yet they were irrevocably commanded to do so.

Duty was duty, and samurai obeyed. Who, then, to bestow this gift upon? There were divisions between them all, old rivalries and grudges between families started in their grandfathers' time, but none so big and encompassing as nineteen men against one. Slowly heads turned towards that individual, and in silence the sacrifice was chosen.

'Gratefully I accept this venerable charge,' said Goemon, and cast his brow to the floor.

Proper words, expected words.

And here he was now, Captain Goemon Inoue, reading auguries in his vomit.

Captain.

How it stuck like a bone in his throat, that he had not even been awarded the position of minister so that at least his terminal plummet might be gilded with a comet's tail of ice and diamond. That title hoisted off on some cousin of a cousin within the clan who ruled in name only. The fop stayed in the splendour of the estates around the famed Silver Pavilion out in the hills west of the city where he larked about the many gardens like some addled young buck stag, all directionless and lustful, fucking whomsoever he should come across.

Goemon knew this because the gardening workforce harangued him every time he visited to make his reports. They demanded coin in return for secrecy, and this he reluctantly had to pay them. Though the minister was of noble blood and was within his right to do as he pleased to lowerborn, if the story of this had escaped how easy and vivid a metaphor it would make as it spread and exaggerated across the city – the Insatiably Rapacious Tokugawa.

This, the duty of a captain.

So far below what he once had. He put it from his mind. He

had lingered here in the alley too long. He straightened and then limped back towards the light of the Goat's lantern, wiping bile from his chin.

'You are well, sir?' his adjutant asked.

'I am fine,' said Goemon, and struggled for an excuse. 'My stomach has not set well since the explosion.'

'Of course, sir.'

The captain took the lantern once more, and on they walked. The Goat's sword rattled in its scabbard as he pressed it into the earth again and again. The old samurai spat and then said, 'I saw that fire, sir, it spread far too quickly to be caused solely by the detonation. Then all those tea-coloured Yoshioka dogs arrive so quickly, so prepared? Saboteurs, my bet. Where did those swordless men get the black powder from to begin with? They couldn't have smuggled it in themselves. If you wish to root out sedition . . .'

'Any definite proof of that is nought but ash now,' said Goemon, and a smile crept across his face, almost of the kind that he had worn when the swordmaster of his youth had pierced his defence. Pain from the blow and yet a simultaneous envious admiration at the ability. 'That sly knave.'

Chapter Fourteen

Ameku sang that night on Hiei.

Ostensibly it was for Yae, who lay verging upon sleep after a meal of warm rice for the first time in months, but Musashi sat close to the hearth also. The blind woman knew that he was there and did not protest his presence. If she had not forgiven him for his outburst before the gates of the city, she did not continue to persecute him for it. Perhaps she held no grudges, or perhaps she held such a fundamentally large one that she had no room to bear the petty also.

Thus she sang with her alien beauty and ability, and the smoke of fading coals was in the air, and as always he became captivated by the song. He could not explain his enchantment fully. When he listened, an ache formed within him that he never felt at other times. And yet it was a good ache, an ache like prodding a hard-won bruise. A deep satisfaction.

There were moments, a few fleeting moments, when he had experienced something akin to this before. Moments that were not remembered coherently with logical memory as much as felt. Known. To try to describe them was like trying to examine the darkness by a holding a torch to it. Moments invariably that came in that somnolent interval where the body kicks at the first images of dreams. The period of hovering consciousness, the mind unneeding of the flesh, yet the escape from it not quite completed.

Caught in the depths of night, say, insects singing as they sang in the forest outside now. Lying nestled in some soft cleft in the earth surrounded by noise so loud, life in the fullest splendour of the year, and he fading into slumber, becoming no more than another aspect of that life enveloped in the grand darkness that stole all sense of shape and barrier. Lay there listening to the insects that thrived in the trees and the grasses. Listening to the smallest crickets tick, to the hum of the larger suzumushi, to the howls of cicadas that fervently beseeched in unerring dedication. Listening to it all come together, each disparate sound unified by the unfettered mind, the egoless thing that defined itself by seeking order and recognition in all it objectively imbibed.

The crickets became the percussion keeping time, the suzumushi insects the chorus holding all in tune, and the cicadas loudest of all the melody, the thing around which the others arranged themselves. When their final rising-falling-rising vibrato trilled itself out the entire thing looped around and began again, a loop as long as the night, as long as the summer.

There was rhythm there, the pulse of creation that all things unwittingly shared. The unwitting mind absorbed into it, perhaps the beat of his heart changing without his consent, and how wonderful to be carried so, to feel without any hint of doubt or higher reason that things had meaning and purpose, that at some fundamental point all connected.

Listening to her sing, it was like an observance of this. It was humbling. The beauty of the song revealed to him in contrast what a low thing he himself was, a skull atop a spine atop a pelvis and no more, and yet despite this – because of this – it was exalting at the same time. A joy felt vibrating within the bones each and every time her voice slid between notes so fluidly, a joy at the fact that there was something higher in the world, a joy that, even though they were low and crude things, here was proof that they were capable of raising themselves.

The ache, sweet ache. An indescribable, lonely longing. He sat enthralled, watching, listening in his strange piety, and it came to him then that no man could hold this power. This was a thing of women and women alone. He watched the moving of her lips and the movement of her throat, and for the first time he became aware on a deeper level that she was a woman. Saw her such.

Ameku's song trailed out, the last note held until it was no more than a sigh. Yae stirred in her sleep. All was peaceful.

He had to speak to her. He could not bear the silence. But all he could think to say was, 'What do the words mean?'

Part of him was surprised that she obliged him. The slight tilt of her head as she considered the translation. 'Many words,' she said eventually. 'But this is the main words: Storm comes. Flowers fall. Sadness again over sea waves. Storm comes. Men all drown. Women find new love at spring.'

'It sounded happier.'

'Ryukyu song,' she said. 'True, no?'

'Nnn.'

A mirth of gentle cruelty upon her lips: 'You like it more or less, knowing?'

The needle stung him, and he was glad that she was unable to see him as he sat there embarrassed at his inability to summon a riposte. But any words eluded him and so Ameku presumed him satisfied for the night. The woman made as if she were about to sleep herself, hands searching for the pillow of dried beans the monks had provided for them.

This could not be.

'Would you comb my hair for me?' he blurted.

'What?' she said.

'My hair.'

Before she had a chance to answer or refuse he rose and crossed the small room to sit with his back to her. She adjusted herself for a long time, perhaps caught in indecision. He held himself tense, drew a breath in, and then he felt her fingers reach out to touch him between the shoulder blades, searching.

They were harder than he would have thought.

Up those fingers went to the nape of his neck. She began to run them tentatively through his hair from the roots to the tips. Unbound, his hair hung to below his clavicle. He had shaved his head entirely after Sekigahara to tend to the wound on his scalp, and had simply let it grow back fully after that; never would he wear a topknot again. The tresses were coarse and Ameku's fingers found many knots. She parted these before she brought out her whalebone comb, and then the woman began to brush its fine teeth through the hair.

There was a lot of resistance, and yet somehow it felt smooth and soothing. The teeth grazed his scalp, caressed it, and he felt a hot flash of prickling sensation run down from the crown of his head all the way to the hairs of his arms.

Suddenly he was embarrassed, ultra-conscious of himself.

'Thank you,' he said as she continued to work, trying to muster some excuse. 'I must look fine. Tomorrow I face the Yoshioka.'

She said nothing for a while, brought the comb through a matted patch. Then she said, 'Do you like to kill?'

'What?' he asked, surprised. 'No.'

Ameku took the answer evenly and continued to comb as though it made no difference to her.

'Why would you think that?' he asked her.

'A man that wants to look good, have fine hair as he kills . . . Killing must be a thing he likes.'

'It's not . . .' said Musashi, and he tried to turn to face her. 'I did not mean it in that manner.'

'Today, you wanted to kill.'

'You're wrong,' he said. 'No, I wanted to fight that samurai. To cast him down. Humble him, not cut him down. Different entirely.'

She gave a little gesture of ambivalence and took another lock of hair in her hands. She did not seem invested in the conversation, not as he was, and he wanted her attention. Her agreement. 'Don't you understand the difference?' he pressed.

'A sword is a sword,' she said simply.

'No.'

'It . . .' she said, and struggled for a word, 'lives to cut.'

'What it cuts . . . *Why* it cuts matters.'

'So, why do you come to cut the Yoshioka?'

'Because . . .' he said, and now it was he that struggled for words in his own language, 'they too need humbling. They sent Akiyama to kill me, over some slight years ago I do not recall, that they do not recall. That is the Way. Killing because they cannot do anything but kill. If I cut, if I . . .' *kill* '. . . that is different. It is my hand against them, me choosing to raise my hand for myself. That is . . . Look at Akiyama. He sees this. He's awake now. Alive. Truly alive, and . . . honest, as am I, and . . .'

His words faded away. She said nothing, and it was maddening in a way that he had never felt before. Not the kind of rage that the sight of topknots drew from him. It was that long ache of her songs magnified. He needed to know if he was right, if what he suspected was true: if she was truly like him and hated as he hated.

But he did not want to argue about the meaning of swords and justify himself any longer, not with her, and so he thought about what to say, and eventually he announced: 'Love is a delusion.'

He thought it was a fine statement and he spoke it with as much profundity as he could muster, and yet there it hung in the air without response. He waited for as long as he could bear it, three slow strokes of her comb, before he realized he was exposed, that he was committed now to explaining it lest it seem meaningless.

'Your song,' he said, 'the words. How did it go . . . ? Flowers fall, and the women find new love in spring? Love – it's not real. Not between a man and a woman. It is no more than an idea. Something for fools to believe in, to write poems about. To drown themselves with. Don't you agree? No more than a delusion . . . Like the Way. Something to fool yourself into believing has relevance, or significance, or worth. No?'

Ameku thought about her answer for some time.

'It is something that I have never felt,' she said eventually.

'Neither have I,' said Musashi.

And there was union in that, and he was satisfied, or told

himself that he was. He sat there with his legs crossed, nodding slowly to himself, and he felt her hands and he heard her breathing. The teeth of the comb dug deep and parted. Yae rolled over in her sleep with her eyes moving beneath her lids, perhaps seeing some dream, and outside the insects hummed with the pulse of creation entirely ambivalently.

In the morning Musashi was woken by the single toll of a great bell. The strike of it was low and resonant as it unfurled over the slopes of Hiei, and it raised him back into the world as if he were borne upwards on the languid surging bloom of some metallic bubble.

It was a strange awakening. Hiei had an aura about it that he had only sensed briefly yesterday, but now in the sober light of morning it seemed to him to hang heavy as mist. He found himself guarded, but he could not tell if this was due to the Mount itself or the fact that he could not stop thinking of the conversation the night before. He took to wondering if it had gone as well as he had convinced himself before he slept, and he brooded on it as he dressed and left his dormitory.

Musashi found that the grounds outside were already thriving with the ordained brothers going about their duties, the bell that had woken him in fact the end of the morning sermon and they having risen with the dawn. They ignored him as they had mostly ignored him the day before. The monks had welcomed their party into their enclave willingly, but with little warmth. Charity was part of their doctrine but not their enthusiasm.

The devout men had abandoned their formal black robes for plain grey jerkins as they worked now, shaven heads glistening beneath the morning sun. Musashi watched them for a while, and saw that they had a focus and determination not unlike that of samurai: sweepers swept the garden paths mindful of the precision of the strokes of their brooms, dust beaten from tatami flooring mats with a thorough, contained aggression, holy artefacts cleaned and polished almost as lovingly as swords.

Scarce those artefacts, though, and scarce any sense of grandeur here. The buildings were not as any temple he had seen before, ornate or imposing, but rather squat utilitarian things of plain grey wood and thatched roof. There were no Zen gardens, no ponds of lotuses, no shaped trees, the belfry no more than a humble platform with a plain iron bell weathered brown and a log on a rope hung from a gallows.

Across the way he saw a group of near twenty young men stripped almost naked pacing around and around an idol of the Amida Buddha. The men were deep in the throes of a circumambulatory rite, had been since before the dawn, their hands clasped before their faces, their eyes shut tightly as they chanted feverishly over and over, voices hoarse and dry, words compressed and coalescing:

'*PraisebetotheinfinitelightofAmida, praisebetotheinfinitelightofAmida, praisebetotheinfinitelight* . . .'

The rough straw sandals they wore cut into the flesh of their feet, blood and sweat mixing, yet on they marched in solipsistic obliviousness both of the pain and of any onlookers. They were in search of the Pure Land, where Amida waited to shepherd their souls, and on this long walk they would call his name ten hundred thousand times, a hundred hundred thousand times, and perhaps by the end he would have heard them, acknowledged them, shown them enlightenment.

Musashi turned from them and his eye fell upon a tender and expertly sculpted statue of the Bodhisattva Jizo, the kindly old saint who cared for the souls of children in the afterlife. From his outstretched hand hung a dozen smooth stones nestled in little red slings, each a prayer for Jizo to care for a stillborn or a child who had died before his soul could affix on the forty-ninth day of life.

Men circling blind in search of the next world, the anonymous grief of a dozen bereaved mothers . . .

Shinto for the living, Buddhism for the dead, as the saying went.

He went and found Akiyama, who had slept secluded.

'The woman and the girl?' he asked Musashi.

The memory of a comb, and a quick dismissal: 'They are tending to themselves this morning.'

Akiyama did not pry. The two swordsmen breakfasted together, a humble gruel of miso broth and dried seaweed. It was the finest thing either of them had eaten in weeks. Musashi ate quickly, and when his bowl was empty he said, 'Let us venture down to the city. The gates must be open. Show me to the school of the Yoshioka.'

Akiyama shook his head. 'You need to steady yourself first. You are gaunt. A week of food and rest upon actual bedding here will put some flesh back upon you, muscle you will need.'

'I don't need a week.'

'Do not underestimate the Yoshioka.'

'I am not. I know how to beat them. There is no point waiting.'

Akiyama's brow furrowed. He looked at his soup. 'What is it you intend to do afterwards, should you triumph? What do you think it is that will happen?'

'He needs to be beaten,' said Musashi, and nothing more.

The expression on Akiyama's face did not change, but he

raised his pale eyes up to peer at Musashi. 'Strategy is vital,' he said. 'The art of strategy is anticipating both your next five steps and the enemy's. Do you not know this?'

Musashi looked away. His arms were itching, and the voices of the circumambulators droned on, agitating him. 'Let us just leave this place,' he said. 'I don't like it here. There is an odd aura.'

'Do you not know the history of Hiei?'

'No.'

'It used to be that forty thousand people lived upon these slopes. Hundreds of shrines and the grand temple Enryaku at the summit. Then, thirty years ago, the warlord Oda set his armies loose. A great battle, the brothers here armed and well studied in strategy, and when it was done Oda's men burnt any building they could find and slaughtered whoever had survived. I was a child then. I remember it rained ash down upon the city for days.'

All knew of the Lord Oda, famed for his military genius and his brutality. It was he who many thought fated to take the mantle of Shogunate and unite the nation, were it not for one of his sworn generals betraying him in his ascendancy and forcing him to commit seppuku. The killing of holy men and women however was an outrage that surprised Musashi: 'Why did Oda turn upon Hiei?'

'The monks here claim he was a rasetsu demon manifested,' said Akiyama. 'An enemy of enlightenment that shepherded the barbarian Christ onto our shores. Believe that if you will. However, as I said, this used to be home to many warrior brethren. Thousands in their white cowls and with their great glaives, driven to interfere with courts and creeds not of their own. They would march down carrying Buddhas above them, march to surround the city in one big snake chasing its tail. This before the Regent built the walls and the moats, so you could get up on the roofs and look out and see the holy warriors every which way you looked, at the height of noon or at night with their lanterns glimmering. Broaching rivers uncaring of the current. They would chant together, so loud, things like, "Break what is bent and widen the path!" over and over. Fearsome . . . And they had a particular umbrage with the ascent of the Lord Oda.'

Musashi heard all that and said, 'So this is a dead place.'

'It seems to live once more to me.'

Musashi shook his head. 'I don't like it.'

Akiyama placed his bowl down, swallowed his last mouthful. 'I have duty to attend to. Let me see to it first.'

They left Ameku and Yae in the enclave whilst one of the monks courteously led the pair of them to the graveyard. He was a young man and he cast glances at Akiyama when the samurai was not looking, staring at his odd appearance. Musashi stared in turn at him until the man became aware that he was caught, and from then on he looked only ahead. The three of them walked in silence.

Musashi found himself looking around the slopes and all that enveloped them. Hiei continued to unsettle him. Not green upon the floor but dark, last year's leaves and this year's petals an entropic carpet through which the nooses of roots emerged. Boughs of ferns compacted into strata as they clambered upwards over one another, those pushed beneath withering into nothing. A raised vein of earth set with stones that held memories of definite edges, once a stairway perhaps, the bulging ground beneath it pushing what remained of the order apart and devouring the rocks themselves. Tall trunks of bamboo, etiolated grey at their bases, the emerald blush of vitality growing rib by incremental rib upwards. Insects upon his flesh drew blood before he could slap them away, the silhouette of a bird of prey gliding silent and eternal.

The nature of this forest, he saw, was to consume.

They passed an obelisk robbed of its dignity, set with some form of parable the letters of which fingers would struggle to feel, let alone eyes perceive a meaning. Up upon the slopes he began to see the burnt remnants of temples and shrines, ugly charcoal smears and stunted beams that were throttled by ivy.

The graveyard was set on a slope where hundreds of square pillars of dark stone stood in erratic rank and file, weathered by years. Evidently they had escaped Oda's desecration. Akiyama led them through the narrow paths. Chiselled names surrounded them, some forgotten and faded or the neat gouges of the recently deceased filled in by fresh red paint. A cat yowled at them as they passed, stub-tailed, grown fat off woodland vermin and the offerings of food that people left for their beloved departed, a contented king basking in his morbid little empire.

They came to the crypt of Akiyama's family. It was in a sorry state. A colony of spiders had woven thick webs between the namestone and its neighbours, the green and yellow creatures the size of a man's palm. Water had pooled and scummed in the hollows of the empty stone candelabras that stood either side of the crypt, itself small and rife with moss.

Akiyama sighed in dismay. The pale-eyed samurai found a stick and began to run it through the webs, scattering the spiders. He swept the moss away, and together he and Musashi picked up the heavy candelabras the best they could and tipped the filthy water from them. Their hands were slick with slime and they rubbed them on leaves and grass until they were clean. Akiyama then produced two pears, yellow and fat, and placed them on the altar. Then he set the candles and incense he had brought before the crypt and lit both.

Smoke curled.

Musashi watched as Akiyama sat down cross-legged preparing to pray, saw the wince his wounds still drew from him. Saw the diligence and sincerity in the man's eyes. Saw what he was faithful to, and felt a twist in his own heart.

'I will grant you solitude. I will meet you back at the enclave with the women,' said Musashi. Akiyama nodded his agreement.

The monk was waiting at the entrance of the graveyard. 'Are there any remaining temples upon Hiei? An altar that I might . . . ?' Musashi asked him.

'There is the hall back from whence we came,' said the monk. 'That is the centre of Hiei now.'

'No. That looks like a stable.'

'It was a stable. All that was left.'

Musashi shook his head. 'It must be . . . proper.'

The monk nodded his head and led him back along the trail. Now that they were but two young and able men, he led Musashi up an arduous shortcut. They wound their way up a steep and narrow little crevice filled with loose rocks and smooth pebbles, what must have once been a stream but the mountain having long since sucked it dry. It led back to the well-travelled trail, and there the monk stopped by the foot of an old stone stairway and pointed upwards.

'There,' he said. 'One of Hiei's last remaining temples.'

Musashi peered through the trees. He could see nothing but the vague sliver of a small roof appearing above the slope of the stairs. 'There's an altar there?'

'Yes.'

'Could you wait here a few moments?'

The monk bowed his head in acquiescence. Musashi set off up the stairs. Echoed upwards, he heard the distant voices of the circumambulators once more, following him softly:

'*Praisebetotheinfinitelightof Amida, praisebetotheinfinitelight-ofAmida, praisebetotheinfinitelightofAmida . . .*'

The stones of the stairway were so old their surface had turned moss green, trembled in the loose earth as he climbed. It was a steep ascent, yet short, no more than fifty steps. The temple he found at the top was also small, perhaps ten paces around either side and set upon a squared dais of stone. The wood of it was almost the same colour as the forest around it, set with scabs of bright moss and fungus. Evidently ancient. Yet when Musashi stepped inside he found new things there – a chest set for coins, a swathe of red cloth draped over an altar, the remnants of recently burnt incense standing in a clay cauldron of sand.

The scent of the smoke could not ward away the underlying stench of the place entirely, the odour like a ditch. The interior was dominated, he was surprised to find, by two large wooden statues of Raijin and Fujin. They were Shinto gods of thunder and wind, ogreish beings that cavorted in chaos, and here they stood in the frozen throes of their dance with their robes blowing around them and panels of smoke and fire rising behind them. They were placed either side of a smaller statue, one of bronze and equally as old, he guessed, showing the Bodhisattva of wisdom Monju sitting cross-legged atop a lotus, this in turn borne on the back of a snarling lion.

Musashi had no coin to offer up to the chest; all he had was the fullness of his heart. He looked around and ensured that the monk had not followed him, that none could see him.

Then he dropped to the knees he had sworn he would never bend for any man, pressed his brow to the ground and rose with his eyes closed and his hands clasped in prayer:

'Raijin. Fujin. Monju. Amaterasu. Enlightened Buddha. Both heavens, please hear me. I ask that you grant my uncle Dorinbo health and life and fortune. He is the best of men, and I ask that you watch over him in my stead.'

He repeated the prayer inwardly a dozen times, more, until the prayer had become wordless, no more than a fervent feeling, and he thought that this was wrong and so he began to speak aloud. He sang the prayer-songs of Shinto that Dorinbo had taught him, warbling in a low resonant monotone, not caring that here was Buddhist ground. His motive was honest, *he* was honest, and the heavens would understand that. And in the singing of it he remembered how his uncle had sung it – how melodies seemed to haunt him now – and he thought deeper of the man, and he was twisted with a profound longing. Wondered what it was Dorinbo was doing at that precise moment. Thought of how he would be standing. Imagined the look in his eyes at the exact moment he would recognize Musashi on the day of his return. That day to come when he was permitted home, that day which had no date, and yet Musashi both vowed and knew was near. Had to be near. Perhaps even before the snows this year. The day when he had attained that nebulous thing he sought, achieved a thing of worth. When all was done in Kyoto, and all was achieved, and all saw and recognized this, and all was right.

Live until that day, Uncle.

Live.

Musashi prayed until his words were spent and he was satisfied that some higher entity could not have failed to hear him. Then he placed his hands upon his thighs, took a steadying breath, bowed a final time, and opened his eyes.

He found himself looking up into the faces of Raijin and Fujin.

The statues were unchanged.

He looked and he saw that the wood they were carved from must have been as old as the temple itself. They had been painted once, but with the rotting of the timber the paint had peeled away and so they were left marred, garish colours outlining dark abscesses of wood-flesh, growths of moss mottled in pallid green; they looked a pair of plague-bearers. They grinned and snarled down at him, delighted in their disease, whilst Monju sat placid, content to be amongst the filthy.

How long had they stood here? How many prayers like this had the three of them heard? How many lives had inadvertently intersected here? How many people were beneath Musashi in the wave he now stood on the cusp of, and would be in time sucked down into just as those before him had been?

Musashi looked up at the pair of statues and something began to formulate within him, somewhere between anger and fear and loneliness at the inkling that perhaps he had mistaken the nature of the forest that surrounded this altar for the nature of existence itself.

It was only the sound of voices from outside that broke his bleak reverie. Men's voices, many of them, distant, growing closer.

Angry.

Demanding him by name.

Chapter Fifteen

Denshichiro Yoshioka rose with the dawn. At the washing trough of the barracks he splashed tepid water over his body, cleaned himself of the sweat of night. He was a man of broad shoulders, forearms coiled with muscle, a square head heavy with bone and lacking neck. To look at him was to see that his ancestors were likely those men who chased and wrestled wild horses to force bridles upon them.

Naked, he went through his exercises. He brought his chin up to a beam thirty times. He clutched a boulder to his chest and dropped into a squat fifty times. He took up a broad training sword weighted to be five times heavier than a true blade and ran through the motions of striking from either side of his body two hundred times.

When he was done, Denshichiro washed himself again. He dressed. He made sure he was alone. Then he went and he brought forth a length of silk from where he kept it in a chest in his chambers. It was one of the standards of the Tokugawa that had fallen in the explosion at the garrison. A member of the school who had fought the fires had recovered it and presented it to him. Yards of it, immaculate and white.

With great care Denshichiro folded it so that the black crest of the Tokugawa was framed in a neat square. He placed this on the ground outside. Then he took out his penis and pissed upon it. Swung his cock back and forth, blighted the emblem with great yellow slashes, grinned to himself.

His duty that morning was to pay a cordial visit to the school of the Kiichi. They were an older school than the Yoshioka, having held a modest compound up by the Ichijo canal for centuries, but their prestige had never risen anywhere near as high. Neither school contested this and their relationship was amiable and well defined as superior–inferior; this was why Denshichiro had come in place of his elder brother Seijuro, who was head of the school, and this was why the master of the Kiichi was not offended by the coming of the second in line.

The master of the Kiichi presented Denshichiro with the quaint antique guard of a cavalry sword. Denshichiro in turn gifted him a cask of fine shochu spirits. They drank a measure each as they ate a plate of satsumas. They spoke platitudes of no real import, commented upon the Shogun's castle and the beheadings there, agreed that next month's arrival of a famed wrestler from distant Kyushu was something to look forward to.

Before midmorning Denshichiro bade his farewells and was on his way out of the school when one of the adepts called out to him. He introduced himself politely as Eijun Yamanaka.

'Sir Yamanaka.' Denshichiro nodded. 'What is it you want?'

'I am sorry to intrude upon your time, Sir Yoshioka, but I happened to witness something strange yesterday. Something in which I think you would have interest. That odd-looking fellow, the Foreigner – does he still serve your most honourable school?'

'I believe so. Though I do not recall seeing him of late.'

'Indeed. I encountered him yesterday before the gates of the city. He looked ragged and worn, and he was not wearing the colour of tea.'

'You are certain it was him?'

'He has a very particular appearance.'

Denshichiro could not argue with this. 'What was he doing?'

'That was the queer thing. He was in strange company. Some kind of witch or devil-woman, and a masterless. A real brute, a dog who tried to cut me down.'

'I am glad to see you remain unharmed,' said Denshichiro, the sentiment entirely perfunctory. 'Have you a name for this masterless?'

'I do: Musashi Miyamoto. I have not heard of him.'

'Neither have I.'

'With good reason I would imagine,' said Eijun. 'He was the definition of indignity. Held my attention with his repugnance – it was only when they were leaving did I recognize your man. Seeing him only compounded the oddity of the whole thing.'

'Indeed,' said Denshichiro. His body settled into a slow contemplative nod.

'The Foreigner,' said Eijun, matching the nod.

'The Foreigner.'

There came an awkward little pause. Denshichiro's expression revealed nothing, and it was Eijun who brought it upon himself to speak first.

'In truth I am not surprised,' the samurai said. 'He came here once, the Foreigner. I looked into his eyes and there was something aberrant about them. It was like looking into a fox's. Made my skin crawl when he smiled, as though he were planning some cruelty for me of which I was unaware.'

'Indeed.'

'In any case,' said Eijun, 'I recalled that your most honourable self would be visiting our school this morn. I thought that you would care to know of a man shirking your colours, and so I sent my squire to follow the pair. The boy said they spent the night upon Mount Hiei, what with those Edo interlopers deciding to bar the gates of the city. I myself had to take lodgings in a room with ten other men, if you can believe that, and, a fine thing, the Edoites relented and opened the gates this morning or I—'

'Where are the pair now?' interrupted Denshichiro. It was easy for a man of his appearance to impose himself, even to his elders.

Eijun recovered his poise adeptly: 'Still upon Hiei. My squire waits there now at the foot of the trails with a few friends of his, either to track them if they move on from there or to point them out to you should you so desire it.'

'This is a great service you have rendered us, Sir Yamanaka,' said Denshichiro, already turning for the door. 'You have my gratitude.'

'It is nothing, Sir Yoshioka,' said Eijun, and he bowed humbly at his departing back. 'A simple matter of respect between our two schools.'

The Foreigner.

He was like a ghost to Denshichiro. Seijuro, five years his elder, had told him with the dark relish that only elder brothers could muster that the man had that reddish skin of his because he bathed in the blood of children. Though

Denshichiro eventually realized this to be nonsense, he had been told it at a young enough age that the sentiment of it was inexorably ingrained in him. Denshichiro remembered nights before he had been awarded the longsword of adulthood when he would stalk the dark halls of the school, placing his feet on their edges to see if he could walk entirely silently like an assassin, and always there would be the light of a solitary candle in the library to spoil his imagined stealth. He would peer in and see the Foreigner there sitting reading, back entirely rigid, eyes shimmering gold.

Denshichiro had wanted to throw salt at him each and every time, as though he himself were some exorcizing priest. That was the Foreigner's realm, darkness and silence. Unsettling, and now rumours of desertion. The thought of desertion in itself unsettling – he could recall no man who had willingly forsaken the colour of tea. He thought it over as the crowded streets parted for him.

He went straight to Ujinari, whom he found working the school's accounts, flicking the beads of an abacus and filling in the waiting columns of a ledger. Ujinari was his closest friend, had been since childhood. They were of an age, born only months apart, and perhaps their fathers had planned this. Ujinari was Tadanari's son, after all, and Tadanari had been as close to Denshichiro's father as a brother. The Kozei and the Yoshioka all but blood, so why not have their two progeny grow up as fraternal kin?

Denshichiro thus sought his counsel above all others. He innately felt that Ujinari understood both his own nature and the world in general better than he himself did – though he would admit this to no one – and he told Ujinari what he had learnt that morning. Ujinari listened and nodded along.

'This Musashi Miyamoto – have you heard any of him?' said Denshichiro.

'No.'

'Then why would he be consorting with the Foreigner? Or the Foreigner with him?'

Ujinari thought about it for a moment, knelt there scratching at the shaven pate of his head out of habit. Both of them wore their topknots in the fashion of the samurai youth of Kyoto, the bared skin no more than the width of two fingers, a mere line cut through the hair instead of the tradition of the full crown and pate bared. Then an idea occurred to him, and he led Denshichiro to the archives room.

At his waist he wore the longsword that Tadanari had bestowed upon him those years past. Walking behind him, Denshichiro cast an unseen envious eye over the weapon as he did every time he saw it. Even the scabbard was a gorgeous thing, misted lacquer capped in burnished copper and set with studs along its length, each one a carved and varnished blonde-wood image of the fierce face of Saint Fudo.

Seijuro, the head, the scion, got the fine things in the Yoshioka family, the cherished heirlooms and the gold-threaded jackets and the ancestral blades.

When they arrived Ujinari set his beautiful sword casually on a waiting stand, and then he quickly searched through the chests of drawers that lined the wall of the archives. He found the scroll he was after, knelt and unrolled it on the tatami mats. He revealed a long row of names written in black ink, most of which were crossed out in red slashes denoting resolution.

Ujinari glanced through the names, and then pointed at one. 'As I thought. Here. Miyamoto is upon the list.'

'An enemy?' said Denshichiro on his feet, squinting down on the document. 'Who did he offend?'

'Sir Ando. Added four years prior. Nothing else is written.'

Nothing else needed to be written, not for Denshichiro. The list was the list, and all fated to have their name written upon it were to be killed without question. The circumstance beyond that did not concern him in the slightest. But who cared for the decapitation of some unheralded knave when something much more troubling presented itself?

'Do you think . . . ?' he barely managed to ask Ujinari.

Ujinari nodded his agreement. 'I would presume Sir Akiyama must have been sent to enact our vengeance upon this Miyamoto. That was often his duty.'

'And now he returns with the cur?' said Denshichiro. 'How is that possible? Why . . . how is that he could abandon the colour of tea?' He put his hand to his face and massaged his cheeks for a stupefied moment. 'He gave oaths. He made vows written in his own blood. How is it that he could break them? What kind of a man . . . ?'

Ujinari sucked air through his teeth. 'You ought to inform my father.'

Denshichiro looked down at him. 'Am I not Yoshioka?'

He summoned eight men to him and led them out towards Hiei. His fingers were rapping off his palms in the first fitful stages of his anger, and he strode at a quick pace.

This was his imperative, and his alone. No need to involve his elder brother or Tadanari. He had seen the way the bald samurai had curbed Seijuro, had made some aspirant monk out of him with his insistence upon meditation and contemplation. These things were like blunting a blade. The Way was one of immediacy; for every problem, the neatest response.

In moods like this everything was an affront. People who did not move out of his way fast enough. People who moved out of his way too fast, lacking the proper reverence. The road that did not shorten itself and draw him immediately to his destination. The crow that flew against his course and offered a poor auspice, rather than flying with him.

At the north-east gate of the city stood a troop of Tokugawa samurai, and the sight of them was akin to throwing bales of straw on a bonfire. The sheer thought of them in his city enough to madden him. They who had killed his father, and not even killed him with honourable blades as the man deserved but with such an insidious and cowardly thing as an insult. He thought of his harrowed father writhing upon his ignominious deathbed, remembered the sweat and the death stench, and Denshichiro stared his hatred at the Tokugawa samurai brazenly. Every time he wanted them to attack, to oblige him in the ecstasy of unrestrained combat, but as always the cowards looked away as though they were trained to do so, and he hated them further for this, and now his fists were clenched.

It was a long walk to the holy mountain and he had time to refocus his thoughts upon the Foreigner. Had time to chase the apparent logic and facts of this absurd and unbelievable scenario that he could scant believe around his head many times over. One made one's vows. One kept one's vows. This was as fundamental as water flowing downhill. Denshichiro had a fighter's eyes that were narrow and difficult to gouge at and usually equally difficult to gauge, but as Hiei rose before them he had worked himself into such a black fury that they shimmered with malice. His broad shoulders tense, his left hand tight upon the scabbards of his swords.

The boy, Yamanaka's squire, was sitting in the shade of a small shrine. He leapt to his feet when he saw the Yoshioka samurai coming and waved to them. Excitedly he told them of everything he had seen. His awe of the colour of tea seemed to shield him from perceiving Denshichiro's mood. Denshichiro commanded the boy to lead, and he set off running up the wide stone stairway that began the ascent.

Denshichiro marched after the squire. He had climbed five stairs when he realized his men had not moved. He turned and looked down at them.

'Why do you falter?' he asked.

'Here is Mount Hiei,' said one of the men.

Denshichiro had not told them their destination. It had not occurred to him to do so, because he should not have to. He did nothing but stare at the man who had spoken.

'Forgive me, Sir Yoshioka,' said the samurai, and he bowed low. 'I pray here. My family has prayed here for generations. If the brothers mark me as a murderer—'

'You cannot murder a dog,' said Denshichiro.

He stated it with such simple, enunciated violence that it quelled any misgiving. The eight men barked their compliance and followed after him. The squire led them to another boy, who had had word from another boy. A little temporary network of spies.

'The strange one, the barbarian, he's in the graveyard, Sir Yoshioka,' the boy said, staring fascinated at Denshichiro's longsword. 'The tall Lord-shirker went away on the trails with another monk. Gengoro knows exactly where . . . I can show you to the graveyard, or I can show you to Gen.'

'I know the way to the graveyard,' said Denshichiro.

He made the decision instantly – ordered six of his men to go with the boy and deal with Miyamoto. He and the remaining two would head to find the Foreigner. He felt no sense of risk in this unbalanced division. The six men were only facing some vagrant of no renown. Denshichiro himself was of the bloodline; he knew that he was worth six men on his own.

*

The conversation between Akiyama and the dead had been long and internal and one-sided. His apologies were manifold and if they were heard they were unanswered.

The glowing ember of the incense worked its way down the stick.

Apologies became justifications. If they could sense his memories, his father, his mother, his grandfather, the legion behind them, then he willed them to share in lying upon that autumn hillside, cut and bleeding and knowing it all to be worthless. Of seeing their own blood seeping into the thirsting earth and realizing their entire transience and simultaneously knowing, fundamentally knowing, the utter waste.

If they experienced that too, then they would understand the path he navigated now. That though he may not know its ultimate destination, he had been granted his reprieve and he would not squander it. Did not the whole world marvel more at shooting stars than the titled constellations through which they blazed?

He thought and thought, and he could not offer them any substantial proof of the worth of this decision, save for what it meant to his own soul. The most profound and personal of urges, of having a similar fundamental knowledge of what was right, or what was desired, or what needed to be, without knowing the exact shape or boundaries of it. Of the act of placing all faith in that.

Yet what were the dead faithful to but silence?

The incense burnt itself out. The ash fell into the bed of sand, arrayed itself into a withered spiral.

'You,' came a voice.

Akiyama stirred.

He turned to find Denshichiro and two other samurai of the Yoshioka standing there between the other gravestones. They had spread themselves out, one at either end of the narrow passage between crypts. Their faces were grim and the colour of tea was a sombre brown upon their shoulders.

The pale-eyed samurai passed through his surprise immediately and instinct took him to his feet. He bowed and he offered them the expression he had given them and all the others his life long, the expression he had cultured in his attempts to belong. A look that he thought friends might give, eager and faithful.

He hated himself for it.

Denshichiro was unmoved. 'What happened to your jacket?' he said. 'What happened to your colours?'

Akiyama straightened his back. He set his face in neutral enmity. He had left the bloodied garment to rot hanging on the wall of the hovel they had spent the winter in. He offered no reply, and wordlessly Denshichiro understood.

Above them, through the boughs, a hawk circled silent and silhouetted.

'I cannot believe this,' Denshichiro said. 'You have forsaken all worth that you might once have held. You. Have you no sense of shame?'

Akiyama held his silence.

'Did you forget the vows you made? Of loyalty unto death?'

Akiyama looked to the two adepts. They looked back. Eyes full of disdain. He did not recognize either. Much younger than he. Denshichiro's generation.

Rage began to reveal itself in Denshichiro's voice. 'Did that mean nothing to you? Is your word hollow? Does a malformed heart beat within your chest? You.'

Akiyama felt the pulling ache of the wounds at his stomach and his shoulder. Even were he perfectly hale, Akiyama doubted he could have triumphed over all three.

'Did you forget my father?' said Denshichiro

Could perhaps kill them all before he succumbed, if he were fortunate. Here, though, enfeebled and surprised, they had him entirely, all advantage theirs.

Trapped amidst them, and hated. What a consummate summation of his life.

'Did you forget my grandfather Naomitsu?' said Denshichiro, shaking his head in disgust and disbelief. 'My great-uncle, Naomoto the progenitor? The Yoshioka dynasty? These great men who took the colour of tea and over the course of a hundred years caused it to mean something? Spat upon by you. You.'

Akiyama had not forgotten. He saw Denshichiro and he saw the lot of them beside him, Seijuro, the master Kozei too, remembered all their myriad expressions. The disdainful commands and the withheld esteem. All the loyalty they had drunk up, drunk never to be quenched. As perpetually thirsting and unchanging as the earth that had drunk his blood.

'You,' said Denshichiro, repeating the word and putting a fresh venom on each utterance, finding new ways to illustrate his anger with each movement of his tongue. 'You. You. You.'

Immune to all this, the hawk, hovering on the whim of an eddy.

'How few the men that are granted the honour of wearing

the colours of our school?' said Denshichiro. 'And you, you ghost, you renounce all that? To do what? Return to this city, our city, as a vagrant and a, a . . . ? You pale-eyed freak. You horse-haired knave.'

The hawk brought its wings in to its body and dived, vanished from sight.

'My family bestows the kindness of admitting an aberration such as you, and you, you wretched degenerate, you—'

Akiyama spoke for the first time.

'What is my name?' he said.

Denshichiro stared at him.

'What is my name?' he asked again.

Silence, save for the insects. Denshichiro stood there unrepentant. Akiyama looked at him, at them, and found his resolution.

A bitter grin of hatred twisted his face, resigned and defiant. Let it rot. Let it all rot, the jacket, the school, the entire colour of tea.

'You damned idiot,' he said. 'We are standing before the grave of my family, and you cannot tell me my name?'

He slid his longsword out of its scabbard.

*

Outside the temple of Monju and Raijin and Fujin where he had prayed, down the ancient stairway Musashi could just about see a group of men. It was their voices that had disturbed him, alerted him, and through the boughs of the trees he counted five, six of them, led by a panting boy. He saw the topknots, saw the bared swords, recognized the colour of tea they all wore. They were crazed with the anticipation of violence, shouting Musashi's name, demanding of the monk who waited diligently still to confirm his location.

Panic. Instant panic. So too the monk. He began gesticulating up the stairs, and before the samurai could turn and see him Musashi had slid back out of sight. Suicide to fight that many. The forest around him too thick to flee through. Inside, back inside the temple, like a rabbit to the hole. Too cramped in here to swing a longsword . . . He looked up at Raijin, his leer mocking, and then he saw the great panel of stylized wind behind him. Big enough? Only one way to see: he clambered up onto the dais and squeezed himself behind it.

His spine was braced against the wall, his nose all but up against the wood of the statue, swords twisted in his belt, guards digging into the flesh of his waist and the scabbard of the longsword tight against his ankle. A haze of questions surrounded him unanswered, ignored.

He heard the Yoshioka coming, footsteps on stone, spreading out as they reached the summit, the panting of their breath.

Then voices.

'Where?' shouted one of them.

'Is he here?' shouted another, his voice outside, then inside, then outside the temple.

'I don't see him.' A third.

'Inside?'

'Empty.'

'In the trees?'

'I see nothing. He could be . . . It's too thick.'

'Up the trees?'

'What is he, a damned monkey?'

'Where else could he be?'

'I'll search the . . .' And this followed by the sounds of branches and boughs being attacked.

'Stop, stop! There's no path beaten through – he'd have made one.'

'He has to be here!'

Reverberating all these sounds in the tight little interior of the temple, the trails of their individual noises tying knots around the building. Musashi held his breath. Beneath his feet, he realized the wood he stood upon was sodden. Malleable.

'Where's the . . . ?' said one of the samurai, outside still, angry. 'Get the lad up here.'

Breaths steadied. Gestures perhaps given; the sound of fresh footsteps soon, these lighter upon the stone.

'You are certain he is here?' said one of the samurai. 'You saw him come up here?'

'That's definitely the monk he left with, sir,' said the new voice, thick with squawking adolescence. 'And he told us he was up here.'

'Then where is he?'

'Is he not here?'

'No!'

'Then I don't know!'

'You followed them?'

'Not all the way.'

'Why not?'

'I had to come and get you!'

Musashi felt the wood beneath his feet begin to move. A poor word. Distort. Give. He tried to spread his weight, but could not do so without revealing himself. He braced his palms on the statue, felt it now pressing on the tip of his nose.

'Are you pulling a jape on us, lad?'

'No! He has to be here!'

'Do you see him?'

'Perhaps he has returned to the enclave,' said another of the samurai. 'He must have slept there. Perhaps we should seek him there.'

'That seems the wisest course.' A third.

'In the enclave proper?' A fourth. 'That's . . . Here on the slopes is foul karma, but . . .'

'We have our orders.'

'Do not doubt my conviction. Just . . . On sanctified ground? Before the monks themselves?'

Leave, bastards! And the wood now wet against Musashi's lip, soft against his feet and he certain, certain that some revealing wooden howl from the statue's strain was imminent.

'You don't have to!' said the boy. 'He's here, he must be!'

'He's not. Are you blind?'

'Have you looked inside?'

'Yes! There's nothing there. Are you suggesting he melted into the shadows?'

'What about those statues? They're big.'

Musashi's heart was bisected a dozen ways by ice.

Footsteps slowly coming in.

One pair only, no doubt the leader gazing up with slow acknowledgement that the size of Raijin or Fujin was great enough to conceal a man.

Which was he looking at? Did it matter? He was here, would check both.

Indecision tortuous.

And then Musashi felt the statue start to tip irrevocably backwards, the groaning of the wood clear.

What a delusion, decision.

Doomed to it, Musashi pushed back with all his strength in

his arms, one foot flat on the wall behind him. Teeth gritted, he shoved the statue forwards, and he felt the weight lift from him suddenly; it lurched away and then toppled forwards. The samurai saw the sickly face of Raijin rush down to meet him, and what Musashi heard was an impact like a bag of wet sand bursting open.

Everything bursting, rushing outwards: fragments of rotten wood, the cauldron of sand and incense shattered, the chest of coins scattered vomiting forth its wealth, Musashi hurling himself off the dais already going for his longsword. He hurtled out of the door of the temple and slashed at the first thing he saw, figures all around him, and kept going, heading for the stairway.

Shouts and screams and none of them moved, too slow, too shocked, and Musashi knew he would leave them behind, felt the thrill of escape until he crested the stairs and saw a samurai standing halfway down them. The motion of his body took him down a half-dozen of the steps before he could stop himself, and there he was, pinned. One Yoshioka in front, and then he turned back and saw three from behind.

From within the temple the sound of screaming, true agony, pleading.

The Yoshioka samurai on the stairs below sank into a taut stance of combat, levelled his sword, and the ones following from above did not rush blindly down after him but rather descended slowly in similar guarded posture. They had him trapped between their jaws and they realized this. Cautiously Musashi matched their descent step for step until he was equidistant between the samurai above and below. He brought his sword down to the defensive position at his waist, realized there were ribbons of blood on it, that he had claimed a victim on his dash outward. He sought what balance there was on the narrow steps. The Yoshioka assumed their postures in turn, readied themselves, grips adjusted, blades raised or lowered. Not a word spoken, concentration ultimate.

Behind and above them all a young face peered down, rapt.

'Come on, you sons of whores,' Musashi snarled, trying to look each of the men in the eye, gauging which would attack first. 'Get what you came for.'

Things happened in a flurry.

One of the samurai above attacked as Musashi turned his gaze away from him, skittering down the steps to slash at him from over his head. Musashi was coiled, prepared, whirled his body to one side and sidestepped the blow.

The samurai misjudged the depth of the stairs, staggered, overextended, now astride three steps with his leading leg hopelessly far forward, thigh exposed. Musashi brought his own sword down through that thigh, felt the bucking of the steel in his hands as it cut, saw man and leg fall separate.

Fresh screams unheard, for the samurai below took his chance, lunged at Musashi instantly. His thrust was too hard, and the old stones of the stairs gave way beneath his feet, rocks and earth tumbling downwards. The samurai stumbled forwards, feet scrabbling at nothing, a hand taken from the sword to catch himself.

Musashi lashed out with a kick, caught the man beneath the chin as he fell. Crack of bone and teeth as the jaw snapped shut. The samurai twisted and fell on his back, and began to tumble down the stairs. Musashi followed his descent dreading the quaking of the stones beneath him, making his feet as light as he could.

The two Yoshioka samurai above gave shouting chase, and

down the stairs now an avalanche cascaded, bodies, stones, swords. Ten steps from the bottom the ground went out from under Musashi, and the first he knew of this was when his shoulder met the earth. Overbalanced in his motion, he rolled completely over and rattled down the rest of the way.

When he came to rest it took long moments to right himself, to sort his legs from his arms, to find his sword. Rising, a Yoshioka samurai was upon him. The man bounded over the last handful of the steps and the debris at the base of the stairway and rushed him, met the point of Musashi's blade with his own and brushed it aside. He followed through the gap he made with his body, keeping Musashi's sword away, crashed into Musashi hip to hip. The samurai sought to drive him backwards or knock him prone once more, but Musashi was heavier, stronger, absorbed the force of the blow, felt it in the hollow of his chest, and then pushed back.

An ankle hooked behind the Yoshioka's robbed him of his feet, the samurai's spine to earth and his sword without strength. Musashi stabbed down, took the samurai through the chest, but rather than scream the man abandoned his longsword, reached up and grabbed Musashi's wrists. The other Yoshioka coming – two of them, not one, how? – and the dying man hung on even though he was impaled, held Musashi tight. Fatal glee in his eyes, defiant, and Musashi snarled and put his foot on the man's stomach and hauled, pulled his sword and his hands free.

But too late, surrounded now by the other two samurai in the small clearing at the foot of the stairway. The pair of samurai were cautious, knew he was dangerous, kept their distance. Musashi moved one way and so would they, rotating around him, keeping him directly between them. One bled freely from the mouth, red flecks flying with the heaving of his breath; the man Musashi had kicked, likely bitten through his tongue.

'Kill him,' sputtered the dying samurai on the floor. 'Finish him!'

They heeded him, but they did not come blindly. They came instead probingly, one an instant after another, and frantically Musashi parried their attacks. Again. Again. He would greet the first one, turn his sword away, and then, before he could exploit the opening in a riposte, he would have to turn and swing wildly to repel the partner behind, flailing or skipping away to keep them both at distance. Defend only, no chance to finish them. Slowly they would grind him down, he knew, far more exhausting for him than them. This perhaps their strategy, not even really trying to take him, merely provoking further exhausting flurries from him at the reaches of his sword without real risk to themselves.

No doubt they were wondering how long it would be before his hands became numb and he fumbled with his weapon. Not long, it felt. The breath was rasping between his teeth now, his shoulder thrumming where it had connected with stone, knees, ankles taut and harrowed.

Here on a Buddhist mountain? Musashi thought. *Ahh, Shinto for the living, and Buddhism for the—*

No.

Doomed. No choice. Go. Move. Last chance. He threw himself at the samurai with the bloody mouth, screamed as he went, final cadence of his lungs. Down came his sword and up came the man's, met, locked and Musashi snarled as though they were caught in bitter ultimate contest, he trying to force his blade into the crown of the man's head.

From behind the other samurai came, one pace, two paces, and then Musashi let go of his longsword with his right hand, maintained the hold with his left, spun and hurled his shortsword in the motion of its draw. The blade hit the rushing samurai, met him on his knuckles clasped on his weapon, glanced away. Not lethal, not even grievous, but blood drawn, the samurai stumbling, his sword falling.

Instantly, Musashi's right hand back to his longsword, attention to the first man, and in the lapse the samurai had pushed Musashi's longsword wildly up. The samurai had not expected the vanishing of the downward force, now staggered forwards in his thrust, sought purchase in the ground, and he and Musashi whirled around each other. Musashi quicker, close, very close, down to one knee and his longsword slashed across, taking the belly from collar to point.

The other, the last samurai, had picked up his sword, but his left hand was mangled, bleeding, unable to hold the weapon, only cradle it in his palm. Right hand only. Fear in his eyes at this. But he did not run, levelled the point of his sword at Musashi. Musashi in turn snarled and charged, and he had no mercy in his heart, only anger, drew his sword back and smashed it across, leading with the blunt edge, aiming not for flesh but for steel. Two hands against one; the Yoshioka's sword was battered from his grip. Musashi did not prolong it, rotated the sword in his grip, drew it back and then hewed it down through the man's shoulder.

The blade wedged itself to rest level with the sternum.

Perhaps the samurai screamed. Musashi could not tell, pulse rushing around his ears stealing any other sound. When the man fell he took Musashi's sword with him, wedged still, prying it from numb hands. Musashi in turn collapsed to his knees, gasping for breath. He felt as though the length of him was trembling. Sweat warm upon his brow and yet pooled cold on his back. He pressed his head to the earth for some time, and simply enjoyed the feel of the hard stones there, the leaves.

In the trees around him the insects had not noticed at all, singing on, the rhythm of the universe undisturbed. This calmness, this ambivalence when he heard it sent fresh rage into his heart, and he stared upwards at the sky, at the heavens and the gods to whom he had prayed.

'That was your answer?' he howled. 'That was your answer?'

The shouting of that ended it, left him feeling empty. Musashi could think once more. On the trail he saw other monks coming, dark robes flowing behind them. He left them the bodies. He got to his feet and hauled his longsword free of the Yoshioka corpse and ran.

Musashi arrived at the graveyard. He called out. No one answered. He moved through the rows and columns of the tombs, exhausted feet stumbling on the worn stones. He rounded the corner where he had left the pale-eyed samurai in peaceful contemplation.

Took it all in. Stood there panting, sheathed his sword, put his hands upon his thighs and did no more than simply behold for some time.

Beheld Akiyama's corpse where it had been left.

Ruined beyond all dignity, cut to pieces in a frenzy, dismembered utterly. All that held it in semblance of a whole were the tatters of his clothes. His crypt was spattered with the violence, gouted streaks of blood gathered in the stone gouges that formed the two characters of his name.

Of his head, there was no sign.

Chapter Sixteen

The Katsura in the west and the river Kamo in the east, veins around the heart of Kyoto, as the summer star Orihime has her Hikoboshi. The surface of the Kamo a languid opal mirror set with mother ducks leading fledglings in flightless chains, breached by the poles of pagodas and the stones of bored children, and around the Shijo bridge a series of little islands upon which people gathered to watch plays from afternoon to evening.

The land of the islands was technically the river and so legally untaxable. Troupes of aspirant actors would duly set up stages there, lay out narrow planks from shore to island to island across which the city folk would balance, coming all summer long to be entertained. No high art of the noh theatre here, the actors not in masks but in caricature makeup, the plays mostly bawdy and lewd and quick, an entire scene gone by in the time it would take a noh actor to enunciate his entrance in achingly protracted song.

Tadanari liked this. There was art and then there was art. He was a patron of the higher theatres over in west Hongan ward, too, but for now he stood fanning himself at the back of a seated crowd watching a tale unfold with women playing men and men playing women. A courtier of rank had slept with a sea nymph, a forbidden taboo, and consequently his penis had fallen off. Now he and his servant were conducting a search through the palace covertly trying to locate it, asking others if they had seen it without revealing the proud courtier's emasculation.

When the phallus-errant was at last found and the play was done, Tadanari put some money into the bowl they handed around, and then, still smiling, made his way back into the city. He wanted to take it all in, a memory to last until autumn, for tomorrow he left for his estate upon the coast and the breeze there. The heat here in Kyoto's high summer was unbearable, and so he would depart and return with the dry heat and the red leaves and the susuki grasses caressing the sky.

Imbibe, then, the things that mattered: the streets themselves, close enough that a man could just about hold a spear horizontally. He passed a maker of noodles with his uncooked wares cut from wafer thin to wider than a thumb draped over racks of bamboo poles like willow branches; a crafter of sandals painting patterns of blue flowers upon a white field on the wooden insole of a woman's sandal, behind him shelves and shelves of all designs; an artisan who worked in gold leaf hoping for commissions, examples of his works laid out glittering – screen doors, vases, shrine cabinets – and a big man in his employ who loomed, imposing, to anyone who stared too salaciously upon the gold.

Look upon the noodle maker's chopping boards, Tadanari knew, and you would see faint forms of crucifixes that the man absently scratched with his cleavers, he a devout Christian, but this concealed for fear of driving conservative customers away; the crafter of sandals and his wife were often seen to have shouting matches that carried out onto the street, sometimes tools even thrown, and yet in the quiet of the night when no one ought to be watching she rested with her head upon his shoulder and he smelt the hairs upon the back of her neck; of the man who worked with gold leaf Tadanari knew nothing yet for the business was recently opened, and yet he knew that the building the man occupied used to be a front for a gambling ring that threw dice in the backrooms, and that in the yard behind it the profits of the scattered ring might lie still buried beneath the thorny yuzu tree there.

Did anyone else know all this, these little facts that one could wander blithely by? He hoped not. That was what made a city a city, these connections, and if they happened to come together in him alone then that made him a kind of nexus-apex, and in that uniqueness was a power and a worth that he cherished.

Onto Muromachi avenue now, this the central divide of the old capital centuries ago but now just a street marginally wider than the others. Along the length of it a water-scarce canal ran in which people loitered, trying to escape the heat. The trenches cut as deep as the height of three men and in a month or two when the typhoon season blew in these channels would roar white and likely burst, but down there now children splashed what they could at one another, their mothers scolding them standing ankle deep, the water falling over the bodies of labourers and beggars lying down on their backs trying in vain to submerge themselves entirely

The avenue itself was filled with stalls and shacks that sold trinkets and refections: tofu fried quickly in a shallow skillet, forming a pancake that would be wrapped around gooey rice flavoured with sweet vinegar; a nail impassively driven beneath the eye of a writhing eel, pinning it to a board so that it could be scaled, butchered and then skewered on wooden sticks to be tossed upon a cast iron grill to roast; cheap woodprints hawked, weak colours on coarse paper bleeding into one another, depicting the romance of the old Chinese kingdoms, the tale of the boy who came from a peach, of Sekigahara.

Tadanari stopped to buy a bag of sugarcane imported from the Ryukyu isles, broke a piece of the pale, brittle flesh off and then chewed upon it as he went, enjoying the sweetness.

Was it wrong to love a city? He did not think so.

You love a woman, say, and the course of duty takes you from her in your youth and her from you in what comes after; what she was, all she was could never be again. All that remains of this love is an unbridgeable absence that you cannot quite fathom, and your one son who was dear to you before but now . . .

You love a man, say, as a brother, and though this man is strong and proud the whim of fate and his own treacherous flesh conspire to lay him low, to strip him of everything in which he held pride, and then like a whisper of wind he is gone too. All that remains of this separate love is a portrait hung on a dojo wall, the dearth of a friendship once held so fundamental, the school this man guided all his life and his three sons also.

But Kyoto . . .

Ah, it would hurt to leave, even for a month. But she was a cruel mistress with this heat, and he supposed it would make it all the sweeter on his return.

His meander drew its way to its zenith, and, as he crossed the long hump of the Shichijo bridge across the Kamo once more, there ahead of him the hall of the Great Buddha of the Hoko temple revealed itself like Fuji reigning over the plains of Kanto. The tallest structure in the city, likely even the nation, the great statue of the Buddha within the height of fifteen men, the hall around it a two-tiered thing worn like a mantle by the seated giant, the first tier coming up to his shoulders and the second one enshrining his colossal and serene face. The beams of the structure were red and its walls white, the two roofs black-tiled and sloping, majestic, imposing, and yet reassuring; as they always were in fair weather, the doors upon the second tier were cast wide open so that an enlightened gaze peered out endlessly across the city.

Tadanari met the pupilless eyes of the Buddha at the peak of the bridge's arc, and he bowed as one might to a friend, as did the people around him, an idiosyncrasy of the denizens of the city. There at the Hoko temple beneath the statue he intended to offer prayer for safe travel, for the health of his family and of his school in his absence, and then his business in Kyoto would be completed for the summer. He bowed once more at the gate, a mark of respect as he prepared to cross the liminal threshold, and he had not taken five paces within when he happened into Goemon Inoue.

The Tokugawa samurai was in the process of leaving, but stopped as he recognized Tadanari. The pair of them stood for an uncertain moment there on sanctified ground, both bereft of the many men they could command but swords still at their sides.

'Captain Inoue.'

'Sir Kozei.'

They bowed to each other, formally, respectfully, rose to stand rigid. Goemon in his black Shogunate livery and Tadanari in the civic colour of tea. This observed by the lowerborn around them, illicit glances cast in passing. Tadanari made the first move: he saw that from both their belts hung smoking pipes, and so he put the sugarcane away and offered up a case of kizami tobacco to the captain.

Goemon had to accept.

The pair of them shuffled over to stand clear of the thoroughfare, stood beneath the eaves of some lowly building. Their pipes were long and slender things, like assassin's darts, a metal mouthpiece and bowl either end of a thin tube of wood. Tadanari pinched a measure of kizami into each, the long fine threads of which were reminiscent of auburn cat's hair, and then, bereft of fire, went and took a taper from a brazier that burnt nearby, this ostensibly there for the sole purpose of igniting holy incense.

Nobody complained.

'Obliged,' said Goemon around his pipe.

'A pleasure,' said Tadanari. 'A happy coincidence to encounter you here. What draws you to Hoko this day, Captain? What might you be praying for?'

Goemon gave a motion with his shoulders, eyes to the distance, drew a long lungful in.

The pair of them stood smoking in silence for some time, looked out across the expanse of the temple enclave. Opposite the hall of the great Buddha perhaps fifty paces away stood a stupa about the half its height. The hump of it was covered in grass and a stairway led to its summit, where a modest stone pagoda lay. This was called the Mound of Noses, and beneath the grass and the pretty ornaments lay thousands and thousands of trophies that had been hacked from the corpses of the enemy dead in the great invasions of the mainland almost a decade previous. Brine-preserved and stolen away from their homeland to be piled and entombed here in grand testament to a nation's failure.

Between these two monuments, dwarfed, all the people walked.

'The Regent Toyotomi had vision, did he not?' said Tadanari.

'I am aware the Regent ordered these built,' said Goemon. He sounded like a child professing the ability to read.

'I did not claim otherwise, Captain,' said Tadanari. 'But, yes, both of these monuments were his work. I assume you know that, though the great Buddha is carved of wood, the segments of it are pinned together by stakes forged from the steel of all the swords and spears he captured on his conquests?'

'I am aware.'

'These things here then he built, and all the bridges that span the broad Kamo, the walls that surround the city, the moats . . . Truly, the Regent enriched Kyoto immeasurably.'

'Your tone does not ring deep with admiration.'

A slow blue ribbon emerged from Tadanari's mouth, coiled upwards. 'Will you permit me to speak something of my true thoughts upon your master's master?'

'I stand currently in your debt.'

'About seven, eight years ago now, our city was struck by a terrible earthquake. The worst that I can remember. Perhaps you and your folk, though, could not feel it, way up in . . . In any case, that great Buddha was destroyed. The stakes could not hold and it shook itself to pieces. The hall collapsed around it. Can you imagine something of such colossal stature being scattered as though it were no more than dice? Its head, it rolled forty paces away. I could scarcely believe it, but I swear to you it is truth. I saw it lying there afterwards, red beams and tiles all around. It was obscene, face down there in the dirt. The Regent himself came to see the damage, stood just over yonder. This was the last year of the Bunroku era, just before the second invasion of Korea . . . The Regent was not enfeebled, but he was old, small.

'Our school contributed to the construction of the hall, and to its restoration. But we were permitted to witness him only, not permitted to be acknowledged. I and the dear late Naokata Yoshioka stood towards the back of the crowd, and over that crowd what we saw was the most honourable Regent Toyotomi's anger – real honest anger, unbridled, unhidden. I could not hear all his words, but some came clear, and what I remember him saying most is, "Accursed thing! Accursed thing! I formed your legs that you might sit! Why do you defy me? Raise yourself! Raise yourself!" There was little dignity to him. An old man's futility like a fish trying to thrash itself free of a barbed hook . . . Please remember, good Captain, this is just my small observation upon what I witnessed of your master's master.'

Goemon's eyebrows absolved him.

'The Buddha did not raise itself, but nor was the Regent entirely powerless: he ordered thousands of men to work upon its repairs immediately, and before he died he saw the statue restored and the hall stand again as it had been. But I knew that day, seeing him, that for all the effort, all the thought, all the money he put into elevating Kyoto higher still, he did not understand the city. The essence of it. Let us say a fire came . . . Forgive me, Captain, I understand the thought of fire must be a sore point for you at this time.'

Goemon's teeth clacked upon the metal of his pipe's mouthpiece.

'But a fire comes say – and it will come one day – and eradicates all, spreads from east to west to north to south, and all the ashes of the temples mix with all the ashes of the brothels.

Is that the end of Kyoto? No. One act ends, the scenery upon the stage is changed, the next one begins. Men will rebuild and Kyoto will continue to be. The form of it altered, the incidental shapes collude into fresh arrangement, but the soul of it . . . The Regent sought to make the city indelibly his by pinning it into place with structures wrought by his hand, and screamed and raged when those structures failed him, and, though this hall stands so wonderfully tall and I marvel at it, it is not Kyoto. Wood and iron are not Kyoto. Kyoto endures in hearts, is summoned and defined by those who know it, an immortal with a million different facets and yet the same conclusion reached. Therein lies the truth the Regent never realized: what is a city but its people?'

Tadanari drew in the last glowing remnants of his pipe, exhaled, then smiled slyly: 'How fares your master's castle over at Nijo?'

'Construction advances,' said Goemon, and he even managed to return the smile.

The torment in him! The captain yearning to simply draw his sword and cut at the man who he knew was undoubtedly responsible for all his troubles, his yearning to be as samurai. Yet there he stood, had to stand, a half-man gelded by his allegiances to distant despots.

Tadanari could feel it, see it, and he revelled in it. Never would he forget the arrogance of the man who had come to his school those years back and refuted the iron-clad right of the Yoshioka to their rightful office. Never would he grant him respite. He opened a separate compartment on his case of kizami and held it up to Goemon with a flourish. So small a thing and yet the captain, forced to fulfil his part, could do nothing but empty the ash of his pipe as a supplicant would.

Magnanimity sometimes the keenest insult, complicity the greatest humiliation.

Tadanari emptied his own pipe and then placed the case neatly away in its velvet bag. Then he and Goemon bowed politely to each other, traded perfectly insincere farewells, and went their opposite ways.

At the altar of the temple Tadanari dropped a golden coin into the waiting chest, the ovoid ryo of enough value to keep a family in rice for a year, and then he clasped his hands and bowed his head and asked what he would ask of the Buddhas and the Bodhisattvas, the serene faces of which stared back at him. He could read no hint of favour of scorn upon them, but in the mood he was in he could do nothing but assume the former. Then he started on his journey back to the school.

Before he had reached the Shichijo bridge once more, the children saw him and came up to him, and to them he gave the rest of the sugarcane that he still had about himself. Children saw things, and over their sticky mastication he expected them to tell him perhaps of a scandal of some local drunk who had vomited over himself, or of a shamed wife forced to shave herself bald in public, things of the sort they always told him.

They brought to him instead the first winds of a storm that was beginning to blow over the city. Something that would be met with shock or outrage or illicit amusement by every tongue that passed it on until it had reached even the meanest of gutters and the most gilded of chambers.

They told him of a band of Yoshioka violating the sanctity of holy Mount Hiei to try to kill a masterless swordsman, and failing.

Chapter Seventeen

The head of the Foreigner was set upon a spike above the gates of the Yoshioka school. There was no breeze to blow the shaggy locks of red hair. His eyes and his mouth were open, and his dead skin seemed to sweat.

'Do you see?' said Denshichiro.

He spoke to his younger brother, Matashichiro. They stood beneath the gates looking up at the head. Near a decade separated the pair of them but the blood of the Yoshioka was strong and the resemblance was budding keen. Matashichiro had been a heavy child, a round face without definition of cheek or nose or chin, arms that seemed fat, and this softness was only just starting to harden into muscle like that of both of his brothers, his shoulders widening, ears growing callused from wrestling, lithic masculinity forcing its way onto his brow as the dimple of his smile grew shallower.

'Do you see?' said Denshichiro again. He had both his hands on the boy's shoulders.

'I see,' said Matashichiro.

'What do you see?'

'A head. I have seen heads before. I am not afraid of it.'

'Good. But this is much more than that.'

'The Foreigner.'

'Yes.'

'Was his blood a different colour?'

'No. Red as yours or mine.'

'Then why do you make me stare at it?'

'Because he was a traitor, and now the city can mark him as such.'

'Is that important?'

Denshichiro patted his shoulders. 'Here is a thing our father told me when I was your age: you have no true existence of your own. Do you understand that?'

Matashichiro did not want to admit any fallibility. Stubbornly he tried to formulate an answer but the words did not come. Denshichiro spun the boy around to face him.

'In my dreams, I dream of flying,' he said, reciting his father's words as he saw them in his memory, even the tone of his voice warping to try to replicate the profundity he had felt as a child. 'I am certain I can fly. I soar with such grace that even the birds envy me, and all the world is mine to traverse.'

Denshichiro spread his arms and flapped them as though they were the frantic wings of a startled pigeon. Matashichiro did not laugh as the child Denshichiro had laughed, but a glimmer of mirth appeared in the boy's eyes.

'There is my actual flight,' said Denshichiro. 'What I feel of myself, of my own existence or my own virtue in my own heart is of the exact same worth. The only place you find true existence is in the hearts of others.'

Above them a fly landed on the Foreigner's lower lip, furtively broached the ridge of his teeth and crawled inside the fetid cavern of his mouth.

Denshichiro spoke on in warm reminiscence: 'I remember when I was young, very young, well before your birth, I stood outside those gates and I watched our father return from a duel. The sun was setting and everything was orange. The man he had killed was called Mitsusue Watari. I remember that well, I have a fine memory for names. Father came up the avenue with Watari's head held in one hand. Blood was dripping from the neck onto the earth, and the spatters of it were treated like clusters of fragile flowers by the crowd that followed him, things to be stepped delicately around.

'I swear to you, though, Father looked as though he deserved that wake behind him. What finer thing had been done in the city that day, that year? He did not look at Seijuro or me as he approached the gates. What mattered to him was the head of Watari and the very same spike up there that now holds that traitor's head. That alone. When he pressed Watari's head down on the spike his mouth opened, and I swear to you again I felt the breath of glory blow from it. Felt it pass across my face, and it blew through all those watching people too. Father turned to them, and he said, "Naokata Yoshioka, proud servant of Kyoto!"'

Denshichiro had dropped into a squat now to look levelly into his brother's eyes. 'Then and there, he lived. Lived not in the manner of drawing breath or eating food, but *lived*. I understood what he meant. If he had killed Watari in solitude and had no witness but for himself, what worth his ability? As substantial as a dream of flight. Father, though, brought his own existence into being, enkindled it in every watching heart. The blood on his hands was not blood, but the chrism of the city. Do you understand, Matashichiro?'

The boy thought about it. 'A crime is not a crime, then, unless others are there to witness it?'

A momentary irritation flickered across Denshichiro's face. 'Sin is sin,' he said. 'What the Foreigner did was unpardonable. A crime regardless. What I have humbly done is ensure that all will remember the traitor how one such as he ought to be remembered . . .' *and the worth of my own hand substantiated*. 'This is right and just.'

'And what of the six men that failed to return with you?' called Seijuro.

The eldest of the Yoshioka brothers was sitting within earshot on the wooden steps of the forehall, both hands resting on the pommel of his longsword and the point of its scabbard in the dirt. He had the same eyes as Denshichiro, the same line of his jaw, but he was slightly leaner and taller and his features settled more naturally into a cold expression rather than the permanent simmering glower that beset his brother.

He had been staring grimly up at the head of the Foreigner since it had been raised.

Denshichiro rose to stand. 'As I told you, brother, when I became aware of their failure, the monks were already roused into a furore, and I assume the masterless was amongst them.'

'Heed this lesson, Matashichiro,' said Seijuro. 'When you commit to something, see it through to its entire completion. Vague resolve, dishonest resolve is the scourge of this world.'

'What was I to do?' said Denshichiro. 'Cut down the holy men to get to him?'

Seijuro sucked air through his teeth scornfully. 'You made the initial choice to broach the holy mountain.'

The brothers looked at each other. Words went unspoken in the blackening silence. It was then that Tadanari entered the yard. He was staring at the head of the Foreigner, his eyes wide and scandalized.

'What madness has gone on this day?' he breathed.

'That one returned in the company of a masterless,' said Denshichiro jerking his chin at the trophy. 'I punished him for his renunciation. You needn't concern yourself.'

'On Mount Hiei,' stated Tadanari.

Denshichiro's pupils vanished up into his skull for a moment. 'You as well?' he said. 'Our right of vengeance supersedes any stigma. The Lord Oda scoured Hiei. Why not I also?'

'A million voices proclaimed Hiei holy before the Lord Oda raised his sole objection. Which of them lives yet, the mountain or the man?'

Denshichiro grunted, waved a dismissive hand.

Tadanari said, 'The city speaks of outrage, of desecrators and violators. Streets ringing with it. I have heard laughter also, mockery of a pompous hubris.'

'Let them talk,' snarled Denshichiro. 'They will come to their senses when they realize the cause. Let them look upon that head. Faithful to the Way, I.'

Tadanari could put an authority of years in his eyes when he so desired. He let silence break those words apart. Denshichiro looked away, crossed his arms and stared up at the head of the Foreigner.

'Very soon,' said Tadanari to the side of his skull, 'you and I shall talk. But now your negligence to your own wild desire has left us with an issue of a greater urgency. I heard that this masterless overcame ten of our adepts in a single encounter. I shall assume that this is an exaggeration.'

'Six,' said Seijuro.

'Six?' said Tadanari. 'Impossible.'

'Apparently not.'

'What is his name?'

'Musashi Miyamoto.'

'Of which school?'

Seijuro shrugged.

'Do we know anything of him at all?' Tadanari demanded, aghast.

'Were you not the one who sent the Foreigner out after this man?' sneered Denshichiro.

'Years prior,' said Tadanari. 'It is not my duty to delve into the pasts of the low men that earn their place upon the list, only to assure myself of their end.'

'Well,' said Denshichiro, turning his eyes back to the flies that clouded about the Foreigner, 'the boys who scoured Miyamoto out for me told me he was as tall a man as they had ever seen, but slender like he was starved. Long arms, big reach, but frailty in this I should expect.'

Tadanari clasped his hands before him, took a breath and looked at the dust at his feet to level himself. 'Miyamoto must have been aided by an unknown agent. Overcoming six men is absurd. But neither can we dismiss him as unskilled. How long were they in collusion, Sir Akiyama and this masterless? How much of our Way did Akiyama divulge, how many secrets?'

'Revered counsel,' said Seijuro to Tadanari, and Denshichiro seethed inwardly at the obsequiousness, 'what course do you think the school should pursue?'

'I am not the head of the school,' said the bald samurai. 'Here is the weight you must learn to bear, Seijuro. How is it you intend to steer us through another's tempest?'

A group of adepts came into the yard through the main gate. They were agitated, striding quickly, all of them wearing expressions of varying degrees of anger. At their head was Ujinari. He saw his father and the three Yoshioka brothers, and came over immediately. In his hands he carried a folded bolt of cloth.

'We found this nailed to the public notice board by the gates of the Hokyo temple,' he said. 'Nailed with a shortsword.'

Ujinari unfurled what he held. It was a jacket of the school, bloodied and torn. He held it by the shoulders and spread it wide, and then showed them the back of it. There, written in a wild hand, black on the colour of tea, were the words:

Violated Hiei to try to kill Musashi Miyamoto.

Failed, with five other men.

Musashi Miyamoto awaits you now, Seijuro Yoshioka!

'It was quite a crowd that beheld it,' said Ujinari.

Seijuro looked at the slashes that had split the silk, at the stains that had crisped it.

'Well,' he said, and took a slow, deep breath, 'the resolution to this seems fairly obvious.'

Chapter Eighteen

The city saw them nailed up where bloodied jackets had hung not hours before and on each and every street beside. Written in two dozen neat and cultured hands, the curvature of the letters different but the message the same:

Tomorrow

The Moor at the Temple of Rendai

The Hour of the Rooster

Adept of the sword, Seijuro Yoshioka of Kyoto, commands the masterless Musashi Miyamoto to present himself for a duel, to account for the recent disturbance he caused at Mt Hiei.

Should he not appear, all will know his cowardice.

These up before the coming of night and with the dawn a response was found beneath the eaves of the grand gate of the

Hongan temple where it could not be missed. None dared touch it, not even the priests, all staring at it until tea-coloured samurai came and tore it down, bore it away:

The time of your humbling is nigh, Seijuro!

Await me!

*

It began, for Seijuro, with earth. Earth of the dojo hall, which he stood barefoot upon, clawed his toes into. Squatted down, pushed his fingers through it, brought it up to his cheeks, his brow, his lips.

Earth my father walked, he said within, *Earth my grandfather walked. Do you contain some remnant echo of their spirits?*

Daubed in dust, he knelt now before the shrine upon the wall, before the portraits of those two men, as well as his great uncle Naomoto. There Seijuro stayed for a long time.

Though he remembered little of his great-uncle he knew that this was the man who had raised the Yoshioka to their pinnacle, who had won the admiration and the patronage of the Ashikaga Shogunate, and this he revered.

His grandfather he tangibly recalled, he the man who had first let Seijuro hold the longsword, the old man wrapping his hands around his own still infant soft, showing him the method of grip with the little finger, the ring finger, the squeeze of Grandfather's hands strong then but in the memory now an infallible strength, an eternal strength.

And his father, he whom Seijuro had followed more than any other man, literally followed with every muscle of the body as he memorized taught technique, methods of the blade, no kindness given, none asked, only knowledge, raw knowledge with which Seijuro had adorned himself, let form around him as surely as the flesh atop his bones.

I need not your strength this day, he said to the three of them, *I wish only for your acknowledgement.*

To his sword, then, which lay stripped and naked by a large vat of water. He set his whetstone into the liquid, then let it rest upon a thin plank dripping down, circles forming on the surface, receding, vanishing. The blade he wrapped in tough cloth and then took in both hands, and so Seijuro set about sharpening the steel upon the stone, using short little buff-strokes that gradually became long and slow, long and slow from base to glistening wet point, the sound like the seething of the sea.

The sea, he thought, *Miyamoto is tall and he has reach. Picture him as the rock, the cliff unmoving, and I the sea. Surging closer, breaching, dashing myself against him, unstoppable, unrelenting force. The sea shall consume all eventually. The sea is indefatigable.*

The steel dried now, powdered, oiled, the blade set back with grip and guard and scabbarded. Time for himself. He washed his body, washed his hair, combed it out meticulously, then shaved his scalp. The tresses oiled, drawn up into the topknot. He looked in the copper mirror and decided to shave his beard, too, so that he would look entirely unmarred. Fresh. The opposite of what a vagrant would be.

Drawing the blade across his flesh suddenly he felt a thrill twisting through him, a base rush of blood, the shimmering warmth of which was indescribably wonderful. He saw it flare in his own reflected eyes, his jaw tight as though it were biting, and why not bite? Today he could kill, today he was permitted to kill, today a day in which he was allowed to fulfil what he was honed to be, to avenge himself against those who doubted and scorned, unleash every slight he bore within him garnered over the vast span since the last such permitted moment, a day to show himself as he was, truly was, in the tearing of the head from the neck and in the feeling of the edge of steel biting through flesh and the dull clip of it parting bone and . . .

Joy. Rage. Whatever he felt, whatever composite of the two, these were undignified things. There had to be propriety, as Tadanari had taught him, and he thought of the methods the master had shown him to level his spirit, to become serene, of meditation and the search for nothingness, of mantras deigned to him since the age of fifteen, and slowly the grip on his razor lessened and he could continue once more.

Fingers; important. Nails clipped and filed, dirt scraped out from under them.

Now armour, the only concession to armour he would make: a belt of a thousand stitches tied around his stomach. His mother had begged by the gates of the Gion temple for passing pilgrims to add to the band of white silk, row after row of little red *x*'s threaded slowly, she not drinking, not eating, not sleeping until the thousandth stitch was achieved. He wore it now both to honour her and because it was lined with eight gold ryo coins, ovoid, finger-length, thick and warding, protecting his stomach, which he knew to be the centre of his essence; men argued for the head or the heart, but all pleasurable feelings he found emanated from there, of good food, of sex, of victory.

Lastly, the jacket. The symbol. The hem of it hanging to midthigh, the sleeves wide and billowing, lapels bound loose at the sternum with a single elaborate knot, the braided cord tasselled at its ends. This as every other jacket the school wore, and of course, as every other, the silk of it the colour of tea. But here that colour only the field onto which a pattern of gold had been woven, wreathes of leaves encircling blooming whorls of flowers. He remembered seeing his father in it, his grandfather. Only twice before had Seijuro worn this jacket, but today permitted. So light he could barely feel it on his shoulders. Smelt old; a good smell, like faith.

In his mind Miyamoto had the face of a tengu demon and he lunged, overstepped. Seijuro slid around him, brought his longsword down through the shoulder, brought Miyamoto to his knees, felt the tremors of the dog's heart thrum along the length of his blade, felt them sweet as the beating of his own heart, felt them slow, stop . . .

The acolytes awaited him, a score of the boys lined up in ranks. Matashichiro was not amongst them: why waste a shining memory on someone whose loyalty was already assured? To one of the boys he awarded the stool upon which he would sit prior to the duel. To another he awarded a platter on which a blackened iron spike had been set, this for Miyamoto's head after. Lastly, to the one he had ensured beforehand was most worthy, he awarded the standard of the school.

This was twice the height of a man, a frame of wood lacquered black forming a right-angle, vertical five times that of the horizontal. Affixed to the peak a banner head in the form of the flower of the konnyaku, long petals parting vulval from which the phallic stigma jutted upwards, a humble plant of meagre sustenance to remind the school of its origins. In nature it was a deep red, tongue red, but here a shining aureate. The banner it sat atop, pinned to the frame with metal rings, read simply:

School of Yoshioka, Head Adept Seijuro Yoshioka.

The boy clutched it reverently in his hands and they followed the standard as they set out onto the street. Seijuro, his two pages, a dozen men. The dead eyes of the Foreigner watched them go. Each pace measured, every gaze upon the horizon. The men not identical, but to those who beheld them no detail of individual face could be recalled, no deviation in height or weight, just them, there as a whole, unified in step and soul and colour, except for Seijuro, marked as he was, anointed.

Around them the city seemed to bend itself, the people aware of their coming without the apparent need of sight. Warping away in Seijuro's eyes like the images within a broad copper bowl, pulling to the sides, forced there, belonging there, and yet their colours warm and magnificent. Silence enveloped the streets like an aura around the samurai, embracing, then releasing, no words to sully, and, though he did not look at the faces around him, eyes only ahead as was proper, as was manly, behind the gold coins of his thousand-stitch belt, Seijuro felt a stirring.

This only the prelude, he thought. *When the sun has set, when the head is affixed, the return – that the glory yet to be.*

They made their slow way north to the moor of the Rendai temple, gathering people behind as the fisherman's net gathers weight, the sun heavy, sinking, quivering behind the haze of its heat, the red eye of heaven descending as though eager to bear witness also. More men of the school awaited them there, having left earlier, and they had erected a palisade of tea-coloured silk. The boy with the stool ran ahead, set it down and awaited on his knees. Seijuro took the longsword from his belt and surrendered it to the page's waiting hands before he sat down, assumed the militant-regal pose of legs spread wide, left palm broad upon left thigh, point of his right elbow upon the other thigh and this fist balled to cradle his chin with his knuckles.

Silently his men arrayed themselves around him. The standard was set into its waiting stand, hung above them still, no breeze to move it. Distant, the crowd gathered, and Seijuro welcomed them. They ought to see. They ought to understand. Simple theatre with a simple moral.

The Rendai temple humble, unassuming, silent. The torii gate of its entrance monolithic, two upright pillars, two curved beams at the top, shadow cast so long it was like that of a man's almost, slender legs leading to the mass of shoulders. In the trees about the temple were scores of birds and Seijuro looked at them, looked at the entire span of what lay before him and thought how wonderful it was to be alive, to be born exactly him and no other.

The hour of the rooster was imminent.

*

Imminent, then gone. Miyamoto did not appear. The edges of the coins in his belt began to dig into the flesh of his stomach. Seijuro sat back, unfolded a paper fan upon which the cityscape of Kyoto was drawn in ink, began to fan himself. In the grass, on the trunks of the trees, the cicadas howled.

*

The sun vanished but the heat did not relent. Sweat collected in the hairs of his eyebrows, accumulating slowly, a trembling bead threatening to burst, grew and grew until it did so, splattered salty upon the waxed surface of his fan; Kyoto blighted by sudden flood. His belt, his kimono drenched, the creep inexorable. No choice but to remove his fine jacket for fear of sullying it. Rendered plain, Seijuro resumed his seat whilst his men lit braziers and lanterns all around.

*

The darkness behind him gradually became total; the only thing beyond the moor the city wall, the moat, and the mountains. With the creep of time what Seijuro became unavoidably aware of was that against this vast expanse he and his palisade and his standard were lit up, and to the crowd, they clustered at the edge of the city's light facing the void, were surely dwarfed by the blackness, marked as feeble, small.

*

Sullied, sullied, silk and moments and potential, and the birds were no longer in the trees, or not visible to Seijuro, and he had long since abandoned sitting, stood now. His mother's belt sodden around his waist like a tepid noose edged with metal. His sword still held upright in the hands of his page, and the boy would not meet Seijuro's eyes, kept his own downcast. The shrieking of the cicadas piercing him, they bawling at the rising summer moon. Blaring, shrill, to him entirely discordant.

*

'Master Yoshioka,' one of the samurai dared to say eventually, 'it is clear Miyamoto is not coming. He has fled.'

Seijuro did not answer. He was counting faces, calculating witnesses. It was a fine thing for his palms that he had filed his nails earlier.

'I took Miyamoto's response from the board myself,' said another. 'I saw it. All saw it.'

That, the manacle; abandon the field and be thought of as

an equal coward. The proper length of time nebulous, but, if it was endurable, unequivocally to be endured.

The crowd had grown. Men and women, rich and poor, artisans and merchants and samurai from other schools. Some wanting to see simple carnage, some wanting to see rival methods of the sword, some wanting to see a humbling. None of these thoughts or urges voiced, however. Just watching. A hundred conclusions being drawn. Seijuro pinned before them, certain he was being pierced.

From behind them a crier came, clacking two blocks of wood together, their tone musical.

'Hour of the dog!' was his call, and then he shrank at the sudden attention he garnered, he being used to being treated almost as furniture. 'Hour of the dog . . .'

Lanterns flickered. Seijuro was not alone in his sweating. People shifted weight from foot to foot, legs growing tired of standing. A young boy dozed draped across his father's shoulders. One of the Yoshioka cracked the knuckles of his hand. An old man hawked and spat. Distant, the low bells of temples could be heard tolling a confirmation of the crier's claims.

And then he came.

Oh, he was different, not the samurai the mass were expecting. An outsider, certainly, not of Kyoto. The tallest man that most of them had ever seen, young, though, face mottled more with pox-born scars than with beard. His hair, pulled back into a wild tail that hung down to his shoulders, jutted out behind his skull a palm's breadth where it was bound in the coils of a leather cord, an obnoxious and deliberate opposite to the dignified topknot. Dressed like a destitute with no apparent sense of shame at it, the sleeves of his clothing cut entirely away, recently and clumsily it seemed, coarse torn threads hanging down his bared arms over muscles lean and tight.

And yet they parted for him as they would have done the Yoshioka, followed after him without thinking as he headed towards Seijuro, he swaggering at his own pace, they wanting to hear now his explanation as much as see. Seijuro could wait no longer, snatched his sword from his page and strode out to meet him.

'Musashi Miyamoto!' he snarled, fifteen paces away.

'Seijuro Yoshioka.'

They stopped no more than a sword's length away from each other. Neither of them bowed. Seijuro saw how young the man was, younger even than Denshichiro, it seemed, and this fresh ignominy all but caused his shoulders to quiver.

'The duel was set for the hour of the rooster,' he said.

'Loud voices,' said Miyamoto. 'Long necks. You chose the hour that suits you best. But this? This is my time.'

The arrogance of it; the gathered Yoshioka samurai snarled, even the young pages, moved as if to surround him. Seijuro waved them back. 'This is the moment of your death,' he said to Miyamoto. 'I'll not visit the same insult of tarrying upon you as you have me. Prepare.'

'Why is it you sent a man to kill me in your stead?'

'Because you need to be fought.'

'You could hate me so for such a reason?'

'I could hate a man like you for much less of one. Prepare!'

A single hiss of a mocking laugh: 'I need no preparation.'

'I am the fourth head of the Yoshioka dynasty! You have no conception of the skill I wield.'

'The skill of the men of yours I already killed did not impress me greatly.'

Silence then, deepening. Seijuro took a cord and began to bind his sleeves up, held it in his mouth, teeth clenched savage on the braids. The moment drew out into a long appraisal between the two.

'Akiyama,' said Miyamoto, 'was it you who took his head?'

'My brother had that honour.'

'Proxies. All proxies with you. Be felled on their account, then; let us call it justice. For him. For all the other thralls.'

'Your head will rot alongside the Foreigner's tonight, cur.'

'I do not think so,' said Miyamoto, and he laughed, let open disgust write itself across his features. 'There is no challenge here. I need no more than a single strike to best you.'

'What?' said Seijuro.

'One strike,' said Miyamoto. The sheer gall of him was staggering, him in his rags and his gaunt pox-twisted face.

'I'll cleave your head from your shoulders in one strike!' said Seijuro.

'Let's make these the rules, then,' said Miyamoto. 'One strike each. Do you agree, or would you rather have one of your men here bleed for you?'

'I agree! Prepare to die!'

'Do you all hear that?' said Miyamoto to the other Yoshioka samurai. 'Do you abide by this agreement between myself and your master?' They snarled their assent. 'Good. Come, then, and I shall teach you.'

'Shut your mouth and let's end this.'

The anger in the Lord-King Yoshioka's eyes was perfect right then. Musashi beheld it and felt a gardener's pride, that of having carefully nourished something that was sprouting into a full and vivid bloom.

The samurai of the Yoshioka stepped back and the crowd stepped forward eagerly. Neither Musashi nor Seijuro moved. So very close, lethally close. Seijuro spread his legs and sank into the fighting stance. Musashi remained as he was, obnoxiously neutral.

To describe these kinds of instants was something Musashi could never do, these times that were potentially the summation of his life. The focus came, the deep focus he longed for, and with it left feeling, and all there was was himself and Seijuro in the long and empty universe. He looked at his opponent, saw the tenseness in him, saw the blotch of a birthmark just below his ear, saw his eyes that were yearning, yearning, yearning, and right then he knew for certain that

he
does
not
know
it
as
you
do

and Seijuro was inhumanly angry, anger entirely, and so as the Yoshioka man went for his sword, he turned his shoulders to put strength into the blow where none was needed, sucked in a fierce hiss of breath, and with these signals it was so easy for Musashi to read. Seijuro aimed for the throat with a wild slash, trying to lop off of his head as he said he would, and though he was fast Musashi simply stepped backwards and let the blow come to nought.

Seijuro overswung in his rage, anticipating resistance of flesh and bone, and he staggered almost entirely around.

Over his shoulder he looked at Musashi, who had not moved for his sword the slightest, arms at his side still. Instantly, Seijuro's sword was around and up into a guard, but there was nothing for him to ward: Musashi did no more than watch him levelly. Seijuro had given his word, and both men knew it. Indecision in Seijuro's eyes, the urge to fight on, but conflicted, receding, quelled.

He lowered his sword and spread his arms wide.

Musashi stepped back into the range of his sword. Seijuro did no more than grit his teeth and lift his chin to bare his throat. His men behind him aghast yet bound by dogma, spectators only to the magnificent futility, and in the crowd a father whispered to the son upon his shoulders, 'That is being samurai.'

How Musashi would have agreed. He did not prolong it, lashed his sword from the scabbard and struck Seijuro across the chest from pit to pit. But no killing blow this, his strength tempered, seeking not to cleave but to rake the blade across the flesh, splitting muscle but sparing the vital innards.

Seijuro, expecting death, reacted to the pain with surprise more than anything. He grunted somewhere between a whimper and a further snarl of anger, and fell to his hands and knees. There he remained. The cord he had bound his sleeves up with had been split, slid off his back like a serpent, hiss and all.

Musashi looked down at him. It was better than he had imagined it could go. Everything planned, calculated to shatter Seijuro's concentration, as his father Munisai had once goaded Kihei Arima back in his home village years ago. That man, Musashi had killed, but there would be no murder this night.

He became aware of the crowd, realized that he had them. That he should justify himself. Slowly he raised his sword, showed them the blood upon it.

'Do you see?' he said to them. 'Do you see, Kyoto?'

The crowd said nothing.

'My name is Musashi Miyamoto,' he said. 'And I have come. Of no school, I. Of no Lord. But here I am. You thought this man here invulnerable. His school untouchable. Look now at what I have done. Look now at your truth. Here was a man who sent others to kill me. But look at him, here, the mighty, the powerful, look at his majesty when he is forced to fight his own fights. This is the Way! Can you not see it for what it is?'

Behind him Seijuro was crawling away. The breath was rasping from him. Some of his men, the three boys, were kneeling by him, trying to pull his clothes back to see the wound, and he lashed feebly at them.

'Everything you hold is false!' shouted Musashi, the words sounding pure and fine to him. 'Everything you believe is profane!' he cried, the victory thrumming warm in his throat. 'Do not accept what you have been told, what you are told!' he told them. 'Men who do not understand death, who would bare their throat to it, these are the men to whom you bow? Why? Why follow—'

'You couldn't kill him, could you?' snarled one of the Yoshioka samurai behind him, tears of rage in his eyes. 'Couldn't even give him that dignity.'

Musashi turned to face them.

Those that weren't tending to Seijuro drew their swords.

Chapter Nineteen

How quickly the warmth of victory could vanish, and how quickly the Yoshioka came. The first threw himself at Musashi with a shriek. Musashi stepped back, dodged, lunged in with immediate riposte. The samurai was quick, though, agile, swerved his body out of the path of his sword just as Musashi had done, and then the other Yoshioka were coming, enveloping, and so Musashi turned and ran.

Instinct drove him towards light and so he fled towards the city proper. The crowd parted for him, panicking at what they thought themselves immune from now amongst them, the swords and the blood upon them suddenly real, and the Yoshioka samurai followed close behind.

Sprinting silent, sprinting grim, the streets beyond the crowd bereft of all but the odd startled bystander. The northern fringes of the city nought but the plain hulks of import company warehouses and sake breweries closed up for the night. Lights though, oil lanterns burning, candle-glow spilling from windows and doorways, flicking past him. Behind him bellowed accusations of cowardice, commands to stand

and fight, the Yoshioka fanning out behind him. How many? Glimpses over his shoulder revealed only motion in the gloom; more than eight, the best he could tell.

Vibration carried through bone from foot to jaw told him he was running at his true limit, teeth jarring with each step. Musashi had no inkling of where he was heading. Took corners as they came. Found identical streets. He bigger, younger, faster, and the chain of the Yoshioka behind Musashi began to distend. What use distance running to men who fought willing enemies at arm's length? Only the youngest, the fittest, remained immediately behind him.

They would hound him through the streets they knew so much better than he. Exhaust him eventually, or corner him. Musashi made his decision. He stopped, turned, held his sword out before him. The lead Yoshioka did not break his stride, came straight at Musashi, he screaming now. Went for Musashi's blade, brushed it nimbly out of his path, the motions of it familiar, and familiar too the way he rammed into Musashi, tried to push him back hip to hip. Encountered before on Hiei; dogmatic offence, found no give, and Musashi lunged with his elbows, his shoulders, drove the samurai backwards and slew him as he staggered.

Other Yoshioka imminent, three of them at least. Turn, run again. This his only option. Scatter them, pick them off in segregated violence. Breath heaving, curses seething inward. The hand of Seijuro manifold. On the gates of a Shinto shrine faces of wooden foxes leered at him, malevolent, mischievous, passed. Growing narrower, the streets, buildings pressed tight, more lights, more voices; residential, mercantile, indiscernible.

Round a corner, a group of men sat grilling fish. Smoke smell, fat smell. Musashi stopped, waited. No time for proper stance or form, vestiges of it only, now came the Yoshioka and he leapt forward to meet the first of them. Fast, the man caught Musashi's sword on the flat of his blade, but his resistance only momentary. Musashi overwhelmed him, forced the samurai backwards off his feet. In stunned watching mouths fish flesh went unchewed.

Second man, sword high,

see

it

and Musashi's blade around to catch him under his arms, perhaps not lethal but enough; sword dropped, not reclaimed. First man rising, third man near. In a doorway came more onlookers, summoned by screaming, none intervening. First samurai came horizontal, Musashi's sword inverted, greeting, once again the two of them locked, then his arms up forcing the Yoshioka sword above his head, rainbow arc, swords apart and all force dissipated. Tea-coloured back exposed, Musashi's grip tight, prepared to cut, but denied – third man here now, interrupting.

Slow, that interruption. Musashi saw him coming. His sword swerved in its path from the first man to him, took the samurai's right hand off at the wrist. Appetites were lost. The hand fell to the ground, and Musashi felt a spatter of blood on his cheek as the lessened arm began its flailing. Ignored. First man whirling, stabbing, missing, barrelling into Musashi's stomach still crouched low, snarling like a boar goring at guts. Spine shining upwards to Musashi, too close to him to cleave, but rakeable; edge of the longsword pressed through silk into flesh, drawing a neat and bloody chasm from hip to shoulder.

Pushed the samurai down to the earth, and now away, go! These three done but more coming. Wrong. Not done. First man, back split, writhing in the dust, swiped at Musashi as he fled, practically flopping on his belly to reach, nicked him on the back of the calf. The wound went unnoticed for ten paces, a razor cut so fine it was unfelt, but then Musashi's stride began to break without his consent. Warmer than sweat around his ankle. Pace slowed, resorted to lunging gait, still going, still, still . . .

Turned, threw his shortsword at the nearest Yoshioka samurai. Near but too distant. Saw the blade coming, batted it aside. Curse sucked down with taste of bile, hint of blood, the gift of tortured lungs. Eyes looked out from windows, silhouettes in doorways, dozens of witnesses watching his faltering defiance.

Another corner, and now Musashi found himself alongside a canal, a balustrade running its length. There, ahead, he saw his chance: a bridge, hump-backed, narrow. He could run no more, all but hopping now, but there, there he could force them to come to him one at a time. Funnelling salvation. On, on, his blood-sodden straw sandal squelching beneath his feet.

Other footsteps, unhindered, not fresh but fast, faster. At first from behind but then to the side, looping around him. The man he had thrown his shortsword at. Must have realized what he was attempting, ran to put himself between the bridge and Musashi. Grinning, shepherding, waiting for others to arrive.

So close behind him, the Yoshioka not as scattered as Musashi had thought. Into an arc arrayed around him now, eight men, sounds of more still coming, they caging him in against the balustrade of the canal. No rush now. Breath gathered. Swords steadied. Moving forward in half-steps, feet never leaving the correct positioning. Beneath the wound Musashi's own foot unfeelable. Tighter. Closer. Touch of wood from behind.

The balustrade.

One quick stolen glance, behind, down into the canal's depths. The drop was long, the water shallow. Moon caught a dozen times in separate little pools, white moon, not scarlet, not his sign, not his assurance, and this moon dancing also in the feeble vein that flowed still. Walls smoothly set stone, bed riddled with rocks and pebbles of all sizes.

Eyes back up to the Yoshioka. Closer. Some happier. Some angrier. Some devoid of anything. Swords out before them or above their heads, eight swords just aching to get closer still, to break his guard, to cleave his flesh . . .

No choice. Musashi sat his weight on the balustrade, swung his legs over and jumped down into the canal.

Further than it looked, an extra sliver of breath stolen before impact. Feet found no purchase, stones slick and wet, went right out from under him with the speed of his fall barely checked. Head whipped down, cracked against a rock, his shoulder, his temple, couldn't tell. Hurt. Left eye lost entirely to wild colour, ear feeling as though it had been ground to gristle. Stunned, unable to rise, lying sprawled in the water, stared up at Yoshioka staring down at him.

Shouting, shouts. Through the ringing he recognized the word 'stairway', saw the Yoshioka pointing along the canal. Beyond the bridge, carved into the wall, and most of the samurai rushing along to it. One remained keeping vigil, as though Musashi might vanish. Vanish? Vanish.

Up, fool.

Obeyed whatever it was that commanded him. Hauled himself up, grabbed his sword as he rose. Tried running.

Water splashing. World unsteady. Head addled, leg dead, staggering too erratic. No more running. Turned. Saw the many Yoshioka now down in the canal with him. Raised his sword, saw it quivering wildly, water falling from its point.

Seven of them. No room for them to spread out properly. Snarled at them. Tried to spit. No coordination, not even for that. Something at the back of his throat, behind his nose perhaps, clicking as he breathed. His sword felt weightless, as though his hands were clasping nothing but air, and with this air he would swipe at them, try to cut them.

Wounded leg curved the path of his retreat, found stone at his side, at his back. Once again trapped. Urge to lean against it, to relent. Ignored. Seven samurai, seven swords all of them where he could see them. Coming at him from the front, and through them he would wade, through the pain and the blows until he succumbed, see how many of them he could drag down to writhe alongside him in the puddles. Writhing like landed fish. No more. No less.

Uncle, he thought. *Know that I tried. Know that I tried. Know that I—*

'Cease!' bellowed a voice. 'All of you will cease this breach of the peace in the name of the most noble Shogun Tokugawa!'

Up on the street, light and movement. The arc of the bridge suddenly swarming with samurai, helmeted, uniformed black. Swords, spears, men with bows now lining up along the balustrade, arrows nocked, aimed down into the canal. At the Yoshioka, at Musashi. One man carried a lantern, stood at the arc's peak:

'I am Goemon Inoue, honoured with the rank of captain in the service of my most noble Lord, the Shogun Tokugawa, given jurisdiction of all Kyoto in his name! It is my duty to keep the peace, and I order all of you to sheathe your weapons immediately!'

No swords were moved. The Yoshioka said nothing. Musashi said nothing save for his ragged, clicking panting. Unquestionably outnumbered, the tea-coloured samurai, those still on the street quelled also. Those in the canal looking up at the Tokugawa, looking at Musashi. He so close. Points of arrows so black they seemed edged with obsidian. Yet the proximity of Musashi was tantalizing.

'No,' said one of them to Goemon. 'You would not overstep yourself so.'

He began the motion of drawing his sword back, foot beginning to rise. One of the archers loosed. So close but a fine shot regardless, the arrow's flight straight as light. It took the Yoshioka samurai in the side of the throat and passed straight through, the shaft the length of an arm yet piercing so entirely that the fletching was all but swallowed by flesh.

A moment of shock as the Yoshioka samurai fell to one knee, grasping at the arrow, hissing blood from his mouth, a moment that Musashi was certain Goemon shared. Then, the reaction: shouting, weapons bristling, bow strings drawn tauter and swords gripped tighter.

'Outrage!' one of the Yoshioka samurai was screaming. 'Outrage!'

'See how much more I am willing to commit,' said Goemon, and his face, his voice were level now, any surprise vanished as though it had never been. 'Please do.'

Three of them did. Goemon lashed his hand forward in clear command and they were riddled with arrows instantly. Two collapsed before they had taken but a step, the third reached Musashi but there was no strength in his arms; Musashi turned his sword aside and the samurai followed after it as though it were his anchor, guiding him down into the water's embrace.

The remaining three Yoshioka howled their anger, demanded the Tokugawa to come down and fight them fairly, but they had judged it impossible to reach Musashi and thus attain glory a moment prior and they did not change their minds now. They backed away, sheathed their swords. The other few men of the Yoshioka came down from the street and together they bore the bodies away, up and out of the canal all the while with the arrows of the Tokugawa aimed at them, and where they went after that Musashi could not care.

Only when they were out of sight did he allow himself to slump backwards, rest his weight against the wall, sheathe his sword. Suddenly he could feel the water flowing around his toes and the pain of all his wounds, his leg, his head, he realized the skin upon the back of his left arm had been grazed clean away, sticky with blood, and how wonderful that was.

'You,' called Goemon down to him, opening his eyes. 'You would be the duellist Miyamoto, correct?'

'Yes,' said Musashi. His voice was rasping, his throat still clicking oddly.

'You should come, spend the night in the garrison with us,' said Goemon, the rim of his circular helmet lit up like a halo. 'For your own safety.'

'Have I a choice?' said Musashi, looking up at him and all his men.

'No,' said Goemon, and he smiled. 'I rather think you haven't.'

Interlude I

The sky is blue and the sea is blue, but different types of blue, the names of which she never learns. Only half-remembered this chain of images, soundless, she so very young, the figures on the white gold of the beach distended and blurry in her recalled sight, but she remembers the shape: two legs, two arms, five fingers, two eyes, one nose, one mouth, yellow teeth, black hair blowing in the wind, white gulls eddying above. All these things she knows she has seen, actually seen, that she could not have possibly conjured in a pleading dream.

Then darkness.

'In we go,' comes Mother's voice. On the girl's shoulder a hand materializes, tender, ushering her forwards. Toes feel the pebble-edges of earthen steps, and she descends.

'Who's here?' says the girl, after the gentle squeeze of Mother's hand tells her to stop.

'Kind old lady Rimi,' says Mother, 'who brings us the ropes she weaves. Tamagusuku, who brought us that nice turtle shell he found last summer. Wibaru, who brings us the fruit from his tree. Arakachi, who brings us the razor clams he finds upon the beach. And Shimabuku, who cuts the lumber for us.'

'Can you help us?' says a man in front of her.

There is something in the voice that the girl has not heard before, that she does not like; a desperate deference. She waits for Mother to answer. Mother, though, does not, and the discomfort grows as the girl starts to wonder in the silence just to whom the man, the adult, is being deferent and desperate to.

'What's wrong?' the girl asks eventually.

'It's old Fija,' says Mother, above and behind. 'He's sick. He's been sick for a long time now. We all want to help him. Do you want to help him?'

'Yes,' says the girl out of childish instinct to please before she actually considers it, and then she quails. 'How?'

Mother places a hand on either one of her shoulder blades and leads her forward once more. After a few shuffled steps, soles on ash and sand, the girl is pressed gently down to her knees. Hands take her hands and place them upon something clammy and coarse; the girl's fingers slowly map out and recognize a palm much larger than her own, find a thumb onto which they clasp.

'Closer,' says Mother.

Fingertips on the back of her head. The girl's face is lowered. She hears a wheezing, sad, short, like the tiniest length of paper being torn again and again. Closer, because she still does not understand. What assaults her then is a smell, so revolting that it takes a moment for the scale of the disgust to register, vile, violating in its closeness.

'She grimaces!' came old lady Rimi's sudden voice, hysteric and loud. 'Oh, she sees them upon him! Devil-spirits clinging to him, dragging him away from this life! He's doomed! He's doomed!'

Later the girl sniffles into Sister's lap. The difference in the scent of the salt of her own tears and the sea salt worn into Sister's clothes is stark. Sister's fingers feel like lapping lagoon waves as they run through her hair again and again, soothing in their repetition.

'I wanted to help,' says the girl. 'I really did.'

'It's over now,' says Sister.

'They didn't tell me how.'

'They didn't tell you because they don't know either.'

'But that's not fair.'

'It's not, is it?' says Sister, and now her fingers part and straighten, the girl feeling a familiar tugging on her scalp as she begins to plait.

'Is Fija going to die?'

'Perhaps.'

'Because I couldn't help him?'

'Perhaps.'

'What?' wails the girl. Fresh sobbing.

'You're wiping your nose all over my skirts,' says Sister soon enough. 'Please stop.'

'It's not fair,' says the girl again.

'You mustn't be angry about it. It is what it is. The sadness repeats itself across the waves.'

'You heard that from the song.'

'It's true though, isn't it?' says Sister, but she herself does not sound sad. 'Women are the source of life. They are a bridge from the other world to this one. But the bridge is very long, so long and dark that we can only see one end of it. Most women look one way, but you, your sight was taken from you in this life, so . . .'

'So?' begs the girl.

'When Mother took you in to old man Fija's room,' says Sister, 'what did you see?'

The girl doesn't understand the question. She thinks for a long time how to answer, and then says honestly, 'Nothing.'

'One day, then.'

Fija dies and becomes nothing and Sister becomes a young woman and the girl an adolescent, and that promised day of comprehension eludes her yet. Across the years Sister conspires to bring her to where she is claimed to be needed. The adolescent keeps her silence in hope that they will relent, but this in itself is greeted as some form of message.

They will not let her be blind.

They refuse to let her be blind.

Around them now is a smell of smoke so overpowering, and yet beneath it, undeniable and unignorable, the scent of cooking, of roasting.

'Why?' wails the wife, her voice so harrowed with grief the word is barely formed through the tears. 'Why?'

'She has come,' says Sister to the wife, soft, repeating her words. The shrieking of the wife lessens, and then there is frantic scrabbling across the earth. The hem of the adolescent's skirts are grabbed, and she feels unbound hair tickling the tops of her feet.

'Please,' says the wife hysterically, 'tell me what is the cause of this? Can you see? Is it some ghost tormenting me for its own amusement? Am I victim? Please? Can you see?'

The adolescent cannot answer.

'Or have I brought this upon myself? Is this punishment? What have I done? What essence have I offended so? How can I atone? How? Tell me! Please!'

A way distant, a man snarls: 'Away, you! Away!' There follows the stomping of feet and a flurry of large wings.

The tugging on the adolescent's skirts grows fiercer.

'Is it the spirit of the Chiyo grove?' says the wife. 'Does it think us desecrators? We had it pacified before we took wood from it, we thought it safe to use. It cannot be because of that! We had it blessed and sanctified!'

The shells the adolescent wears as a necklace rattle against one another with the pulling of her clothes. The wife's voice drops lower into a hiss almost, her depths revealed in her desperation.

'Is it because of what I did?' she says. 'You know. You can see. You know what I did. Is it because of that? Is that sin what drew the spirits to me, all these years waiting? It is! I see! Forgive me! What can I do to make them forgive me, to make them spare me? I'll, I'll, shave my head, I'll raise a cairn of a thousand stones, I'll—'

On she speaks, maddened, and, oh, the pure, heartbreaking agony in her voice. It is terrifying to the adolescent. To be clung to as though she were the sole outcrop of land in a sea beset by an unending typhoon. The adolescent wants to run, to be a child once more that she might hide behind Sister, but that will never be again. Sister is there, always there ready to bear witness, foremost of those awaiting. All of them silent and awed around her, willing her, willing her, and still the wife is broken by the passion of her lamentation. Still she pleads for mercy with the intensity of the burning, still she claws at the adolescent's clothes, and no one is coming to relieve the adolescent, to tell her what to do, and now the wife finds a new level, starts offering up fingers and strips of her own flesh in appeasement, and the adolescent can bear it no longer. She speaks as they want for the first time.

What she says – murmurs – is, 'That will be enough. No flesh. No blood drawn. The cairn. The hair. That will be enough.'

There is silence all around. Long heartbeats of it as her judgement is heeded. Then the adolescent feels the hair upon her feet spooling and then warm flesh, a brow perhaps, charcoal dry upon her toes.

'Thank you,' utters the wife, and does so again and again and again.

In her voice is a piteous earnestness, a maniacal gratitude, and the adolescent can do nothing but stand there and receive these things knowing she has given false medicine to the woman. The shame wrings her innards, and still the wife persists in thanking her, over and over, and each kiss upon her feet revolts the adolescent anew. Eventually, Sister comes and coos the wife away. The adolescent is left shuddering, hoping she can return to solitude. That, her duty done, they will at last leave her be.

But what she has done is change things irrevocably.

'She shivers,' says a man.

'It's them,' says a woman. 'They move her.'

There is a low sigh of awed agreement that seems to come from every angle. Enough of them to drown in. The true pain, however, is withheld until she and Sister are walking home, hand on elbow. A monkey chirrups above, agitated or joyous. Sister has such pride in her voice, shaming enough that it blinds even the sightless.

'You see them now,' she says, overjoyed and oblivious. 'You spoke to them!'

The adolescent wants to cry. But neither can she bring herself to confess to Sister why she spoke, and so the words wash over her as they go, meaningless as colour.

Now that they know she has awoken, they craft for her a headdress, somewhere between a hat and a wig. All she knows of it is that it is big and wide and heavy, hard to balance, and either dry grass or dead hair tickles at her neck constantly.

This headdress is the anchor that binds her to what she has become, for they have awarded the adolescent a title alongside it.

Now, they call her yuta.

She who sees.

PART IV

The Two Heavens as One

Chapter Twenty

The heat, the heat. Even indoors, even in the shade, skin clammy and yet mouth dry, and all so formal; vestments of silk sticking, a constant sense of peeling with any motion, body contorted into the dignified pose with all weight resting on the heels tucked beneath thighs, strain on the knees threatening to tear, between calf and hamstring a pressure vile and viscous.

But maintained, always maintained.

'Captain Inoue, humbly I submit myself to your judgement,' said the samurai before Goemon, his hands and face pressed to the floor. 'My actions were unforgiveable. By loosing upon the Yoshioka without command, I have failed you unequivocally. I beg of you a chance to atone: my immolation through seppuku is hereby offered, should you be so merciful to grant me such.'

The samurai forced his brow down further. He could not have been more than twenty. Goemon watched, kept the immaculate façade.

'Raise your head,' the captain said eventually.

The young samurai did so hesitantly, a ghostly residue of

his brow and the bridge of his nose left upon the varnished hardwood beneath him, fading quick.

'I ordered you to loose,' said Goemon, with low and utmost conviction. 'Understand this. There is not a thing in this city I do not command. Therefore I gave you the command. Repeat this.'

'Sir?'

'Repeat.'

'You gave me the command.'

'Indeed,' said Goemon. 'And it was a fine shot. You fulfilled your duty exact. The fate of the slain Yoshioka was entirely of their own determination. There is no need for punishment or atonement here.'

The samurai threw his face to the ground once more, honorific gratitude spilling from his mouth unchecked. Goemon let the man speak his submission and thanks until he had satiated himself, and then ordered him to be about his duty. The young samurai left backwards on his knees, shuffling out through the doorway, which was closed by unseen hands behind him, and then Goemon was alone.

A sort of ashen amusement took him. The mercy of the damned thus extended.

He let it pass through him, counted thirty heartbeats of stillness in his bearing before he called the Goat. The old samurai, when he appeared in the doorway, found his captain's manner inscrutable:

'Bring him up.'

It was the lowliest of Goemon's men who had brought Musashi to the cells the night before, this done on instinct before they had considered that their charge had not been proclaimed officially a prisoner. There they had stood in wordless debate on what to do with him, unwilling either to insult or to trust, these hard men with harder weapons at their side growing silently flustered, refusing to take an authority they had not been granted. Musashi, exhausted, had eventually crawled through the low door of the wooden cage of his own volition, collapsed upon the mat there and slept immediately.

The Tokugawa samurai duly reached a compromise: they kept the door of the cage open, but stood guard outside it the night long.

At some point someone had come to tend to Musashi's wounds with a soldier's sympathy. He had with him distilled spirits with which he soaked a rag to rub upon the grazes on Musashi's face and arm, then peeled open his slashed calf and doused it thoroughly, grinning all the while at Musashi's hissing and writhing. A needle and a thread closed the wound, a crude technique that Dorinbo would have scorned, and then Musashi was left to sleep once more until morning.

And now in that morning, marked by scab and bruise and suture, he felt ecstatic.

His body ached whichever way he tried to sit or lie, and this was the spur of his joy. His wounds prodded, his stitches picked at, the pain magnified and pleasing; all of it proof of what he had achieved, of whom he had beaten, the knowledge of it burning sunlike within him, and heliolatrous to this he sat.

He hoped that through the mortal veil Akiyama's spirit, wherever it may be, appreciated the achievement also.

Rage had driven everything after he had found the pale-eyed samurai's body. A day had passed in a blur of pulsing moments. There had been no words, no reasoning. There were only things to do. He had hacked the sleeves from his jacket and the kimono beneath, both liberating his arms for unhindered movement should any further ambush appear, and more than this because he had simply wanted to hack, to cut. The sweat sliding down his bared arms had felt as the temperature of blood and the thought of that was invigorating, and, having entered the city anonymously, driving the shortsword of one of his perished assassins into the wood to pin his challenge up, felt equally fine.

Then came Seijuro's reply. Had Musashi not been sodden with his fury the language of it would have made him laugh: *Adept of the sword, Seijuro Yoshioka of Kyoto, commands the masterless Musashi Miyamoto to present himself for a duel.* 'Commands'! Commanding, as though Seijuro had some compulsion or control over Musashi. The pompous Yoshioka scion perhaps bred to assume so, perhaps never denied or contradicted before in his life.

Perhaps never even had to wait for something, and in that his undoing.

And it had worked! He had laid the smug Lord-King low, made the smug Lord-King lay himself low, and then Musashi had forced his mercy upon Seijuro. Had made the man choke on glorious clemency. Proved himself better before the eyes of those watching, a humane victor.

How could they, all of them, fail to see the fallibility of the Way now? That morning, the logic of it was flawless. The conjecture immaculate. The worth undoubted.

Fearlessly he met the gaze of the samurai who eventually came to escort him from his cell. Every further man he passed on the way he looked square in the face, trying to gauge the impact of what he had done. He saw not much of anything, but then here was the source of the scourge. That every face turned to him regardless was enough; his eyes bright as crimson moons above his lesions.

Musashi expected a public hearing, perhaps out beneath the sun in the courtyard. Instead he was commanded to climb a ladder up to the second floor, and from there led to Goemon's personal chambers. The Goat was waiting by the door, leaning on his sword. He held his hand out for Musashi's own longsword. When it was surrendered, the old man cast a grim eye over the shambolic state of it.

'A pair indeed,' he said, and then slid open the heavy door.

Goemon's eyes had Musashi's immediately, the captain sitting rigid, cross-legged. The room around him was militant, sparsely lit, large windows being indefensible in case of war or siege and so only a row of arrow-slits let the sun in. The ceiling a matrix of hard black beams like the intersections of armour, the floor beneath it just as callous. No decoration present, no vases, no paintings or tapestries, no potted plants, nothing save for the crest of the Tokugawa ensconced paramount on the wall behind the captain. Each of the three inward-facing leaves varnished proud auburn, inset into the black regal and dominating.

On the floor was a platter of food: a bowl of rice, another of miso broth and two slim fish grilled unto cremation. Goemon gestured to Musashi that it was for him. With neither comment nor thanks, Musashi strode over, sat down and began to push the food into his mouth. The rice was old, the soup bland and lukewarm.

The captain said nothing at his lack of manners, watched him gorge in silence. At no apparent signal he picked up a black velvet bag from his side and withdrew what lay within: Musashi's shortsword.

He leant forward and carefully placed it equidistant between them. The steel of it was murky in the dim light, a leather cord wrapped as crude grip around the weathered wood of the handle in place of the cultured cloth that had once been there, that long lost to rot.

'Found in the street,' said Goemon. 'Now returned.'

Musashi did not move for the weapon, gave it no more an interested glance than he had the captain, continued eating. He felt Goemon look closer at him, begin to study.

'You are very young,' the captain said. 'I had not heard the name Musashi Miyamoto prior to two nights ago. You possess no renown, neither a house nor a master, and nor are you the prodigy of a rival school. I have to therefore confess to some degree of surprise that the scion of the Yoshioka bloodline would consent to duelling you.'

Musashi kept his eyes upon his food, said nothing.

'It is quite an aptitude for chaos you seem to possess. Might you explain your reasons for this debacle, this whole series of the events – the incident on Hiei also?'

A sliver of green onion was stuck to Musashi's lips; he sucked it in, swallowed, then dug into the rice once more. 'Not my reasons.'

'Then you lay the blame of instigation upon the school of Yoshioka?'

Musashi grunted. The fish now held his interest, clutched between his sticks and then its head sucked right off.

Goemon clucked his tongue. 'Sir Miyamoto, I understand you may be suspicious, but I would take it as a courtesy if you would deign me the gift of a conversation. You in turn understand that I have the full authority of my most noble Lord Tokugawa within the boundaries of this city. I would likely be commended in Edo for having you tortured to death in the name of quelling unrest and restoring peace. Instead, I feed you, have your wounds tended, not worsened.'

Musashi's chewing stopped for a moment. 'Can't remember the last time someone called me Sir Miyamoto,' he said.

'I wonder why that would be. Rags in the silken city, a brutish temperament in the heart of all culture. You do not belong in Kyoto,' said the captain, and his fingertips met their vague reflections upon the varnished floor, eyes down to them and then up to Musashi. 'In this, I think, we are alike.'

'Did you not just say it was your city?'

'I'd raze it flat were I permitted.'

There was conviction in him, gaze distant for a moment as though he were already beholding pillars of smoke bisecting the sky. He found something in it, a sudden inspiration, and he turned to Musashi and let loose with a long stream of language, a brogue so thick it spewed from his mouth like fog, formless and mystifying, Musashi understanding but one word in three, one word in five, and seeing this Goemon grinned wider, spoke faster, threw fresh incomprehensible idiom out with the joy of a man mid-congress.

'There,' he said, softening, slowing now, but still a world apart from how he had spoken before. 'That was how I was taught to speak. Them, the true words of my father, and, oh, how many the moons I've yearned to speak as such again. But here, for you, I'll use the polite form. Culled and clipped for softer ears. Yet even this, here in this city, this tongue too base. Every word of mine I have to twist. To them that live here, all things that aren't of Kyoto, they aren't no thing at all. Improper. Fraudulent. I learnt that but quick at the time of my arrival. All the people yonder in the streets heard this voice of mine, thought me a farmer. Started calling me the "Rice Humper". All of them, carpenters and spinsters and the coolies who lug the shit barrels about. Do they mean I just lug bushels, or do they mean I thrust my cock into them? This I haven't scried, and like as not I never will. But these the sorts of minds abundant here, in the beams, the foundations. This, Kyoto.'

'I've never heard men speak as you before,' said Musashi. 'From where do you hail?'

'Province of Mutsu.'

'Where's that? Michinoku?'

Goemon laughed blackly: '"Michinoku". Another thing that's done around here; so too in your southern heart I see. "Michinoku". Half the country dismissed with one little word. Hundreds of leagues of land, a dozen realms of storied history and character, but no. Everything north of Edo: Michinoku. Only Michinoku. Where the snow is. Where the Ainu are and the Yamato blood falters. All truth ignored.'

'I meant no slight upon you.'

'No one ever does, ne'er they damn well do,' said Goemon. 'But always there it is, just seething away behind the eyes.'

'If you're of the north then, of Yutsu—'

'Mutsu.'

'—of Mutsu, why is it Tokugawa's crest you sit before now?'

'There's a tale and no mistake,' said the captain. 'Clan of my birth: the Date clan. Centuries my family in service to them, and the Lord of my youth was the most noble Masamune Date. One-Eyed Dragon, as we called him. Pulled his own eye out in his childhood when rot took it – is that not the Way manifest? This I'd kithe to any man round here who doubted the samurai spirit of the north. Trusted bannermen of the Date, we Inoue, enfeoffed upon the rich plains of Mutsu and the privilege mine of riding in the personal guard of my Lord. This, how once I was cherished . . . Were you at Sekigahara?'

'Yes.'

'Of the west?'

'Yes. Ukita.'

'Must have been no more than a child, you, then.'

'I killed a man in a duel,' said Musashi. 'One of theirs, the Yoshioka.'

'Is that so?' said the captain, but he was preoccupied with his own circumstance, dismissed the boast. 'A chance that you and I have met before, then, or at least shared a horizon once of a morn. The clan Date swore allegiance to my most noble Lord Tokugawa, rode to that valley together. Fine day. Not for you, as like, but for me . . . For our clans, for our cause, a fine day. Then the aftermath. The reassessment. The Date were allies, but allies only have worth after centuries, do they not? A union born of war is perilously fragile at the war's end . . . The north there looming unknown. Untrustworthy. Intolerable to my Lord Tokugawa, so to planning: an exchange of the bannermen between the clans.

'"A show of unity and strength" were the words spoken most, over and over, "fresh brotherhood fostered" and the like, but the tactic was clear. And respectable. Take the man you think enemy's sword away, put your own to his throat. The Lord Date could not refuse. Tokugawa had the numbers on him, and other more enduring allies still. Therefore . . . Ahh, the thing I'd like to scry most is who was it exact that put forth my name? Was I of such renown and reputation that the Tokugawa demanded me, or did the Date think low enough of me to consider me expendable? Which truth softer, which truth finer to my ears?

'It matters not. A score of us went south, made our vows. Scattered quickly, sent to separate posts the length of the country so that we'd not form some little faction canker-like in the bosom of Edo. Me, the last to be designated duty, and thus' – and now his brogue vanished, snapped back into the rigidity of the Kyoto tongue – 'here I am demoted so, a captain of alien streets that loathe and mock me where once I ruled a swathe of land from the mountains to the sea as I saw fit, using words comfortable to me.'

There was a melancholy mirth on his face. Musashi pulled a fish bone from his teeth and wiped it upon his thighs.

'In your estimation this makes us alike?' he said.

'We are both outsiders here, are we not?' said Goemon.

'But you follow what you hate. Why? Do you see any future for yourself here in Kyoto?'

Goemon did not answer.

'And it will lead to what? Your head on a spike. If you stay here, then, you are complicit in your own annihilation. Why not renounce Tokugawa and return home? You think he cares the slightest whether you live or die?'

'I would not expect him to. This is service.'

'That is the Way, and the Way is a lie forced upon us all,' said Musashi. 'Here is what I have learnt: true strength is in independence, not in having men to do things for you. A babe can summon its mother to tend on its every whim with a single wordless cry – that is what all Lords are, truly, and you must not empower them in their weakness with your acquiescence.'

'You are saying that my most noble Lord Tokugawa is a weak man, then?' said Goemon. 'A bold thing to do in a stronghold of his men.'

'Weak, incapable, unworthy,' said Musashi, 'all of these things he must be, and all Lords, for anyone who wants to tell others what to do is inherently unfit to be followed.'

'And presumably you offer yourself in contrast?'

'I felled Seijuro Yoshioka. I felled a half-dozen of his men. Myself. Me. Because I chose to, and it was I who wielded the sword. Thus, this victory has infinitely more meaning than Tokugawa's triumph from his distant inviolate saddle at Sekigahara.'

He meant it. At that moment, he truly meant it.

Goemon looked at him curiously. 'But how did you earn this victory?' the captain asked. 'Take your sword then, as example; this sword that lies between us now. Did you earn this with your independence? Did you dig the ore and smelt it and forge it yourself? Or what of the rice you are eating now? Did you grow it for yourself?'

'Those are insubstantial things of no worth.'

'Those are the things of the greatest substance.'

'You're wrong,' said Musashi, slashing the air with his chopsticks. 'Look at Seijuro. Thrall to the Way. Where is he this morning? Where is the code he believes in? Do not waste your time doubting me – I am honest. Ask your questions of the Way instead, for that is the abomination that will claim your life. Can you even explain to me why it is you follow?'

To Musashi's surprise Goemon thought about it, then spoke honestly.

'Imagine a hundred men in a line,' he said. 'There is space between them. The first man carries something precious. Let us say it is an icon of glass, and he must toss this icon to the next man in the line. It sails through the air, perilous and fragile, and then is caught. What was valuable before becomes even more so, inherently, thanks to that risk. It could have been shattered, but survived. And that value magnifies as that man tosses it to the next man, who tosses it to the next man, and so on and so on. Accumulating countless merit yet still as easily broken as it was in the air that first time. Immeasurable, precarious worth.

'I am the hundredth man in the line. The icon is the name Inoue, and it is falling in the air towards me now. I must catch it and pass it on, lest the lives of all those men also be for naught. I cannot be the one to let that happen. I cannot be the one to shatter it, for when I die I shall have to present myself before all those men of worth and account to them my failure. That I cannot bear.'

'But that death will be hastened if you continue to follow,' said Musashi

'That is the way of things,' said Goemon. 'I had the privilege of being born samurai, of being born Inoue. My fate is what it is.'

'So you are content to die?'

'Never once have I found my dinner bowl wanting, yet the calluses upon my hands are born not of the field but of the grips of swords. This luxury I did not question; it would be a cowardly man indeed who acted thus and then reneged upon the hardship.'

'That does not answer my question.'

Silence from Goemon.

'Do you not see?' said Musashi. 'The only people who would call you coward are men in the exact same place as you, who could suffer the exact same fate. Unless we smash this idiocy that binds us, limits us, and start anew. Otherwise we're no more than, than, men in a mire, pushing each other down by the shoulders, content in the fact that those around us have an equal mouthful of shit when we could all of us be free of it entirely. That is why I came to Kyoto. To scour it out from the heart. The Yoshioka its embodiment, and now they are humbled. Now they are ended. Let all in the nation take that as proof, and let a better realm grow from it.'

It was spoken aloud then for the first time. The thing of worth he had envisioned in the winter months tending to Akiyama, the thing that he had now achieved. His pride was boundless and golden as the sun that he felt shone within him, but the captain looked at him and it seemed, just for a moment, that of all things he might actually laugh.

'Ended?' was all he said.

'Ended,' repeated Musashi hotly.

The room, though, was cold and hard, and the word seemed if anything to possess a sort of anti-reverberation. It was both there between them, and nothing. Goemon stared at Musashi through narrowed eyes. Stared as though he were trying discern the extents of a mirage in a distant haze, and how silence could be the most pressing inquisition, the most invasive.

'Let Inoue be damned,' said Musashi, for attack was always preferable to parrying. 'Live for Goemon. It is that simple.'

Goemon Inoue turned his head slightly. 'Does the name Miyamoto mean nothing to you? Do you not fear the inquisition of your ancestors beyond the Sanzu river?'

'Miyamoto is *my* name, and in these rags, in the blood I shed, I am honouring the one member of my family I value.'

'This, presumably, includes pushing statues of the Buddha onto your foes?'

'It wasn't a Buddha, it was a Raijin!' said Musashi, and then he glowered as he realized the ridiculousness of the statement. 'And it was not my intention to do so.'

Goemon let amusement pass again across his face for a moment, and whatever empathy Musashi had gained for the captain vanished as though it had never been. He realized the waste of trying to reach such a man here in his sombre crypt of a room. His topknots. His swords. His Tokugawa livery. The outrage spiralled ever outwards.

'Am I captive, or have I liberty?' he said bluntly.

'What are your intentions?' said Goemon. 'I speak now in the interests of Kyoto. There must be peace. Another lawless incident such as last night is impermissible.'

'I will do as I will do.'

'Your feud with the Yoshioka.'

'This fight was of their choosing, entirely them. They started it years ago, and I ended it last night.'

'Again, you seem to think that this is somehow over,' said Goemon. 'Were it not for my intervention, your head would be up on a spear over Imadegawa avenue. You cannot deny this. And you do know Seijuro has two younger brothers, no? That the four or five men you killed last night are but a fraction of the whole? What of them? Do you think they will politely accede to you the rights of the victor? Or will they speak of vengeance? Does that not daunt you?'

'Daunt me?' said Musashi, angry, goaded, the sun within scorching wrathful and every syllable felt so utterly. 'I'll not leave, not if it's unfinished. Not until what I came for is achieved. They started this and if they continue I will not stop until they're all humbled at my feet. And all the world will know that it was done in my name, that it was not a clan, not a Lord, not a family that felled the Yoshioka – me. Musashi Miyamoto, enemy of the Way, the one man truly alive in the realm of the willing dead . . . And when they see my victory, know my name, then they will know which is the superior path.'

Goemon said nothing, but Musashi saw in the captain's eyes a sudden intensity, something piqued, and took it for a challenge, an insult. He tried to think of something further to say, when through the arrow slits the sound of a commotion disturbed them. Noise in the courtyard below, an inchoate roar of masculine confrontation that was soon quelled and then defined by one voice screaming above the others, furious, utterly furious:

'Outrage! Outrage!'

Chapter Twenty-one

Hard of brow and wide of shoulder, Denshichiro Yoshioka, and he also gifted of a supreme set of lungs. His voice so loud and so fierce the edge of it was almost like paper ripping:

'This is unforgivable! Outrage! I demand justice! Where is he? Bring him out, bring out the captain so that he can beg forgiveness!'

Goemon peered unseen out of an arrow loop, assessed the situation in the courtyard before he emerged. Denshichiro had with him two dozen swordsmen of the Yoshioka, they arrayed for something more than shouting, sleeves of their tea-coloured jackets bound up and the material a vivid green in the morning sun. They were outnumbered by men of the Tokugawa, these carrying bow and spear, yet the men of Kyoto stood defiant and dismissive of any threat.

Tadanari Kozei was with them. He alone wore his sleeves loose, something less than total conviction on his face. The bald samurai stood there and watched guardedly as Denshichiro stalked back and forth in fury, found his way back to his refrain.

'Outrage!' Denshichiro howled again and again, face reddening, hands clawed, and yet bellowed with such a perfect honesty and belief that Goemon found it remarkable. 'Outrage!'

The captain could delay no longer, though he was tempted to see just how long this display could be sustained without faltering. He took all emotion from his face, and stepped outside with measured steps of authority.

Denshichiro's eyes bulged at his emergence. 'At last!' he said. 'Account for yourself, Inoue! Four of our men slain last night at your command! What gives you the right to spill our blood, the blood of Kyoto itself? Outrage!'

The captain spoke coldly: 'I was merely fulfilling my remit to keep the peace in the name of my most noble Lord Tokugawa, he being the high protector of this entire country, Kyoto included. The duel was lawful. Everything afterwards, however, was in violation of it. Your men were given clear orders to cease and disband, and refused. Thus I ordered them killed.'

'Lies!' said Denshichiro, the volume and intensity maintained flawless. 'They were not interfering with any man of the Tokugawa, but still you slew them! They were ridding the city of a masterless vagrant, in fact, doing your job for you, and yet you chose to kill them! This your scheme no doubt to bring us all under the yoke of Edo!'

'The yoke of Edo is already upon you,' said Goemon. 'Do not suggest otherwise, Sir Yoshioka. Perhaps if Seijuro had beaten that masterless vagrant, I would have not had to intervene at all. But, alas . . .'

It took a moment for Denshichiro to recognize the jibe. He all but shuddered, voice now threatening to crack as an adolescent's might.

'You dare to speak thus to me?' he spat. 'Belittle the Yoshioka? The things I could do to you with these swords of mine, you son of a—'

'Denshichiro,' said Tadanari to his side.

It was not this that silenced Denshichiro, but rather the emergence of Miyamoto from behind Goemon. A pointed entrance, arm draped casual over the hilt of the longsword at his waist. A silent countenance so studiously obnoxious Goemon found himself marvelling at it in the same black way he had marvelled at Denshichiro's anger.

Yet for all the broad swagger, close as he was the captain could not avoid noticing the stiffness of Miyamoto's body, the way the young man tried to hide the tenderness of his wounded leg.

Denshichiro saw only his enemy – both his enemies together. He drew in a long breath as his mind performed the obvious calculation. 'Collusion!' he shouted, finger darting between Goemon and Miyamoto. 'Collusion! I see the plot now! Insidious!'

'I am the thrall of no man,' said Musashi.

'Horseshit!' said Denshichiro. 'Clear to me now! You, you sit on your knees and you guzzle down whatever the Tokugawa fling into your mouth!'

'Miyamoto speaks the truth,' said Goemon. 'He is masterless. Does he look as though he has enjoyed any form of luxury lately? But know that to prevent a reoccurrence of last night's chaos, for the sake of the peace of the city I am placing him temporarily under protection.'

'Shield him, then!' said Denshichiro, and he sank down now, veins bulging like leeches upon the muscles of his arms, hands going for his swords. 'We'll kill him, and we'll slaughter every last one of you cursed intruders to get—'

'Denshichiro!' snarled Tadanari, and he grabbed Denshichiro's right wrist, checked the motion.

This was interesting to Goemon. Younger, broader, stronger, it was clear that Denshichiro could have shaken Tadanari off if he wanted to. Yet the young samurai relented. He shut his mouth and stood straight. Tadanari held the grip until he was well past certain that his ward was in control of himself once more.

There was utter silence in the yard. Tadanari released his hold, and then, isolated in such fierce attention, slowly walked to stand before Goemon. There he dropped into a low and grovelling bow, arms by his side, legs straight, chest parallel to the ground.

'Most honourable Captain Inoue,' said Tadanari, 'humbly I apologize for the words of the young master Yoshioka. I beg you consider the duress he is under, distraught over the fate of his brother. He is not of sound mind this morning, and I implore you to temper your response with that compassion in mind. We are at your mercy, as we always are.'

Goemon said nothing. Tadanari could not rise until his apology was acknowledged. The captain stood there for some time, and watched dew beads of sweat shatter and arc the paths of lightning bolts down the dome of the Yoshioka master's bald crown.

Magnanimity the greatest insult, complicity the greatest humiliation.

Eventually the captain had had his fill.

'There is no insult here, Sir Kozei,' he said. 'I, however, ask that you disperse now, and return to the grounds of your school where you can grieve in private. A harrowing day for the Yoshioka, no doubt, to be so exposed in front of the city.'

'Humbly, I thank you for your consideration, Captain Inoue,' said Tadanari, and he rose with his eyes closed no doubt to hide the hatred there, Goemon supposed, opened them entirely neutral. 'We obey your just ruling.'

'Now heed me all of you present,' said Goemon, voice loud. 'This ends here. Peace must reign. I am the enemy of chaos. Unsanctioned bloodshed cannot be permitted. Unsanctioned violence—'

'Do you understand,' said Denshichiro, speaking to Miyamoto, looking only at the ragged swordsman, 'how little time you have left? My sword has already claimed your head.'

Miyamoto, equally focused, equally young: 'I felled the first thing that your father squirted out, I am in no fear of the second.'

'Wretched vermin, your eyes I'll pull out afore I raise your skull up above our gates to rot alongside the Foreigner's.'

'See the blinded thrall who cites his ambush of a wounded man as a shining triumph. You'll find me harder to—'

'Silence!' shouted Goemon. 'You will heed the word of his most noble Lord Tokugawa! Unsanctioned madness is intolerable and any violator—'

'Then sanction it,' said Denshichiro.

Goemon blinked. He allowed the tip of his tongue to emerge and dance across his lower lip. 'I . . .'

'Sanction it, Captain,' said Denshichiro. 'I formally challenge Musashi Miyamoto to a duel of the sword. As a samurai, as a citizen of Kyoto, that is my right, is it not?'

'But the law . . . I . . . It is not for . . .'

'Do you accept, dog?' asked Denshichiro of Miyamoto.

'Of course.'

'Then come die now.'

He jerked his brow towards the street, and Miyamoto matched the hatred in his eyes, started to walk hobbled on his sutured leg, but Goemon put a hand on his shoulder, pulled him back. 'No!' he said with little decorum. 'This cannot be!'

'It is my right,' said Denshichiro. 'Do you not know your own law, Inoue?'

'But—'

'It is my right.'

'I consent,' said Miyamoto. 'Let me go.'

'No,' said Goemon, eyelids like the wings of dragonflies. 'No. There has been enough chaos to last the summer long and—'

'Do not deny me what is lawfully mine!' said Denshichiro.

Goemon yielded: 'A . . . a fortnight, then. I sanction a duel between the two of you in a fortnight. That is an auspicious day, the ides of the month. The serenity of the heavens and the harmony of the earth shall not be disrupted on such a day.'

'I demand vengeance for my brother now!'

'A fortnight,' said Goemon, and he raised a hand. The men of the Tokugawa made their presence known, arrows nocked to strings but not pulled taut, not yet. 'I concede that you know your law well, Sir Yoshioka, and this the compromise I offer. Accept.'

Denshichiro's eyes went across the courtyard replete with longbow and able arms, then back to Goemon's: 'A fortnight, then.' And on to Miyamoto's: 'Before the Hall of the Thirty Three Doors at the hour of the monkey. Do you accept?'

'I accept,' said Miyamoto.

'It is sanctioned,' said Goemon, his tone reluctant, his expression that of the defeated. 'This shall be made public.

Should Miyamoto fall foul of some violence before this, the integrity and honour of the school of Yoshioka will be sorely tarnished.'

'I know the Way,' snarled Denshichiro, jerked his chin at Miyamoto. 'He's the dog that needs leashing.'

'Two weeks and I'll bite your throat out.'

'Enough,' said Goemon. 'Disperse.'

Denshichiro might have said something further, but again Tadanari marshalled him, took him by the shoulder and led him away out the gate. Neither one of them bowed or even looked back. Their men followed them, into the street, where they marched away before the ruins of the fire-claimed block opposite, ashes and charred beams still waiting to be cleared.

Goemon turned to Miyamoto: 'This then what you wanted?'

'Good enough,' he said, rolled his shoulders, and in his eyes Goemon saw the infallible certainty of youth.

Miyamoto left then, limped the opposite way the Yoshioka had gone. Goemon followed him to the gate, its frame still damaged, its roof still bare of tiles, watched him go. He could feel that the Goat was hesitant to approach him as duty dictated, either fearful of his mood or vicariously embarrassed at the outwitting of his superior.

'You may draw near, Onodera,' he called.

The Goat hobbled over on his ersatz cane. Tentatively, he asked, 'Are you not dispirited, sir?'

'No more than my usual temperament.'

The Goat nodded, then stood in silence for ten heartbeats just to be certain. When he felt he could speak once more, he said, 'We could have slaughtered them there, sir. There was open threat and insult.'

'No, we couldn't,' said Goemon, 'not here. People would forget those, and remember solely that the massacre took place on our ground. It would become part of the history of Kyoto, an irreversible and sordid legend of the Tokugawa.'

'They'd be wrong.'

'It wouldn't matter. What is a city but its people?'

He smiled blackly. The Goat did not understand his captain's apparent pleasure in saying such a thing. Instead he followed Goemon's gaze to Miyamoto, the tall swordsman's shoulders visible above the crowd, lurching with his limp like a ship on the ocean.

'Ragged odd cur, that one,' the old samurai said. 'Forgive me for the intrusion, but I could not help but hear him ranting in your chambers, sir. A lot of words, but the weight of their meaning I would not wager against a single chicken feather.'

'He is young.'

'Young in a way I wasn't. Can't believe he of all people bested Seijuro. Can't believe that nick on his leg is all he suffered.'

'A fortnight will see him stand right once more,' said Goemon as Miyamoto vanished from his sight. 'Mark him well, Onodera. Do you understand me? Mark him very well.'

Chapter Twenty-two

Inevitably today upon the streets an added fascination, and a lurid one at that. People still bowed, still yielded the way for the Yoshioka, but once they had risen from their deference their eyes followed after. What ideas coalesced within their multitude hearts, Tadanari wondered, found himself angered by. Things they should not be feeling. Things he should not be feeling.

Denshichiro marched at the head of the two columns, proud, oblivious. Tadanari glared at the back of his head, and what was within him waxed whiter and whiter. The very moment the gates of the school closed behind them, Tadanari grabbed Denshichiro by the back of his neck and dragged him away, heading for a place of even further privacy.

'Fool!' he hissed in his ear. 'Have your wits fled you? Provoking the Tokugawa like that! Idiot!'

'Do not talk to me in such a—'

'I'll talk to you as you damn deserve!'

Alongside the hall of the dojo and the long buildings of the barracks they went, heading for the inner sanctum. Those they passed knew to keep their ears closed, melted to the sides, scarred men in rough vestments of sparring or lower-born girls in jerkins carrying basins of water, each bowing regardless, ceding, heeding nothing.

'Your brother lies stricken and you seek to join him immediately!'

'We must have vengeance for the men they killed!'

Grip held tight around the neck as they broached the cloistered domain of the elders of the school, an enclave within an enclave where Tadanari and the Yoshioka family had their residency. At the centre of it was a private garden, a secret little oasis nestled between high walls and the boughs of green trees and bushes, in which lay a bordered bed of grey sand immaculately raked into pristine ridges.

Into this were set thirteen boulders, some smooth, some pointed, some set with moss or inlaid pattern of the earth's creation. They were placed with expert artistry around each other so that only twelve could ever be seen at once from any level angle. At the head of the bed was a wide low wooden dais, a place for seated contemplation towards which Tadanari gave his ward one final push: 'Sit.'

'I will not,' said Denshichiro, rounding on him, voice unchecked. 'This is not a time for passive things.'

'I ask you not to be passive. I ask you to think. Is it not enough that you scandalize the school with your violation of Hiei, you go and insult the Shogunate?'

'What is there to think about? Enemies abound. We face them. We take their heads. That is the Way.'

'The Tokugawa are a hundred thousand men, two hundred thousand. Who knows their numbers? And what are we? Less than a hundred, spread across the country. Balance that math in your head, before you go threatening to kill their captain in their garrison.'

'They turn my stomach, the thought of them here in this city.'

'Mine also. And because of you I had to bow to them, boy.'

Tadanari was speaking in rare coldness. Denshichiro's voice dropped to match it.

'You fault my reasoning?' he said.

'I question its very existence.'

'I acted as I ought to act. They slew four of our men. That is unforgivable.'

'And we shall not forgive them. But neither can we punish them.'

'You scorn me but in confronting the Tokugawa I act no different from you.'

'What do you imply?'

'Do you think I do not know it was you who armed those provincial men with the gunpowder, organized that whole incident with the fire? Your insidious little arsonists hidden amongst the lowerborn too—'

'Where was my hand visible in all of that?' said Tadanari. 'Nowhere. Nowhere. No aggressor wore the colours of the school.'

'Then why attack them at all?'

'It was no attack! The black powder was not placed in the garrison itself; I did not want to kill them. I was reminding the city of who it ought to hate.'

'What is the difference?'

'Can you not see?'

Perhaps Denshichiro could. Perhaps he was just being obstinate, but Tadanari doubted it. The young man stalked off cursing, feet heavy on the dais beneath him, stood and looked over the boulders and the bed of sand until he remembered that was what Tadanari wanted him to do. Then he simply turned away with his arms crossed.

In this rage he stood as a true inheritor of the Yoshioka line. Rage of this sort as deep within their blood as the span of their shoulders or the hardness of their brows. Tadanari had seen it and where it led. Had seen it break Naokata, father of Seijuro, father of Denshichiro and the truest friend Tadanari had known.

It was just after the War when Naokata had first shown signs of his illness. Struck with a convulsive fit the likes of which he had never had before, and yet by the time the moon had grown anew he had experienced the spasms twice more. A pain in his side developed, just below his ribcage on his waist. Grew so vivid that soon Naokata would talk of splitting himself open, a merciful seppuku of sorts, certain that whatever it was was a solid thing like a tick or a leech lurking there, something that he could pull from himself. Mad words uttered under the throes of agony.

Within six months his muscle had faded into nought but skin that hung across him like a shroud of leather. All that ability, all that strength that he had worked for decades to hone, hollowed out so thoroughly and so ruthlessly. Tadanari had wanted to weep when he looked upon Naokata in his repose.

Then, of course, Captain Inoue had come on behalf of his master. Had traipsed around the hall of the finest school in the nation with his foolish iron hat on, halfway between a warrior and a diplomat and without the dignity of either. Had acted as though the divine mandate of the Son of Heaven did not grant the Yoshioka immutable precedent as sword-masters to the Shogunate. Had demanded, should the Yoshioka care to audition for what was rightfully theirs, Naokata present himself in Edo; no less than the head for the head of the nation.

Tadanari had raised a bureaucratic tempest, sent missive after missive to Edo pleading for time, hoping that some miracle would manifest and Naokata would suddenly and immediately regain his health. He found Edo exactly as the mould their man must have been cast from: not dismissive, not angry, just completely impassive to the absence of the true inheritors.

From his bed Naokata demanded to know what was happening, and when he might expect to receive the Tokugawa honour. Tadanari had to tell him the true state of things eventually. Immediately Naokata had demanded his horse to be saddled, as though he would ride to Edo himself. A skeleton's conceit, Seijuro and Denshichiro had hoisted their father up onto his mount, the thumbs and fingers of their hands encircling his shins entirely. Naokata had steadied himself, brought his whip down on the flank of the horse. The beast did not notice, so feeble was the blow. Again, again, Naokata pinned immobile like some harrowed, withered child trapped in the boughs of a tree, fists no more than an irritant where they pounded.

There the Yoshioka rage ignited, but the first time Tadanari had seen it unleashed without any care for others witnessing it. How his heart had broken for the indignity of it all.

The decision was made to send Seijuro instead. The heir apparent. Whatever happened in Edo, Tadanari didn't know. Seijuro never spoke of it, and when he eventually returned he wore the composure of a man who had been shamed, or who felt it keenly. He returned too late, though, a month or so after the final missive from Edo had arrived. Naokata had made Denshichiro read it to him, the Tokugawa informing the school of Yoshioka that they had deigned to favour the Yagyu instead.

'Precedent!' Naokata had howled as Denshichiro had, of outrage in the Tokugawa garrison, only with all the force and vigour excised, no more than a look in the eyes and the sound like a boot pressing down upon a lung. 'We have the precedent!'

This was his great and final anger, what undid Naokata as a man, as a human being. Those were his last coherent words. He endured for a perhaps a week after, a collection of organs in a bed clawing at strands of light and nothing more. Then he died.

That the rage of the Yoshioka. More and more apparent with each generation. Tadanari had considered Naokata's father Naomitsu completely inscrutable; Naokata had told him that the old man had a taste for drink, and only then what had lain within had been exposed. Naokata himself wore it as a clam wore a pearl, a secret that those who dived deep enough knew about, yet only truly prised from him when everything else had been hollowed out from within him.

But in Seijuro and his brother manifested so clearly. Seijuro undone on the Rendai moor because of it, and now Denshichiro seething and seething and Tadanari let him, knowing that the only thing that would expunge the anger would be itself. He forced it out of himself in turn, felt the pressure lessening on his throat, his chest.

'What news of Seijuro?' Denshichiro asked.

'He is out of the city already, sent to healers at the Hozoin temple. If he lives – if – he will be crippled, however. Lamed arms, if not a malformed posture. He will no longer be able to wield a sword, and thus he can no longer lead the school of Yoshioka.'

'Then I am now the head.'

'Yes,' said Tadanari. 'And now you must behave worthy of that stature.'

'I am acting in a worthy manner. Are not the Tokugawa to be hated?'

'They are. But you must not make hatred your entire definition; it is a vile and short thing to live in thrall to.'

'You read the reports of our men in Edo just as I did. The Tokugawa are going to move the capital there. This aberration cannot come to pass.'

'It cannot be stopped.'

'Our prestige will be lessened.'

'Lessened, but not entirely vanquished. Skill will always be respected. Our school will continue to send our swordmasters out elsewhere across the nation, speaking in halls to Lords and samurai who will listen keen and attentive, and there they can start whispering against the Tokugawa. One man turns another, that man turns two, their sons are many and learn their lessons well, and eventually, though it may take generations, the numbers will balance out. Then the Tokugawa can be punished.'

'But I want—'

'Is not the concept of "I" itself against the Way? You bear the name Yoshioka. Your duty is foremost to that. You and I are bested. Accept this, bear the humiliation. We – the school, the Yoshioka, the Kozei – will endure long after you and I are individually dead, and that is the "we" that will prosper. Unless you dash all that attempting to seek a selfish, violent satisfaction you cannot achieve.'

The thought of being denied enkindled the rage anew in Denshichiro, eyes flaring, lip curling. Tadanari said, 'And you have Miyamoto. As the Tokugawa are to us, we are to him.'

That quelled him. His eyes went distant, no doubt images of tremendous violence calming him. It in turn brought forth the swordsman in Tadanari, the teacher who had made countless assessments of the ability of men. He asked Denshichiro earnestly, 'Can you beat him?'

'Of course I can. You doubt me?'

'The sword free of thought cuts with the keenest meaning. Are these not your father's words?'

'I know them.'

'So sit,' said Tadanari, indicated the dais, the bed of sand. 'Consider.'

Denshichiro obeyed. He sat on the dais and assumed a meditative pose with his legs entwined, soles and palms upwards. This the posture of inner peace, and yet upon Denshichiro it looked a crossbow primed to fire, his shoulders taut and coiled. Diligently he set his eyes upon the foremost boulder in front of him, stared waiting to see beyond, to see nothing.

The boulder he looked at was crested with a knife-ridge of obsidian, set like a sundial so that at noon either side would be illuminated equal but here in the morning a shadow cast on the western face, black and blacker, differences in the black that Tadanari knew would guide and lull the conscious mind into egoless contemplation.

But no peace in Tadanari. Not the obsidian he looked at now but rather Denshichiro. Could he truly be taught? Seijuro had only earnestly listened to Tadanari's urgings for meditative discipline only after he had returned from Edo and whatever disgrace he had faced there, when he had been made aware of something lacking in him.

Even then what good had that done? Provoked by the simplest trick, and now maimed.

And here, Denshichiro. Denshichiro who had heard that haunting final tirade of his father's, the toneless invective against the Tokugawa, which had degenerated into no more than a rattle of pure pathetic anger, feeble and heart-destroying. What chance for him to forget that? Or in those hisses had he found the definition of his nature calcified, had his fury made indelible?

Denshichiro turned from the rock, looked up at Tadanari: 'I already know the answer here. Twelve of the thirteen boulders only visible – no man can achieve everything. Humility, things like that. Must I sit here longer?'

'Do you really think,' said Tadanari, 'your father, and his father before him, would have sat here for so long, if the answer was so simple?'

Even if he didn't, Denshichiro turned back, rolled his shoulders, stared into the obsidian once more.

Patience. Patience a virtue.

Chapter Twenty-three

Unleashed from the Tokugawa garrison, Musashi walked the streets of Kyoto on his wounded leg. Into the crowds that swarmed as thick as he had ever seen he went as an individual, and he went in search of evidence of his achievement.

The day before on the way to the Rendai moor he had barely noticed the city around him, focus entirely on the duel. It overwhelmed him now. Between the buildings the heat was channelled, billowing, a swaddling embrace like a pillow across the mouth, the nose. Musashi felt drops of sweat begin to collect in his eyebrows, taste the salt of it on his lips. Unrelenting, turning corners expecting the relief of a breeze and finding none, hundreds of fans in hundreds of hands fighting hundreds of battles in vain.

Around him colour: brocades and silk curtains covering the entrances to storefronts, myriad designs; there three white ume plum blossoms atop a field of red; there a great crane with its wings flaring atop a striped ivory-blue background; there a pattern of small circles arrayed around a larger one, black on green. These family or guild crests, their trades oblique, knowledge of what they purveyed like a code of the city, proof of belonging. Ribbed paper lanterns of white and red hung unlit from roofs of jade-green tiles beneath which courtesans draped in panchromatic layers of silk passed. Even the heat itself seemed to add a shade to all that he saw, a subtle glow of reflection from stone or metal making his eyes feel as though they were burning.

All these tones a disparate collection that in their fleeting incongruence never truly coalesced into a whole, like a shattered handful of coloured glass atop a mound of ashes. The underlying colours, the primary colours of Kyoto as it seemed to him, were plain and lowly: the greys and deep blues of the common hemp clothing of the lowerborn, beams of buildings, charcoal-black, smoke-hardened to protect against flame, dusty and tan the earthen streets starved of rain.

A sense of containment began to fester, at his throat, at his ribs. Each of the structures here was of two storeys and the thoroughfares no more than eight or nine strides across, the sky above devoured either side by cantilever ribs of eaves. Always someone looking down from beneath these, their arms draped across bamboo railings or fingers parting wooden blinds, they idly drinking or eating or simply watching, and every time his eyes met theirs, man or woman, they looked away, and then looked back when he looked elsewhere.

This was the wondrous golden city he had looked across from the slopes of Hiei?

A heavy gate lined with murderholes that obliged the thrusting of spears at interloping stomachs loomed, and he thought that he had come across what he sought. This marked the boundary to the higher wards where distant Lords held estates they seldom visited and samurai bodyguards congregated before it, their eyes as murderholes also as Musashi approached them.

He cast his arms wide and told them of how he had beaten Seijuro, and he expected from these swordsmen at the very least a form of martial respect. Instead they jeered him, jeered his clothes, his wounds. Swords restrained by mandate of peace upon the streets, voices their only weapons. Accents as disparate as the extents of the nation but the words the same.

Jeered him for abusing the sanctity of the duel by arriving late.

Jeered him for running from a dozen men who would have surely cut him down.

Each of them oblivious of the arguments that Musashi repeated hotter and hotter, that it was better to live, that he was not afraid of death for if he was he would not have attended the duel at all, that he fled because the sole point of fighting was victory and victory alone and, this achieved, he had nothing more to gain upon the moor of Rendai.

How they tore these reasons down, or rather repelled them without sinking any cognizant part of themselves into them, spat that by his reckoning the rabbit was worthier than the tiger, that if he believed what he said then surely he ought to abandon the sword entirely and resort to European knavery, arm himself with pistols alone and put holes in people at inviolate distance and proclaim himself the mightiest warrior the world had ever known, a charlatan champion.

He looked at them all, at their topknots and their swords, and he did not understand. How could this be? How was it they were failing to see? He felt some part within himself tarnish. It was as though he were back in his exile with Jiro, that he was nothing, that he was the black and formless waters once more.

Seething, he left them by their iron and oaken barriers as solid as ever.

A cumulative aggravation now swelled within Musashi, born of every step he had to clip for the passing of another oblivious of him. The braying laugh of some drunk drifting from above, the sounds of an old man sucking his sickly sinuses into the back of his throat, the shriek of a young woman entreating people to come and sample her family's konyakku gelatin. Sweat now in the corners of his eyes, stinging, the wiping only exacerbating, a snarl threatening to break across his lips.

He rounded a corner and there revealed to him was the vast form of a pagoda that towered upwards. Five tiers of symmetrical beauty, the sheer size of it stopped him in his place and he gazed up at it. He wondered how many years it had stood – decades? centuries? – and then thought of all the earthquakes, all the bolts of lightning, all the great fires and all the wars that could have possibly occurred and yet had failed to consume it in that span of time.

He had marvelled at it from a distance, and yet how different the pagoda seemed in such close proximity. Near like this Musashi could not avoid how the tower dwarfed him, both in stature and in everything that it stood proudly athwart to, and suddenly he could not bear to look at the beautiful thing, and he turned from it as the eye shirks the fullness of the sun.

A street away he happened across an exhumation; a great shrine brought out into the clearing of a square and peeled from under layers of hemp sheets. The shrine was made to be borne aloft on shoulders, yokes long enough that four score men would share the weight. A beautiful thing hung with bells and cymbals, the wood lacquered vermillion, a sloped roof from which a spire styled like a pagoda thrust upwards and around the eaves of which a slender dragon was carved clutching its orbs of wisdom. The shrine itself aureate, torii gates and whorls of clouds dazzling.

There were murmurs in the crowd, first of wonder and admiration, then of the memory of the last time it was seen and those who had carried it then. Calls of good-natured rivalry began, men and women claiming that theirs would be grander, would be raised higher, and those who owned this shrine calling back they were undoubtedly wrong. This, they said, was the pride of Daikokuya ward and nothing else could compare.

To things of this sort were the people drawn, falling into bands and teams possessed of purpose, inspired. A street away from the shrine wide circles of tanned hide were being hung across laundry poles. These the skins of taiko drums awaiting lashing to the wooden barrels of the instruments now being rolled or carried out into the sun, soon to be washed and polished until they gleamed. Already men were practising the strokes they would play, beating out the patterns on the floor, on tables, on walls with the heavy sticks, remembering how it ought to go, how it always went.

Tentative, the rhythm: *attata-attata-ta-ta attata-ta-ta.*

A joyous industry waking and coalescing, and through all this emerging beauty and effort Musashi walked, ignored in his rags and his wounds. Two boys ran around him wielding drumsticks as swords, oblivious of the real ones at his side. He asked a passing man what was occurring, he with a bolt of vivid blue cloth in his arms. The man bowed, spoke demurely, no recognition of Musashi in his eyes.

'Lord Regent Toyotomi's commemoration festival at the

end of the month, sir,' the man said, 'seven years ago to the day he died.'

He bowed again and quickly left. Musashi watched him go, rubbed sweat from the corner of his eye.

Dead men and dogma; all he had achieved ignored for dead men and dogma.

'What of Akiyama's head?' asked Ameku in the evening.

Musashi sat at her feet stirring a pot of rice gruel over a hearth. The blind woman was sitting at a crude loom, a mat half-woven already. Yae and she had sought and found work and lodgings in quick time.

They were in the slums of Maruta, where Akiyama had said they would find shelter away from the Yoshioka, a low and ignoble place. Musashi had brought them down from Hiei before the duel. The Yoshioka had attacked the mountain before and it did not feel safe to him to return there, and more than that he found the monks now repulsed him.

The ordained brothers had proven themselves as selfless as merchants. They had come to him like carrion birds in the wake of the Yoshioka ambush, had taken Akiyama's remains for cremation and then had demanded payment. Only when Musashi had surrendered Akiyama's horse in lieu of coin had they lit the pyre and sung the prayers that needed to be sung.

But this was to be expected. The true insult came whilst the flames were blazing and ash was upon the air. One of the brothers had come to speak to Musashi, an old man all taut motion as he strode up, his feet bare and calloused and on his head the square-topped white cowl of a warrior zealot.

'You!' he said to Musashi, exultant. 'A great thing you have done, repelling desecrators in defence of what is holy. Six men you overcame! A true feat, the will of the heavens no doubt! Something higher moves your hand!'

Musashi had rounded on him, held his palm up before the man's face and hissed, 'This is mine and mine alone, and what moves it is my will alone, you old fool.'

He spoke with the profound fury of betrayal. In that small temple prior to the Yoshioka ambush he had knelt and prayed to the heavens, prayed with the kind of fervent earnestness it embarrassed him to think about, and in reply immediately the heavens had sent men with swords to kill him. If that was how they chose to communicate, then he was done with them. From here on only on himself and himself alone could he rely, he saw this now, and so he had no more time for cruel or absent things, or those that chose to worship them.

But one more facet of a flawed world. The outrage spiralled ever outwards.

The old monk of course had hardened like frost forming and he went on to level a tirade at Musashi, commanded him to open his mind to the Teachings and accused him of being complicit in his own ignorance and damnation, and Musashi watched the pyre and heard not a single word of it. He left them all behind. Left them to chant hollow names and to live on dead slopes.

'What of Akiyama's head?' Ameku asked again.

Musashi rapped the wooden ladle on the rim of the pot, scratched at the back of his neck. Eventually, he admitted: 'It did not occur to me to . . . There was nothing I could do.'

'Ugly,' she said, and shuddered, 'to be not whole. Like an animal. Terrible.'

'I honoured him in a finer way,' said Musashi. 'Wherever he is, he will appreciate that.'

'He is nowhere.'

Musashi had no answer. Yae came in with a pail of water which they set to boiling for tea. Ameku continued to work, the machine clacking percussive and slow as she wove the tatami cover. Her feet pressing pedals of the loom, her hands hooking rushes onto levers, her whole body in rhythm.

'How is that loom?' he asked.

'It is . . .' she said, and that familiar pause as she tried to translate herself, a slash in the air with a hand as it frustrated her, 'shit, utter shit. This tatami will sell for nothing. You tell me in the capital, many machines, many money.'

'Well, do not fret. We have coin left over from trading the horse to those greedy bald fools, so we won't starve for the next few weeks.'

'"We"', pronounced Ameku.

'Your meaning?'

'We get to Kyoto. Yae and me, here is good. Why do you stay with us? Want to stay?'

Musashi felt the weight of something like fingers at the pulse points of his throat, invisible things that stole his voice.

Ameku did not press. Her mind returned to other things, for she clucked her tongue and shook her head. 'It is a terrible thing, Akiyama. To do that to a body. Makes my skin feel cold, to think about it. The nothing beyond is the nothing beyond where the . . .' She did not know the correct word for soul or essence or spirit, and so she tapped over her heart. 'That is that, but the body – the body can be proper, can be made proper. Must be.'

'This, the Ryukyu way?' asked Musashi.

'Is it not the human way?'

'You did not much seem to like him whilst he lived.'

'Another swordsman,' said Ameku, and Musashi could not tell if this was a jibe at him as well. 'But the dead are the dead, and things like this are of more . . . are more important, no?'

Her words brought his uncle Dorinbo to mind.

Always, Dorinbo had said, the dead must be treated with complete propriety. The dead, after all, were the most helpless.

Yae spoke up as she poured dried tealeaves into clay dishes. 'I liked Akiyama,' she said. 'He tried to talk to me, when you were away in the winter. But I was scared of him, and I ran away. I wish I hadn't, now.'

'It is not a matter of . . .' said Musashi. 'The Yoshioka are not going to yield the head to me. Not that Denshichiro.'

Ameku's fingers pinched a reed into a noose. 'They have it still?'

'Up above their gates, as he said it. There'll be twenty of them there at least. There's no method of standing against that number, and I'll—'

For the first time then, it occurred to him that Denshichiro might bring that number of men to their coming duel. He had barely escaped Seijuro's bodyguard when they elected to swarm him, and then Musashi recalled the anger and hatred in Denshichiro and wondered if there would be a duel at all – if they all would not just simply rush him from the off. Their honour nebulous.

How would he triumph? How would he survive?

He sat in grim contemplation. A mosquito landed on his irritated ankles and tried to feed where others had. It was fat and slow and Musashi slapped it, and a rivulet of watery blood coursed a thin trail towards his sole.

Ameku shared his mood, but her thoughts ran as cyclical as the machine she worked. 'Up above the gates?' she said. 'Beneath the sun? Up to the sun, in this heat . . . Left to . . .'

Again she did not know the right words, and again her hand irately conjured nothing in the air. But then why should she know these kinds of words? What sad world was it where rot or decay or putrefaction of a severed stolen head should ever have to be translated?

Their world. Their Way.

Musashi looked at her, and wished that she would sing this night instead of shudder. Sing for him, and him alone.

'I'll get his head back,' Musashi said. 'He will be at peace. All will be.'

Ameku did not answer; Yae did not understand.

Musashi left them, went outside and there by the light of an oil lantern stripped both his swords and sharpened them.

This was familiar and finite and gave him satisfaction.

Chapter Twenty-four

Tadanari knelt with a book before him. It was wide as the blade of a shortsword was long and fat with hundreds of sheaves of paper, the front and back covers made of thin polished cedar. It was a thing of decades past and decades to be.

Upon each page were handprints and names all in shades of brown and red. Each a solemn vow of the adepts of the school, cast in their own blood. Tadanari remembered cutting himself upon the left forearm and letting the blood drain into a shallow tray. The dojo hall dark, past midnight at the solemn hour of the ox with the elders watching, the hand pressed against the page designated his and his name written in the blood left over, all the while uttering vows of utmost loyalty spoken so truthfully it felt as though his sternum was being wrung.

Each and every member of the school was recorded there. Himself, his son Ujinari, Seijuro, Denshichiro, friends current, friends gone.

He came to the page of Nagayoshi Akiyama. With great care he began to cut the sheaf of paper from the annals. No one had thought to remove it until now. When he had done so for a while he did no more than kneel there and hold the page in his hands, contemplated the palmprint and the lines therein to the sound of distant cicadas. In truth he had come here to the archival room like a pipe to the lips, the private garden too hot beneath the sun and he in search of solitude from the upheaval of the past days.

As his eyes languidly traced the heel of Akiyama's thumb, something occurred to him. He summoned a servant and told him what he wanted, and within a short time the man returned carrying a small chest of dark persimmon wood. He set this down before Tadanari, bowed with his brow to the tatami mat, and then departed and left the master alone once more. The bald samurai unhooked the latch and cast the hinged lid back.

Inside were all the missives Akiyama had sent to the school upon his hunt of Miyamoto. There were three dozen, more than that, perhaps even fifty. Faithfully he had written at least once a month, and on each and every one of the folded sheaves the wax seal stamped with the two characters of his name remained unbroken.

Tadanari dug his hands in and scattered a handful of them across the floor as though he were sifting through sand. All words were dust eventually, as Saint Fudo taught, but even though he knew this, recognized this, accepted this, the fact that the severed head of the writer of all these unheeded thoughts was set above the gates of the school caused a strange melancholy to momentarily seize Tadanari.

It was not that Akiyama had not deserved to die for his betrayal, it was that perhaps it should not have been so callous and so sudden. Or that perhaps the retribution ought to have been by Tadanari's hands, and not by Denshichiro's. The young killing their elders had always struck him as an abomination.

Or that perhaps, ultimately, he should have recalled sending Akiyama out on his duty, that perhaps if he had done so he might have understood Miyamoto better, that perhaps Seijuro, whom he had groomed so meticulously, would not have found his ruin.

Here now a chance to rectify that. Tadanari picked one of the missives at random and broke the seal. He began to read. Akiyama had exquisite calligraphy. It was a report of Miyamoto intruding upon a seppuku, and Akiyama's observations therein. Another letter opened. Now Akiyama was upon the southern coast certain he would encounter his target soon. Another, and the stanza of a poem about summer's equilibrium, which Akiyama hoped might be read and appreciated at some evening gathering at the school.

On he read, and over the course of an hour Tadanari began to learn of this strange masterless savage, this Musashi Miyamoto, until something intruded upon his solace. A sound, close and immediate and violent. He listened, and recognized it as the whip and slap of bamboo, again, again. It persisted until he could ignore it no more.

Tadanari rose, went and sought the source of it. Outside in the courtyard an adolescent novice was on his hands and knees stripped to his waist, being lashed across his back by an adept of the school with a training sword. The blows he struck were vicious, ribbed sword scything through the air, the crack of impact across the knobs of the spine sharp but the acolyte bore it all. He gave no sound but the merest of whimpers.

The dead eyes of Akiyama oversaw all.

Tadanari tried to ignore the gaze.

On, the adept struck. It appeared at first to be a matter of corporal discipline, but something seemed odd to Tadanari the longer he watched. There was no measured rhythm to the adept's strokes, his hands clutched too tight around his ersatz lash. The novice's eyes were red, his teeth clenched, lips murmuring something unspoken.

Tadanari stepped outside. The sunlight made him squint. 'What is occurring here?'

'Master Kozei!' barked the adept, snapped his body down in a low bow. The acolyte too swivelled in the dirt, forced his brow to the ground, his back a glistening tiger's hide of scarlet welts and sweat. 'Punishment!'

'What infraction warranted it?'

'Young Yuzen neglected his duties this morning, sir. Water was not in the troughs for the adepts to wash with when they rose. Furthermore his area of the barracks was unkempt.'

'I sullied the premises of the school and hindered the adepts egregiously, master Kozei,' said Yuzen, speaking into the earth. 'This is unforgiveable. I begged the most honourable Sokuemon to help me atone for this, and graciously he has obliged me.'

'He came to you?' Tadanari asked of the adult.

'He did, sir.'

'How is that you failed to notice the infractions yourself?'

'I—' said Sokuemon, and nothing further.

'Did you not wash this morning?' asked Tadanari. The only response he received the lowering of Sokuemon's head. Tadanari did not care about a matter of simple cleanliness, all attempts at it foiled by sweat in this weather regardless, and yet the man could not answer, which meant he hadn't. Routine shattered. Tadanari turned his attention to Yuzen.

'You,' he said, 'is there a reason for your dereliction?'

He too was reticent.

'I ask of you a direct question, and expect an answer.'

'Answer!' shrieked Sokuemon, raised the bamboo sword needlessly.

'Forgive me, Master Kozei,' babbled Yuzen. 'I am shamefully negligent and worthy of punishment, that is all.'

'You were the one who bore Seijuro's stool to the Rendai moor, were you not?'

'That honour was mine, sir. Undeserved. Undeserved.'

'And are you aggrieved by Seijuro's fate?'

'Of course, sir,' said Yuzen, hesitant, heard no response, wavered, attempted. 'No.'

Tadanari looked at the pair of them. Neither looked back. Eventually the elder of the school of Yoshioka stepped back into the shade, gave a small gesture with his hand: 'As you will.'

Yuzen brought his face up from the floor and spread his back level for Sokuemon to resume striking. This the adept did with the same zeal as before, little hisses of more than punitive diligence escaping him, droplets of sweat rising from the acolyte's back with each blow. The pair of them men, or man and boy who walked the Way, which was the Way of emptiness and denied the existence of what might lie within a human heart. Disquiet, shame, grief . . . These ought not to be felt.

But to strike and be struck were acceptable emotions, acceptable desires. The paramount two perhaps; Yuzen and Sokuemon here channelling, paragons of a sort.

Tadanari watched them because he understood the necessity of it, watched until blood was drawn and Yuzen was forced down to his elbows, and yet behind his level eyes a worry. Something was afire in their collective spirit – was this not the reason for his own queer mood, his sympathetic musings to a traitor? – and he began to wonder how deep the malady ran.

The steadying hand, the steadying plane; this Tadanari knew he needed to be.

For them.

For himself.

He called them all to assembly in the dojo hall. Light of the late afternoon sun streamed through the mullions of the westerly narrow windows above, half the hall lit brilliantly and half in shadow; the adepts and novices knelt on the eastern side gifted halos of loose hairs and skin albescent, the faces of those on the west difficult to discern.

Uniform, though, the tough, dark sparring clothes, the wooden swords laid before each, the expressions.

'Turbulent,' said Tadanari, his words careful and slow. 'Turbulent, these past few days. It has come to pass that Seijuro Yoshioka, first son of honoured Naokata, grandson of honoured Naomitsu, is no longer able to lead the school. This you all know. He is not, however, dead – I beseech you all to visit shrines of whatever creed you follow to pray for his health. Perhaps fate will bestow a miracle upon us. Such an occurrence withstanding, however, Denshichiro Yoshioka, second child of honoured Naokata Yoshioka, has assumed leadership of the school, as is proper.'

'Hail Master Denshichiro!' shouted the most senior of the adepts there.

'Hail!'

All bowed to the ancestral shrine of the school, which was set into the wall. An effigy of a red Shinto torii gate, a fat rope woven of women's hair and two vases of pink hydrangeas, and beneath this were hung portraits of the previous heads of the school. Two of them faded, the wood showing through the paint where the decades told, one vivid still, scowling fresh and unyielding.

The mood amongst the men was as Tadanari expected it to be, faces still, the façade striven for, and yet something beneath this: the eyes not inquisitive or attentive but guarded, spines rigid out of more than the protocol of posture.

'Perhaps,' he said to them all, 'the idea of defeat the likes of which Seijuro suffered was unthinkable to you. Nestled deep in the depths of your delusion. Shed your conceptions of individual invulnerability. The storm comes. Branches are torn away. The tree stands resolute. I ask of you: what truly has changed?'

Silence, not one man wanting to risk exposing ignorance. Expected, respectful. But still uneasy. The heat in here, penned between door and wall, all but pulsating. Tadanari wished for autumn, wished for winter, but summoned all he could to quash the throttling grasp of it; advanced onto levity.

'Has our flesh suddenly become enfeebled? Hollow the arms we have trained so long? What of our ability – has that been stolen from us? Kappa sprites maybe, crawling from the river Kamo in the night to suck it straight out of our sleeping arseholes?'

A simple joke, something easy to affix to. As he hoped, the youngest novices were unable to keep straight faces at the crudity, and he turned on them now, pointed at the youngest boy he could see, hoped that the unchastened would lead where the taciturnly trained had long forgotten how to tread.

'You,' he said, and the boy assumed the dignified posture instantly, face hardened, 'tell me, why does the floor of this dojo remain earthen when we could easily afford all the wood and varnish we might need for flooring?'

Immediately recited: 'This dojo was built by the founder Naomoto when the school was ascendant. He could not afford such then. If upon earth was how he learnt it, than on earth so too shall we, master.'

'Good,' said Tadanari. 'A flawless answer, and flawless reasoning. All of you, remember this. Beneath you is the earth trodden by dozens of great men, who bested champions the length of the country, who taught Shoguns . . . Ashikaga Shoguns. This earth has not changed. This earth is still the same as it was a week ago. Know this. Feel this.'

Some, the younger, obeyed literally, palms placed broad and reverent.

'And what of the sword?' he said, drawing his longsword and holding it up so that the blade shimmered in the light. 'Is this now empty of the souls of my ancestors? Has this now no more worth than a sickle, than a fish-gutting cleaver? No. It is immutable. Still just as bright as before. Of its methods? Unaltered. Two hands still hold it, the right hand at the guard, the left at the pommel, the same as before. Find assurance in this.'

He pointed at three men, ordered them to stand, take up their wooden swords and assume the stance of combat. Around them he walked, pointing out their fine observation of technique to those still kneeling: the way they braced their ankles, the firmness of their forearms, the steadiness of the weapon in their hands. He bade all present to stand and do the same, to feel the confidence of familiarity.

'Has our philosophy changed?' asked Tadanari, walking amongst them now. 'Why do our longswords bear a shorter blade than other schools?'

'So that they are easier to wield close,' said the adolescent he patted on the shoulder. 'We break the guard, advance so that we stand hip to hip with the enemy, and then bring our longsword within his tract of shielding to rake or stab at artery or joint, master.'

'Exactly,' said Tadanari. 'This is the flawless wisdom. We are not spearmen prodding from range. We are not bowmen, cowards who kill with no risk to themselves. We are swordsmen. Swordsmen who stand close to our foes, close enough that our spirits meet and shatter theirs with the focus, the magnitude of ours. This is the wisdom that has bested men from the Yagyu, the Kashima-Shinto, the Itto. This has not changed.'

He set down his true swords upon a stand and took up a mock blade of his own, spread his legs and dropped into a stance before the original three commanded samurai. They in turn grew tauter, anticipating, moved to surround him. Tadanari rotated slowly between them, feet never crossing, moving his sword pointedly through many different positions: above his head, by his waist, braced across his collarbone.

'Where are you looking?' asked Tadanari, the question unnecessary but voiced all the same.

'At your blade, master,' said the man, the eyes of all three men following it unwavering.

'Why?'

'Eyes can deceive easier than steel. Feet cannot harm you. The blade is where the danger lies, and so on that we focus.'

'Indeed,' said Tadanari.

He darted forward suddenly at one of the samurai, knocked his sword aside and ghosted down the length of it until their bodies met. There Tadanari forced the edge of his own sword across the man's chest and turned immediately to meet the coming of the second man, tapping the point of his lunge away with a deft and almost imperceptible manoeuvre. The motion of his sword did not cease, lancing forward to run half its length across the jugular, before Tadanari swivelled on his heel and dropped to one knee in a slash that connected with the third man's thigh. Three lethal blows, had they been using steel, delivered in less than three heartbeats.

The students barked their respect. The pride Tadanari felt, as perhaps any swordsman did at the sensation of impact upon the palms of his hands, was carefully hidden from his face. He looked around at them all, saw them all now in the light, all eyes gleaming, all skin pure, and he mustered all the gravitas he could and put it into his voice.

'These are the fundaments of our Way,' he said, looking from man to man once more, encouraging, ensuring. 'Know that they are unchanged. Know that if you follow them with honest dedication, if you are prepared to offer the years, mastery and the serenity that comes with it shall be yours. Keep your heads and your hearts calm. The school has stood for a hundred years, and will stand for a hundred more should we behave properly, behave as men. Turbulent though this wave is, it has come and we must ride it. We must not kick against it, or worse yet kick up another one. Faith: have faith in what has come before. Have faith in the Yoshioka. Have faith, as I do, in the steady and just nature of Master Denshichiro.'

They, all of them in the light, shouted their obedience,

their joyful, emboldened obedience, and within his breast Tadanari felt only a hollowness.

He could not escape the mood. That evening Tadanari was sitting in the private inner garden of the school, stripped to the waist and his body slick with sweat. Before him in the bed of sand surrounded by the thirteen boulders was a tortoise. Idly he was tearing leaves from a head of spinach and tossing them down for the creature to eat. He watched its face as it devoured levelly, gnarled and grey with eyes implacably dark, and he envied the perfect stillness of it

Envied more than that.

The tortoise was a sort of mascot-pet of the school, an exotic oddity in a nation of sea turtles and river terrapins only. It had come from over the waves on a trader's ship long ago, from China or perhaps even further, and had been here for as long as Tadanari could remember. It looked exactly the same as it had the first time he had seen it in his childhood, its shell as broad as a man's torso, its step as calm and assured as the creeping of moss.

Implacable to time.

He fed the tortoise often, liked to feed it, and tonight for every leaf he gave it he took a swig from a clay jar of sake in turn. Stared down at his own bared chest and his stomach in bleak contrast to the unchanging creature. Moist and scrub with hair, repulsive for a moment, lined with the sagging of a skin apparently abhorrent of the muscle beneath. He pulled at it with a thumb and forefinger, staring with amused disgust at the length he could stretch it. An old man's webbing.

Another drink sucked through his teeth only heightened his amusement, smiling grimly at nothing. He was not enfeebled yet, far from it, but in him now the mourning of his youth, both wondering and knowing exactly where it had gone.

The sound of a door being slid open from within the building behind him caused him to tense; too late for the domestic staff, it could only be one of two people.

'Father?' came a voice.

'Here,' said Tadanari, relieved.

Ujinari came out into the garden, wide black trousers flowing like skirts, the tea-coloured jacket of the school rendered a kind of sienna by the lanterns.

There, Tadanari thought, *there*.

Distant youth, or youth that this night seemed distant, summoned. All his years spent travelling in the name of the school, to study other methods of the blade and then to prove the Yoshioka Way superior to them, he seeking Lords in search of swordmasters for their clans and armies. Imperative that he did this, he, Tadanari Kozei, for his blood was trusted more than any other and the Yoshioka themselves could not be seen to roam. They in Kyoto, always Kyoto, whilst he travelled from hall to hall after hall on Honshu and Kyushu and Shikoku, demonstrating cross-handed grips and the Strike of the Springtime Tide and whatsoever else was demanded of him.

On and on, raising esteem of the name Yoshioka, and meanwhile the name Kozei faltering. His wife Ejima waiting childless as he roved far across the country for all but a few days a year. In these nights they were granted they were as husband and wife ought, but no babe ever resulted. Ejima enduring in her solitude until she was old enough that another woman so bereft would have been called a spinster, and absent Tadanari growing older, too, no longer needing to shave his scalp.

Naomitsu died. Naokata inherited, and his first decree as head of the school was to adjudge Tadanari's days as envoy over. Talk of having proven himself a master of the Yoshioka methods and thus fit to teach within the dojo of the school, and so on, and so on, and yet Tadanari knowing it was born both of Naokata's loneliness for his friend and to relieve himself of the burden of the teaching he found onerous. Men like Naokata made solely to achieve, not to foster achievement in others. Tadanari did not care. The school was the school, what he served, and so back to the city he loved and to the woman with whom he was failing.

He and blossom-wilted Ejima now permitted the time, and yet propagation unattained. It is I, it is I, she would say, my meadow is stony, and he would sit there and see her tears and not contradict her.

Would sit there and think of a time down on forested Shikoku where a sickness had swept across the land, a hot swelling between the legs, behind the genitals. A realm of stricken men and women waddling to spatter the trunks of the vast trees with crimson urine, Tadanari these years later still revolted and fearful at the memory of that colour he emitted in agonizing ropes. Gory vandals, and what it was within him swelling and pulsating, and then gone overnight. Gone, and after the relief of its passing the worry that it had taken something with it, that it had hollowed some vital part, and now Ejima crying and begging him to forgive her for the failure she assumed was hers.

And he a man and she a woman, and so he gave her nothing more than silence.

Perhaps both of them faulty, perhaps one of them, perhaps neither. They were united in resolution and were rewarded: Ujinari. But no easy birth, not for a woman of Ejima's age. A night spent shrieking and howling and bloodied rags and cloths being taken out again and again in front of Tadanari, he waiting outside petrified by the sound. The midwife's tone was grave even as she informed him that the child had emerged, was of a healthy blue behind, but of the wife she would not say anything, would not meet his eyes.

Somehow Ejima lived. A week in her bed, and then she was up and holding Ujinari in her arms; a strong heart, a hale samurai spirit as the people remarked. Vital and loving of her child, and Tadanari was joyous as he saw her with his son, and yet the memory of the harrowing night of the birth lingered, led to the question what exactly was to follow.

She still had her monthly bleeding, was still capable, and yet the risk. The danger and the chance.

Would not a swordsman commit himself to death if he saw the chance to slay his foe at the same time? Man and woman, samurai both; they both knew themselves fundamentally to be no more than prisms, the multitude rays of their respective families converging in them, Kozei and Chosokabe, passed through them unified and focused and strengthened. The glass itself was unimportant. The light was.

Ujinari less than a year old, and she came to him one night without his asking and without her speaking. She was wearing his chainmail shirt, a gift that he himself had never worn, having never taken to the chaotic field of battle. She was swathed in it, her thin shoulders enveloped, not the first time she had worn it, and the eroticism of it he never could explain. The way the light shimmered down her side in seams, perhaps.

The point of her chin enveloped in the cowls at the neck. Soft hair over hard steel.

Absent all these sensations as they had lain down and coupled there in silence. His palms flat upon the tatami mats, arms locked straight, looking down at her with the chain-mail shirt hiked up around her waist, links of it rattling softly. He remembering the screams of Ujinari's birth, she in her eyes remembering the pain. No lust in them, no desire, yet still he thrust. No desire and no questions. Rhythmic and steady, a carp upstream. No questions, no questioning, the mail clanking cold and her skin beneath it warm, she sheathed in it like a sword, implement of life and death, and this their familial duty.

This unquestioned.

This what had to be done.

The second child, the conception of it a miracle really, grew for six months, came out already dead and dragged Ejima across the Sanzu river with it, and now Ujinari here a man before him.

Benighted, the centremost boulder in the garden's sand bed stood a pygmy monolith, its cresting ridge of obsidian a sharp steeple. Tadanari smiled, smiled at all that his son represented, and gestured for him to come and join him on the dais. Ujinari did so, slid his longsword out of his belt as he prepared to sit.

'You have your mother's hands,' said Tadanari, watching him. To him it sounded profound.

'You're drunk,' said Ujinari.

Tadanari shook his head dismissively, and then gestured for the longsword before his son set it upon the nearby stand. Took it with no decorum, pulled the blade out of the scabbard a hand's breadth and stared at it through one eye. He twisted it back and forth and the steel shimmered in the golden light. He remembered the moment he first saw it in the hall of the Forger of Souls. He remembered the joy of bestowing.

'This serves you well?' he asked his son.

'Flawlessly,' said Ujinari. 'I still cannot thank you.'

'Have you cut with it yet?'

Ujinari did not answer.

'Four years, and still the edge has not tasted blood. Men would argue whether that was the finest of swords, or the very worst.'

Tadanari meant it as no more than a statement to himself, a drunk reaffirmation of the state of things, and yet Ujinari took it as criticism.

'It would be inauspicious to cut simply for the sake of cutting,' he said. 'A bad omen, no?'

'Of course, of course,' said Tadanari, nodding vaguely. 'Wise.'

Ujinari calmed. Tadanari held on to the sword. He looked down upon the flat of the blade at the image of the sword of Fudo carved so masterfully there. Single-handed, double-edged, a bulbous pommel and an eldritch guard. Perfectly weird, befitting the otherworldly.

Houken, it was called. The Cutter of Delusions.

Ujinari saw his father's fascination with the engraving. 'I had a question about that, if I might ask it of you.'

'Ask.'

'I have heard say that swords so marked with Fudo's symbol are conduits, that men wielding them can call down his strength or his protection in battle. Do you know this to be true?'

'The only men who could answer that truly are those that have claimed to have felt it. I have not experienced such myself. Perhaps such a thing has occurred, but I would express scepticism.'

'Then why . . . ?'

'Why did I have it put upon the blade?' said Tadanari.

Ujinari nodded. Tadanari smiled at his son.

'Fudo is the patron saint of swordsmen, a manifestation of the Buddha's wisdom and wrath,' he said. 'He takes the form of a pale ogre that burns constantly with the flames of mankind's suffering, which he bears out of love and his duty to free us all from that which misleads us. His sword is the implement of this, and, when the saint passes the celestial blade through a mortal, the mortal is thus cleansed of his mire of delusions and enlightened.'

'Delusions,' said Ujinari. 'Greed? Ego? Lust?'

Tadanari nodded to each, and then he added, 'Permanency.'

Ujinari reached down to pat the tortoise as he thought. 'So the wielder of the sword is to act as Fudo, cutting such delusions where they find it?'

'It would be a rash and arrogant man who sets himself as the divine, compelled to cast judgement on other mortals just as flawed as he. A more humble and righteous goal would be to look at the image of the sword there upon that blade, and strive to cut these things from oneself.'

'Permanency,' repeated Ujinari.

Tadanari nodded. 'You and I, Tadanari and Ujinari, are fleet things. If we are extremely fortunate, we will see nine decades pass before us. Tell that figure to the trees, to the mountains, see how it compares. When you draw that sword forth and see the Cutter of Delusions, remember that it is not your sword alone. That there many of the bloodline Kozei yet to be who hold equal possession over it.'

'And that is why you deigned to give the sword to me?'

Tadanari did not answer. The sword of Fudo had driven his thoughts deeper, and he spoke of what truly occupied his mind: 'I want you to be honest with me,' he said. 'Do you think Denshichiro can beat Miyamoto?'

'He should be able to,' said Ujinari. 'But I did not see Miyamoto fight, so I cannot say for certain.'

'Seijuro was a finer swordsman.'

'He worked harder on his technique, but Denshichiro is stronger and faster, and will be prepared for trickery.'

'Trickery,' pronounced Tadanari, curling his lip. 'Do you know, I read about Miyamoto this afternoon, of what the Foreigner thought of him. Do you know what it is he hates above all things?'

'What?'

'Seppuku,' said Tadanari. 'Seppuku, if you can believe that. Let that tell you the sort of man he is. Opposed to the ultimate dignity. Men like that, you cannot reason with. Predict. And I saw him at the garrison of the Tokugawa. He is a giant. Slender and half-starved, but I do not think Denshichiro will have strength in his favour. Definitely not reach.'

'Tall trees fall the hardest.'

'Is he focused?' asked Tadanari. 'Is Denshichiro focused on the duel?'

'Yes,' said Ujinari. 'Yes.'

'You are making sure he is focused?'

'Of course I am—'

'You shouldn't have to be,' snapped Tadanari, suddenly

angry. 'He should be preparing of his own accord. Rock-headed fool. Your "friend". Why are you friends with him?'

'That's an odd question to ask someone.'

'Why?'

'Why were you friends with Naokata?'

'Naokata and Denshichiro are different. Naokata had focus, knew the Way. But Denshichiro . . . With his . . . Attacking Mount Hiei and . . . All his bravado unearned and . . . Why do you copy his ridiculous hair, that little sliver of scalp? You appear as some prostitute whoring himself out upon a theatre stage.'

Ujinari said nothing. He took up what was left of the spinach and held the leaves directly to the tortoise's mouth, its hard beak mashing away. Tadanari watched him, felt the bubbling encroachment of shame.

'I apologize,' said the father.

'I am not one to be offended over my appearance, and you are not yourself when you drink,' said Ujinari. 'What has set you in this black mood?'

'Getting old. Becoming a miser,' he said, trying to joke, but the sword of Fudo there in his lap, scything away to the truth. 'There is the third brother, Matashichiro.'

'What do you mean by that?'

'You sail away from the tempest, you do not set course after it.'

'I do not like the implication of that, Father.'

'Denshichiro, as the head of the school, cannot lose to Miyamoto. Cannot. We have already lost more than enough face with Seijuro . . . With this scandal upon Hiei, and the enmity of the Tokugawa . . . To lose again to a masterless man of no school, of savage technique . . . No. Irrecoverable.

Which Lord would want to learn those methods? Where the renown then? Fading out like some sputtering lantern devoid of oil. This school to which I have given my faithful decades of service, to which I have sworn you willingly, my son, I will not . . . I cannot let that come to pass. I refuse.'

'But you cannot simply pass him over to give the leadership of the school to Matashichiro.'

'"Pass over".'

The words were growled, and the tone of it set Ujinari looking around as though he were hunted: 'What are you thinking?'

'I think only of the school.'

'Father, are you mad? Is he not the son of the man you took as a brother?'

'Barely,' said Tadanari, 'I'll—'

'Have faith in him. He is preparing properly. He will defeat Miyamoto. Have faith.'

'The only man I have faith in is you, my son.'

'Then have faith in me. I vow it to you, when he takes the field at the Hall of the Thirty-Three Doors, Denshichiro Yoshioka shall make the school proud.'

Tadanari looked at Ujinari for a long time. Then he slid the sword back into its scabbard, handed it back to his son.

'I believe you,' he said.

The tortoise looked up at the pair of them. Spinach had ceased; no more manna from heaven, yet the abeyance of divine favour did not set its slow-beating heart to quailing. Off it walked on its even exile across the barren bed of sand, footsteps left dark.

Chapter Twenty-five

The calluses upon Musashi's palms were raw from training of the sword, and they burnt as he hauled himself up onto the roof.

It was broad and sloped and tiled with curved clay slabs that were warm still from the day. What lay beneath the roof he did not know. Some kind of store or artisan's workshop perhaps. He had picked it simply for the shadows that lingered in the alley beside it. The tiles sounded hollow beneath him, and he spread his weight and moved as quietly across them as he could, ruing every stumble and heavy misstep. The waxing moon was bright above, all but full, and he kept his body low to avoid silhouetting himself to any who might be watching from below.

Kyoto at night was quieted, but never silent. There was a mandated curfew upon all but a few designated wards and those venturing out upon the streets were scarce. Musashi heard the murmur of voices through paper walls or doors cast wide open in attempt to catch a breeze that wasn't there. The roof was alive with the vivid pleas of insects, lonesome and beseeching.

He had scouted his prospective path from the ground in the day and he moved quickly. His swords were at his waist and across his back hung an empty rice-straw stack. He passed from roof to roof easily, buildings built as tight as they could be in the confines of the city. A dog barked in his wake, no hiding his scent. Somewhere a baby cried out in response, once, twice, and then was silenced by the smothering of a breast.

Ahead of him rose the vast swell of a warehouse or a brewery of some sort. It was easily a hundred paces long, and its roof lay higher than the ones he was currently on. He stepped out and braced his weight with his foot on the wall and then scrambled upwards to grab for the edge above. The cut upon his leg protested, his ascent frantic and graceless, and when he had made it he lay sprawled upon the tiles feeling the throbbing of his calf beneath his sutures.

The injury worried him.

He had spent the day assessing himself, trying to think of some way that he might stand against the numbers of the Yoshioka. All the things unfelt in the wake of his victory were now felt, the grazes on his arm and face hot, one ear raw, knees swollen. He found, however, that he could move through the patterns of the sword well enough, that his forearms and wrists were fine, and that his legs were strong enough to brace him in the stance of combat for as long as he needed.

He could not run, though.

Walking was possible with but a slight limp, but running, true running, was denied him. The best he could muster was a lopsided lunging gait that would surely not outpace the Yoshioka should they choose to swarm him. He knew it would not heal in a fortnight, and so if he went to the duel he would be committed to facing however many of them that chose to attack.

There were no methods or techniques he could recall to aid him. His father Munisai had taught him mostly individual duelling form, and had spoken of the chaos of the battlefield as something survived through sheer physicality and luck; the man himself crippled in testament to this. No wisdom or technique there. Everything else Musashi had learnt for himself, or observed from others, and what he had learnt was that against multiple opponents the longsword was a desperate thing. His survival on Hiei and in the streets had been frantic and barely won. One edge, one point upon the weapon, to attack or to defend with it to leave your back exposed. A whirling flurry where surely his luck would expire eventually.

After twenty heartbeats the leg felt as good as it ever would, and he rose and crossed the expanse of the great roof, advanced half-crawling, straw soles spattering thuds upon the clay and hands grasping at the serried ridges of the tiles. The higher vantage afforded him a view across the city, and he saw the warm glow of a thousand lanterns light up the towers of pagodas and the tops of trees a hundred years old and the forms of crows alighted for the night.

Musashi swung himself down back onto the lower roofs of humbler structures. Ahead was noise. Ahead was Yanagi, the quarter of the licensed illicit, where men and women came in the evening to satiate whatever lust they so desired, be it flesh or drink or food or song or poetry.

He skittered along the rooftops of the quarter and he cast his eyes down to the street as he passed. He saw silhouettes lithe upon silk screens enticing, heard a miasma of wild delight, of voices joined in discordant but joyful song, of hands clapping along, of the deftly slapped twang of shamisen strings, of epicene poets eulogizing violet morns of spring, of a sudden boisterous cheer as a drunk man burst onto the street stripped to the waist and his nipples painted with ink, one red, one black. The drunk danced a dance of no pattern at all and his friends laughed and spurred him on, and if any of it had any meaning it was lost on Musashi.

Bamboo scaffolding encased and supported a building gutted by a fire. Musashi clambered around on the matrix of the lashed green trunks, swung his body out over the street and moved sideways, hand to hand and foot to foot. He smelt the stench of charcoal and ash mixed with the tantalizing grease of fish fat cooking elsewhere, and beneath him erupted the excited shrieking of women as a rising actor appeared upon a balcony.

The actor's face was white still from that evening's performance, streaked where his sweat had run across the hours. He had ventured out on a measured foray, designed to enhance his aura. He wore a broad-shouldered parody of a courtly robe, and he stood with one fist on his waist and the other holding a pipe to his lips in mock pompous pride, and as the women laughed he wiped his brow with a silken kerchief and then threw the paint-smeared garment down to them. The actor retired inside as the clamour for his token raged, and in the darkness above them all Musashi dismounted unnoticed from the scaffold.

On like a ghost, balancing on beams and the scabbards of his swords rattling where they glanced and twisted. On the edge of the ward he halted for a moment to catch his breath, checked the sack was still across his back and that he had not lost it to some unfelt snag. Over the raucous revelry, he heard a lower rhythmic noise. Not music, not song, caught his ear in its insistent steadiness.

A brothel window left open, a woman upon her back on lush tatami mats, the seven layers of her kimonos spread like the petals of lotus flowers and her body bared to the patron between her legs.

Here, a secret glance into that floating world so unknown to him, and Musashi could do nothing but stare for a few sordid moments.

Saw the way the man tensed his back as he thrust, the curvature of his spine, heard his hisses, saw the woman's unbound hair coiled upon the floor like the delineations of some chaotic map to nowhere. Her legs were around him and her thighs were white and the man buried his face upon her chest as he thrust, thrust again, he contorting like the penitent and the woman bore it all, looked up over his oblivious shoulder at nothing as he sought his ecstasy.

Musashi saw in them the fallacy of love and decried it to himself as he had done before, and yet he could not break his voyeuristic vigil. He looked at the woman, looked as well as he could not at her body but at her face. He saw the charcoal smudges of her painted eyebrows, even and placid, barely moving. Looked beneath them, stared, and saw too that she seldom blinked. That she held her eyes wide and sightless.

Wide and sightless, like the blinded.

It stirred thoughts in Musashi. Only then did he find that he could turn his back to it and advance, and neither of the spied-upon was aware of his intrusion or his passing.

He left wild Yanagi behind him, moved on to the desolate artisan wards and the company of cicada choirs once more. The well-ordered buildings of duplicate design and even roofing became as a road for him, and here he advanced so quickly in his hunched posture that he found his breath escaping him.

Drawing closer, drawing nearer.

The echoes of wooden sandals from below halted him. He saw the figures of two Tokugawa samurai out upon a placid patrol. They walked a guard of mere protocol, inattentive and unmindful of anything but what lay before them, and yet Musashi dared not move until they passed. His wariness of them and all like them was the reason he had chosen to forego the streets; curfews violently enforced. He held his breath and watched.

Their shadows danced upon the earth as the paper lantern one of them held up before him swung pendulously on a chain, and the spears they both held became as gnomons for this erratic sun, and Musashi looked at the weapons and thought of the Yoshioka.

If the longsword was of ill suit against a mob, then what of the spear, or another polearm like a glaive? Weapons of greater defensive potential; perhaps he could hold the Yoshioka at a distance and kill them slowly.

No. Visions of him stabbing at a Yoshioka only for another to come in from the side to grab the shaft, entangling it and leaving him helpless came to Musashi. The cloud burst and the other faults became apparent, he realizing that his technique with the spear was rudimentary, that in his height he had reach on the Yoshioka regardless, and finally the question of where he would even acquire such a weapon.

Unhurried, the Tokugawa samurai segued around the corner to hunt for nothing elsewhere. Musashi's wounded leg was reticent to move once more, congealed in the contortion in which he had held it. He forced motion, felt the burn up to his knee, and his sigh of pain was the only breeze that blew through the humid air. Even his hands were slick with sweat, moist palmprints left invisible in the dark.

Evidence of the coming Regent's festival seemed to be upon each street corner. Yokes for shoulder-borne shrines were stacked against walls half wrapped with cushioning, simple carts in the process of being painted, herds of taiko drums corralled in rows, tattooed skins hooked and lashed onto the barrels and then doused with water to pull themselves into taut tune through the night.

All passed beneath him. This rooftop passage offered him fresh perspective on the city, and he thought how different it was to look down rather than up. No feeling of constriction, no dwarfing, no sense of humility. Was there tacit purpose in constructing storeyed buildings so close to one another? Impossible for the street-level inhabitant to gain a sense of space or self, reminded always of one's smallness. Was there another Way in architecture? Was it inherent in all things?

Pondering, he slipped on guano and he overran the boundaries of the kingdoms of riled cats and his feet brushed against a lost paper kite, sent it floating back down to earth.

An apprentice sat hard at candlelight labour in the yard of his master's property. He was young, perhaps even of an age with Musashi, and he stopped his work and looked around as Musashi passed, searching for the sound that disturbed him. But he did not think that the source of it lay above, and he turned almost immediately back to the task that engrossed him.

Musashi, taken with his own sense of invisibility, tarried to watch a moment.

The young man was carving a slab of wood on his lap with a small chisel, scraping away thin curls bit by bit revealing letters writ in reverse awaiting ink and the press. So intricate and so dexterous his hands, shaping out the myriad characters and their complex forms effortlessly. Musashi stared at the ability, wondered how many hours' honing lay within the apprentice's flesh and bones as lay within his own at the sword, and he wondered what it was all this talent was being given over to.

He found the answer on the opposite side of the yard. There, scores of test prints had been hung over taut lines to dry, and he read the title in a myriad botched attempts:

Virtuous Manual for the Comportment of Faithful and Upstanding Wives.

His heart despaired. Hands so able forming something so trite.

Musashi moved on. He was close now, but his mind was afire. How many like the apprentice in the city? He thought of all he had seen in the days. Every trade of every possible imagining. Old men that made no more than buckets, and young boys who earned their trade by filling such buckets with safflower oil and conveying them across the city, delivering them to ladies wise in cosmetics. So common, so plain and yet here intersecting the accumulated expertise of woodcraft and metallurgy and agriculture and mechanism and amalgamation; the planks of the bucket sanded and shaped flush, the ring of iron that noosed them to form the bucket, the growing of the safflower seeds, the construction of the press that squeezed the oil from them and the combining of the oil with the right measures of powders and pigments. Then consider the production of those powders and pigments equally, the trees that were cultivated and hewn and their transport to the city also. So too the claiming of the iron ore from the earth. See the scale of it boggle outwards. Each facet born of wisdom the depth of which Musashi could only wonder at, admire, and the result of all this?

Something for an actor to smear from his sweating brow onto a kerchief and toss away into a crowd. Something for a woman to paint her face with, that she might feign innocence.

Or consider the fabrication of that kerchief also – or that innocence – no doubt equal in mastery and scope. Consider it all, see it continue in all directions, all linking, uniting. Clay brought whatever distance to potters who would shape and harden it using mastery of kiln, pass it off to the painter who coated and varnished it brilliant white, and what this yielded was a spoon that would dig of gruel. Prodigies of mechanism and lever lying on their backs in the dust repairing presses that would print no more than vacuous *Virtuous Manuals* or crude erotica shilled cheap, the lewd depictions of which were a long-trained artist's base summation. Men able of number and mathematics instead calculating the profit of kelp, flicking abaci beads lathed adroitly spherical, brushes dipping into ink concocted of soot and bones and the effort therein. Or consider the brushes: on distant meadows horses reared, shorn of hair that was glued to wood lathed as the beads. Or the paper they used: mulberry bark boiled in lye and then . . .

All this effort, chasing around itself, leading nowhere. Beneath pagodas of ancient beauty and emergent castles of magnificent stature capable people instead making the icon of their lives trivial and insubstantial things. Each ability worthy of praise and yet rendered moot by their tessellation. The intersection of their delusions of purpose shackling; fetishes of knucklebones bound together there in the shaman's palm, all illusory and yet interpreted as grand and meaningful conjuration.

The zero sum of all this human knowledge and ability, the waste, the indignity of it. Was that ultimately a city? Was that ultimately what he hated?

No time to map the depths of it. He had arrived and what lay ahead of him now dwarfed all in his loathing – the gates of the Yoshioka school.

They were as fine a structure as any he had seen. The gatehouse stood twice as high as the wall they broached, doors of thick wooden planks studded with iron barred for the night and impenetrable to anything shy of a cannon. The roof was narrow and tiled, and on either end of it a stone komainu lion-dog held a vigilant and unerring guard, one snarling and one roaring.

Between their mythic forms, just visible by the light of braziers that burnt within the school, lay the mortal remnants of Akiyama.

His head was impaled upon a spike, and his face had been set to look outwards upon the street. His hair was loose behind him and shielded his features from the light, the benighted head indefinable in anything but its ghastliness. Shooting-star flickers came and went as swarming flies caught the light for brief instants.

Musashi stared at it as he readied himself, perched predatory on the roof opposite. He wiped his hands dry, peeled back sodden strands of hair that had stuck to his brow, ensured the sack's mouth was pulled as wide as it could be. Speed was of the utmost necessity – jump across, place the head into the sack, jump back, escape.

This, the only real choice. He could well have tried climbing up the gatehouse from its base, stolen a ladder from somewhere even, but that would doubtlessly expose him to the Yoshioka within the school on the ascent. The gap between this roof and the gatehouse's was only five paces, maybe six or seven, and he had a slight advantage of height.

It was not a daunting leap.

Possible, he was certain.

He steeled himself, took a run-up and threw himself outwards.

Except he had not thought to plan his steps and so he launched himself off of his wounded leg. The limb was exhausted, had no strength whatsoever with which to propel him, and as soon as his toes left the tiles he knew he would not make it across. He went out and down instead of up and forwards. Primal instantaneous terror surged as gravity imposed itself and in a panic he flailed and cast his arms forward in a desperate attempt to grasp the roof opposite. His elbows clattered into the tiles and his ribs met the edge of the roof square as a hammer upon an anvil. His breath was forced entirely from him in a low and guttural moan, and he scrabbled at clay with his fingers and kicked at air with his feet.

In the brief moment he managed to hang, Musashi saw a samurai within the courtyard turn at the noise and then cry out in alarm. Then the weight of his dangling legs swung in wild momentum and pulled him away from the roof. He landed on his side and lay in the dust for long moments, listening to the noise that erupted within the compound.

By the time the Yoshioka unbarred the gates, he had managed to rise and drag himself into the shadows three streets away.

The failure hurt more than the breaths he struggled to gather.

Chapter Twenty-six

Each morning found Goemon fetid with sweat from the night. He slept on a mattress that retained a wet shadow of his body, rested the nape of his neck on a lacquer platter that was crested with a narrow strip of a pillow made of dried beans. Even in sleep, his posture was rigid and set in proper etiquette.

The Goat brought him breakfast in his chambers. Goemon could manage no more than a mouthful of rice without his stomach twisting in nausea. Each time he would mutter excuses about the heat putting him off his food, and the Goat would stand there knowing that Goemon was lying and yet not questioning him, stand there leaning on his sword and nodding his head in sympathy to his captain's actual plight.

He was a good man, the Goat, and Goemon appreciated his efforts. It was absurd that such a stoic and loyal retainer should be stuck with a sobriquet like the Goat and not referred to by his true name of Kiyomori Onodera, but this too was in a way part of the old samurai's duty.

It was his cloven foot that had first led the men of Tokugawa to call him so. The Goat would get it out when they were drunk, peel his stocking off to reveal his mangling. How they would all gather around to peer at it as boys did at captured insects, his foot split between the toes almost all the way to his shin and healed twisted into a form fascinating in its repulsiveness.

'It's amazing,' the Goat would say, when someone asked the inevitable question. 'The ways you'll think of defending yourself when you're on your arse in the mud and someone's swinging a sword down at you.'

It was probably through one of these drunken sessions that the moniker originated, long before Goemon had arrived in Kyoto, some comparative jest that somehow got adapted in sober life also. Was it derogatory then? Was it derogatory now? It sounded it, but men did not sneer it nor belittle him, and the Goat himself accepted its use evenly. More than this – Goemon had once seen him cutting erratic clumps out of his beard when the old man thought he was alone, crafting it so that it curled wiry from his chin much like the animal's. The Goat actively cultured the Goat.

He did this, Goemon knew, because it was good for the group to have such terms. They helped to build a unity, an inner collective idiosyncrasy of no real meaning that nevertheless helped define against the outer by its very being. In this he was faithful to the way of things. As a man of the warlord Oda, Onodera had been young and strong, had fought in the wars of conquest and had stormed Mount Hiei and taken three rebel-heretic heads and burnt whatever icon he could find. As a man of middle years and sworn to the Regent Toyotomi he had suffered his maiming. And now, as an old man of the Shogun Tokugawa, he was the Goat.

The tree bears fruit until it fails to do so, and then it is cut down and made into furniture to enthrone and comfort the young.

This was fact, this was duty. All they could do was endure it.

The familiar sound of the Goat's scabbard-cane rattling across the wooden floor preceded his arrival. Goemon heard it approaching his chambers, and he wondered for a moment if the man did not exaggerate his limp also. The old samurai barked his presence from outside. Goemon gave him permission to enter. He slid the heavy door open and stepped inside, bowed. It was still before midmorning.

'Something has arrived for you, sir,' he said. 'From Edo.'

'Edo?'

'Yes, sir.'

That was odd, and the Goat's expression did nothing to encourage Goemon. 'Bring it up to my chambers.'

A team of men hauled the arrival up the ladder and placed it reverently upon the hard floor of Goemon's room, bowed to it and then to their captain, and left. It was a cube of about knee-height and even sides, wrapped in a sheet of blackened hemp patterned with the Tokugawa crest.

He and the Goat looked at it for some time.

'A gift,' said Goemon.

'Yes, sir.'

'Specifically addressed to me?'

'Yes.'

'To whom do I owe gratitude?'

'No name was attached.'

'From the clan itself, perhaps.'

The Goat said nothing.

Goemon cast back the sheet. Revealed within was a thing of beauty. It was ostensibly a board for playing go, but that would be doing a disservice to the craft and art that had gone into its construction. It was a perfect cube of matte ebony wood, the grid of the game carved into the topmost surface barely seen black-on-black. Wrapping around three of the sides was the image of a tree painted in vivid gold leaf, the trunk of it gnarled and curved and its branches wide, grasping and bare.

The captain beheld the wonderful object for a long moment, and then a low groaning sigh escaped him. He sank down into a squat and wrapped his hands over the back of his neck, clawed his fingers into his flesh. 'You may as well line a cask with salt now, Onodera,' he said. 'It seems my head is due in Edo imminently.'

The gift was a veiled message. A game board indicated strategy. It had been given to him in pointed anonymity, save for that it had come from the Tokugawa, and that designated Goemon's strategy in relation to the duty he had been assigned by that body. The tree so elegantly depicted upon its sides was bare, meaning they believed his strategy was failing, or had failed. Had withered and died. Was entirely fruitless.

All these things it meant, and Goemon did not move, just crouched there with his hands now upon his cheeks, pulling the lower lids of his eyes down.

'It must be the riot at the castle, they must have heard about it,' he muttered. 'The architects told them, or some spy, or . . . Did the scandal truly reach that far?'

The Goat did not reply. He read the hidden message just as well as his captain. Yet, faithful adjutant that he was, eventually the old samurai was compelled to move forward and examine the go board more closely. Stiffly, he sank down to his knees.

'Ah,' he said happily. 'Look here, sir.'

'What?'

'The branches of the tree – don't you see? They are rife with buds about to bloom.'

His gnarled finger ran itself over a swathe of branches at the very extremities of the tree's reach. Goemon looked carefully. There were little nubs there, perhaps, but whether they were intended or simply mistakes in the manufacture of it, a brush slipped or a twist of gold that fell unwanted, he could not tell.

'Do you not think this is encouragement, sir?' said the Goat. 'That they are faithful in the imminent flowering of your strategy?'

It was a mercy he was offering, another lie he was pretending to believe. The kindness of it hurt Goemon such that he dismissed the man, and sat in baleful solitude for the rest of the morning staring at the portent of his doom.

In the afternoon he set out upon the streets. The Goat accompanied him. Goemon's mood had not relented and he felt alien to the sun. His belt was tight around his waist and beneath the iron of his helmet the tiger's claw of his sodden topknot toyed with his scalp, ran its needle points back and forth with a malicious joy at his helplessness.

The level countenance the captain maintained upon his own face almost faltered. He took to fidgeting to try to distract himself, pulling at the cords of the helmet beneath his chin, setting his thumbs into his belt, rippling his fingers across the grip of his longsword.

'Where are we meeting this fellow?' he asked the Goat, eyes roving back and forth in search of nothing.

'Somewhere furtive, sir. Can't have a man such as he present himself in the higher wards.'

'You are certain he is trustworthy? Men of this calibre . . .'

The Goat sucked air through his teeth. 'He was drunk when he suffered his disgrace. That's why he was spared seppuku. In the years since then, he has served faithfully. Perhaps he'll be given his swords back soon.'

'Or perhaps he has been forgotten.'

'The clan never forgets, sir.'

'No,' said Goemon, 'it doesn't.'

On the intersection of Kamanza and Koromonotana there was violence brewing. Two teams of taiko drummers were squaring up to one another, and all was rendered absurd because they were growling grave curses into the faces of one another whilst wearing the gaily coloured jackets and head-scarves they would wear in the coming Regent's festival. For weapons they had the thick drumsticks they clutched in either hand, and their instruments stood silent and ignored. The band clad in striped yellow were accusing the cherry-blossom-pink gang of stealing a jar of polishing wax from them overnight, and threats were uttered and shoulders were rolled and some grave pugilistic rhythm was threatening to break out until Goemon bellowed for order.

The sight of samurai and swords quelled them, and they stood before him like sullen children. The striped yellow men were obstinate and would not disband until their wax was returned to them, that their drums might shine to properly honour the Regent, they said, and they were entirely unafraid of Goemon. Stood there demanding petty justice of a blooded warrior, and the captain simply looked at them in disgusted disbelief.

These were the kinds of men and these were the kinds of things he would be beheaded for.

The captain could bear it no longer, and neither did he have the time to investigate and resolve some probably errant suspicion. He reached into his pouch of money and threw a handful of coins at their feet, many times over what a new jar of wax would cost, and turned and left the striped yellow men scrabbling in the dust.

But of course – inevitably – as he left, a hidden voice yelled at him from behind and above: 'Why not just murder them as you murdered the Yoshioka, Edoite?'

And there it was. He was a buffoon to some and a tyrant to others.

What was a city but its people?

He didn't look back, didn't try to scour out the source of the voice. Whoever it was would be hidden by some bamboo blind, and probably revel in how foolish he would look trying to locate them. Goemon walked on. Over his shoulder the cherry-blossom troupe began to practise once more. The sound of the drums came to him, the pounding bass driving out a low rhythm: *a-bom, a-bom, a-bombombom*.

Shortly, the Goat pointed out the mouth of an alley. It was shaded and unremarkable. He had Goemon stop and wait at its mouth as he hobbled in to confirm all was according to plan. Up against one of the walls a man was sprawled as though in a drunken slumber. The Goat peered down at this apparent malingerer, prodded at him with the point of his scabbarded longsword. The man stirred angrily, yet calm words were exchanged, perhaps some codes or passwords of verification. Then the man rose to his feet, entirely sober and steady, and the Goat looked to Goemon and gestured for him to come.

'Here he is,' said the Goat as the captain drew near. 'Our surreptitious riverman.'

The agent was disguised so well that Goemon wondered if it even was a disguise any longer. He wore a filthy old sleeveless jerkin and short leggings that ended at his shins. His flesh was dirty and jaundiced and his hair was short and matted. Yet in his eyes remained something of the samurai he had once been, some remnant pride, and his face was marked by a scar that could only have come from a sword, a neat straight line that parted his beard and ran from the corner of his mouth to below his ear.

'Sir Inoue,' the man said, bowing.

Goemon looked him up and down. 'On your knees,' he said.

The agent was surprised by this. He hesitated, looked to the Goat for confirmation. The Goat in turn looked to Goemon.

'If we are discovered, if people witness this,' said the captain, 'I'll not have them thinking I am conversing eye-to-eye with a vagrant.'

The agent was reluctant. It seemed he was disappointed. Perhaps he had been relishing the opportunity to talk equally with swordsmen as he once had. But he was condemned to penance and he swallowed his objections and sank to his knees, placed both palms out upon the earth.

'Now then,' said Goemon. 'The man you are watching—'

'Draw your sword,' said the agent in a low voice, daring to look up for a moment.

'What?' asked Goemon.

'Draw your sword and hold it to my throat,' said the agent. 'If we are discovered, it will appear you are imparting justice on some lowly scapegrace.'

Goemon looked at him for a moment, perfectly affronted.

'Do it,' implored the man. 'A finer image, no?'

'I will not relegate the sword my father wielded into becoming some prop in a clandestine charade!' Goemon hissed.

The agent said nothing more, and the Goat looked at his captain as though it were a reasonable idea. Goemon bridled for three furious heartbeats, but then he saw it for what it was – just another facet of this absurd city and risible circumstance, and what use pride for the already disgraced, the already dead? He slid his longsword out of its scabbard, this marvellous icon that he had wielded at Sekigahara, that his father had in the campaign against the Ashina, and placed its brilliant edge at the filthy throat.

Very carefully, the Goat spread his legs and then began heaving his shoulders with his breath as though he had either just delivered some form of violence or was just about to.

'The subject,' said Goemon to the agent. 'Your vigil over him is constant?'

'Save for this sole moment, sir.'

'He has no idea of your presence?'

'He walks always with eyes on the horizon,' the agent said, and Goemon could feel the man's voice through his sword, the words humming up the length of the blade. 'Everyone in Maruta gives him a wide berth, scared of him. He is quite safe, I believe, but I remain vigilant for any attempt upon him.'

'Good,' said Goemon. 'And of the other pertinent elements as discussed with Sir Onodera?'

'He's found a common place, a low place, nothing suspicious growing there, I believe. I walked freely through it without challenge. Speaks often with a blight-eyed islander woman, nothing more.'

'Blight-eyed islander?'

'From over the seas, sir. Ryukyu. Taken of a sickness.'

'Is he smitten with her?'

The agent shrugged. 'He tends to her nightly. Why else would a man spend time in the company of a woman?'

'Do you believe she will suffice?'

The agent nodded.

Goemon sniffed, rubbed the sweat from either side of the bridge of his nose. Then he made the decision that had weighed upon his mind for days. 'Very well. When you get the order . . . make it vivid.'

The agent peeled his throat away from the sword and, through a mime of grovelling for clemency, bowed his understanding. Curtly, Goemon raised his weapon and sheathed it, and then jerked his chin away in command. Dismissed, the agent ran to the mouth of the alley as though he were terrified and vanished into the streets outside.

'Cherish the mercy of the benevolent Shogun!' the Goat shouted after him for good measure.

The two samurai were left standing in the murk. Goemon took a breath and steadied himself. The Goat turned to look at his captain, and there was genuine concern in his old eyes.

'This is a desperate strategy, sir,' he said.

'What else is there I can do, Onodera?'

The Goat might have answered, but at that moment further into the alley something moved and caught Goemon's attention. The Goat tensed at the sudden turn of his captain's head, brought his sword up as if to draw it, but Goemon gestured at him for calm. It had been small, an animal of some sort. Now that he listened intently he thought he could hear its panting, and curiously he went to look for it, moving slowly so as not to startle whatever it was.

Behind a stack of old abandoned rice-straw casks he found a small dog sitting. It was evidently a stray, a mangy-looking thing of a wretchedly sparse tan hide and one of its ears torn away. It sat there with its tongue lolling and its mouth wide in what seemed an idiot's smile, fighting its battle against the afternoon's heat with the constant heaving of its lungs.

Goemon squatted down before it and reached out. With one hand he began to gently stroke the dog, and then, seeing its calm reaction, the second also.

The dog sat there and panted and yawned and rolled its sickly tongue, and Goemon, hidden away from the streets and all who might judge him, watched all this and smiled. He felt a rare moment of calmness. He had always felt a liking for dogs. Back in distant Mutsu, back across leagues and years, it had been his pleasure to own an entire pack of hounds, great hale things with their heads up to his waist more similar to wolves than this tattered little mongrel.

Of course, then had come the glorious summoning from his most noble Lord Tokugawa. He had left the dogs in their pen, and they had howled for him as he departed, yelped with such a clamour that he heard their cries long after his estate had passed from his sight. It would be nice to think that they remembered him still, that if his scent no longer lingered in the air some remnant trace of it remained within their hearts.

Goemon though never let himself be fooled; he knew well the nature of dogs.

The Goat stood watch. He was pleased to see some measure of contentment upon his captain. 'Seems you've made a friend, sir,' he said happily.

Goemon gave a grunt, the barest of nods. He looked at the dog, and the dog looked back.

Its sickly eyes gleamed with a sheen like spilt lantern-oil.

Goemon sighed sadly. 'The law states quite clearly that stray dogs found within the city limits are to be killed,' he said.

Beneath the captain's hands, the dog panted on. Eventually, the Goat asked, 'Should I fetch a spear, sir?'

Chapter Twenty-seven

Musashi slept like the hunted.

He did not trust the Yoshioka not to mount another attempt on his life, regardless of any word given to Goemon. Each night he would barricade the door of his room with the rudimentary furniture within and wedge his scabbard between the jamb and the frame. Likely the door could still be opened with enough force, but it would create a clamour and wake him should he be sleeping, and whoever was there would then have to stumble over the pile of furniture to enter, all of which would give Musashi time to rise and greet the intruder with his longsword in hand.

Barred and sealed, his room became what he imagined the inside of a stilled lung might be, tight and humid and chokingly warm, and even the walls themselves seemed to sweat. His hours of repose spent hunched up in the corner with his swords bared before him, alternating between moments of the frail slumber of expectant prey and a torpid, viscous consciousness.

Fatigue was beginning to tell, eyes bleared and heavy, but all endured, all endured.

Musashi did not know how many other rooms there were in this lodgings or how many destitute were in them. Some rooms even cheaper than the pittance Musashi was paying for his, these set with a half-dozen mats slept on inevitably by decrepit men. A lingering stench of sake and sweat and distrust abounded, pitiful things like straw sandals or copper coins scabbed entirely green guarded like jewels. Halls that bumped and breathed around him, an old man's voice murmuring to no one.

His ribs were hurt. The impact against the gate of the Yoshioka had been harder than he thought at the time. His chest was mottled with ugly bruises, and if he took a full breath he felt a sharp pain lance along one side. Sharp enough that it stole that breath from him. The act of rising or sitting was laborious.

It was night. Ameku was singing. Her song that seemed to him to never end. With a chest of throbbing bones he sat against the wall and listened, and willed for the melody to null his pain.

She was working her loom as she sang, singing in time to the slow clacking of the levers with her back to him. He had not told her about his failure to recover Akiyama's head. That too would hurt. Through her hair he could just about see the nape of her neck. In the candlelight her skin was the colour of something fine he hadn't the words to describe.

He thought of that benighted lake and the red moon hovering above it. The reflection of it shimmering on the calm black and formless waters, the sound of gentle lapping. Of which thing he was to her, and which he wanted to become.

'Tell me of Ryukyu,' he said. 'Tell me how you learnt to sing like that. Tell me . . . Tell me *how*.'

'That you too might sing?' she said, and still she taunted him. Still the barrier she had made for herself persisted, and it maddened him. It was a wall that stood before him, and by that very fact he was compelled to attempt to breach it even though he could not possibly know what lay upon the other side.

'I . . .' he said, grasping at things he could not explain to himself. 'No. What you do . . . It is ability, and . . . A thing of worth . . . And I would . . .'

'Ryukyu,' said Ameku, 'was a long time ago, and then my time ended there.'

'But,' said Musashi, 'what was it you did there? Why did you leave?' *Why are you here now? Why is it we happened to meet?*

Ameku just shook her head. 'Still, Musashi, still you have to know the meaning of the words,' she said. 'Stubborn, you. Do not change.'

'Tell me,' he said.

She did not. Instead she started working back at her loom, and sang once more. He sat there listening, feeling the nag of that half-unknown, unasked, unanswered question.

The days passed in humid exhaustion, and they offered him no respite.

He set himself to the sword and the felling of the Yoshioka. One of them. All of them. Cast them down. Disperse the swarm. The fortnight until the duel passing both too slowly and too quickly, caught between savage anticipation and logical wariness, knowing that he was yet to devise a method of victory. Taunted by this also, another barrier.

But it was there, it was achievable, he was certain of it, if only he could reach out and grasp it . . .

Around him the slums of Maruta. Outside the walls of Kyoto proper, outside the cultured zone, Maruta lay upon the banks of the north-easterly forking of the river Kamo. It was the docks of the city, as much as an inland holding could possess such, for the river was an artery and brought goods of all sorts to the capital. Rice or salt or ore arriving daily, but the greatest traffic in lumber, the city so vulnerable to fire, constantly rebuilding or building anew, and also the centre of so many industries that hungered for fresh fodder to mulch into paper or shape into scabbards or palanquins or doors or ladles or umbrellas or sandals.

The wood arrived sometimes chopped and stacked in a boat, or sometimes men simply rode huge logs as vessels themselves, prodding their course with poles. Maruta itself meant 'log'; here known as Log Town in the vernacular.

The rivermen coming, the rivermen going constant, and when they left they left with their boats just as burdened as when they had arrived, merely changed their cargo. When they departed they took the effluence of the city with them in stinking, sloppy casks, villages along the river's course needing fertilizer for paddy fields and hamlets of the corpsehandlers needing piss for tanning. Goods in, waste out, in, out, a cycle of excretion and construction: the mouth and the arsehole of the city, as Maruta was also known in even lower vernacular.

A transitory place where men drifted in under twilight skies and were gone upon the current in the morn. Faces unnoticed, things here built cheap, hovels and slovenly lodgings crammed up against one another, no temples or garrisons or emporiums. Where Kyoto had pagodas Maruta had pyramids of casks of shit stacked high, emitting a pervading stench that was magnified in the humidity. Mistlike, never quite subsiding, all here enveloped in it, the men and women shovelling or labouring or casting off, sawing, lashing, sorting, drinking, malingering, begging.

Stagnant.

Stagnant as his mind, Maruta, and in frustration he abandoned it in search of somewhere else, as though that might suddenly grant him what he strived towards. A half-hour's walk north of the slums Musashi found isolation on the banks of the Kamo, a little copse of trees right up by the waterside, and it was peaceful and serene and the air clean enough that one might even practise meditation here, and yet he found the exact same problem persisted.

Cranes waded past him through the shallows, and they beheld him in his futile exercise and the flashing of his longsword with their yellow eyes round and uncaring.

Summon your enemies, his father Munisai had once told him of the theories of duelling; summon them before you exact in your mind and over a thousand still breaths examine them until you have assumed their form and see out from their eyes. A wisdom indefatigable through century and nation, and yet useless here, for every time he summoned Denshichiro to his mind he simply wanted to slash the spectre to pieces.

Made him want to spit, the thought of the man's face and all he was, and then the frustration that this was all he could summon made him actually spit, or throw a rock into the river, or kick out at the stumps of trees. A vicious and infuriating gyre from which he could not escape.

Months he had spent with Akiyama, an adept of the Yoshioka style, and never once had he thought to speak with him about its merits and philosophy. He had beaten the man and so he had innately assumed he had surpassed his entire school by virtue of this victory, and now he cursed the callousness of this.

Seek and grasp, force through, overcome: if not the spear against the numbers of the Yoshioka, if not the sword, what then, of guns?

At Sekigahara he had seen their terrible capabilities, seen them snub out entire lines of men in easy instants. If you allowed as he did that the sole point of fighting was victory, then surely its achievement through any means was permissible, was worthy. The samurai in the city had jeered him with the idea of using foreign mechanism, but their jeers born of the Way. What Musashi fought for was no less than the Way's entire destruction. What was the very symbol of the Way but the sword? If these two things were true then should not his first action be to abandon its fetishes, take up modern potential instead?

He stared at his longsword in his hands for some time.

Musashi realized it belonged there, belonged on some level fundamental to him, and then of course the same practical flaws arising: where would he get a gun? Or the dozen guns he would need to shoot all the Yoshioka down in quick succession? Or a longbow? Or throwing daggers? Or anything else?

He snarled, and then felt foolish for snarling. Stood there landlocked and envious of the river that flowed so effortlessly. Dragonflies were in the air before him, their wings shimmering crucifixes, the water beneath them pooled and still. Mottled blue bodies glanced upon the black surface, sent rings dilating outwards, and these rings, they had no correlation, served only to annihilate one another in their expansion again and again. Caught his eye, the way the patterns did not intersect, did not correlate. Seemed marred to him, unnatural.

Anger at his inability faded from him, only to be replaced by a separate tormenting gyre that was goaded by every pained breath he took. The bruises on his ribs led him to thinking of Akiyama's head, and his failure to recover it.

He decided to head for the city.

The Tokugawa samurai on the gates to Kyoto stopped and searched others seeking to enter, but they did not even meet Musashi's eyes. Turned away as though they were deliberately avoiding him, and he sneered at them for this evident cowardice and loathed them for their submission and oppression both.

Beyond them the streets of the city were rife with drumbeat, each thoroughfare throbbing with a different pulse. Pounding of the bass skins offset with the rolling patterns of the smaller drums, a quick middle timbre: *atta-ta-tata, ta-tata, ta-tata.*

The sound of it carried Musashi along through the meaningless noise and clamour. Lithe forms of stub-tailed cats ghosted over overhanging roofs, peered down with eyes wide and green and cynical. The arc of a bridge lined with neophyte monks, bell-shaped straw baskets over their heads smothering the mantras they uttered low, bowls held out pleading in bony hands, they living their years of avowed poverty seeking to learn the charity and meanness of the world. The sweet stink of a sake brewery with its broad doors cast wide open and the vats within exposed. Imposing shrieks of the peddlers of goods, tempting potential customers to partake of sweet bean paste, of imported incense, of intricately carved netsuke beads to hang from the belt, inutile shit, inutile shit, inutile shit.

Another shrine for the Regent's festival was being readied. It was of a brilliant blue lacquer that had been polished to a sheen, and now men were testing the hardness of its yokes upon their shoulders. Forty of them bore it upwards with a great wheeze of effort, and they and the watching crowd cheered as they found the weight bearable. They began to teeter it back and forth between them, the shrine rising and falling like a boat upon rough seas, cymbals and gongs and chimes attached to it rattling in a great cacophony.

Those on the left of the mob went: *Hwaja!*

Those on the right of the mob went: *Hoja!*

The left went: *Hwaja!*

The right went: *Hoja!*

The chant went on and on, and people in the crowd clapped in time, and apart from this was Musashi, silent and watching. Always apart.

He walked on. Like a bruise to be prodded, a burn to be squeezed, the school of the Yoshioka drew him in. Surpassing all thought of danger, the grim curiosity, the necessity. He told himself that he would look on it for but a moment, and then retreat. Glimpse and see Akiyama's head, and in its piteous state find the inspiration he needed, or simply convince himself that he had made some progress towards its liberation, or both, or neither.

Something, anything.

As a sealed lagoon amidst a squall, the street before the school was quieted and residual noise from elsewhere washed like spraying spume over the crowd that had gathered. They were giving the gates a wide and fearful berth. Cautioned,

Musashi peered covertly out over their heads from the corner of an alley.

Beneath the maw of their compound he saw Denshichiro sitting upon a stool. The leader of the Yoshioka had his tea-coloured sleeves bound back and his thick arms crossed, and at his side eight adepts stood equally dressed. They had evidently been there some time, for they were standing watch over the head of Akiyama.

Still impaled upon the spike, the head had been taken down from the gatehouse and was now set on the street before them all. The sun and the heat had done to it what Ameku had not been able to describe.

The crowd watched the head, and the head watched back.

In those few moments of his botched attempt at a righteous larceny, the Yoshioka must have recognized Musashi. Or perhaps they had simply surmised who it must have been in its aftermath, and then duly extrapolated what it was Musashi had been seeking on top of the gatehouse, and thus they found their lure.

Had they spent each day since then in this manner? The trap was so apparent, and yet Musashi could not walk away. Stood there for far longer than the moment he had promised himself, observing all he needed to.

He was taller than most of those in the crowd and, even in his obscured position and even in his stillness, one of the Yoshioka eventually spotted Musashi. He spoke to his fellows and their heads turned, Denshichiro's last of all.

The smile that broke across his face, once he had confirmed to himself it was Musashi, was visible at distance.

Denshichiro rose to his feet. Those close to Musashi grew nervous as they realized who it was who had attracted the samurai's attention. Musashi abandoned any pretence of hiding and stepped out onto the street. The crowd drew back.

Instants unfurled devoid of sound or rhythm as each man watched the other. Denshichiro's smile faded. He cocked his head and held his hand out in gesture to Akiyama's head.

Come and claim it, his spread palm said. *Charge and give us the excuse and shield of your instigation to wield at the Tokugawa.*

Nine men there. Nine men, nine swords, and Musashi's leg imperfect and his ribs painted purple and yellow and his mind still without any idea on how he might surpass them. Yet he could not force himself to walk away.

Denshichiro turned to his men. He held his hand out. One of them tossed him a bamboo training sword. He caught it and held it up to Musashi.

Musashi saw.

Denshichiro took it by the grip and then turned to Akiyama's head. He looked to Musashi. He looked to the head. He ran the blunted point through the brittle curls of the dead man's hair. He looked to Musashi.

Musashi saw this, too.

Denshichiro drew the sword up to rest across his shoulder, and slowly he went to stand behind the head. He stood there with his off-hand on his hip, and still he looked at Musashi.

Musashi's thumb dug its way between the rope that served as his belt and his waist, clawed itself.

Denshichiro drew his right arm back and swung the sword around one-handed. A gentle parody of a blow, the shaft slapped against Akiyama's right cheek, rested there.

Musashi saw. Saw nine of them. Nine of them, and he alone.

Denshichiro drew the sword back once more, and this time swung backhanded. Bamboo connected in the same demeaning manner against Akiyama's left cheek.

Steel swords at Musashi's waist, and what was it that held them back? The Yoshioka were there and he was here, and, if he had not the method or the logic that would best them, then what of will, or of justice, or of bloody-minded ambition?

Denshichiro swung forehanded again, then backhanded once more, forehanded, backhanded, growing stronger. The head rocked and twisted and flies raged at each impact.

Or if those things would not suffice, what of a complete and utter hatred?

Forehanded, backhanded, forehanded, backhanded, and the outrage spiralled ever outwards. The anger that had carried him this far could take him further surely. The soles of Musashi's feet parted the dust of the street and a curse parted his teeth as his lips drew back into a snarl, and from his side a girl whispered his name, and there was Denshichiro not fifteen paces away, scion, heir, Lord of all that was wrong, and bamboo broke skin and painted a rotten welt upon a desecrated cheek, and Musashi's palm was upon the grip of his sword, calluses sliding between the leather cords, and then Yae, with no other choice, stepped into his path.

An hour later in the workroom of the lodgings Musashi and Ameku were at erratic war, he striding back and forth and tearing at his clothes and she stilled and sitting at her loom and not offering him her face.

It was she who had sent Yae to watch over him.

'What in all the hells were you thinking?' he shouted at her. 'What your intent? You think I need guarding?'

'Yae, she stopped you, no?'

'She stopped me from recovering Akiyama's head!'

'Yae, how many men, Yoshioka men?'

'A lot,' said the girl. She was standing by the woman, clutching at her sleeve, afraid of Musashi in his fury.

He waved a scornful hand. 'They could not have stopped me.'

'They would kill you,' said Ameku.

'I was there to get Akiyama's head, to set him at peace. I was trying to right that wrong.'

'They would kill you.'

'Do you know what it was they were doing? Denshichiro, that arrogant son of a whore?'

'I do not care about this man.'

'That you knew you him, you would. Worthy of his head being struck from his shoulders, and his school torn down and—'

'And then his men kill you.'

'Was it not you who spoke so candidly about how wrong and terrible and ugly it was, that Akiyama's head was not laid to rest with his body?'

'I said . . .' she said, struggled to keep up with the pace of his words. 'I said it is bad, but, but, do not die, do not kill . . . Can you not understand this?'

'Get the head, and all at peace, and them that need laying low laid low,' he spat.

'You die.'

'And so what if I did?' he cried. 'What matter that? Better I die killing them than, than . . . I hid for two years from them after Sekigahara, and they intruded upon me, and killed those just like me. Their world, their Way. Two years as nothing I, as black water at night, and still the injustice. Better to kill and to be killed, to, to live in moments where I can say that I was definite, that I was real . . . A separate entity to them, defined by my striking at them and they striking me than to hide and acquiesce to all their ordurous shit and achieve the same end.'

'Truly, you think this?' she said. 'Better to die?'

He faltered for a moment, the fuel of his stubborn arguments sputtering before the wind of logic.

'Please forgive me, Musashi,' said Yae in the disjointed lull. 'I'm sorry that—'

'You have no cause to apologize,' he snarled in a manner that made her feel she had to apologize. Wind could extinguish or it could ignite. 'Neither one of you can tell me that they, those samurai, do not deserve to die. Neither one of you can say that my coming here, of my felling Seijuro, of what I shall do to Denshichiro, none can deny that these are worthy things, things that need to be done. That I will do.'

'Revenge . . .' said Ameku. 'It is this important to you?'

'This is not revenge,' said Musashi. 'What are you talking of?'

'Yoshioka try to kill you,' said the woman. 'So, you come to Kyoto to kill them. And Akiyama dies, and now here you are.'

'This is not a matter of vengeance! I am no samurai. I overcame that – vengeance is no saintly thing to me. Or, if it is a vengeance, it is no vengeance for myself. This is for Akiyama, and all like him, for Jiro, for all those thousands at Sekigahara, and the centuries before.'

Ameku said nothing. Perhaps she could not think of anything to say, or perhaps she could not think of how to translate what she thought, or perhaps she meant to mock him. The outrage spiralled ever outwards; in this kind of mood all were against him.

'If you only understood the Way,' he said. 'If you understood it, if you felt it . . . Felt it as I did, who was born to it. Do you know what I almost did because of it, where it almost led me on some supposed shining path? What I was made to do, when I was no more than a child? I watched my father pull his own intestines out in agony, and watched other men condemn him for this. Then I was set upon a path of vengeance, and committed myself to die at its end. Do you understand this? I came so close . . . For years I struggled through hardship, all for a single chance – and I succeeded! I got so near to him, I had the dagger all but at that son of a whore Nakata's throat. Prepared to kill to him, knowing I would be cut down after, or have to kill myself, and all this because dogma demanded it. I was a sliver from death – I, a child, ready to die. To waste all I had. The Way made me want to do so – want to! Have you ever felt such a hold upon you? But no . . . I failed to kill him then, I could not do it, but even so I was not freed. I hated myself for the gall of surviving. Hated myself for living – the Way made me shamed of my own breath! Do you know what it is like to wake in the morning and to loathe yourself entirely, to wish the flesh to be scoured from your hands and the bones beneath unto dust? That, I felt for years, on account of some ancient code. Some scabrous accursed dogma. That is the Way. The dream that I was given. That was forced upon me. Where is the justice that such a thing should reign highest in the world? What sort of man is it that could look out and see statues of his enemy raised to the sky, and not seek the satisfaction of—'

'And this is not revenge?' said Ameku.

Musashi stood there with his jaw clenched and his hands as fists, and no words escaped him. Outside still the drums played, growing in scale, growing in urgency – *atta-ta-tata, ta-tata, ta-tata atta-ta-ta* – and they were there and easy to blame and so he snarled and turned his rage upon them instead.

'How can anyone abide the city?' he said, lashed his arms at the unseen players. 'This accursed noise, these drums. To the myriad hells with it all. I cannot think. I cannot breathe.'

Expended, he went and sat down with his back against the wall, turned his head away and looked at nothing. Yae had tears in her eyes. Ameku sensed or heard this, and moved along the bench. The girl climbed up to sit beside her and leant her head on the woman's shoulder, and for a time her sniffling was the only sound from those within the room.

Outside the drums played on.

Ameku began to knock a fist into a palm in time. 'This,' she said, meaning her pounding, 'what is the word for this . . . ?'

'Rhythm,' said Musashi.

'Rhythm,' said Ameku. 'This is not a bad thing. Do not hate it. All ideas from rhythm. All ideas from music. I told you before, in Ryukyu we have no iron, so no swords. Instead of swords, we have instruments. Men, women, both. Drum, or flute, or voice, or three-string . . .' She made a motion as though she were strumming a shamisen or a biwa lute. 'Everyone, an instrument. Everyone, rhythm. Better this way, I feel.'

He looked at her. As always her hair was long and immaculately combed, caught echoes of the light. Her words stayed with him through the haze of his sleep that night the way the melodies of her songs had stayed with him through prior darkness.

The next morning found him on the streets of Kyoto, caught in a somnolent stupor born of a vampiric heat and the toll of restless nights. Crowds passed dreamlike around him, the taste of sweat salt on his lips, sounds passing through his body as ethereal as the sounds of bells beneath water.

On the streets he saw groups of young women forming, learning to dance the dance they would dance for the Regent soon. Standing in ranks, and on their heads were lanterns worn as hats, empty of candles at present, symmetrical fronds shaped from cheap wood to form arcane crowns. They all following the movement of the leader, legs extending, cavorting, the fans held in either hand twirling, rising, falling, spinning. The motion of them all in their tentative unison mesmerizing to the desperately tired eye searching for comforting recognition of pattern.

On the steps sat the old women watching, teeth like lead and fingers like the husks of millet. They, these grandmothers, holding the wrists of the youngest girls that were corralled between their legs, moving their little hands through the motions of the dance, simultaneously teaching and remembering how it had been when they were young, when they had danced as they had been taught in turn by their own grandmothers.

Nudged and bumped, his body in the bustle. Would have driven him to anger usually, or given the sense of entrapment, an enclosing pressure, but now Musashi found ambivalence. His reserves of fury perhaps temporarily spent the day before, his flesh now at the whim of the world as much as his mind, all just equal forces buffeting equally.

The drums, the drums. The skins lashed now, and the great bands forming. The rhythm permeating. Some big double-skinned instruments borne on a yoke between two men facing one another, and as they would each strike a separate side of it they would caper, lifting one another up, flipping and cavorting. A young man on his knees with two small sticks in his hands, beating frantically on a snare no bigger than a bowl, the tone of it high and pitched.

All things from music. All ideas from rhythm. Ameku's words constant in his mind like the chanting of circumambulating monks.

Musashi stopped and watched a group of ten men with ten drums out before them on stands at waist height, bodies and instruments set out in a perfect line. What they were practising was a dance as well as music, the motions of their arms as they played regimented and flourishing, one arm held high, the other flicking the wrist and the stick in spirals and curls. Or one leg sliding out behind them and dipping into a crouch – *just like a sword stance* – or interlocking their arms with their neighbour and playing with one hand on their drum and one hand on the adjacent instrument, striking out two concurrent parts and yet the one, whole true rhythm held flawless.

Now realized properly, their noise was not repulsing or irritating but rather mesmerizing, enthralling, he drawn to watch them closer, drawn to observe rather than see. Natural, the natural state of things to be carried such, the rhythm of the universe that he had felt only fleeting before manifested here. Observing their technique, the muscles moving beneath the skin, the wrists rolling and rolling on and on untempered and yet methodical, free yet precise.

The right hand kept the rhythm, pulsing, pounding deep: *bom, a-bom, a-bombombom*.

The left hand beat out the counter, the urgency: *atta-ta-tata ta-ta-ta ta-tata-atta-ta-tata*.

The girls nearby chanted: *Sore! Sore! Sore sore sore sore sore!*

The entwining, the interplay of the hands of the drummers entrancing, two hands together in unison. Something forming quivering and invisible between the hairs on the back of Musashi's own hands. His mind deprived of the concept of ego beyond simple endurance, of rationality, now sparked and inspired to blaze off on an abstract angle of pure conjecture.

He saw drums and thought of longswords, and how a longsword worked was this: the right hand held up near the guard pushed and the left hand held near the pommel pulled. It was this controlled motion that gave the ability to cut properly, not some great swipe with the shoulders but rather the sword utilizing the body as no more than a fulcrum, the potential of the steel by and for itself duly realized as it whipped around. Thus, two hands always on the sword.

Musashi, though, saw the duel with Akiyama: his longsword cutting down across the body held only in one hand. He had summoned enough strength with his right wrist alone to achieve the motion of two. Contra. Impossible. But he had done it, and he had kept training the right arm to this day. But always a strange sense of emptiness as he did so, as if he were pushing at something barely realized.

A feeling as empty as his left hand was during the training.

There before him, the drummers: the two hands together, in unison, forming the rhythm of the universe. One alone would not suffice, the beat of that malformed and unfelt, but two, two together, fulfilling all possible potential.

In them, in him.

Clarity.

Clarity.

On the surface of the water all the rings now passing through one another, perfect circles cast immaculate and interlocking, and here, now, not in the solitude of wilderness but rather in the finest city upon the earth, at long last amongst his fellow people, Musashi felt a moment of pure wellbeing, of belonging, of righteousness.

Chapter Twenty-eight

The cheer went up for the champion, echoed through the streets of Maruta, continued, grew. A gang of men roving, shouting and waving fists, eyes locked on the warrior that strode ahead of them: a black and red rooster on a leash. Upon the creature's head was placed a miniature samurai helmet, delicate and crested in gold leaf, someone having been to a dollmaker's. Around its bristling chest were loosely collared a tiny pair of swords doubtlessly appropriated from the same set.

Those they passed they gathered up in their wake, itinerant rivermen, drunks, gamblers, Musashi. Before them all the rooster strutted back and forth, not scared by the clamour but thriving in it, his talons and his spurs white and sharp, his tail up resplendent. They made their way to a large shack of some sort down by the river, its true purpose unclear and inside of which more men were crowding. A ring had been formed by crates and planks and all manner of things set into an angular attempt at a circle and within this waited another rooster, this one white and wearing a leather hood, clawing at the earth.

'When that hood comes off, a truly diabolical hellbeast will be unleashed,' the owner of the white bird was shouting. 'Within this rooster beats the heart of a tiger, he'll tear the throat out of a boar, let alone a scrawny old bantam such as he faces this day! Fearless! Your money's safe on him, mark my words!'

'Close your ears to these lies, good men!' said the owner of the avian samurai as they strode in. 'I bring to you my undefeated warrior, victor of seven bouts, the pride of the shit stacks! You cannot argue with experience! You know on which one to bet, wise brothers, oh, how you do!'

Swagger and pomp, and all around the ring money was changing hands, the excitement rising. Musashi let it pass before him. He had focus on the coming duel, his body aching with the pleasant burn of exploring the potential of what he had envisioned in the drums. The thrill of theorizing and creating anew, fervour and anticipation building in him as he found it, this thing of his devising, not only possible but practical. Familiar even, as though his body had walked the steps before, or was always meant to walk them.

He rubbed his tired eyes and leant against the wall at the back of the crowd, his only real interest in this cockfight as a diversion, something to keep him awake and fill the span of time from now until his meeting with Denshichiro.

The black-and-red rooster was carefully divested of its helmet and its swords and then placed into the ring, kept on its leash as the betting was finalized. The white rooster sensed its presence, feathers bristling and its talons beginning to tap with what some argued was nervousness and others claimed was bloodlust. A lengthy debate, the weight of it growing with each additional coin.

'The red one was wearing the helmet, yes?' asked an ageing man to Musashi's side.

He nodded, not interested in meeting the man's eyes.

'Perhaps I best bet on him,' said the man, taking a pouch from his waist and rummaging inside for coins. 'Which one are you going for?'

'I've no money,' said Musashi.

'I'll front you a bet, if you wish.'

'No.'

Ambivalent, the man ambled over to speak with the bookmaker. Inside the ring the two roosters were growing more agitated, the white one beginning to caw beneath its hood, the red one now testing the extent of its leash, cantering at its limits. His bet made, the man returned to Musashi's side with a wooden chit in his hand. He was out of place here, all but bald, his legs bare beneath a plain black kimono belted loosely. This a fine garment compared with the rough jerkins and jackets others wore, with the tattered and sleeveless kimono upon Musashi.

Musashi crossed his bare arms, tried to make his desire for solitude apparent. The man persisted oblivious, flapping the lapels of his clothing to fan his chest: 'Maruta, Maruta. Rare I venture up out here any more, but fun when I do. Not from Kyoto, are you?'

'No.'

'What think you of our fair city?'

'It is what it is.'

'A pity to hear words so jaded from one so young.'

His tone amiable and ignored by Musashi. At the back of the crowd a man turned to look back at the pair of them. Had a good long look this time, having glanced back several times before, and then his eyes went wide. He turned back to the ring without saying anything. It was not Musashi or his swords he had been examining.

'Surely you've been outside of Maruta?' said the man. 'You can't judge Kyoto on what happens here, honest as it is. What have you seen of the true city? Where have you been?'

Musashi rubbed his nose, sniffed, looked only at the roosters.

'You must have been to some of the temples, at least? Even if you're not pious, you have to see them. Beautiful buildings, just beautiful. Achievements. Chionin, Kiyomizu, Tofuku . . . No? None of them?'

'I've been to Hiei.'

'Ah, Hiei.' The man nodded. 'Enryaku temple. That was beautiful, back in the day. What does it look like now?'

'Dead. Burnt.'

'Indeed,' said the man sadly. 'I can't bring myself to go and look. Such a shame. The late Lord Oda's work . . . An outsider lessening Kyoto.'

Above them all the cry went up from the umpire that betting was closed and that the fight was nigh. He stood on a chest and gesturing with a crude imitation of a gourd-shaped fan like a man adjudging a cultured wrestling bout would use. Those clustered closest to the ring were forced to their knees, those behind them into a squat, those at the back onto their straining toes. The two combatants were picked up by their respective owners and taken to opposite sides of the ring. There squatting they made the final preparations, the owner of the red cooing something unheard, the owner of the white repeatedly flicking his bird on the back of the head.

Musashi and his apparent companion alone were bereft of excitement, the ring barely visible to them. The man was unyielding: 'When did you come to the city?'

'A week or two past.'

'Ahh, that's time enough. You must have formed some opinion, however small. I'd like to hear it, just for the sake of idle curiosity. Mine the fortune to have been here so long I forget how others view what is common to me.'

Musashi exhaled through his nose: 'If you want to know, I hate the cleanliness there. People always brushing, sweeping, polishing. Staring at you if you dare to defile it. Wasting so much time fighting against what is natural.'

'So you would prefer a city dusty and falling into disrepair?'

'I would prefer a city full of people concerned with things higher than appearance. A city clean from the inside.'

'A lofty desire.'

Musashi grunted, crossed his arms anew.

The fight was imminent now. The umpire of the contest stood in a wide squat, raised his rickety bamboo approximation of a fan high in one hand. Hush fell, breaths were held. The two owners nodded their readiness. The fan slashed down, the hood upon the white bird was ripped off and then the two roosters were hurled into the centre of the ring to wild cheers.

They met in the air in a scrabbling flurry of claws and wings and beaks and then fell to the ground still fighting. The white one jumped and the red one rose to meet it, necks extending, feet gouging, feathers on end, and when they clattered to the ground for the second time they backed apart from one another. The men roared and started to beat upon the crates, goading them on. The roosters, though, were wary, circled each other as around them their feathers drifted slowly down.

'Evenly matched, it seems,' muttered the man. 'I thought the red one had weight on the other. I suppose white is a misleading colour, lessening. Tell me: after that opening flurry, which one has your favour?'

'I don't know. I haven't seen a cockfight before.'

'You're a samurai, aren't you? Can you not discern their fighting spirits?'

'They're just birds.'

'But surely they have some telltale—'

'What are you doing out here?' snapped Musashi. 'Can't find this in the city proper?'

'In truth I came to speak to you, Sir Miyamoto.'

In an instant, in the saying of that sentence, the man's entire comportment changed, his guise shed. Musashi looked at him anew and the image of Denshichiro screaming in the garrison of the Tokugawa came to him, of a voice commanding him into silence.

'I know you,' said Musashi, alarmed. 'You're of the Yoshioka.'

'Tadanari Kozei, of the ward of—' he began, but did not finish as Musashi made for his swords anticipating a rush of tea-coloured samurai from outside. Kozei placed a hand on the young man's wrist before he could draw his weapons, neither gentle nor restraining, spoke evenly: 'I came alone, and I came unarmed. I only wish to speak with you.'

'You are without swords. I doubt you are unarmed.'

Tadanari released Musashi, smiled. From his belt he took a folding fan, which he revealed to be plated with iron, strong and thick enough to parry a sword, and his long tobacco pipe the metal mouthpiece of which ended in a point sharp enough to stab.

'These are only the tools of common sense,' he said. 'But, as you see, you have your swords and I do not. Furthermore you bested Seijuro, who was half my age and a superior swordsman. I am quite at your mercy. Will you calm yourself, and listen to what I have to say?'

In the ring the white rooster sank down, spread its wings, flared its tail and brayed long and piercing. Musashi leant back against the wall.

'Thank you,' said the bald samurai. He replaced the fan and the pipe at his belt, and then he too turned to look at the fight once more. 'It is clear you are a man of skill with the blade. Firstly I must ask, as a matter of martial respect: who did you study under?'

'Munisai Shinmen.'

'Is that so? I saw Munisai fight in Osaka, when he was named the Nation's Finest. Your style had been described to me. It does not sound much like his methods.'

'He died when I was a child. Since then I have taught myself.'

'Of course. Might I ask of Munisai's death? I was suspicious of—'

'He chose it for himself.'

The red rooster suddenly dashed towards the white one and butted it backwards, and the low men of Maruta all sensing blood, longing for it, began a roar that died feeble when the two roosters did not follow through with claw or beak, settled for merely shrieking at one another and circling once more.

'Tadanari Kozei,' said Musashi, 'Akiyama spoke of you. You're the one who sent him to kill me. Is it you who wields the power at the school?'

'My counsel is valued.'

'But not your hand. What worth that? Do you value it yourself, or is that why you sent another to enact your will? Coward.'

Tadanari bore the insult entirely impassively. In the crowd an errant flailing elbow knocked a hand clutched full of coins open, copper scattering across the earth amongst feet. The owner of the money sank desperately to his knees, began to grope blindly with clawed hands through the legs around him.

'I read the late Sir Akiyama's thoughts upon you, of your character,' said Tadanari, 'of how you think, of what you value, and I do not think the school of Yoshioka are who you believe us to be. We are not high-born, you know. We are not the inheritors of centuries of prestige. No noble bloodline flows through me: my great grandfather was a cobbler. The great-great-grandfather of the young heirs Denshichiro and Seijuro was in turn a dyer of silk. That, the roots of the Yoshioka. A humble craftsman who discovered the shades of the colour of tea, and from the rolling of the presses and the hauling of vats found strength and dexterity in his arms, which he turned to the sword. Raised himself up, won renown, founded the school of which my ancestor was the first student. Is this not what you speak so highly of?'

'Then bring out your ancestors to meet me,' said Musashi. 'You cannot? Then do not speak of their virtue to me. I am concerned with you. You now ruling the Yoshioka, the inheritors of that "virtuous struggle". Are you humble? Tell me: would you have a man perform seppuku for you?'

'Seppuku is a noble choice.'

'It is an abomination! The greatest abomination! And you, all like you, revel in it. Not humble but fancy yourselves gods; you are a devourer of decent men, of men who could be decent given the chance.'

The vehemence of his words broke Tadanari's façade for but an instant, the slighest muscle rippling beneath the corner of his eye: 'That, the source of your hatred?'

'I hate it all, everything you stand for.'

'Hate is a very short and sad thing to live your life in thrall to.'

'In this world it is necessary.'

Tadanari said nothing for a while. One of the owners was lashing a whip, cracking it down on the dais beneath him again and again as though his rooster would understand the threat and throw itself forward. 'You will think as you will think,' he said. 'But I do not believe that we should be enemies. Duly I have come to negotiate an ending to our feud.'

'Negotiate?' snorted Musashi. 'Where were the negotiations when you sent Akiyama on my trail? Or on Mount Hiei?'

Tadanari ignored the question. 'We are both disciples of the blade, are we not? It is evident you are a man of rare skill. Our school is always searching for exceptional talent. Your ability and our renown together could be a formidable combination.'

'Are you offering me a place amongst you?'

Tadanari looked at him earnestly. In the ring wings were thrashed wide to intimidate, to boast, yet the roosters circled still. Musashi laughed bitterly.

'If the thought of working with us in particular has grown too distasteful,' said Tadanari carefully, 'we have fine relations with Lords the length of the country. There are always positions as swordmasters available somewhere, not necessarily in Yoshioka colours. We could recommend you thoroughly to one of them, far from Kyoto if you so desire. Honshu, Kyushu, Shikoku . . . Wealth and prestige on all of them.'

'I have no desire to serve.'

'I see,' said Tadanari.

'From where has this urge for bargaining sprung?' said Musashi. 'It was Denshichiro who demanded the coming duel. Adamant upon it. Does he even know you are here?'

'I speak on his behalf, whether he is aware of it or not.'

'Then why do you want to bargain now?'

The bald samurai was spared answering by a flurry from within the ring; the owner of the red rooster hooked a staff under the body of his champion and flicked it towards the white. The two creatures engaged in another frantic exchange, squawking and thrashing as the pair of them climbed up each other, and then upon the earth amidst the shed feathers a spatter of blood fell. The crowd roared, even though they could not tell from which cockerel it had fallen.

'Sir Miyamoto—'

'Stop calling me "sir",' spat Musashi. 'I don't need it. I don't need to be meaninglessly flattered to know my own worth. Do you, Kozei?'

'Musashi, then,' said Tadanari. 'Where do you see this ending, really, should you pursue it? What do you stand to gain personally from, say, killing Denshichiro? What do you think that would prove?'

'That you, and all that think like you, can be beaten. That this world made in your despicable image is finite – can be finite. The perversity of the Way, which is a cult of death, which swallows all hope and goodness. Nebulous and foglike and corrupt to the core. But my way! I show my way, which is as light. Is not codified, not taught and driven into unwilling skulls but felt. Known. True. All these things beating in the hearts of all men. That the reason I fight, I speak, to show that if it is believed it must be dispelled. If it is written it must be unwritten. If it stands tall it must be burnt low. This the only recourse for your world, and then the world will be as it ought. Living. Alive. Honest.'

Oh, the saying of these words, of words like these at the times they conjured themselves, felt so wonderful to Musashi. The heat that burnt in the throat, in the heart, it was the absolute perfect certainty of youth. When he spat them everything was clear, explained, elucidated by their very being. He did not need to consider their meaning or ponder the depths of himself: all he needed was to say and to find his vindication.

Tadanari heard these words, and said, 'But are *you* honest, Musashi?'

'What?' said Musashi, unsettled for a moment, pierced, and then a sneer deflected the spoken blow as surely as a sword against a sword. 'Of course I am. Counter to you, to all of you.'

'Honesty is purity,' said Tadanari. 'Purity is focus. You, however, set your rage and your enemies as broad as the sky.'

'Nothing easier to read than the sky. Nothing more honest.'

'Indeed,' said Tadanari. 'Then would your true satisfaction lie in killing every last man of the Yoshioka? There is a third brother, too, a child. Would you kill him also on account of his name? You who speak so passionately of the abomination of seppuku, of the sanctity of life? Are you at your base a charlatan bent on nothing more than selfish murder?'

The white rooster suddenly dashed and soared through the air, too quick for the red one, clawing fierce at its eyes. Its spur gouged deep, bursting, and the red rooster shrieked and bolted half blinded. It skittered and leapt in a mad flapping of wings, vaulting the boundary of the ring, and then it was amongst the spectators. Men staggered back and fell over one another in a mess of limbs and feathers as the rooster thrashed frenzied over all their prostrate forms, scrabbled until it found earth beyond the bodies and then gone, out of the hall and out of sight.

In the ring the white rooster shrieked and bristled triumphant, and then from the mess of men somebody uttered, 'Frost of hells, what just happened?'

'That bantam's got a tiny arsehole is what.'

'Coward,' agreed another.

'He wouldn't have fled if you fools hadn't fallen over,' said the owner of the red rooster. 'Anyway, the match is postponed. An impasse. All wagers are quashed.'

'To the hells with you, an impasse!' said the owner of the white.

'These bouts are to the death, are they not? Your bird was unable to kill mine. So – a draw.'

'What's the ruling?' said the bookmaker to the umpire.

'I . . .' said the umpire, his crude fan now a ridiculous mockery in his hand, he searching in his mind for some form of precedent that he could draw upon. 'It's . . .'

'It's victory for the white!' shouted someone in the crowd.

'Impasse! Impasse!' shouted another.

The hall erupted in noise once more. A lot of shouting that grew uglier quickly, men suddenly remembering the tools at their waists, things of common labour like hammers or pry bars or razor strops had other, more primal uses. Fingers jabbing into chests, noses pressed into the sides of faces, phlegm brought forth from old sinuses. Around the feet now in the ring the white rooster capered, ignored.

'Dignity!' bellowed Tadanari.

He was shorter than most of the men there, swordless and wearing the garb of some old fop out for a summer afternoon of fun, but his tone was obeyed, had to be obeyed. All turned to look at him, found his posture regal, his eyes deadened into perfect objectivity.

Nevertheless, someone spat, 'Who are you, old man?'

'I am Tadanari Kozei,' he said, no trace of anger in his voice, 'swordmaster of the school of Yoshioka. All of you will cease this shameful outrage immediately, and behave as citizens of Kyoto ought.'

The silence manifested freezing in the hollows of chests as he was recognized, verified. The man who had questioned him threw himself to his knees and drove his face grovelling into the dust.

Tadanari ignored his prostrate form. He pointed a finger at the umpire. 'You, are you not in command? We shall resolve this civilly. Make a ruling.'

'Sir,' said the umpire, stared at the ground sprent with feathers.

'I would suggest,' said Tadanari, seeing the futility of waiting, 'that victory be given to the white rooster. He is, after all, the only one left standing in the ring of combat.'

'Sir.' That meant he agreed.

'Declare the red rooster killed.'

'It was killed,' said the umpire, swallowed. 'The red rooster was killed.'

'So it shall be,' said Tadanari, but even with a samurai present a shout of protest began. Before it could devolve entirely once more, Tadanari held up his betting chit for all to see: 'In case any of you doubt my impartiality, look at this.'

Money on the red.

'The red rooster was killed. There shall be no challenging of this, no repercussions,' said Tadanari. 'The rooster died within that ring.'

There was a low mutter of agreement. Those that collected winnings collected them without gloating, and those that had lost began to leave sullenly. In the gathered hearts the rooster was slaughtered in a multitude of ways, and any actual breath it might yet continue to draw counted for nil.

The master of the Yoshioka turned to Musashi. 'Do you see?' he said. 'Left to themselves, blood would have been shed. But no – here now, life and civilization.'

A curl on Musashi's lips. 'This is your conception of honesty?'

'What of yours?' Tadanari said.

Again he probed, and again Musashi was taken back to the village of Miyamoto and to Dorinbo, to what he aspired to be.

After a moment he said, 'I offer you this compromise. First of all, you will take the head of Akiyama, wherever it is now, and return it to Mount Hiei to be cremated and interred in full propriety with the rest of his remains. Secondly, in place of duelling at the Hall of Thirty-Three Doors, Denshichiro must apologize to me. He must get on his knees and beg forgiveness for himself and his brother and for the entire school instigating this, in front of all in the city who would care to witness it. Then it will be over, and I will leave Kyoto. Bloodlessly.'

Tadanari sucked air through his teeth as he considered the likelihood of it, and after a moment he nodded a nod that started tentative and grew definite.

'Thank you, Musashi,' he said. 'I should truly like to see your style of swordsmanship one day, regardless.'

'I'll await your word. You know where I am.'

They stood looking at one another for a moment. Neither one of them bowed. Tadanari turned and left the hall, began to head back towards the city proper. After a moment Musashi followed, called to him outside amongst the dissipating crowd. Tadanari stopped and looked back.

'Your man at Sekigahara,' Musashi said. 'I beat him fair. He was wounded but the duel was of his urging, not mine. I offered no insult to the body.'

The Yoshioka samurai gave no reaction. Soon he was lost amongst the bodies and Musashi was left in Maruta, simmering still.

Chapter Twenty-nine

The tortoise advanced one ponderous foot after the other through the halls of the school. Though it was well cared for and could not remember the sensation of hunger, the drive for food was perpetual and it headed now to a place where it knew sustenance was always plenty. Unneedful of the light, steady through dark corridors and hard floors treading a route decades familiar, it came now to the room it sought and found two shadows splayed across the glowing paper.

The tension and posture in them was warding even at a primal, reptile level. The tortoise fled at its torpid pace for somewhere calmer.

Inside that room, Denshichiro all but paced in his rage: 'You mean to strip me of the glory? This past week of which I have devoted myself, my spirit to the thought of felling Miyamoto? Seen it in dreams with such clarity? All that tossed away on your whim, that potential majesty wasted. Your decision, old man, with neither my knowledge nor my consent, to annul this.'

'You have heard me wrong,' said Tadanari, his arms crossed and his hands up the sleeves of his kimono. 'I have annulled nothing. You will still attend the Hall, as will Miyamoto. There you will bow to him and you will apologize to him on behalf of the school regarding our attempts to assassinate him.'

So levelly spoken that it took a moment for Denshichiro to understand.

'No!' the young samurai said, so shocked he could only snarl the thoughts as they came to him. 'How can you . . . ? How can you even have considered that? In the name of Yoshioka you sanctioned this? That's not your name, old man! You may have seen the beams of this building being raised but that is not your name! My name! My name! No! Unthinkable! Miyamoto, that . . . I will not bow to the low son of a whore that felled my brother!'

'You must.'

'No!' said Denshichiro. 'How will the people ever respect us again, if they see me bowing to him?'

'The tide will cover the sand,' said Tadanari. 'Do you not understand this? We have been here a hundred years. Miyamoto a handful of weeks. There will be scandal and rumour and low jokes for a few months, but when they have exhausted themselves things will resume as they have always been. Consider Mount Hiei—'

'Cease wielding that as a weapon against me!'

'I speak not of your actions. Consider the Lord Oda, who wanted Hiei eradicated. He succeeded, until he was betrayed and killed, and now monks inhabit the slopes once more because all remember that monks always inhabited Hiei. I went and spoke to Miyamoto, listened to him speak. He is nought but meaningless rage, all of what he says no more than ranting. Do you know what he stands against the most, what he waves before all as proof of the world's wrongness?'

'What?'

'Seppuku,' said Tadanari, and he repeated it once more shaking his head in disgust. 'I could hardly believe Akiyama's missives, but it is true. That propriety to him is an affront, and do you not see that that is the kind of man with which we are engaged? Base lunacy, he no more than a maddened dog, and no sympathy will be given to him – he's merely abnormally good with a sword. And when he is gone everything he did here will be forgotten, and everything we are and everything we have been will be remembered.'

'Why not you that goes and bows to him, then?'

'Because,' said Tadanari thinly, 'I do not carry the name Yoshioka.'

'I will kill him,' said Denshichiro. 'I'll take his head, and there will be no need to wait for any tide of any kind to restore any . . . I will kill him. Of this there is no doubt. I will not be bested by tricks like Seijuro was.'

'Miyamoto is skilled,' said Tadanari. 'Your brother's humiliation and the ten other men he killed beside stand in testament to that. You are skilled also, but not overwhelmingly so. The match would be an even contest. This is fact. Admit this. Through your pride, admit this. Either of you could prevail. If you win, we gain what will be ours anyway, what we already have. You lose, and not only do you die—'

'I'm not afraid of death.'

'Not only do you die, but the school is plunged further into scandal. The name Yoshioka, which your father and your grandfathers bore before you, is sullied. We are already deeper into this outrage than we ought to be. But it is salvageable, of this I am sure. If it worsens . . . There is nothing to be gained by fighting him, Denshichiro, but everything to lose. The risk is entirely ours. Why roll a die you know to be weighted?'

'Because he felled my brother,' said Denshichiro. 'Because I am samurai, and I demand even the chance of vengeance.'

'Miyamoto will find his own end regardless of our intervention.'

'Dying is not enough!' said Denshichiro. 'He has to be killed, by me! And all have to know it! The respect the city holds for us is faltering. In their hearts, their image of us is tarnishing, rotting away with each step that dog or a bastard Tokugawa samurai takes upon our streets. I can tell. I'm attuned.'

'What does the inside of their hearts matter?' said Tadanari. 'When has a single human heart ever altered anything outside of the confines of the ribcage?'

'We deserve to be beloved,' said Denshichiro, and he said it with such conviction, such personal umbrage in the eyes that it galled Tadanari. 'We are this city!'

'We deserve to be followed because their fathers followed us. That is the sole logic that we reap the benefit of. The logic you scorn now. Heed me: Miyamoto is a snow in the late spring, nothing more. He will be remembered here only with a passing curiosity, if at all. Nothing enduring, nothing permanent. Not like we can be. Not like we are.'

'Have you no trust in the Way of the Yoshioka? In me? How did my father ever tolerate the advice of a man as gelded as you?'

'Because he was not a boar-headed idiot intent on his family's destruction.'

'You call me idiot? Well I call you coward!' shouted Denshichiro, and he raised a hand to point at Tadanari, jabbed his finger savagely again and again. 'I will eat shit before I bow to Miyamoto, and I will eat shit before I take counsel from you again!'

Tadanari found it hard to contain his own fury. Somehow he managed to force the words out levelly: 'Bear a little shame now and your great-grandchildren will thank you.'

'I'll earn a great glory and they will thank me more,' said Denshichiro, and he turned and made for the door, the frail frame of which nearly shattered as he hauled it open. He stormed off down the corridor still cursing, feet graceless and heavy.

There in the silence Tadanari stood. Looked around at the walls, at the floor. Wondered why it was they stood.

Some time later Ujinari appeared as lithe and silent as a ghost and asked what it was that had set Denshichiro's temper ablaze. Tadanari explained.

'I shall speak to him,' said Ujinari. 'You're in no mood to. Your counsel, your strategy is wise, I'm sure he will see that. He just is as he is. Once the tempest of his blood has ceased I am certain he too will agree.'

'Thank you.'

'Strange times.' Ujinari smiled. 'I wish this summer would end, this heat would break. But we are the Yoshioka. We will endure.'

'We are the Kozei.'

'One and the same.'

Tadanari looked at his son and saw the confidence there, the loyalty. He wished that he could share in it, that Denshichiro could share in it too.

* * *

Later, within the private garden of the school, a pretty cask of lacquered persimmon wood sat upon the dais. It looked like something fine sake would be kept in. On its side was painted an image of a flowing river, a catfish rearing its head between gourds being carried merrily downstream. Tadanari had unscrewed the lid of the cask, and this lay to one side. On the rim flies congregated.

Inside was Akiyama's head, awaiting transport to Mount Hiei in the morning.

The cask had been packed with cloves and mugwort and the ashes of incense, and yet still the smell of rot pervaded. This macabre company was the only kind Tadanari could tolerate that night. Yet he could not bring himself to bring the head fully out.

He simply sat there. staring at the tip of a peeled nose and the locks of curled red hair that hung over the lip.

'What was it that caused you to break from us?' Tadanari asked Akiyama. It was an honest question and he waited some time for an answer. When he received none, he spoke on: 'It cannot be the nonsense that masterless spouts. I listened to that. That could not have swayed you. For all your aberrations you were steady. You, of all the adepts, might have been the most loyal. Up until the moment you weren't. Much like a murderer, I suppose. What was it, Nagayoshi? Revealed to you in an instant, like a Bodhisattva seeing suddenly the path to the pure lands? A moment when things you knew to be stone became as liquid? Can all men experience such a thing? An instant when unseen bells are struck and things that were thought jewels resonate fit to shatter?'

He realized he was speaking aloud to an incomplete corpse.

Tadanari turned his eyes away in embarrassment at his

own unrest. He looked to his hands, where between a thumb and a forefinger he was rubbing one of his ivory netsuke pouch-clasps anxiously. He moved the thumb and saw the image of Saint Fudo looking back.

In the devil-saint's right hand, the Cutter of Delusions.

At the sight of the purging sword for a moment he wavered, quailed, and he thought that all was dashed, that the celestial edge was passing through him at that instant. He rebelled, dropped the clasp, covered it with a palm on his thigh and then forced calm upon himself. His eyes found their way to the centremost boulder in the bed of sand. Always cool the surface of obsidian, the knife-ridge of it enamelled like ice unmelting, beguiling the ego away to nothingness. Formed of millennia and sharp enough to break the span of a mere handful of decades across, to rack a human life brazen for examination.

Candles burnt. His unseeing eyes did not notice his son's arrival. Ujinari did not disturb him, waited for his father to become aware of his presence in his own time. There was a near-startled moment when he did, then informal bows exchanged.

'Deep in thought,' the son said.

'Nnn.'

Ujinari looked at the cask and the sliver of Akiyama's head that was visible. Tadanari grunted again, waved the flies away and then replaced the lid.

'Let me ease your mind, Father, turn it away from such morbid things. I have spoken with Denshichiro: he will do it. For the betterment of the school, he will apologize to Miyamoto.'

'He agreed?'

'He is not happy, but he sees the wisdom of it.'

'How long did it take to convince him?'

'Not long. You misjudge him. Once he was calm, he was willing to listen.'

'To you, perhaps. It seems you have the gift of diplomacy. Perhaps we ought to send you out as envoy for the school.'

'Hold your praise, for regrettably I am not that talented,' said Ujinari. 'There was one thing Denshichiro demanded.'

'His acquiescence not total, then?'

Ujinari chose his words carefully: 'He is aggrieved by your acting on his behalf without his consent. Greatly. I think it is irrational, but it is how he is. He will only apologize to Miyamoto if you are not present, and then, the matter settled, you agree to retire from the city until the spring.'

'Unthinkable,' said Tadanari. 'He cannot be left to govern himself, not with the Tokugawa situation so volatile. Look what he did—'

'Father, I believe I can temper him.'

'You?'

'I am his friend. As you were to Naokata. Kozei and Yoshioka, stronger together, no?'

'Naokata and Denshichiro are not . . .' said Tadanari, but did not finish. He eyed his son levelly. 'How sure of this are you?'

'Relatively,' said Ujinari. 'I convinced him to agree to this, did I not?'

'But he is tempestuous,' said Tadanari. 'What of the incident upon Hiei, say? That came out of nothing. Could you have stopped that?'

'I could have, yes, if I had put it upon myself to act as counsel,' said Ujinari. 'I was lax. I beg your forgiveness for my error. But I swear from this moment forth I will be vigilant.'

'You would have to be with him as constant as a hawk on the hand.'

'In your stead, I would do so. For the future of the school.'

Tadanari looked at his son, saw the responsibility in his eyes. Ujinari had worn a longsword for seven years now, but under the shadow of Seijuro Tadanari had always thought of him and of Denshichiro as latently younger, or perhaps simply young. No truth to the thought, just felt inherent. Now, though, that shadow cast aside and Ujinari raised up into the light, Tadanari saw him perhaps for the first time as a man proper.

It was both humbling and exalting.

'Very well,' he said. 'I shall make my preparations to leave. It will be good to escape this heat, I suppose.'

'Thank you for the honour of your trust, Father,' said Ujinari, pressed his brow to the floor, his voice full of candour and spirit and all the things Tadanari knew to be good. 'I swear, I vow to you with all that I can vow that Denshichiro and I will make you proud of us.'

Chapter Thirty

'I did it,' said Musashi. 'Akiyama's head is being taken to Hiei. It will be cremated and interred . . . It will be burnt, and put with the rest of the body. He is whole again.'

'Good,' said Ameku, and nothing more.

She was working on the loom. The mat hung before her was nearly complete, a delicate shade of green as broad either way as a man's outstretched arms. The wooden levers of the machine counted instances as faithfully as the beating of a heart.

'I made arrangements peacefully,' said Musashi.

She nodded.

She was not moved as he thought she would have been moved. The set of his shoulders lessened. He took his scabbarded swords from out of his belt and sat down upon the two wooden steps that led down into the room where she worked, wanting to sit closer to her, wanting to provoke something from her.

'Will you sing for me?' he tried.

Ameku laughed. 'You, who cry "too much noise in Kyoto, too much noise!" want a song?'

'It's just tonight. The silence here now is . . .' He could not find the words to explain.

'I do not want to sing tonight,' she said. 'So, no song. A song that you are made to sing, it is no true song.'

He accepted this. Ameku pinched a reed into a noose, hooked it upon the loom, and her fingers were calloused and worn and yet he saw them as lithe and delicate.

This mood had hung over him since he had spoken to Tadanari at the cockfight. He felt achievement, and no achievement at all. He felt as though someone had stolen words from his throat and left him mouthing like a carp in silence. The method he had envisioned in the drums fated to be witnessed only by his imagination.

'Tomorrow,' he said, 'Denshichiro Yoshioka bows to me before the whole city.'

'What?' she said, and he explained himself further. She stopped working, and he could see the confusion in her in the tilting of her head. 'Why, you want this?'

'Because it needs to be . . .' he said.

'Akiyama's head is safe. It is done. So do not go there. You trust him? You think he will do this, bow in peace?'

'I have the word of his master.'

'You do not trust this man,' she said, all but laughing in scorn. 'I know you do not. So why do you go?'

'What else am I to do? This has to be done.'

'You need to . . . to win?'

He did not answer, and in that silence gave her one.

'If he bows . . . then what? What do you do?'

'I suppose I shall take my freedom. Go where it dictates.'

'Freedom is a stupid word,' she said. 'It is a stupid word in Ryukyu tongue too. Men on Ryukyu say they got freedom, those who go out on the sea. Feel the wind. Think he can go anywhere. What does he do? He comes back to land and the town and the house and the wife and the child, or the sea eats him and the sea is not changed. That, freedom?'

'That is how you think,' he said entirely neutrally, speaking simply for the sake of filling the void between them.

Outside a drunk vomited away his misery.

'Go, don't go,' she said. 'It is the same. This hour tomorrow, you have the same future. The only reason to go – hope of sword. The only reason – revenge.'

'It is no revenge, said Musashi. 'Won't you listen to me? I have told you that I am not killing. Denshichiro is bowing to me. He is the symbol of all that is wrong in this world, the pompous fools who demand all kneel before them. Those that take all and offer nothing, the unworthy bloated sons of whores that—'

Ameku cut him off before his fury ignited itself inextinguishable. 'Musashi, stop your . . . raf raf raf like a dog,' she said. 'On and on and on so many words you shout. Every day. Every day. Shout and shout and make for you a nice little wall, build around your heart. Armour.'

Effortlessly, she cast him down. He sat with his elbows on his thighs, looking up at her. The loom clacked and clacked, a dolorous rhythm. He looked at his swords where they lay before him. He took a breath.

'I cannot return home without having attained a thing of worth,' he said quietly.

'You think this is such a thing?'

'It must be,' he said. 'It must be. The world is wrong and the Way is obscene, and all this must be fought. Someone must fight it. Someone must humble them. Even if I cannot express it fully, if I feel it, if I know it to be right – is it not worthy?'

'Why do *you* need to speak? Why do *you* need to tell? If it is good, it is good. Nothing to be said, nothing you say changes it.'

'Because *you* think me false.'

He had let more emotion into his voice than he had meant to, and he was embarrassed for this slip, and yet even so she did not answer. Her silence maddened him. He did not know whether he would have preferred her to agree or disagree, only that she would speak. Acknowledge him. She that created so enviously easy with her voice. She with her voice that seemed to him to breach the heavens, that brought beads of dew to the embers and made all as smoke. If only she would sing for him now, perhaps he might be able to pull an answer from the mire.

But the back of her head was all she offered him.

Chapter Thirty-one

On the eastern banks of the river Kamo the Hall of Thirty-Three Doors had stood for four hundred years. At its creation it had been painted brilliant blue and red but this had faded with time and none could bring themselves to risk sullying the memory of what it had been, and so it had been left to assume a grand and sombre darkness. The peak of its sloped and tiled roof was high and its structure immensely long, the eponymous doors contiguous along one side, each five paces across and twice the height of a man separated by a thick beam. To fire an arrow accurately the length of it was considered a challenge, and yearly men would compete in day-long marathons to hit a target at the opposite end, loosing ten thousand arrows or more and hitting six, seven, eight thousand times.

These thousands of arrows without, and within a thousand and one statues of the Buddha Kannon. A thousand of these for the thousand dimensions of the mortal chiliocosm stood in ten raised ranks. Carved of dark cypress and brushed with gold, each the height of a man with robes flowing from narrow shoulders, epicene faces full of love and behind each of them like a peacock's tail a halo of arms clutching the myriad implements of Kannon's grace: lanterns, brushes, icons of swastikas, lotuses, jars of balm, rosaries.

They arrayed five hundred either side of a great effigy of the enlightened one in the centre, sat cross-legged and representative of the thousand and first dimension, the pure lands beyond to which Kannon had ascended. It dwarfed the others, his golden head from which nine smaller golden heads sprouted surrounded by golden bells hung on golden chains; aureate, so flawlessly aureate his body, his aura. Before him a sheen of incense smoke and the flickering of tall candles, prayers daubed upon the wax in ink, letters slowly devolving with the melting.

And there shielding this divine host on the lowest rank stood the twenty-eight guardians of Tenbu, their statues of plain and humble darkwood. There Raijin and Fujin cavorting in their tempests, there proud Nanda around whom the dragon of wisdom coiled, four-eyed Hibakara playing his warding biwa lute, fierce Gobujo with a sword in either hand as a symbol of his inhuman might.

All frozen and still and looking outwards through the thirty-three doors of the hall cast wide open. Compassionate gazes and furious scowls taking in the grounds of the temple and the silent crowd of hundreds of men and women and children that had gathered opposite.

Between these two hosts, immortal on his right and mortal on his left, stood Denshichiro Yoshioka.

He waited in solitude. No mark of rank or prestige had the head of the Yoshioka brought with him, no silk awning nor standard of the school nor fine paper parasol held by an attendant to shield him from the light and the heat. He waited with only the sweat upon his brow, his swords at his side and the plain tea-coloured jacket he had always worn.

Unasked the question amongst those watching, eyes upon Denshichiro's knees, imagining dust upon them, wondering. The only noise that of the city drifting over the walls of the compound; the beating of the drums at practice, oblivious of any form of observance.

Musashi strode over the hundred paces of the Shichijo bridge, the wooden planks ringing beneath his feet. He too heard the drums, impossible not to in the streets, passing from the radius of one group to another to another with the separate beats and patterns converging, merging and then separating in his ears.

The right hand kept the rhythm: *bom, a-bom, a-bombombom.*

From the crest of the bridge's arch he saw the blunted peak of Mount Higashi deep and green, saw the face of Toyotomi's colossal Buddha gazing out of the massive hall that enshrined it at the Hoko temple, saw the tiers of pagodas reaching skywards. Lastly, saw the red-and-white gate of Rengeo temple, and behind it the mottled roof of the Hall of Thirty-Three Doors.

On this he focused. His eyes felt as if they were pulsing, throbbing. Perhaps tonight he could sleep.

He had hauled his rope belt around himself thrice, so tight around him that it cut into his waist, wedged his swords into his flesh, hardened his posture into something taut and unshakeable. It felt good. Prepared him.

The closer he got to the gate the more people took notice of him, they perhaps gathering to bear witness to the apology and knowing who he was. Some fell in behind him, saying nothing, followed his steps expectantly.

He crossed the liminal threshold and entered the grounds of the temple beneath a great hanging awning of the Buddhist colours, vertical bands of white-red-yellow-green-purple repeated. Those behind him followed. The enclave was sparse of greenery, no more than a clearly delineated garden and pond in one corner and disparate trees segregated amidst an expanse of grey gravel. Pebbles crunched beneath Musashi's feet as he walked, dust rising, and habitually he tested it for balance and grip as he walked, dragging his straw sandals.

The crowd ahead waiting at the Hall were unavoidable. They saw him, or perhaps the smaller mass of those walking behind him, the turning of their heads like wind through grass.

Distant, the drums still, the left hand batting out the urgency: *atta-ta-tata, ta-tata*.

Rounding the corner, and there Denshichiro stood alone beneath the gaze of the great Buddha Kannon. The head of the Yoshioka drew himself up as Musashi approached, swept his jacket back to put his left hand on the scabbards at his waist. The timeless dignified pose. Musashi was glad to see the Yoshioka samurai held it until he came to stop ten paces away from him; pompous idiot would only make falling to his knees appear even more of a concession.

The pair of them stood looking at each other. There was loathing in Denshichiro's eyes, identical to that which his brother had worn. Musashi matched it.

'Get on with it, then,' he snarled. 'Loud voice, so all can hear.'

Denshichiro said, 'I thank you for deigning to grant me the respect of punctuality, Sir Miyamoto.'

He gave no signal but as he finished speaking there was sudden motion from the crowd, from around the sides of the Hall. Men emerged, samurai. They were not wearing the livery of the school but they were obviously Denshichiro's men disguised, drawing their swords and quickly moving to surround Musashi in a loose ring. Eight of them.

Denshichiro, the ninth, said, 'No fleeing this time.'

Of course he would say that. Of course he would do this. Fated, and Musashi knew this, had known this despite whatever he might have protested to Ameku. There was black glee on Denshichiro's face, and Musashi mirrored it.

Now a real test, a real vindication, and, if he persevered, real proof, real victory.

The Yoshioka made no move to rush him, confident in their numbers. Denshichiro began binding his sleeves up, jerked his chin for Musashi to ready himself also. A conceited concession born of the certainty of triumph. His sleeves cut away and his arms already bared, Musashi dropped down and sank his sweat-slick hands into the gravel, coated them with the pallid dust. Rendered them corpselike; here the absolute trial, a theory so keenly felt he was staking his life on it.

He rose, took a breath. With his right hand he drew his longsword and with his left he drew his shortsword. Holding both, he sank into the fighting stance.

Distant the right: *a-bom, a-bom, a-bombombom.*

Distant the left: *atta-ta-tata, ta-tata, tata-ta ta atta-ta-tat.*

Together, rhythm.

Envisioned only days ago, the execution of this technique was unheard of but the inspiration pure. A longsword offered only protection from one direction, easily overwhelmed and surrounded. A spear gave safety in its length but its lethality far less, used best against massed immobile ranks on the battlefield where the point could not be dodged. Two swords together, though: reach and edge and mobility.

If, as no one had before, you had the strength.

If, as no one had before, you had the timing.

From the crowd a murmur of surprise at the sight of both blades. From the Yoshioka samurai only the faintest hints of whatever they might be feeling, their faces locked in the concentration of combat. From the swarm of watching Buddhas impossible love, endless love.

Prepared, Denshichiro drew his sword, stepped forward. His men did so too, the noose growing taut. Musashi raised his shortsword above his head, held the longsword out before him and turned in a tense, coiled rotation.

'Here,' said Denshichiro, unheard by Musashi. 'Me.'

A tightening in Musashi's throat, in his spine, in the muscles of his arms. A quivering of his left biceps that he could not contain. Everything balanced now, balanced on the edges of eleven swords, the world seeming to lose colour as the focus came, heat gone, taste gone, smell gone, but touch ultra-aware, the sword grips tight upon either palm, the wrist sensing the balance, waiting, closer, waiting . . .

The scrape of gravel to his side. Musashi whirled at the noise, and whether the man had stumbled or not he could not tell but it was enough to nominate a target, to spark. Musashi burst forward raising both his swords high as if to strike and he could see or sense the indecision in the samurai's trained eyes, caught between the double threat of the swords where he had been ruthlessly taught only to anticipate a single. Musashi brought the shortsword down first and the man brought his blade up to parry it. The steel met and Musashi rode the anticipated impact, twisted his body around and from the side brought the longsword down on the man's arms where they were braced.

One hand doing the work of two. The edge met flesh above both elbows and cut finely, instantly – the Yoshioka man's sword caught the light and Musashi was aware for a vivid moment of the queer image of a sword within the sword, some foreign weapon carved upon the blade – and his own steel bucked as it passed all the way through the momentary obstruction of meat and bone, and then there was blood in the air and the severed limbs were falling still clutching the weapon.

And because they had to understand that this was possible, because Musashi had to understand that this was possible, even though the man was killed he kept going. As the arms and the strangely marked sword clattered to the earth, as the pathetic stumps were spread wide and the scream began, Musashi raked his shortsword across the young samurai's throat and then stepped back and scythed his longsword around, cleaved the man's leg off at the thigh.

Distant, the girls went: *Sore! Sore! Sore sore sore sore sore!*

Gurgling and writhing the pieces lay on the ground around him.

Shock, open now, from the Yoshioka, from the crowd, as he had intended. But, where their hearts seized, Musashi continued unhindered, knowing that rhythm, that momentum, was vital. He turned on the next man instantly, covered the distance between them in two strides, and lashed at him from the right with the longsword. The same folly – the man moved to block the first attack, leaving his left open, and Musashi's shortsword took him across the belly.

One of the samurai leapt in as Musashi righted himself, the Yoshioka man swinging his sword down. Musashi raised both his swords crossed to catch the blade, to cradle it, and then he hauled upwards, stronger, raising the samurai's arms and exposing the body. He lashed out with his knee into the groin or the belly, connected meaty, and then his shortsword hissed as a spectre as he disentangled it and thrust it deep into flesh.

Onwards unbroken, driving the dying Yoshioka man backwards and hurling him at the next closest samurai. This man was young and lithe and danced around the body, but his arms were frail and seeing this – no, knowing this, realizing this without seeing – Musashi smashed his longsword around savagely, pure strength, battering the Yoshioka sword out of the way with the flat of his blade and then, before the motion had even finished, before he or the samurai had had a chance to recover from that blow, the shortsword whipped out and took him across the chest.

Distant the rhythm: *a-bom, a-bom, a-bombombom.*

Close, Musashi's heart: *ka-dum, ka-dum, ka-dum.*

It was working, working, and he felt nothing, only did, manifested what ought to be, had to be. The fifth of the Yoshioka came bravely, fearlessly, tapping Musashi's longsword to the side with a practised feint and closing in so that they were hip to hip. Familiar this move. Already seen on the slopes of Hiei, already repelled. As other men had done before he tried to barge Musashi backwards, and as Musashi had done before he resisted. Looped his right arm over both the man's, pinning them and his sword to his side, and again with the shortsword he killed, sliding it across the side of the samurai's throat, slicing something that caused a thin jet of blood to spurt out and hit Musashi in the face.

Lashes, blood in his lashes, blinking red, on his lips, in his mouth, which hung open with concentration. Ignored, focus on the enemy alone, no taste, no colour. The sixth tried the same as the fifth, as he had been schooled. Musashi saw the feint coming again, let the man move his longsword and then simply held his shortsword out. The samurai impaled himself upon it to the guard, screamed, dropped his sword and clutched at Musashi's wrists.

But Musashi, moving as steady as the tide, hauled himself free, spread his arms wide, headed for the seventh. Invited the attack but the man skittered back with his blade up before him. Two great feinting sweeps of Musashi's longsword in time to the beat that he alone heard and then the true attack, he dropping to one knee and trying to take the samurai's leg. The man got his sword down and braced, parried, but the inversion of his weapon left him tangled. Musashi rose to his feet, advancing, always advancing, and thrust his shortsword through the gap in the knot of his arms.

The eighth screamed as he came with his sword high above his head, committing everything to the charge with magnificent futility. His only thought was to kill, and he was fast. The blade came down and Musashi jinked backwards, twisting his body around in the air to bring the longsword to bear, and then, just as he had done to Akiyama, he leant forward at full stretch and let his reach do the killing, slicing the man upon the chest whilst inviolate himself.

How this focus took moments and dilated them. In the pirouette to right his balance, Musashi found himself with his arms crossed across his body, swords out horizontal, and upon the ground he glimpsed his shadow splayed, stretching away from his feet spread wide. It reminded him of the long sunset shadow of the torii gate at the entrance of the shrine of his youth, of Shinto, holy things, of heaven. But here was Buddhist ground, and did they too not have a heaven, an entirely separate heaven? Two heavens. Two swords. Within him, as one.

Denshichiro remained.

Eight men now scattered across the gravel. Dust in the air and gore on the earth. Musashi moving as he should not be moving, striking as he should not be striking. Blood, not his blood, dripping from Musashi's brow. All this Denshichiro saw, could not hide from his face. Musashi dropped both his swords low, beckoned him in, daring him to attack.

And here, in Kyoto, before the people of Kyoto, Denshichiro could not refuse. Whatever he felt less than the colour of tea. He came steady, not blindly, drew his sword back above his head. Did not try to come close but sought one tremendous cleave from above and right, arms strong, body nimble, feinted as he rolled his body and brought the sword down instead from the left.

Made no difference. Musashi knew it from conception to execution, knew it perhaps without seeing it, in that moment knew everything in the world that mattered. Denshichiro's sword came down. Musashi stepped to the side. Arms exposed, Musashi went for Denshichiro's wrists as they found the nadir of their descent. Ran his shortsword down Denshichiro's forearm, peeled it, held the edge of the blade there nestled at the heel of his thumb. Immobilizing. Then the longsword up and the edge of that held to Denshichiro's throat.

The two of them, so close they could feel each other's breath.

'Walk into it,' hissed Musashi, vicious triumph in his voice. 'Walk into it like your brother.'

Upon his sword was oil, and upon this oil was blood, coiling and coalescing and, Musashi saw, as liquid as Denshichiro's eyes.

The rhythm unbroken: *a-bom, a-bom, a-bombombom.*

The distant left still constant: *atta-ta-tata, ta-ta-tata.*

The leader of the Yoshioka whimpered, dropped his sword, and ran.

Musashi let him go. He was drained of all vigour, could not chase, could not throw his sword. Did not want to. Denshichiro disappeared around the side of the Hall. Musashi turned and looked back, took in the proof of what he had achieved. There in the gravel, glistening on his fists, across his arms, his chest, his face.

There the crowd. What did he expect of them?

They in turn saw him, saw all he had wrought, saw the grin that unfurled across his face. To the last man, the last woman, the last child amongst them, they remained as silent and still as the thousand and one Buddhas looking out from within the Hall.

Victory.

But that night the moon did not rise crimson as he had anticipated, had hoped, and, with the air of Maruta rife with the stench of piss, Musashi sat in the room of his lodgings and stared into the darkness. The thrill of triumph had faded by the time he had washed the blood from himself, the ache of the exertion enfeebling his arms. What was left now was the hollow analysis.

He had bested nine men in combat using a method of his own creation, and there was pride in that. But it was a faint concept, a painting of the sun and no more. What he saw again and again was the first man he had killed. Bereft of arms, the stumps spreading, the horror in his eyes. This Musashi had done to unsettle. This he had done for a tactical advantage.

What troubled him now was that he could not deny that he felt very little guilt about it.

He sat staring for a long time, thinking of goodness, of the definition of worthy things, and of his uncle Dorinbo.

Tadanari wept, and he did not care who saw him. He was on his knees, dust on his clothes, his hands, his face. Tenderly, he tried to fix what was broken.

How morbid his attempts. The watching men of the Yoshioka did nothing to stop him as he gathered the arms and the leg of Ujinari and placed them where they ought to be. His son slain first by Miyamoto, he had been told, and he looked at the ruin, and he saw the ruin, and racking sobs of soundless grief escaped him. Tried to wipe the blood from his son's slit throat with his jacket, found it dried and stubborn and ugly. No dignity possible, and yet he tried to make it so, as though the Buddha Kannon was actually present in the thousand and one statues nearby, would grant divine favour and restore life should Tadanari only arrange the cradle of the soul correctly once more.

It was futile, a mad hope, and he knew it to be so but still Tadanari knelt in the attempt, there caressing his future splayed out slain and helpless. He wept and he wept and he tasted dust and the salt of his tears, and on the earth beside him lay the sword he had bestowed, unbloodied, reflecting the dying sun.

On it the sword of Fudo clear. The Cutter of Delusions, flensing Tadanari to the core.

Interlude II

Five years the young woman has worn the headdress they forced upon her in her adolescence. Five years with the hair of a dead woman tickling at her neck. Five years studying the depths of meaninglessness.

Now she is sitting upon on a cushion of a fine soft material, which she scratches her nails impulsively upon like a cat. The heat is that of the night, the scent that of split aloe. Either side of her other women are kneeling, awaiting.

The men duly come. They step as one at a sonorous pace, until they stop. Then one man continues the dirge of the sole, coming closer, closer, before there is the scraping sound of something being set down before the young woman.

'Blessed yuta,' says the man, voice grizzled and rasping and tremulous. 'Are the heavens placated? Have you divined whether the season of storms has passed?'

The young woman reaches out and feels what the man has set before her. Her fingers find the unpleasant shock of the damp scales of a fish of some size, cold and dead and still, and around it other things doubtless taken from the ocean: a smooth stone, maybe even a pearl, a long feather, a curved brittle thing that might have been a whale bone. All these things her hands rove over slowly and carefully, and, as always, this alone she senses and nothing more.

Eventually she sits up, removes her hands.

'Bounteous, the new season,' she pronounces.

Proper words, expected words.

The men do not cheer. They never do. There is relief, but it is tempered; they are spared the teeth but they are still pinned beneath the tiger.

A length of hair is reverently cut from the young woman's head and then tied around the beam of the prow of the first ship to brave the deep ocean once again, bound north for the Japanese isles.

It is not the peal of warm bells or pleasant chimes that herald the coming of a yuta but rather the rattling of the bones of foxes and monkeys and devious things all lashed to totem poles, and for the first time in her life the young woman hears this morbid applause ripple out not for her.

Another yuta approaches.

This seer is much older than her, much, much older but just as blinded. She has journeyed from the far side of the island to offer her advice on the placing of warding stones, she regarded as the foremost wisdom on this. The young woman is expected to learn from her. She knows instead that this yuta will in fact expose her.

She dreads this damnation. She longs for this liberation.

The young woman wonders if it will be instantaneous. Thus she waits as the condemned, balancing her headdress with Sister nearby, the village elders fearfully present, and there is spectacle, and there is show. The old yuta hisses and howls and draws near, and sea salt is thrown, and her entourage rattle their fetishes, and then a hand lashes out suddenly and grasps the young woman by the wrist.

'Sistren,' the old yuta pronounces fiercely. 'Sistren!'

It is a grasp that throttles, endures beyond physical touch, prevents the young woman from taking in anything further that day. The talk of the properties of jade and obsidian slide over her like oil, and if there is any actual wisdom in them she does not imbibe. Something has been knocked aside within her, and she is waiting solely for that moment that comes later that night, when the two of them are at last alone. When the bones are stilled and the sighted sleep far from them, then the question wells like a canker. It wells through the meagre dinner and the silence beyond, and though she wants to ask it, needs to, still she cannot bring herself to do so for an hour, longer. She wonders how to broach it, to phrase it, and wonders which answer she truly seeks, until eventually it seeps out almost as an accident, a mistake she cannot revoke:

'Do you see them?'

Her voice is frail. The revered yuta breathes through her nose.

'I see things as they are,' she says.

The turn of seasons unseen. Mother walks the conduit bridge that lies within all women, joins tempest-stolen father in the other world.

'Sister?' says Sister, waking her from sleep. 'Sister?'

The young woman hears her insistent voice eventually, rises. 'What is it?'

'I . . .' says Sister. There is wind outside, and whatever she faintly mumbles next is stolen by its blowing.

'I can't hear you. You're far. Come closer.'

Sister hesitates before she says, 'No.'

'What is it?'

'I have the bamboo sickness.'

The young woman takes this in. She knows what the bamboo sickness is: growths erupting the length of body the colour and texture of the inside of a trunk of bamboo. The young woman has no conception at all of how that might appear, but of the disgust and fear in the voices that first told her of the disease she has a very clear and tacit understanding.

'Are you certain?' she says.

'I have five welts upon my left arm,' says Sister. 'A sixth is emerging.'

'Does your husband . . . ?'

'He saw.'

'Your children?'

'They saw. They all saw, they all know, the whole village. I haven't left the house in three days. But now . . .'

'What?'

'I carry it, so I am leaving. I must, before it spreads. This is law. I'm going before they drive me out. Unless . . .'

Sister hesitates.

'Please don't,' says the young woman, dreading what her sister will say next. 'Please, not you also.'

'Can you see the cause of all this upon me?' says Sister. 'Why have I drawn the ire of the other world? How can I appease them? Please, Sister' – and her voice cracks now – 'please, tell me! I don't want to go there. I don't want to be amongst the filthy, I don't want to rot, I don't want to—'

'Nothing! I see nothing!' says the young woman. 'There is nothing there!'

She feels the hot path of tears find their way to the corners of her mouth. Outside, the wind blows.

'I understand,' says Sister softly. 'I am sorry. I love you. Goodbye.'

And she goes.

The bamboo sickness does not leave with her. Two dozen are stricken, three dozen. The air is rife with the scent of warding herbs burning. Some take to their boats and live anchored offshore. Many refuse to leave their houses. The young woman is amongst them, but not through fear of the disease.

A boy whose voice has not yet deepened brings her water and food daily. She hears his laborious approach, the little grunts as he struggles with the weight. Moments later he calls as he always does:

'Blessed yuta?'

Today she hears a new dimension to the fear in his voice.

'Bring it in,' says the young woman.

'Might I?' he tries. 'Might I leave it here? Can you find it here? In the door? May I be excused now?'

'No. Bring it in.'

'But—' he says, but he cannot bring himself to argue further. The water sloshes against the clay as he hauls the jug in. His feet skitter away the instant it is set down.

'Wait,' she says.

The footsteps stop.

'Why do you behave this way today?' asks the young woman.

'Everyone is being strange.'

'That is no real answer,' says the young woman. 'Tell me, child.'

Nothing.

'Do you think that I do not already know?' she says. 'Do you think that I do not already see?'

'Forgive me,' he whimpers. 'It's everything. This year, everything – the baby that was born warped and dead, the storm that destroyed the hall, that man who fell into the sea and was taken off by the seawolf, and now, and now, this, the sickness. It's all getting worse, and yesterday, the elder, he said . . .'

'What?'

'That all this is because of you, blessed yuta,' the boy says. 'He says that some of the women like you can see the bad spirits, and some of you just let them into this world. And all this plague, it started with your sister, the closest to you, but you aren't sick. The man that fell in the sea, he rode on a boat that carried a length of your hair, and, and . . .'

'That is what he said?' says the young woman.

'Yes,' says the boy.

'Do you believe him?'

The boy runs away.

Two nights later they come. Though they try to be silent, a mass of people cannot truly be invisible even to the blind. The volume of sand shifted, the crackle of torches or dry driftwood under accidental foot, these the portents. She has sought out her hated headdress and sits facing where she believes the door to be, awaiting.

The headdress has its effect: she hears a faint gasp that is quickly stifled.

'You saw our arrival,' says a voice she recognizes as the elder himself.

'I see many things.'

'Then you know why we come.'

'Speak it all the same.'

'Know that we are prostrate before you,' says the elder, and his voice does sound lower than it was before. 'We come not as equals but as those entirely at your mercy. We come not with an urge for violence, for you are inviolate, seeing one, but come instead with an earnest plea for clemency.'

'It is so,' echoes a multitude of voices that chain all the way beyond the door and become muffled by the walls.

'Why so many of you here?' says the young woman.

'It is the will of all us,' says the elder. 'We are in agreement.'

'And what is it you have all agreed upon?'

'We ask you to spare us. We ask you, humbly, to leave the village and take with you what you have . . . Take with you the beacon that shines around you in the other world.'

'Leave?' says the young woman.

'We beseech you,' says the elder.

'Where am I to go?' she laughs bitterly. 'How am I to get there?'

'We have considered that,' says the elder.

'What?'

'We have bought passage for you upon a ship to Japan.'

That gives the young woman pause for thought. That was no cheap fare, and the village had no rich families. All of them together, then, a collective sacrifice, such the strength of their desire to see her gone.

'Is Tsutomu amongst you?' says the young woman. 'My sister's husband, are you here?'

There is a sort of whimper, and then Tsutomu answers: 'I am here, blessed yuta.'

'You too agree with this? What would my sister say?'

'Your sister is gone,' says Tsutomu. 'My children remain.'

'We are all in agreement,' says the elder. 'We ask that you show us kindness and consent to this. We are entirely at your mercy. We will force nothing upon you. Doom us or spare us.'

'What if I avow to dispel the spirits?'

'There are things more powerful than vows drawn to you, seeing one. We have seen their mischief already. Please, we beg of you, for the future of the village – choose to leave.'

The young woman takes this in. This is not what she was expecting. The reason why this is unexpected takes a moment for her to find, an old piece of folk wisdom rising in her memory.

'The ship leaves two mornings from now,' says the leader, taking her silence for consent. 'We shall bear you to the bay upon a palanquin.'

'You name me a witch—'

'We do no such thing, seeing one,' says the elder quickly.

'You name me witch, and yet you seek to put me upon a ship. Do you not know what is said to happen should one such as I take sail?'

'We know,' says the elder.

'That a storm will come and the wind will blow and the waves will rise, and the mouth of the sea will open up and drag the ship down to the depths to hover there in the inverted world for all time? Trapped in a moment of perpetual drowning – which amongst you knows this, and is prepared to sail with me on board?'

'We know this,' says the elder, 'but—'

'But?' presses the young woman when the elder stops himself.

It takes a moment before he speaks again, but he knows he cannot lie in front of her. Then he says something so illuminating it is as if she were a child again, on that beach, in that single memory of light.

What he says is:

'But the Japanese do not.'

PART V

Rambo

乱暴(する) noun, suru verb
A state of outrage, (to enact) great violence, (to go) berserk

Chapter Thirty-two

See it as a bird sees it and how peaceful the streets of Kyoto, spread out as a mosaic pattern of rooftop tile and ochre veins of earth, the only violence visible that of the jagged angles of towering pagoda tiers violating the sea of low roofs seeking to impregnate the sky. Yet down amongst these streets the breath of reason and tranquillity failed to blow, repelled by moats and walls and formative castle structures, by perhaps even the encircling mountains themselves, stillness pervading, all that was there already trapped beneath the eaves of roofs, there channelled and flowing, churning ignescent, low and rancid as the sweat it brought forth . . .

. . . the crowd glistening with this as they gathered outside a tavern. A half-curtain hung across the entrance obscuring their view, this made of green hemp and on it printed in white the two characters for evening calm. The gathered people summoned by a sound, a violent sound that had erupted as brief as thunder but had not echoed and died as thunder did, had been torn away as though the iron lid of a crypt had slammed down.

'Did you hear? Did you hear?'

'What?'

'It's them.'

'Who?'

'The Yoshioka.'

'In there?'

'Nnn.'

'Who is it that . . . ?'

'A swordbearer. Masterless.'

Murmurs of this sort, and then the Yoshioka re-emerged onto the street. They wore the looks of men enthralled to some otherworldly beauty. Three of them, each holding a bloody sword and in the hands of the lead man a human head held by the hair. The leader raised this trophy up and let it swing upon its tresses, uncaring of the gore that fell upon his bared arm, his shoulder.

'Musashi Miyamoto!' he snarled exuberant, naming the slain. 'Musashi Miyamoto!'

The head swung back and forth and rotated in his grasp so that all saw the dead man's face well, his mouth lolling and his tongue visible, his eyes open, the wound on the neck ragged. Sawed and pulled free of the body and offered up to the midday sun with such supreme pride and joy, rapture in the eyes.

'Where are they?' came the whispers.

'Who?'

'The black-clad men, the Edoites. The law!'

'They . . . they're the Yoshioka. Do they not have the right?'

The head there paramount and the Yoshioka oblivious of the shock and disgust, the gasp that scythed outwards like the breath of bellows across coals, passing into shouts the further it went, informing or warning or fascinated. The head, the head alone worthy of attention, and from Miyamoto's lip grey moustaches so long that the tips of them were sodden red, hanging like the tails of dead foxes.

How many the men that lay with a woman and thought of another? A common sin or no sin at all, and here the Yoshioka now began to walk as men of this sort, the numb-legged aftermath of a surrogate moment of ecstasy. The crowd parted for them and their trophy, blood running sweet, blood running hot . . .

. . . and here on sanctified ground a scorching heat, dry in its fury, the funeral pyre of Ujinari burning bright. The body was hidden by a white shroud, and Tadanari stood not three paces away, watching as his hidden son was enveloped by the flames. As they grew higher he felt the coming of pain upon every inch of his bare skin, the heat scouring.

Members of the school stood behind him. Tadanari had not commanded them to help bear the body to the site. He had given no command since he had returned from the Hall. These the adepts that felt the glow of rage behind their eyes (or as a noose around the throat through which they tried to swallow comprehension of defeat, or as acid fear hidden in the belly) and yet managed to keep it suppliant had not stormed forth in thrall to it.

The most loyal of men and Tadanari unmindful of them. Ujinari's longsword in his hands and this alone existed to him. He remembered seeing it sitting naked upon the stand on the day of its blessing, admiring the lustre of its metal, and knowing, deeply knowing then, that that lustre would hold true and would be looked at in the same awestruck manner by his descendants in centuries to come.

Fudo snarled unceasing upon the gorgeous scabbard.

What else was being cut, shed from him in that blaze? The last of the Kozei stood humbled, helpless but to stand at the mercy of the fire and let it rape him of all it pleased. And, in the aftermath of that, though brightness was before him his mind went solely to dark places.

Soon he smelt the hair upon his arms begin to singe. He relented, stepped back from the pyre not into relief but only the embrace of the liquid heat of summer. The fire roared upwards, and he looked up through its shimmering haze and saw the sky distorting as though the world were coming apart, and his sole wish was that this were true and that the destruction were the ultimate work of his hand . . .

. . . now heels burning where they slapped upon cedar sandalwood again and again, another separate band of Yoshioka on another street and they in pursuit of Musashi Miyamoto also. The masterless enemy fleeing without even drawing the swords at his side as was his cowardly wont, and they with glee in their tea-coloured hearts. Miyamoto a short man, stubby little legs in miserable little rags, and in at least one of the samurai's minds this jarred with the image of the lithe and slender giant that had faced down Seijuro, but still they chased, still they screamed and cursed at his back.

Hammering a spectre, any spectre, into the grave vengeance had dug in them was better than leaving it empty. Necessary. Righteous.

Miyamoto rounded a corner and crashed into a line of taiko drums set on stands. They tumbled to the floor thudding loud and hollow, rolled, and he slipped and stumbled amongst them. No grace, this Miyamoto, yelped as his forearms met earth. The lowerborn moving to help him as he scrabbled desperate and then receding immediately as the Yoshioka rounded the corner, shrieked their triumph. They did not allow Miyamoto to rise, set upon him with their swords with him still on his hands and knees and hacked and hacked and hacked.

The crowd watched as again a head was eventually brought up, brandished in glory and gore for all to see . . .

. . . and a third head on a third street, a third Miyamoto, his swords scattered unbloodied in the dust of the street. The Yoshioka waving the head at Goemon Inoue, snarling in joy, taunting the captain, and the captain standing there. His iron helmet heavy, his chainmail jacket like an oven upon him, the streets around them silent and staring.

The Yoshioka samurai slung the head underarm towards Goemon and, as it rolled and left a bloody trail, the tea-coloured samurai screamed, 'There your dog! There your dog!'

There the challenge and Goemon fit to burst already, sucking it all up like a volcanic stone sucks up bitter saltwater, and still the Yoshioka dared him. On this street, on every other street where they unleashed their chaos upon the innocent. Every instinct telling him to draw his sword and be as a samurai, and his men at his side as ravenous as a pack of wolves for the fight, and around him the alien city that loathed him smothering him with its delight at his humiliation, and the wrath of the sun even upon all.

'Hold,' he commanded his men, and he hated saying the word. 'Hold.'

They obeyed and let the Yoshioka go. The tea-coloured samurai retreated jeering them as cowards, left them the head and the corpse of the masterless, and Goemon could feel the enmity of his own men at him for forcing them to yield.

But what else could he do?

He looked at the severed head, and he wondered what it was exactly he had unleashed in Miyamoto. A man who stood against nine and triumphed. Both an astonishing portent of this chaos that Goemon could scant contain and his last hope also, the captain here bound by the chains of his duty that he felt so hot around the wrists, the spine, the throat . . .

. . . and a saucerful of water was thrown into the brazier and the coals flared and spat and hissed and steam rose, and Musashi stalked past wanting to feel the heat once more, the heat inside his heart, that wonderful sunlike thing that assured him of all. Where was it? Where had it gone during the night? It had failed to rise with the dawn and now all seemed dimmed.

Oblivious for the moment of Yoshioka violence, shrouded in the streets of the city that became his unwitting armour, avenues and roads in the hundreds and the Yoshioka that rampaged through them few. Divers searching for a single pearl in a reef that spanned a score of leagues, and so many false pearls yet to distract them.

There was blood dried upon his clothes and his muscles still ached from the exertion, but there was no satisfaction in this pain as there had been previously. He ventured forth with no clear direction, trying to quash the doubt of the night before, but of the form of the sign he sought he was not certain. Thus he wandered for the first time as no more than a querent, witnessing the city rather than challenging, hoping that its currents would grant him reassurance in his victory.

He walked the densest alleys, these so narrow that he could spread his arms and touch either wall comfortably, overhanging roofs stealing all sight of the sky. Even here in these unseen places chains of paper bunting and lanterns hung limp and fragile in the humidity arrayed for the Regent's festival. Here Musashi found no welcome, only a solitude, a sightless void of eyes turning away from him, turning down as men and women pressed up against beams and walls to allow him to pass breast to breast. He walking as a beast in the night, unseen but of a volatile size enough to be sensed regardless. A silence that followed him, a roaming and temporary cessation of trade as all the hawkers of the inutile shit he despised so found themselves voiceless.

This caused him no joy.

He came to the gate of the higher wards with its neat row of murderholes, the same samurai standing before it, and he looked at them. A dozen of them, maybe not the same men exactly, the faces indistinct to him but the topknots and silks and the swords identical, and he just stood there. Surely they would recognize him. Surely they would offer him proof. Surely against them which he so despised he would be able to judge some measure of progress. But that day he did not call out to them, he did not beseech them, he did not boast to them. He merely stood there and waited patiently as a fisherman for their reaction. Any reaction.

They gave him none.

His pace slowed as his thoughts drew ever inward. His eyes lost their focus and the hundreds and thousands of the city passed him by like the waters of a river around a rock. Movement drew his eye – a troupe of young women, fans twirling in their hands, stepping through the steps of a dance, practising, practising. They alone having space upon the street, they alone afforded recognition as separate from the throng, and yet they all using this space to move as one.

Musashi stopped to stare sightlessly at them.

After some time a boy appeared at his side, peered up into his face.

'It's you,' the child said, delighted. 'I saw you yesterday, at the long Hall. You killed the Yoshioka!' He was no more than ten, wearing clothes that marked him either an urchin or a member of an impoverished family. 'It was amazing!' continued the boy, excitement gleaming in his eyes. 'I've never seen anyone so amazing as you. Two swords! There was what, fifteen of them? And you just killed them in moments!' He lost himself in a fit of mimicry, slicing away with two imagined blades.

Streets away there was some kind of uproar, echoes of it felt rather than heard. Too distant to carry meaning, stripped of clarifying words such as *head* and *Miyamoto* and *vengeance*, and so the women kept on dancing and the boy kept on talking: 'You cut his arms off and they fell off, and his leg, and blood was everywhere, and they were all screaming and—' And on he spoke like this until he was satisfied he had given a true account.

Only when the boy was done did Musashi look at him. 'Is that all you took from what I did there?' he asked. 'The fight?'

'What else was there?' the child asked.

Musashi turned his eyes back to the women. He stood there trying to think of the answer, or any answer, and the dance was danced and the city flowed past him in a hot haze of colour and motion.

The boy grew quickly bored, and Musashi did not notice him leave.

Chapter Thirty-three

The hour of the ox, the dead time after midnight. The time for vows and oaths and solemnity. Denshichiro opened the door to the dojo hall with his left hand only, struggling with the weight. His right arm was swathed in a bandage, wrapped tight and pink and moist. There inside the dojo he found braziers burning bright, smoke coiling around the beams of the ceiling and the school waiting in expectant silence.

All the adepts and all the acolytes arrayed around the edge of the hall on their knees, they in their number close and intimate, elbows interlocking. He looked around at them, and they looked back.

In the centre of the hall knelt Tadanari.

The old samurai turned his face to Denshichiro. Grief had altered it, hardened it into a thing of shadows and ivory. Slowly, he reached out with one hand and gestured to the space before him. There a long pale strip of cloth was laid out upon the earth of the floor, a band for tying around the head. Before the knees of each member of the school, before Tadanari also, a similar band was spread.

The hand was held out, insistent, steady. Denshichiro approached the centre of the hall. As he drew close he saw that something was written upon the headband in black ink, the strokes savage and quick:

'No,' said Denshichiro.

'Kneel,' said Tadanari.

'We can't,' said Denshichiro. 'Have you any conception of what he wrought, what he—'

'Kneel,' said Tadanari.

Denshichiro obeyed, his legs folding beneath him. He looked at the headband as though it were a stretch of tanned human skin. With the characters of that name upon it the cloth had undergone transubstantiation, evolving from a thing that bound solely the hair to one that bound the soul and the will also; a profound declaration that Musashi Miyamoto would be foremost on all their thoughts until he was dead.

'As head of the school,' said Tadanari, 'you must be the first to take up the mantle.'

'That is folly,' said Denshichiro. 'You did not see him. We must not be his enemy. No. Impossible. We must be done with him . . . He fought as men cannot. He is unbeatable. He'll kill whoever we send after him. Eight men he killed before me, in no more than ten heartbeats! And look, look what he did to me!'

Denshichiro raised his bandaged forearm up to Tadanari's face. The elder samurai was unmoved.

'Are you mad?' said Denshichiro at the silence. 'I am the finest swordsman in this school. And he beat me. Do you not understand? He beat *me*. He beat Seijuro! He beat eight of us at once! There's no shame in saying it . . . Miyamoto is a demon, an abomination, inhuman. To pursue any further feud with him is folly. Is that not what you wanted, Sir Kozei? I bow to your will now. Let us be done with him. He will be forgotten. Snow in spring, as you said.'

The lids of Tadanari's eyes were heavy and still as though they were carved of wax, gazing towards Denshichiro but not at him; through him, beyond him.

'Is this because I ran?' said Denshichiro. 'You too, had you seen, would have run. There was no stopping him. How can I explain this to you any clearer? My duty is to live, as the scion, as the bearer of the blood. Is it not? Is it not?'

He quailed in the silence, found no respite anywhere in the hall. Command withered. Denshichiro placed his palms upon the earth and bowed as low as he could. He held it until he dared to look up once more.

'Or, if you must kill him,' he tried, 'let us hire agents. Assassins. Let's be done with him at a distance. No one will remember how he found his end. Snow in spring. Snow in spring. Yes, or, or . . . Longbows. Let's use the bows. Or arquebuses. We can buy guns and hire a rank of masterless to shoot him. That's how he'll be felled. We cannot beat him with the sword. Do none of you understand this?'

He looked around the room at all the men and boys. There was no submission, only stillness. Hints of something further than that given and stolen by the whim of the firelight. Denshichiro turned back to Tadanari.

He became aware then, perhaps the last place his eyes had

ventured, that the longsword resting by the elder samurai's side was Ujinari's. The gorgeous lacquered scabbard studded with the face of Fudo was blighted by an ugly wound. Through the sleek blackness a vein of bright magnolia wood ravaged a jagged path, the empty scabbard having snapped beneath Ujinari's falling body. Crudely it had been reset to house the unblooded blade once more.

Denshichiro's face hardened. 'Do you blame me for my actions?' he said. 'How can you? There were eight men, and myself. Any other man but Miyamoto would have his head stuck on a spike outside the gate now, and you would be praising my bravery. You can not fault me for behaving as I should. Eight men I had! Whoever heard of one man standing against nine? The risk was minimal, the idea was sound, the tactics, the strategy. I cannot be faulted in my intentions!'

Through the mullions of the high, thin windows smoke billowed, fled.

That you of all people should cause his last words to me to be lies.

'I meant to fight Miyamoto myself,' said Denshichiro. 'A duel between the two of us alone. There was to be no risk to any but myself. The eight were there merely to encircle, to prevent him fleeing. I intended to fight him one on one, truly I did. But the savage, the animal, Miyamoto – he leapt straight into combat before I could engage. There was nothing I could have done, and, and . . .'

You do not name him. Can you not bring yourself to?

In the face of silence, the wheel of Denshichiro's emotions completed a full rotation: 'Why am I facing this inquisition? This is outrageous. Fate sends a punishment like Miyamoto, and you behave as though I am at fault for the, the, the cruelty of the universe. Outrageous!'

'Don the headband, Denshichiro,' said Tadanari. 'Comport yourself like a man.'

'No!' shouted Denshichiro. 'I refuse! It is madness! You are not the head of the school! I am! Yoshioka! Yoshioka! Do you not hear what I am saying? Am I alone left sane? Am I alone thinking of the future?'

'Don the headband. As your father would have done.'

'You dare speak of my father?' said Denshichiro. 'Actually, it is good you do. I have tolerated this insubordination long enough – look at the portraits there hung upon the wall, and ask yourself to whom they deigned to grant command by right of birth? Whose father, whose great-uncle, whose grandfather is venerated at the shrine that we all pray to? Mine! And you will heed me when I order that we shall engage Miyamoto no further!'

Tadanari struck as he rose to one knee, rising and drawing Ujinari's sword from its fractured scabbard in a fluid, beautifully observed motion. Decades of skill summated: he brought the edge swift across Denshichiro's throat, followed the arc through, held the sword high and still as blood fell upon the earth. Denshichiro clutched at his neck with both hands as he fell backwards, legs kicking, fingers glistening red. No shout he made, no shout possible.

The watching samurai were as still as that crimson-spattered sword. The thrashing ceased with an intermittent, fading desperation. In its wake Tadanari rose to stand, looked around at the gathered men, held the blade up to show the blood upon it to all of them.

'The masterless vagrant Musashi Miyamoto has felled both Seijuro and Denshichiro,' he said. 'This, I declare truth.'

No man contested. Those that were most loyal to Denshichiro had gone to the Hall with him, or to Mount Hiei before that. Those that were here were all pupils of Tadanari. The dead man had been the figurehead of the Way they sought, but the one that lived they knew undoubted to be its embodiment.

'The leadership of the school,' continued Tadanari, 'duly falls to the third son of Naokata Yoshioka, Matashichiro.'

Silent assent.

'Matashichiro's reign will be long and virtuous, but for now he remains a child. I therefore propose that, until the young Master comes of a suitable age, I, Tadanari Kozei, Master of the Way of the Yoshioka, assume the mantle of plenipotentiary. This is proper. Does any man here contest this?'

Some last spark of energy forced its way out of Denshichiro, a sad little gurgle emanating from the gorge across his throat. If any man read it as an omen or a protest from the departing spirit, he did not voice it.

Tadanari shook the blood from the sword, wiped it pure again on silk as he slid it smoothly back into the scabbard. He then knelt, placed the weapon reverently on the ground, and took up the headband. With ceremonial stillness and practised motions he placed the characters of his enemy's name against his forehead and then slowly wrapped the length of the cloth around the dome of his skull. Wrapped it tight, tied the knot over his brow so that the name within was forced up against the flesh, the mind.

The men of the Yoshioka followed his motions, hands moving in unison.

'We are avowed,' said Tadanari. 'For his grievous insults to the school, Musashi Miyamoto must die.'

'Death!' echoed the men.

'You have been killing already, and I say unto you: kill. There is nothing left to us but to kill. We will not use guns or arrows or even spears. We shall use the sword. We shall not take him from behind like cowards, but give him warning so that he knows his doom is upon him. We shall observe our vengeance properly, as men that our grandfathers could respect.'

'Sir!'

'He is no force of fate. He is no demon. He is just a man. And even if we must throw ourselves upon his blade to smother him so that another may take his head, this we vow to do, vow before each other, before all our forebears who trod this earth before us now. Do we not?'

'Sir!'

'I have a method to draw him to us,' said Tadanari. 'He will come, and we will kill him certainly. But, should fate render Miyamoto up to us before this, then kill. Kill. Do not hesitate, do not waver, do all you can to kill. I declare this now our Way.'

The men of the Yoshioka barked, bowed to the shrine of the ancestors and Tadanari dismissed them to rest for the dawn. They filed out in silence, none of them looking at the corpse of Denshichiro, at the patterns his blood had made upon the earthen floor. Tadanari was soon alone with the body, and he gazed at it.

Still and ugly as Denshichiro deserved, for the errant fortune that had granted him the privilege of being born as he was without any concurrent merit of the spirit.

Tadanari drew his shortsword. He reached down and cut the topknot from Denshichiro's head. The end of it he dipped into the wound upon the dead man's throat and, using the hair as a brush, wrote the names of Denshichiro and Seijuro upon the headband that Denshichiro should have worn. He cast the gore-sodden knot of hair into a brazier and bore the marked band to the shrine of the dojo and the paintings of the previous generations of the Yoshioka.

There he reached up and draped it around the portrait of Naokata, so that the band hung down as though it fell across his shoulders, Seijuro's name on the right and Denshichiro's on the left.

Tadanari looked up into the approximation of the face of his friend.

'He was not your son,' he said. 'He was nothing like you.'

Naokata did not respond. Tadanari turned and left him with his pallid yoke.

Chapter Thirty-four

The waters of the Kamo slid effortlessly by and over their surface a shakuhachi flautist sent out a melody as lapping and lilting as all that passed before him. His bamboo pipe pale in the sunlight, his eyes closed in concentration. A young man and far from a master yet, he came to these remote banks to practise his instrument without bothering others. Thusly he was unaware that he had an audience: Musashi, Ameku and Yae sat some distance away upon a fallen tree soft with moss.

Musashi had heard the man's playing several times when he himself, for much the same reason, had come here to practise his own silent instrument.

The music was wistful and long. The three of them, man and woman and child, listened. It was Ameku who broke their silence.

'Why do you take us here?' she asked.

Because I cannot abide the city. Musashi wiped sweat from the gaunt hollows beneath his eyes. 'Because someone ought to hear this.'

'If we are not here, the music for the river only, it is not good?'

'Why play at all, if not to perform?' he said. It did not feel an entire answer, and so he offered: 'You sing, and I thought . . . All ideas from music, as you said.'

'Ah,' Ameku said. It was a very pointed syllable, and her lips formed themselves into a familiar formation. But the hint of mockery on them did not last, and eventually she spoke again: 'This man – he has skill. His music is good. So . . . Thank you, Musashi.'

The woman squeezed Yae's shoulder and the girl said her thanks also. For her part Yae seemed thoroughly bored, eyes darting around, heels drumming against the log on which they sat. It was not long before she dropped down and went to busy herself looking at stones at the water's shallow edge.

'Today you are changed, Musashi,' said Ameku. 'Still. Quiet.'

'Nnn,' he said, because he did not know what else to. What he even desired to.

'You are not happy. Though you beat the Yoshioka, you are not happy.'

He had not told her. 'You know?'

'Drunk men in the lodgings, they speak easy, speak loud.'

'They do.'

'You killed,' she said quite easily, and some vestige of decorum turned Musashi towards Yae for a moment. As though he might be ashamed of a child hearing the thing that he had wanted to scream to the heavens in the glory of its execution. The girl though was not listening.

'That was their choice,' he said.

'How many, the Yoshioka?' Ameku said. 'Eight? Nine?'

'Eight dead. One wounded and fled.'

'Fled?'

'Ran away.'

'Ran away. Nine men come to you, but you stand with two swords.'

'It felt natural,' he said, no boast in his voice. 'As though I were just sliding through it, sliding into the right positions again and again. As though I wasn't trying . . . Or rather, I was trying, with so much of my essence that it became nothing. And it simply . . . was.'

He realized, though, that this was not what she had meant.

She said something to herself in her own language. It did not seem complimentary.

'Is that how you say "revenge" in Ryukyuan?' he asked.

Ameku let out a low hiss of a laugh.

'Have you any trust in anything at all? Anyone?' Musashi asked her. It was not condemnatory.

'A blind woman must trust everyone. I am weak, yes, I am the weakest perhaps. You, Musashi, now can do the things you want to me. Anything. Any man who is with me, the same, any woman too. Even Yae, little Yae, she, holding my hand, she can take me to a bad place. If she wants.'

The girl had turned at the mention of her name, and now she wailed in genuine hurt, 'I wouldn't do that, Ameku.'

'I know, I know, my cat. But this is true. No, Musashi?'

'It is true.'

'No argument today too.'

He struggled for words, just as he had struggled in the city, just as he had struggled to himself. He wanted to tell her the excitement he felt at his creation of his new style, of having devised and enacted something that no man had done before. But poetic proof eluded him and he could not quantify the feel of his sword splitting bone with some higher purpose. The purpose not a day ago he had been certain was there.

'I feel hollow,' he said. 'I won, but there is no victory.'

'The city, they play their drums as they did a week before.'

'Yes.'

'You want people to see you.'

Why play at all, if not to perform?

But it was not that, he did not think, and so they sat in silence. The flautist made a mistake, took a breath, repeated a phrase of the melody and then continued. The river flowed on. Ameku's eyes seemed as though they were watching its passage, moving back and forth, back and forth. But they saw nothing, and they were ugly in the light.

'If I speak, you will listen?' she said.

'I will listen.'

'Yae . . . Far? Can she hear?'

The girl was now twenty paces distant and pulling the small purple flowers from the heads of reeds, casting them on the water to flow away. 'She cannot hear,' said Musashi.

'Good,' said Ameku. 'She is too young to know this.' The blind woman took a breath. 'Listen well,' she said. 'I will tell you of Ameku. Ameku, in the Ryukyu tongue, it means the old sky . . . The forever sky. I think you have names like it in Japan. But, a bad name for me, no? Unkind. This is my family name. Mother, father, my sister also. Ameku, all of us, on Ryukyu . . .'

And she did tell him. Told him of her childhood, of her youth deprived of sight and yet supposedly possessed of another form of it that others were errantly envious and awed of. Of what they expected her to have and to be. In the telling of it she was pushed to the very limits of her ability in the language, the frustration of being unable to express herself fully and fluently adding to that of her tale, but within her voice was a growing anger that transcended grammar. Wound its way through her entire life upon those distant islands, culminating in a plague and an ultimatum and an exile.

'I do not see the dead,' she said. 'But they, all of them, man and woman and the old and the young, they *know* I see the dead.'

'But you don't.'

'This is truth. But, to them, on Ryukyu, I could not tell it.'

'But it is truth.'

'It is. If I shout this at them, though, what would change? They would not believe me. It was . . . I was . . . Everything set. Made of stone. What people are is . . .' she said, and here she struggled for a word, mimed bringing something to her mouth and drinking.

'Vessels,' offered Musashi.

'Cups,' she said. 'Cups, and others pour what they want into them. Understand – there is them that are loved and them that are hated. The loved, they do a bad thing, and people say, "He has a reason" and excuse him. The hated, they do a good thing, and people say, "It is false", or, "Why are you not as this all times?" and hate more. This cannot be changed.'

Musashi thought of six helmets hung from the bough of a tree, rusting slowly from rainwater, and then he found himself thinking of Akiyama, of the man's bitter laughter as he thought he lay dying, of the tales he had told across his long winter of recuperation.

'You, Musashi,' said Ameku, 'you kill the Yoshioka. The Yoshioka are the loved. So the man who kills them must be . . . ?'

'That cannot be true.'

Ameku waved a hand and with it took in the span of all before them. 'Sadness again, over sea waves.'

The distant flautist held a high note, resonant and piercing. It brought forth a shudder or a spasm from within Musashi that set the hairs upon his arms on end and kindled something behind his eyes.

'But how can honesty be reviled?' he said.

'Are you honest, Musashi?' she asked.

She said it softly and like smoke permeating through the links of a suit of armour it invaded him, found its mark at his core in the way Tadanari asking him the same thing in hostility had not.

'Always them you curse,' she continued. 'The world. The Way. Never you. Always words and words and more words. What lies beneath the words? Anger. They are wrong, perhaps. But you are wrong also, definitely – and this, you *can* change.'

Musashi struggled to speak. Ameku spared him the torment.

'I did not tell you all my Ryukyu story,' she said.

'Then tell me,' he said, 'please.'

'They, the people of my home, all of them on their knees before me,' she said, 'scared of me, of the sickness they say I bring. *Know* I bring. Tell me that they buy a place on a ship, so that I could go to Japan. And I tell them that they will die should I go on a ship with them, evil magic will do this. And they say that they know this, but . . .'

'But what?'

'"But the Japanese do not,"' said Ameku. 'That is what they say. Japanese ship, they put me on. Japanese crew, who did not know of yuta's magic, these innocents my people are happy to, to . . . let die. Die for them, so they can live.'

'But the ship was fine. There was no curse.'

'It does not matter. They believed, in every heart, that if the yuta goes on a ship, the ship dies. And this was a good thing to them. A fair bargain. *That* is people. All people. Ryukyu, Japan, Middle Kingdoms.'

There was something in the way she said it all, a curl of her lips, a flick of her hand. He understood now what he had wondered over for all these months.

'This is why you hate,' he said.

But he saw immediately that he was wrong, profoundly wrong. 'Hate?' she said, confusion and exasperation and pity in her voice. 'Why do you think I hate? I do not hate. This is what I am trying to tell you – if you hate for this, your hatred has no end.'

'But,' he said, 'it is worthy of hate.'

'It is . . .' said Ameku, and she fought to find the words, relented. 'It *is*! This is what is. All it is as is. You must learn this, learn not to hate it. Or the anger, it will . . . One more fight, one more fight. The Yoshioka did not kill you yesterday, but perhaps tomorrow. Or the next thing you hate. Or the next. Or in the end, you. Yourself. You,' she said, and she looped an invisible noose around her throat.

'I cannot accept that,' said Musashi, shaking his head, blinking furiously. 'Someone must fight it. I feel this. I know this. Someone has to—'

Ameku silenced him by reaching out and taking his wrist in her hand. 'Fighting it changes nothing,' she said. 'Hating it changes nothing. The only thing that this will change is you. You will die. Did you not tell me that, after Sekigahara, you made the choice to live? Then live. Do not die. Do not. I am yuta, the people name me yuta, so me, I see the dead world, no? I tell you, there is nothing. You do not want to go there.'

Her fingers could not quite encircle his wrist, and the touch of them was warm, and she was as close to him as she had ever been.

'Here is a truth,' she said. 'What you can change is you. What you master, all you master, is you. What you can touch with hands, your country. Let the city be the city and the world be the world. Know this. Know this, and then live, Musashi. Just live, far from cities, from people if you must. Live. Be happy.'

Musashi's eyes followed her wrist up to her arm, to her shoulder, and there was her hair, combed and dark and everything her eyes were not, and he wanted at that moment to reach out with his own hand and feel those tresses upon his palm.

But he pulled his hand free of hers.

'I've done nothing of worth,' he said. 'Why do I deserve happiness?'

The flautist drew his music to a close. His fingers were sore and his throat was tired and he had played all the notes that were there to be played. On the banks of the shore, Yae had stripped the reeds bare of flowers and all blossom was now fled upon the current.

Chapter Thirty-five

The third of the Yoshioka brothers, Matashichiro, was roused in the morning and brought to Tadanari in the rock garden at the heart of the school. The boy saw the bands the men all wore around their heads, felt the change in them; a hardening.

They skirted him around the dojo hall rather than through it as they normally would. Of this he asked no questions.

The thirteen boulders were there in the sand arrayed as they always had been. When he had been younger Matashichiro had imagined the centremost boulder peaked as it was with that sharp band of obsidian to be a shed dragon's tooth. Or perhaps his father had told him that, he could not remember. Regardless, he knew that this was a childish thought, and so he put it away, straightened his back, tried to stand before Tadanari as a man. The elder samurai's comportment was grave, his eyes beneath the knot of his band as black as that of the tortoise that looked on.

They bowed to one another, settled on the dais in the formal posture of kneeling. There Tadanari spoke:

'Musashi Miyamoto has felled Denshichiro.'

'What?' said Matashichiro. 'He's dead?'

'Yes.'

'But,' said the boy, 'I . . . I heard his voice. I saw him. He was injured, his arm was skinned, but he wasn't dead.'

'It transpired that Miyamoto had coated his blade with poison. A lingering curse. Denshichiro died in the night. He did not die as a man ought.'

'Are there poisons that can do that?'

'There are, but only those black of heart could bring themselves to use them.'

'Then he's . . .' said the boy, and whatever adulthood there might have been in his voice faltered, 'like Seijuro.'

'No tears,' said Tadanari. 'Not yet. First . . .'

He produced a band like the one he wore with Miyamoto's name upon it and gave it to Matashichiro, watched as the boy wrapped it around his brow with eager compliance. He tied it clumsily, the knot loose, the length and breadth of it cut for a man so it sat upon his ears and rose up above his crown like a priest's hat. Nevertheless Tadanari nodded, satisfied.

'There,' he said. 'Now we are avowed.'

'Avowed to what?' said Matashichiro.

'Vengeance.'

'Of course.'

'I cannot hear force in your voice,' said Tadanari. 'This is the man that slew your brothers. Is that not worthy of vengeance?'

'Yes.'

'Still a lack,' said Tadanari. 'Let me tell you of Miyamoto. He is wicked. He is a man without meaning or cause. He has killed a score of our men alongside your brothers. He kills them not for just cause of duty, not for the pure search for higher understanding of the ways of the sword, but for himself. His name alone he shouts, a leech sucking the blood of decent men, gorging, growing fat. Is this not hateful, Matashichiro?'

'Yes.'

'He is a black thing. A corrupter, as malignant as a canker. He cares solely for selfish glory, fights not for Lord nor school nor father nor son nor brother nor sister nor mother, fights solely to kill those he wants to. He gives nothing and takes everything. Lives for himself and no other. Is that not hateful, boy? Is that not the very definition of hateful?'

'Yes!' barked Matashichiro, as he imagined his brothers would have done should he be the one dead.

'Good,' said Tadanari. 'Now, these are things that require your hand.'

He gestured to a stack of papers by his side, dozens of sheaves with columns of writing upon them. A wide shallow dish filled with liquid red ink also awaited. Matashichiro took one of the papers and attempted to read it.

'What are they?' he said. 'I don't understand all these letters. I haven't learnt how to read them yet.'

'Proclamations, to go out across the city,' said Tadanari. 'These are the methods to draw Miyamoto to us.'

'And they need my hand?'

'You are the head of the school.'

'But I do not understand them.'

'It is my strategy,' said Tadanari. 'It is the wisest course. I know Miyamoto. I have read of him. I spoke to him. It is a challenge to him, to what he stands for. Once he reads this, the dog will be unable to do anything but respond in all his vile excess. Then, when he comes . . .'

'Vengeance,' finished Matashichiro, at the bald samurai's prompting.

Tadanari nodded. 'Dignity shall be restored.'

Matashichiro looked at the unknown characters once more. 'But—'

'Do you not trust me, who served your father?' said Tadanari.

'I trust you.'

'Then do as your father would have done.'

The mention of his father sealed the boy's resolve. He placed his right hand into the dish of ink and then pressed it down with his fingers spread broadly upon the first of the proclamations, anointing each the word of the scion of the Yoshioka. Crimson-fingered, on and on he worked, pressing his palm again and again, the multitude of sheaves then taken and laid out in a long line to dry like blood there in the rising sun.

*

The high priest of the Hall of Thirty-Three Doors stood before Goemon imperious in his purple robes, the yard of the garrison stilled and silenced by the presence of the holy man and his retinue, and how the man could shout. Had shouted for near an hour already, ordering the captain in the name of the ever-loving peace-adoring Buddha to hunt Miyamoto down, to dash him to pieces and claim his head.

'If you had seen this too you would understand why I speak,' the priest said. 'Miyamoto butchered a man where he stood, cut his arms off, slit his throat . . . All the while with his face devoid of anything, as if he were empty inside, as if he were not seeing people before him.'

Goemon was polite as he could be: 'You are suggesting it would be preferable if he wore a look of rage? Of joy?'

'It would make him appear human at least. We would know the way his heart beats. This repugnant brutality of his, though, it seems born of nothing. Intolerable.'

On and on the high priest went, claiming the authority of the heavens, of the Son of Heaven who had ordained him and awarded him the purple robe and to whose court he was a regular attendant, and Goemon stood caught in forced obsequiousness. Not wishing to offend, not permitted to offend, not permitted questions such as why the priest consented to the duel taking place on his grounds in the first place. The sun in the sky and the tiger's claw raking his head, cords of his helmet throttling, swords at his side, and why was it they were there? Why was it he was here?

The Goat limped into the yard as quickly as he could on his maimed leg. Uncaring of decorum or deference to the high priest, he pushed his way through the gathered mob of acolytes directly to Goemon, bowed, and then forced a piece of paper into his captain's hands. It had been torn down from somewhere, and on it was a child's handprint in scarlet ink.

'The Yoshioka are pinning these up, dozens of them all across the city,' whispered the Goat.

Goemon read quickly:

INAUGURAL PROCLAMATION OF MATASHICHIRO YOSHIOKA, SIXTH HEAD OF THE SCHOOL OF YOSHIOKA

Point the First: For his actions, the masterless Musashi Miyamoto is now avowed enemy of the School.

Point the Second: The honourable Matashichiro Yoshioka declares the shame inflicted upon his bloodline by the defeat of his brothers too great to bear, and vows to perform seppuku to atone, as is proper, as is the Way.

Point the Third: The ritual shall be performed at the height of the moon's rising this night, unless the masterless Miyamoto presents himself at the grounds of the school to duel a champion of the honourable Matashichiro's choosing, that order may be restored.
Point the Fourth: If he should fail to present himself, then let the entire city and the entire nation take this as proof of the dishonesty of the masterless Miyamoto.

Goemon read it again, and then looked at the Goat. He saw the proclamation for all it truly was, and his voice was low and incredulous: 'Would this suffice? Is his sense of honour—'

There was further disturbance at the gate and another samurai of the Tokugawa burst into the yard. He too pushed past the high priest heaving for breath, having run half the length of the city, and he dropped to one knee in the dust.

'Captain!' he said. 'Violence at the castle!'

'The Yoshioka?' asked Goemon.

The man nodded.

No rest, no chance for contemplation. The castle was his Lord's territory and any violation on it was as personal an affront as encroaching on Edo itself. Goemon quickly pulled on a chainmail jacket, only scantly concealed it beneath his clothing, and then he was off, they were all off – he, the Goat, a score of men clutching spears – leaving the high priest yelling in impotence in the yard, all running beneath the sun reaching its zenith in the cloudless sky above.

By time they reached the site of the castle, sweat was dripping from his nose, his brow, his chin. All the cranes and pulleys were stilled and all labour halted, the workers retreated. Great shaped stones sitting monolithic, the mounds of seashells gleaming nacreous, above them crows circling.

There were five Yoshioka samurai standing before the scaffolding of the emergent gate. They had nailed something to it, and Goemon recognized the same scarlet handprint as upon the proclamation. One of the samurai clutched a bloodied sword in one hand, and a severed head in the other. A lower-born, the overseer who had protested their intrusion.

The tea-coloured men saw the Tokugawa coming, and though they were outnumbered four to one they did not flee. Indeed, they seemed delighted at their arrival.

'Surrender!' bellowed Goemon at them. 'You have violated the law of the Shogunate! You have murdered his subjects and you will face justice!'

The lead samurai merely sneered. 'This is my right, Captain,' he said, the title an insult in his mouth. 'Our right, our moral right. This man was cut down on account of Musashi Miyamoto.'

He tossed the head towards Goemon. It rolled in the dust and it came to rest with the man's dead eyes looking at him. Goemon looked into them, and then he looked at the Yoshioka samurai. It was open challenge, and he wondered what the true meaning of this defiance was. Some planned suicidal sacrifice designed to spark a chaotic revolt, or merely men in sway to raw bloodlust? Were they that rattled by Denshichiro's defeat that they had lost all sense of reason?

'You will heed my command,' said Goemon. 'I speak with the authority of the Shogunate.'

'We are a long way from Edo,' said the samurai.

'The reach of Edo is infinite. I know this well. Surrender.'

'And we know the dog is in your service. This, all this . . .' said the man, and he licked the blood from his thumb. 'All this is upon you.'

'Surrender! Obey!' said Goemon, and how small these words seemed as they echoed.

'Do you not see?' the Yoshioka samurai called to the watching crowd, perhaps two hundred people, labourers from the site or those caught in passing. 'This is all a plot by the Tokugawa to lay the Yoshioka low. Miyamoto is their agent!'

'Slander and lies,' said Goemon. 'Miyamoto is not sworn to us.'

'Why is it you have not brought him to justice, then? Why is it he roams free?'

'Do not preach of justice – you are the criminal here.'

The samurai laughed, and he spoke on to the crowd, beseeched them to open their eyes and see it as they saw it. They wanted to be killed, or they knew they could not be killed, and though it was obviously their scheme Goemon could summon no other resolution than this because in truth he *wanted* to kill. These were the men that would bring about his death and shame, and he knew this, he had known this for months, had borne their agitations, and the weight of all this seemed now to dwarf all else.

Beneath his helmet the tiger's claw cleft away skin and bone until it was digging right into his mind, into his memories, of how he had once thought, or known, that he would die an old and revered bannerman of the Date and be interred in some grand crypt in a secret grove of perpetual autumn that his family would attend for generations. Not the truth apparent: that he would be disgraced and dismembered by alien hands, his body split into two and both parts finding their ends in separate foreign cities and likely left to rot, no purity of flame to remove the mar . . .

'Silence yourself!' barked Goemon. All he could think of.

On the samurai spoke to the crowd, claiming Miyamoto to be Goemon's sworn blood brother, but in truth it did not matter what he said now.

'Heed my command!'

It was that he wore the colour of tea.

'Damn you, heed me!'

It was that this man would live beyond Goemon, that he perhaps would sire sons and not have them robbed from him as Goemon's had been, and this a personal affront now, the envy and the hatred the dead have for the living.

'Silence yourself and surrender!'

It was when the Goat had pressed that sheaf of paper into his hands that, for a brief glimpse, Goemon had thought he had seen an escape if he could only endure it for a day more, and yet this samurai persisted in all he was.

'With full authority of the Shogunate of the most noble clan Tokugawa,' said Goemon, and something was welling in his throat, pulsing behind his eyes, and the heat, the heat, the heat, 'I hereby order you to—'

The Yoshioka samurai heard the change in Goemon's voice, and he rounded on him: 'Away with you, you Michinoku snow monkey.'

The Goat, standing attendant at his captain's side, saw best the change in him. Like a gale upon a field of ashes, something just gone. Unleashed. Goemon surged forward now, tearing the cords from his helmet and tossing it away to clatter on the earth. Screaming in his northern brogue, and what things Goemon Inoue howled at the Yoshioka samurai. How he shouted. Spat and raved and offered every insult he knew, offered the insults he had only heard and had never uttered before, accused the man of every vice and perversion and promised a vast and terrible retribution. The voice of Mutsu echoing before the castle of Kyoto. Goemon natural now, a northern malefic summoning curses like wind, growing in his rage and finding truth in it, and he spoke not only to the sole samurai before him but to the city entire, to the southern clan to which he was sworn, to the fate that cast him so, everything that had festered within him these years now emerging into the sun. Becoming the sun.

Standing there with his shoulders heaving when his gestures and his words were expended, and the Yoshioka samurai said, 'Is that yelping supposed to have meaning? Speak proper that I can understand you.'

In those words, Goemon found his final resolve. His head was all but forfeit already, and in that moment he saw the freedom of that where before he had seen only the doom; if all actions were meaningless then selfishness and virtue were one and the same.

He went for his sword, began to march forth.

The Goat grabbed his captain's arm, stopped the blade from being drawn. Tried to hiss advice in Goemon's ear but the man could hear nothing in that moment, struggled to advance with his adjutant clinging on to him, and the Goat saw that he would not stop and he knew what it was that he had to do.

He lurched forward ahead of Goemon, hobbled towards the Yoshioka samurai and hauled his own longsword free of his scabbard. Faced the man much younger than he and drew his weapon up and uttered an insult that was low and crude and comprehensible.

This he did because he knew that, if Goemon had engaged the Yoshioka samurai, the captain, young and hale and in the colours of the Tokugawa before the castle of his Lord and the eyes of the people of Kyoto, might very well have triumphed.

No balance on his cloven foot and strength and speed all but fled from his old arms, it was over in a single movement. The Yoshioka man cut the Goat across the chest, split his ribs and his sternum and his stomach before the arc of the Goat's attack was even conceived. This was not surprising but the pain was.

No crime to die, no hand of a tyrant apparent here. This duty. The Goat fell to his knees and then onto his back. Dimly he was aware of some howl of outrage, and this pleased him, that the men he served with might consider his loss an affront.

Above him unseen the Yoshioka began to flee and the Tokugawa made to chase them. 'Halt!' barked Goemon.

'They must—'

'Let them go!'

'But the—'

'Stay yourselves, damn you! I command you!'

'Why? Why!'

Goemon did not answer, quelled them with a look, and reluctantly his men obeyed him, watched the Yoshioka samurai vanish with utter hatred. All eyes turned to the Goat where he lay. One of the men picked up the old man's sword and another his scabbard; they reunited the pair and then placed it in the Goat's right hand. Goemon knelt in the dust and took the other.

'Onodera,' the captain said, a fierce respect in his eyes because he understood what it was the Goat had done for him. 'Thank you.'

He pulled the old man's jacket across to hide the wound and give him a measure of dignity. No red visible on the black. The Goat nodded, his hand grew tight on his captain's. 'It's not enough,' he said. 'Force it. Today. Tonight. Do it.'

Goemon nodded. 'You will be avenged.'

The Goat understood this, but he could say nothing more. After perhaps twenty more breaths his eyes lost their lustre and he died.

The captain rose to his feet, his purpose and resolve reaffirmed. Wordlessly he nominated the first man his eyes met as his new adjutant, and commanded him: 'Fetch me a messenger and scour out the three finest archers from amongst the men. Bring them to me at the garrison. Go! Go!'

Chapter Thirty-six

It was some time after dawn, with the cries of the rivermen outside casting their boats off the shore, when Musashi realized how few farewells he had actually said in his life. To his father, a promise to uphold a dogma he now rejected and reviled. To his uncle, the words too awkward to say aloud. To Akiyama, to Jiro, to all the others now dead, he hadn't even got the chance.

The finest he thought, or perhaps even the only example, was to the Lord Hayato Nakata, right before he beheaded him.

The thought of this sat pulsing within him through the morning as he tried to muster words. He gathered his few belongings together and placed them in the rice-straw sack he used for travel. He set the sack on his back and then stood there facing the door of his room as though he were off immediately for a long time. Then he sat down with it still on his back for at least another hour.

He thought about simply leaving without a final word, simply drifting out of her life as erratically as they had come together. But he knew that he would not permit this of himself. That was simply fleeing. A definite farewell, a definite ending, that demarcated it as a firm decision, and that was worthy, what he wanted. Yae, Yae would be easy. Or hard. Perhaps she would cry. He did not know which, nor which he would prefer.

He remained in his room fretting, restless and yet not wanting to move. The longer this went on, the more he started to feel foolish.

Why was it so hard to tell someone that you were heeding their advice?

Eventually, he simply decided to commit. The day was passing by and he needed to be out upon the roads. Just throw himself in, and let it happen. He took a breath, opened the door, stepped out of his room. There was a tightness in his chest, beneath his purpled ribs. Before the doorway to the hearth room where Ameku worked the loom again he hesitated. He hung there inertly, debating whether to stride in with purpose or simply watch in silence for a while.

It was the sound of a door opening down the corridor behind him that spurred him into movement. He quickly stepped inside, hoped his first words would not waver, and found instead the room entirely empty.

Musashi looked around. The ashes in the hearth pit were cold. The tatami mat Ameku had been weaving hung suspended on the levers of the mechanism, all but finished. But where were the hands to weave those last few reeds?

He called out for her, for Yae. He went to their room and knocked on the door. There was no answer.

They were nowhere to be found.

He went and sought out the owner of the lodgings, the coarse ageing man beating the dust out of a futon mat with an iron poker down by the banks of the river.

'Where's Ameku?' Musashi asked him.

'Who?'

'The blinded woman.'

'Is she not on the loom?'

'No.'

The owner shrugged.

'What about the girl, the young girl with her?'

Again, the same nonplussed gesture. 'Neither of them I haven't seen all day.'

'They haven't departed, have they?' he asked.

'They best not have,' said the owner. 'That tatami she is weaving is due tomorrow.'

Musashi gave a low grunt of puzzlement. He stood scratching at the hairs upon his cheeks as he thought, sucked the inside of his lower lip. In truth he did not know their usual routine, he having been focused on his sword these past weeks. He knew they bathed together. Perhaps they were off to the river to find a measure of privacy.

This felt wrong. He felt denied. Yet perhaps it was better this way. Perhaps even fated to be so – had she not told him of the futility of such gestures, that what was known and what was right and what was ultimately good did not need to be said?

The owner stood there with his poker in his hand as Musashi deliberated, wanting to return to his work. He saw the sack that was slung over the swordsman's shoulder. 'Are you on your way, sir?' he prodded politely.

Roused, Musashi grunted affirmation. He paid what was owed to the man, and then, after a moment's consideration, he also gave him half of the coins he had left over. 'You see that the blind woman gets this.'

'Of course, sir.'

The man had agreed too eagerly. Musashi looked down at him, adjusted the swords at his hips. 'I'll be coming back through here in a month or so,' he lied. 'I'll check with her then that she received it.'

The owner understood what was implicit there, and this time he bowed a more compliant, respectful bow. 'Have you a message for her along with the coin?'

Musashi thought about it again for a final longing moment. Then he simply shook his head and went.

He left Maruta and headed north-east on the Nakasendo road. His swords were at his sides. His hair was matted with salt. His bare arms sweated and the threads of his cutaway sleeves curled like the marks of tattoos.

He did not stride. There was no confidence in his steps. The road ahead ran all the way to Edo, but that was not his destination. He had none – he was simply going. Could not face his uncle, not yet. Merely leaving Kyoto and the Yoshioka behind, as Ameku had told him.

Better to live.

He repeated this to himself as he walked.

Live.

Live.

Repetition robbed it of its status as a word.

He tried to hum one of the songs Ameku had sung. His voice was crude and it made a mockery of the melody as it was in his mind, as he knew and felt it, and he did not find the solace he wanted to find in it, and eventually he admitted this and resigned himself to silence, and longed for inner emptiness.

But such a thing was impossible. All the while he tried not to look back at the city he could no longer see. His fingers wrung at the rope lashes of his pack. He told himself that it was done, that he had proven all he could, and yet for all this at his most inner place something still rebelled against this notion. He saw in his mind the duel, remembered both his arms in their perfect unison, and the rightness of this . . .

He was west of Mount Hiei when he stopped of no particular spur.

He turned and looked back down the road. He was caught in indecision. Surely there had to be something he could do. He had been so certain these prior weeks. Certain in himself, in his course. What if felling Denshichiro was not quite enough? What if he admitted to himself that some part of him was not entirely honest? What if there was a further gesture, a gesture of complete and utter honesty that none could fail to recognize as such? If only he had dug further, fought harder; if only he had rejected the black and formless waters of the night.

It had to be there.

Somewhere

But then Akiyama was dead, and all was chaos, and what Ameku said made sense, and there was no clarity. He had no conception of the meaning of all this any more, and yet he stubbornly persisted that either he did, or he did not need to. Did he heed her words because they were sound, or did he heed them purely because *she* said them? And he stood there on the road with pilgrims and merchants passing him, rejecting those words, accepting them, rejecting them, on and on and on and if only there was some conviction either way, and he thought all this, and he was so tired, just then.

It was as though some damming wall within gave out, vanished in an instant, and suddenly he was unavoidably aware of just how exhausted he truly was. The travail of the past weeks weighed down upon him. Eyes so heavy that holding them open was like chiselling away at stone. Sutured leg and all his other wounds oozing and aching in their various ways, beseeching him to rest.

Musashi became aware that he was standing before the stone gates of a temple. The wooden sign hung from the crossbeam gave its name as Ichijo. Musashi had not heard of it. It was of no particular holy renown, and in such proximity to the vast halls within the city the modest shrine he could see nestled in a grove of trees was diminished.

Just inside the gates, he saw a pond that shimmered green, reflected light where it played between the leaves of trees. Musashi limped over to its banks. He set his pack and his swords down, and then dropped to his knees and brought handfuls of water to his face. The water was cool and felt fine upon his brow, his lips, and yet it bought no decision forth.

Cicadas howled and marked the crawl of time.

Within the grounds there was also a great spreading pine tree, centuries old, needles the length of his hand and its bark ridged and mossed. Beneath its boughs was shade. Face glistening, he went and sat on one of its roots, and stared at nothing.

If only he had said farewell.

He thought of this, thought of everything, and the heat persisted warm as his body, as his blood. He placed his elbows on his thighs, and he found that perhaps the heat was sharing his blood, his body, for his pain was receding, growing distant, and on the insects sang.

A hand shook him roughly awake. Musashi started. He had slept sitting and almost tipped backwards off the root.

'Up, you,' an old man was saying. 'Up.'

It was daylight still, but the shadows had grown long. The old man had on the sombre dragonfly-green robes of a Shinto priest, and he persisted in his shaking.

'What do you want?' said Musashi, pushing the priest's hand from his shoulder. 'I've no coin to throw in prayer, if that's what you desire, you covetous old wretch.'

The priest blew air from his cheeks and stood up, affronted. 'Got a temper on you, don't you?' he said. 'Ungrateful shit of a pup.'

Musashi grunted an inchoate retort, rubbed the doze from his eyes.

'If you've a mind for it,' said the priest, 'that fellow bade me wake you. Said he wished to speak with you.'

The priest pointed over to the gates. Standing beneath the double beams beyond the holy threshold was a samurai, and he wore a jacket the colour of tea.

Musashi rose immediately. He drew both his swords and strode over, blades held ready for ambush. The samurai though was perfectly level, mockingly level. He did not even go for his own sword. He simply stepped backwards again and again, keeping a clear ten paces between them. The road was wide around him, and no other seemed to be with him. Musashi's aggression seemed to amuse him blackly.

'Leaving Kyoto, Miyamoto?' he called. 'You think it finished?'

Musashi moved cautiously to stand just outside the gate,

looked along either wall. He held his longsword out in guard before him and had the short above his head readied to strike. Yet no swarming attack revealed itself.

'I felled your master,' Musashi called eventually, 'and your subsequent master proved himself a coward. What more is there for me to do?'

'Matashichiro reigns now.'

A moment of confusion, wondering what it was that had happened to Denshichiro. Then Musashi said, 'The third one is just a child. If he has umbrage with the manner I dealt with his brothers, tell him to find me later in his life – he and himself alone.'

The man tilted his head to one side. 'You're leaving with less than you came with, no?' His smile widened. 'The master Kozei bids you farewell.'

Then the samurai turned and ran back down the road towards Kyoto.

The oddness of his flight masked the meaning of his words for but a moment.

Musashi ran a ragged and desperate lurch on his wounded leg. The samurai, hale and fleet, had long since vanished from his sight, but that was irrelevant. He ran not in pursuit, but instead to Maruta. Those he passed either coming or going upon the road saw his determination and gave him a wide berth.

Night had fallen by the time he returned to the slums.

The long boats were all drawn up on shore and the sentinel pyramids of the casks of effluence stood stoic in the dark. The only noise that of the river's flowing and the few trees there were rattling brittle with the cries of insects. No drunks, no gamblers, no men returning exhausted from their toil, no women squatting down in doorways and talking as they fanned themselves, no children chasing. The street leading up to Musashi's lodgings was desolate and petrified.

A sense of wrongness twisted down his spine. Musashi had his eye upon every shadow, his shoulders rolling with his breath. The door of the building revealed itself smashed, utterly smashed, far beyond simply gaining entry but rather ruined in some fit of rampant destruction, the entirety of it splintered and scattered about. No light burnt within the halls inside. He peered inwards, seeking some skulking form, and then out at the street itself.

Seeing nothing, he took a street lantern down from the post it was hung from, tossed its ribbed paper cover aside and moved to stand in the doorway.

'Ameku?' he called inside. 'Yae?'

There was no response. The light of the oil lantern stuttered and hissed. He caught his breath and called again.

'Ameku?'

Musashi ducked his head and stepped inside. His footsteps rang dead upon the wood of the floor. Slowly he advanced, anticipating, anticipating. He came to the workroom and cast the light of the flame in. A chaos of pots and pans thrown everywhere, a sack of rice split open and the little white grains forming an erratic starscape across the floor. Even the hearth had been dug into, coals and ash scattered wantonly.

These things he had no interest in. His eyes were drawn to the loom where Ameku had worked these past days, and it was revealed to him now entirely destroyed. Pulled from the wall, the bench upended, the ruins of the mechanism spread about still attached by the gears like a serpent's skeleton.

The basket of rushes that had sat by her feet had fallen over, and on the pale bundle of the stalks he saw the vivid red of blood.

The colour of it, lantern-lit, stole Musashi's thought for a while.

When he walked back out onto the street he found a man waiting for him. He was a lowerborn in patched-up hemp clothing, glancing around fearfully.

'You,' he said. 'You're Sir Miyamoto, are you not?'

'Yes.'

'I am bound to tell you something.'

'What?'

'That it was the Yoshioka who did this. They told me I had to tell you this, that you had to know it was them.'

'What did they do?'

'They . . .' said the man, and he cringed. 'Do you really want to know?'

'Yes.'

'They . . ,' he said, and he stopped and steeled himself, and then spoke on quickly, as though he thought speed might spare him any reprisal: 'A mob of them came. They told us all to stay out of their way. They were looking for you. They knew you stayed here. But they found her, the blight-eyed islander, and, and . . . What they did was . . .'

'What?'

'They thought you were hiding. So what they did was they . . . They brought her out here onto the street. And they called out to you to reveal yourself. And when you didn't, they . . . They cut her hand off. And you didn't come, so they did it again. More and more. Small parts. Bit by bit. And . . . We all heard her screaming. We all saw. And, and you didn't come. So . . .'

'So?'

'It was a long time. My children heard, they were crying and . . . When it was finally over, they threw her body in the river,' said the man, and then his courage broke and he dropped to his knees. 'Please do not grow angry with me, sir. They told me to tell you this, all of it. They said they would come back for me and my family if I didn't.'

The lantern sputtered and hissed in Musashi's hand.

'You all just watched,' he said, looking down at him.

The lowerborn quivered, a scar that parted his beard twisting ugly, but he remained prostrate.

Musashi turned his eyes away. 'What of the girl?'

'Girl?'

'A young girl stays with her. Yae, she's called.'

'Fled. She must have fled. I . . . It was the blight-eyed woman they slew, sir.'

Just visible at the end of the street was the hall where he and Kozei had watched the cockfight together. The Yoshioka master's offerings of peace false, and he knowing where Musashi abided. This Musashi had known but had not thought of it beyond risk to himself, built his little nightly barricade just big enough for his room alone.

And now . . .

His eyes turned towards the city. The glow of it visible over the walls, constant, eternal, the ten-thousand-year city, and he of twenty years only with a single torch in his hand.

When was it ever any different?

When was it ever any purer?

He left the lowerborn on his knees, and headed for Kyoto.

Chapter Thirty-seven

The pale rising moon was on the wane, just past full, a sliver taken, imperfect. Hour of the dog, most likely.

It hung above Tadanari Kozei where he stood in the garden at the centre of his school. He was upon the dais overlooking the thirteen boulders set neat in the sand. Beneath the band lashed around his brow his eyes were on the ridge of obsidian, marking distinctions in the blackness.

In his hands he held Ujinari's sword in its scabbard.

The sword marked with the sword of Fudo. The devil-saint. The purger of delusions, enemy of greed, of ego, of lust, of ignorance.

Of permanency.

In the vast abyss of these past days Tadanari had come to realize something about himself. He saw that for all his life until this point he had held himself timeless, thought himself free of the doom of the mere handful of decades of life that other men were condemned to, because the more of him belonged to two things he thought immortal:

The name Kozei and the name Yoshioka.

One of these was dashed already. One of these was marred but could prove itself true yet.

How he pleaded.

Matashichiro knelt at his feet, dressed in white, a sheet of white hemp out before him. Upon a platter a dagger awaited, this too wrapped in a white length of silk. The youth knew all the regalia, what it all meant, but he had swallowed his surprise at the sight of it, had donned the garments, had come without protest. These were the paths of manliness.

There they waited moments of no end together, drowning in the cries of the cicadas, until a bellowing voice burst the shroud of night.

'My name is Musashi Miyamoto!' it echoed. 'Here I am, you sons of whores! I have come, so let us end this as it needs to be ended! You murderers! You cowards! You thralls!'

In the main courtyard of the compound there was confusion. There the adepts of the school had been waiting, eyes upon the gate, muscles quivering, stomachs humming like the reverberation of bells as they imagined the man that would appear and the cuts they would rend him with. The shouting, however, had come from behind them, from within the compound of the school.

'I await you!' yelled the voice. 'Come and die, for I await you!'

The braziers burnt bright, crackled and spat embers upwards. Then decision: the seniormost adept barked command and the group splintered, adepts running to find the source of the noise, disbelieving that they had been bypassed.

In the garden, Tadanari closed his eyes. He had wavered, thought that the lure of Matashichiro's suicide might prove resistible, but no – here the self-righteous young fool had presented himself, ready to kill and die for the sake of his maddened ideas of justice and his vainglorious pride.

When he opened his eyes he found Matashichiro looking up at him.

'Do I do it now?' asked the boy.

'No,' said Tadanari. 'Not yet.'

He had meant to say *you may not have to*, but those words had not come.

The ordeal was now at hand, all his hopes votive. He willed with every mote of his being to overcome, and as he heard the night erupt in sound and motion he found himself breaking loose of time, roaming the length of what he had been damned to, all vivid and present.

His hands grew tight around his sword as though he might throttle the image of Fudo there.

Musashi rushed into the darkness. They had made it about darkness. They had killed her in darkness.

Moving even before his cry had finished, knowing they would be coming. Knowing as he had known they would be crowding the front gate, expecting him to present himself into their maw like a samurai braced for death. Not a samurai, he, everything in his life offered in proof of this. Hauled himself over the low wall at the rear of the compound, and now what he wanted to become, what he needed to become, was chaos.

Chaos against their order, their Way.

Loping as fast as his sutured leg would carry him, not knowing where he was heading, listening to the shouts of the Yoshioka as they converged upon where he had been, their footsteps, the rattling of doors being thrown open, the sounds of the scattering of their swarm. Round the corners of buildings, pressed up into the shadows, and the first of the samurai appeared, two of them running to where they thought he was, oblivious of him until he stepped out with his longsword in his right hand and his shortsword in his left.

The steel of his blades was cerise in the low light and the first of them yelped at his sudden appearance. Musashi swung his longsword into the side of that man's throat, silenced his cry. The samurai dropped his own sword and cut his palms and his fingers open as he grasped at the edge of the weapon, fumbled in vain against it, and as the second man did nought but gape at this Musashi lunged forward with his shortsword and stabbed up under his sternum and twisted savagely.

He left the pair screaming, a fresh lure.

Up he went through the building he had hidden against, blood dripping from either blade. A long hall set with dozens of simple mats of bedding. A barracks. The nest. The hive.

He thought of Ameku on her knees in the street and knowing pain, pain only – was it worse to be blind to your mutilation, to be spared seeing your fingers or limbs or whatever they took taken away, or was it a form of hell to exist in a realm where your only sensation was ever-increasing agony?

Enact it upon them, let them all see, feel. The other side of the building revealed the space of a communal wash trough, the light of a brazier and three Yoshioka samurai heading across his path. Focused on the distant commotion, they too were blind to his emergence.

'Here!' he snarled.

He leapt down on them before shock had even passed across their faces, and he saw that one of them was old and two of them were young, perhaps as young as himself. The first youth he cast down with his falling strike, splitting the length of his ribs, and before this man had fallen Musashi stabbed immediately into the second's throat with his shortsword. The third, the old one, managed to get his legs braced and his sword up to parry Musashi's blow, but, though their longswords locked and negated one another, Musashi's short remained free. Down into a crouch, then the blade of that lashed across the samurai's taut old stomach.

'Was it you who killed her?' he snarled at the samurai as he collapsed. 'Was it you?'

No answer was given. Blood on his fist, now, warm, warmer than sweat. Musashi shook it off, surged onwards, for the outrage spiralled ever outwards.

These the trail of sensations the mind wanders down when it is loosed such: Tadanari saw hydrangeas blooming wild before him in a remote meadow he had discovered by chance on the travels of his youth, and he remembered a separate time and the taste of them drunk as tea far too sweet for his tongue, and also his hand reaching out to cup a head of the flowers and bring them closer to his eyes.

The feel of their petals on his sword-calloused palms and the blooming of pity and loathing within himself at their frail beauty.

Frail and soft as well the long tresses of hair pressed upon the hardness of chainmail that rattled in the night.

The bloody palms of a hundred different men pressed into a book and oaths to the Yoshioka uttered, filling the pages over years and so many pages empty yet, so many yet to be, which must come to be, that could not fail to come to be.

Faith in this.

Matashichiro, the heir, knelt at his side. His palm red also, red with ink from earlier. No one had told him to wash it. Wearing white and hearing from within the school screams of a type that he had never heard before, screams that grew in their number . . .

Musashi spoke of her and thought of her and yet it was more than she. This was everything. Akiyama and Jiro and the Way and all the world. Everything as simple as it needed to be. He had thought himself honest before the Hall of Thirty-Three Doors, but that paled to the truth. That paled to now. Let the anger carry him and realize itself, a moment that none could deny in its earnestness.

His longsword bucked as it bit into the flesh of another throat, lodged itself against the knobs of the spine. The Yoshioka samurai collapsed thrashing, but Musashi did not see him fall, left him behind, eyes always ahead.

A tea-coloured thrall rounded the corner of a building and Musashi hurled a stolen shortsword through the air. The man was screaming something even before he was struck, not of Musashi, not at Musashi, and then the spinning sword impaled him through his chest, silenced him and forced him to his knees, and as Musashi ran past he struck the samurai across the face with his longsword.

No drumbeat now but the rhythm of the universe was within him, he was sure. He carried it, the spark, whatever it was it was within him. Drove him, his scope solely upon the finite range of his swords, and this he understood and could control. Could communicate with as clearly as he needed to this night.

A glimpse of orange light like a shooting star as he went,

seen out of the corner of his eye and quickly gone, vanished somewhere behind him. Ignored. Meaningless.

The Yoshioka howling in confusion and he drifted through them, amongst them, and he could not believe how quickly he alone had caused them to descend into panic and scatter. They charged past him without realizing, and he could not be caught, and he was invincible, and he was truth.

He found himself broaching the main courtyard. There braziers burning so bright he had to squint for a moment, forms of the Yoshioka blurred. Perhaps six of them, and they looked so thoroughly shaken it was as though they were surrounded, facing not one enemy but an unseen horde the origin of which they could not fathom.

A systolic instant of surprise, even, where it seemed Musashi's arrival drew their attention away from some other threat.

He went for them without hesitation. The closest samurai held a bucket of water, which he dropped to spill into the dust, drew forth his own longsword and rushed to meet him. His eyes were upon Musashi's longsword and so Musashi cleaved with the short. The second man came through his comrade, barging him out of the way in a desperate frenzy to get at Musashi, succeeded only in staggering himself, died in the arc of Musashi's longsword.

'It was Kozei that ordered it, wasn't it?' spat Musashi, weaving his way around the braziers, the sting of smoke in his eyes, embers rising, keeping the building to his back and the remaining Yoshioka before him. 'Where is he? Bring him out to face me! Bring him out to face me! Bring him out to—'

And he broke the rhythm of his words and lunged at the nearest man mid-sentence, he reading the heaving of Musashi's lungs and the movement of his lips. He caught

Musashi's longsword upon the flat of his own inverted sword but fell to the short, and outwards Musashi threw himself, heading for the centre of the yard.

He rushed inside the arc of the next samurai's sword before it could descend and hammered his longsword into the side of the Yoshioka chest, the edge sinking deep enough to surely cut the heart. Spun, crossed his blades, caught the subsequent sword from the subsequent man with gore-gobbed steel, twisted, stabbed with the short and the blade slid in below the collar bone.

Fatigue was starting to rob his motions of any grace, Musashi aware of this on a visceral level, and yet he felt no sense of desperation. A warmness pervaded, the warmness of the lack of identity. He was barely Musashi any longer; all there was was the fight, and he was no more and no less than a participant in it, a wave of its ocean. Nameless, formless

unfindable

and he felt drool upon his chin, or perhaps blood.

A flurry of motion, a parry, his own elbow driven into his side and his breath escaping him, and then Musashi's longsword looping from above guided barely by thought or intention. Aimed for the Yoshioka's shoulder but found the crown of his head and the crack of the skull's splitting was wet. The Yoshioka samurai's headband, cut through, fell to earth before he did, the man collapsing and twisting split-legged.

. . . Above Tadanari and Matashichiro both, the wide boughs of a spreading pine were lit like veins of bronze through thick smoke, the tree taller than the school itself and its branches reaching out over the walls of the garden, so massive and encompassing, and yet Tadanari remembered it, saw it, as no more than a seed, and every stage between.

Did any of those years hold meaning?

The cry of victory did not come this night and the mouths that howled were growing as Miyamoto killed, and now Tadanari stood in time's abrogation and from this vantage he looked at his Way anew, the Way in which he had held a complete faith for his entire life, and thus found himself akin to a man who felt his feet sinking into stone.

With as much of his soul as he could give he begged for the men of the Yoshioka to kill Miyamoto. To prove to him that the decades of his instructing them had not been in vain; that the dozens of the pairs of arms that he had strengthened and imbued with skill had not been set with false ability; that although his progeny was slain he, Tadanari Kozei, had managed to create something that would outspan his flesh. How he begged, and Fudo on the scabbard and his infinite snarl . . .

Such was Musashi's frenzied elation that the night itself seemed to be glowing; the paper doors and walls of the corridor he loped along now lucent, his footsteps heavy and his breath ragged. Screams constant from outside, of panic, of agony.

Into this building scouring them out wherever they might be hiding, every last one, and he was rewarded – a single samurai delivered himself to Musashi. Charged at him immediately along the hallway, and Musashi jerked onwards to meet him, knees stiff, sutured calf throbbing. Could not hesitate, to hesitate was to be surrounded, and Musashi feinted with the short, tried to provoke the Yoshioka into lunging, and the samurai fell for it, drew his sword back to strike, and Musashi snarled delighted, and then the Yoshioka samurai drove forward with the pommel of his sword.

A feint of his own that had duped Musashi entirely, and the blunt steel smashed into his unbraced face clean. Musashi both heard and felt his nose break, and as he staggered blinded the Yoshioka samurai screamed his triumph, let it rule him, and brought his sword around in a decapitating slash only to find the sword burying its edge into the beam of a constricting pillar.

A spastic form of combat now, one of them weaponless and one of them sightless. Musashi slashed wildly with his sword, slow and heavy and the Yoshioka read the path of it and caught him by the wrists. They grappled, wrestled, and though the samurai was smaller he knew the methods of unarmed combat and found Musashi unbalanced, and so the Yoshioka man rolled his hip, drove on with his feet and sent the pair of them crashing through the door to their side.

Paper tearing, frail wood of the frame shattering. Musashi's swords fell from his hands as they landed, scattered amongst the wreckage, and he kicked and thrashed and tried to find them. The Yoshioka samurai writhed to his knees, drew his shortsword and stabbed it down desperately towards Musashi with no concern for finesse. It was Musashi, now weaponless, who caught the wrist, he pinned on his back, struggled to keep the point from finding his throat.

The Yoshioka samurai managed to squirm on top of Musashi as he tried to force the blade down, and, spluttering in blind pain, Musashi tried to resist. Blood in his mouth, blood behind his nose, the sensation of drowning, yet Musashi fought, held him, and then the stomp of footsteps coming, closing in.

'I've got him!' the Yoshioka samurai was screaming. 'I've got him! Cut through me! Kill him! Cut through me!'

Little grunts escaping Musashi born of savage will. Relinquished his right hand from the struggle, sought a weapon on the floor beside him. The Yoshioka samurai now with his freed left hand took Musashi's skull and grasped at it, clawed, thumb gouging at the eye, footsteps coming, imminent, Musashi groping, groping, found a splinter of wood.

Thrust upwards at the head and the point of it met skull, too soft to pierce bone, to kill, yet sharp enough to rake the flesh. Bashed with it, bashed with it, heel of hand on temple, Yoshioka samurai screams now wordless, splinter gouging its way along, footsteps coming, had to be here, had to be here, and the point of the splinter sank somewhere soft. Eye or ear or mouth. Samurai's strength faltered and Musashi kicked out from under.

New samurai in the doorway.

Shortsword stolen from the splinter-stabbed foe, Musashi on his knees, rising.

Blade up into the standing man's throat, he not even cognisant of the scene before him.

Musashi turned, intending to bring the shortsword down upon the first.

Bloodslick hands slipped upon the handle, came away empty, and the second samurai vanished backwards into the corridor, his throat still rent with the weapon.

Bereft, Musashi saw the first man seizing Musashi's own fallen longsword.

Hands closing.

Theft complete.

No time, no time, samurai rising.

There – there! Upon the floor, dark form of rock.

Rock taken up with both hands.

Up behind head and then down into the back of the Yoshioka's.

Before he could stand, before he could bring the blade to bear.

Hollow crack, again, again, frantic, frenzy of motion, stone to skull, stone to skull.

Not stopping until the samurai abandoned all hope of using the sword upon its owner.

Not stopping until the Yoshioka abandoned hope of breath.

Body down, body suppliant, body still.

The paper walls glowing and Musashi looked down at the corpse, he on his knees panting, struggling to conceive of his survival. Then sudden motion in his hands: somehow the rock itself was squirming in his grasp, and he looked at it and realized that the rock in fact had legs, a head, and that these stubby things were all writhing and kicking. Shocked, revolted, he dropped it.

The rock continued to thrash upon the floor, and Musashi peered at it in the gloom. It was alive, he realized, a creature he had never seen before, some kind of land turtle. It had fallen on its back, and now it kicked and kicked in a vain attempt to right itself with its pale and segmented belly rocking back and forth.

A snort of disbelieving laughter escaped him.

How far could this take him? How far could he go?

Slowly Musashi rose to his feet, touched his shattered nose, found the pain too much. Spat blood, sucked it from his sinuses. Arms numb, felt hollow from the shoulder down, yet he bent and forced them to retrieve his swords.

There was noise yet. Not finished.

At his feet, the land turtle continued to thrash. Before he advanced Musashi hooked a foot beneath its shell and flipped it over.

It began to crawl away, and he wished it life.

. . . Kozei and Yoshioka, Yoshioka and Kozei, revealed to Tadanari the mutuality of the two. One had fitted within the other and both had served the opposite, both living in their entwined reflections.

Had it always been such? When he was a young man, he had been bound by friendship to Naokata, and such was that friendship that he might even have had held a belief that Yoshioka held the greater place within in his heart. He had served willingly, obsequiously, as men who have nought but themselves can pledge.

But in a memory Naokata lay on his death bed and pulled on strands of light and howled of precedent and Tadanari's heart broke anew, and Naokata's sons had proven false, thoughtlessly provoking or shamelessly running, and the screams were coming still and they said that Miyamoto lived yet, sacred ground trampled and sundered and how many men had he killed, how many of Tadanari's disciples were slain in the desecration of his faith in them?

The Yoshioka his buoyancy and his shield – the honour fine enough second in line, for him and for his bloodline, but spared the full indignity should the jewel shatter. At least so he had thought. At least so he had been certain. But the jewel had been struck, and now everything was perilous and vibrating fit to fragment. Kozei and Yoshioka, Kozei and Yoshioka, one of these might endure, must endure, and in that one both survived.

He looked up into the sky, did Tadanari Kozei, as if to find certainty from the nacre of the moon. A reassurance the twin of that found by boneless oddities that ventured up from ocean depths on nocturnal egressions to stare at that same orb with their eyeless gazes. But the moon was robbed of pre-eminence and what he saw put him in mind of a skyline that he had seen twice in his life before, skylines that followed great shakings of the earth. A hue of red and orange, a hint of it there forming. He tried to discern its emergence above the roofs of the school, his school, his last hope, felt inevitability come like a wind . . .

Again, the falling-star flicker barely seen. The encroachment of complete exhaustion perhaps, invading Musashi's vision. No. No. Not exhausted. Gripped his swords anew.

Ahead, the grand door of the dojo.

Licked his lips, tasted his own blood, lurched inwards. There he found what must be the last of the Yoshioka, and as he saw the number of them his heart contorted. Gathered here, perhaps, the final bastion, and it cut through his calmness, his anger, so many more of them it was as though he had felled none. For an instant he saw standing amongst them the thralls of the Tokugawa and the monks of Hiei and the consenting masses of the lowerborn, scores of them, all faceless together whether in their topknots or their shaved heads or their cowed eyes, all of them together, all arrayed against him, and he did not care.

'All of you,' he said, his voice breaking with his breaths, 'thralls. Where are those that killed her? Bring their throats to me.'

'Arsonist!' howled one of them, and he charged and aimed a slash as savage as his shout at Musashi's neck. Up his shortsword, greeting the blow, diverting its path and sending it arcing over his head, and his longsword was already in motion in the opposite direction. It met the samurai in the side of the chest, sank in between his ribs.

'Where?' shouted Musashi over the scream. 'Where?'

They came unheeding, perhaps emboldened by the surroundings, hallowed ground to them. The möbial sweep of a Yoshioka sword, arms twisting, blade from up to down then up, trying to split Musashi along the sternum, fine feint, the breeze of its whipping passage felt upon his chin, then Musashi's shortsword hacking into the samurai's waist.

The moments of frantic fight unfurled like the smoke that billowed from the braziers. Smashing a blade aside with the flat of his longsword, the short in perfect rhythm killing in the opening. Evading, shoulders coiling, and then the long-sword around to knock a stomach out.

And here it was, and he was realizing it, and the anger had carried him this far, and now it would carry him all the way, and how could he have ever doubted it, this feeling, moments like this, for here was honesty, perfect honesty, an honesty that could not be denied by the world, and he flailed and battered with desperate speed, lunged with his shoulders and the weight of his body, weight of his heart, and on, and on, and he saw it all and he knew it all, defined it all, and a samu-rai attempted a familiar attack, brushing Musashi's sword aside, rushing close, chest to chest, and Musashi repelled as he had repelled before, and slew as he had slain, and the next man who had seen it fail so thoroughly used the exact same manoeuvre, as he was taught, unable to think, to conceive of nought else, and Musashi saw it all: he creation, they entropy! He creation, they entropy! Envisioning this, enacting it, thing of pure will, bones of his wrists singing with the cumulative ache of the impacts, swords moving where they needed to be and Musashi saw the openings as and when they came, there, his shortsword at a throat, there the long cleaving across the belly, there the feel of a Yoshioka blade passing so very close. Hacking down on proffered wrists with wild strength and hewing both hands away entirely, and every sword stroke now a repudiation, cutting the world that he had been offered, cutting himself free of it, for truth was truth, felt entirely and exactly here and now, and if he could only use the raw sensation of these instants as his proof in place of fumbling with the curse of inutile verb and noun then all would be as it ought, this, what he felt, what he knew to be right, honest and good as he had ever wanted to be, achieving, achieving, let this be the definition of who he was, his proof to the world, let them see when it was done, let them know.

Stood on something fleshy with his rear foot, a hand perhaps or the roundness of a calf, and he slipped, his legs spreading wide. As he sprawled they attacked, frantic the parry he offered, a sharp crack of steel, a Yoshioka sword fulcrummed and a razor kiss down his back. Rolled, found purchase, his longsword lashed around and severed a leg beneath the knee.

Up, charging, hacking. Pure inspiration. Pure motive. He, for himself. Individual. Fighting because he chose. All that mattered. Youth offered, youth votive, everything given, everything offered for their ruination, the ruination of the hateful world that was.

Turned to find only a single samurai left, and the man was parrying, and his hands were weak, could not stand against Musashi in his rage, and Musashi struck with a downwards blow that tore the sword from the man's grip and continued, painted a ragged wound from his collarbone to his groin. The samurai fell to his knees and then rose again out of stubborn instinct, but took no more than two steps before he fell once more.

He flailed and grabbed at what he could, and his hands found a long strip of white cloth draped around the painting of the former master Naokata. He managed to grip either end in one hand, forming a noose of sorts, yet still it was too frail to bear his weight; he tumbled and he brought the cloth and the painting down on top of him, all clattering in an ugly heap.

Clutched in the samurai's dying hand, Musashi glimpsed what appeared to be letters smeared on the cloth, but what they were he could not read, their meaning stolen quickly away by the encroachment of fresh blood.

Through his ruined nose he snorted gore.

. . . The glow now fiercely luminescent up above the school, a column of smoke belching upwards. Tadanari stared up at it, dwarfed, powerless to stop its growth. The school was ablaze, the barracks, the dojo, all burning wild, and the pulsing corona of the fire seemed to him to mimic the shape of a lotus flower.

Buddhism. Inevitably it all returned to Buddhism. Shinto for the living, and Buddhism for the dead. Fudo apparent in his glory. He with his sword Houken, the Cutter of Delusions. Always searching, and always finding fresh targets in this world of limitless delusions conjured by limitless numbers of limitlessly fallible men. Men like Tadanari, and here and now with all the adepts of his school dead or dying and the fire burning high, Houken swung celestial through him and he was truly flensed of the last vestiges of his subjective fantasies.

Stripped from him the permanency to which he had never admitted he had been beholden.

Rendered Kozei and Yoshioka, these two things that had been like wings to him, no more than blackened remnants. Where once he had been a thing of centuries, now he was no more than a single finite body, withered down into the lowest, most detestable form:

An individual.

The only thing left to live for himself, and how black and meaningless that was.

What kind of man was it that could find pride in such a life? To be only the fire, igniting that which other hands had built over time? A wicked, loathsome man, a murderer, a bane of meaning.

Downwards, earthly now, screams drawing closer. A clamour of pain. Over quickly, and no loyal voice called that the interloper had been felled. Aching moments passed, and then a figure emerged out into the garden. A part of Tadanari thought it might be Fudo himself, summoned from the scabbard by the fire, by the destruction of all this, all Tadanari had struggled to build. All he had believed would last.

But no. No god or saint for him so humbled. What emerged from the darkness of the doorway into the inferno-painted night was just a man. A sword in either hand. Bloodied face. Lacerated rags upon his body. Staggering almost.

The killer of his son, the ruination of his vision, this despicable, decrepit thing.

'Kozei!' snarled Musashi.

At last he had found him, here in some neat and secret little garden, surrounded by the boughs of trees and a manicured sandbed set with boulders artfully placed. A murderer enshrined, a torturer bedecked in a garland of flowers. Musashi forced himself out towards him, feet heavy on the wooden porchway.

Tadanari stood, arms bared, band around his head, and as Musashi approached his face pinched itself into a look of sheer abhorrence, the lines formed in its creation suddenly revealing the path of time upon his features.

'Not enough solely to slaughter,' he spat. 'You had to burn it too.'

Musashi did not know what the man was talking about, did not care, matched the samurai's venom: 'And you had to kill her, just because you could.'

'I have never killed a woman.'

'Ordered it, then,' said Musashi. 'All the same, the same.'

The enmity upon Tadanari's face somehow grew deeper. By his feet a figure in white knelt, a seppuku platter before him; Matashichiro, pledged to die.

It took Musashi a moment to recognize the regalia and what it all meant. Why seppuku? Why here? It was mad. They were all mad. Maddened by the Way. He looked closer at the figurehead of the Yoshioka. From what he had heard he had presumed him a boy, no more than a child, yet here Musashi saw the hardness of Matashichiro's brow, the first signs of a beard forming on his chin, a man emergent.

'How old are you?' he asked.

'Thirteen,' said Matashichiro.

Musashi considered it: 'Off your knees, then.'

'I can?' said Matashichiro, eyes rising to Tadanari, further words forming on his lips. These, though, never heard, for Tadanari slashed his longsword down and took his head in one clean blow.

The body fell, the head came to rest, the white hemp turned red.

Musashi watched it, and he wanted to feel something: a fresh snarl, a fresh outrage. But after all he had seen this night, all he had felt, there was no such spark left within him.

Tadanari too a husk. He drew back the bloody longsword and hurled it high and far beyond Musashi. Musashi watched its path as it vanished and became aware only then of the colour of the sky, of the roar of flames behind him. The sound of something collapsing distant.

The school was irrevocably ablaze.

Tadanari picked up the scabbard, intricately carved with some pattern, and hurled it in the same direction. Hurled it hellwards. It was snapped and it bent in the air as it plunged into the flames. From his side Tadanari drew another longsword, this a far humbler and far duller thing.

'It's all ended,' he said. 'Come, then. Find your end too.'

The loathing in his eyes was boundless. He waiting, longsword out by his side, and there were no more words now that Musashi could speak, not for himself, not for Ameku, not for anyone.

All there was was to do.

Musashi raised his swords. The weapons quivered in his grasp. He made for Tadanari upon the platform, and his feet moved not in the position of perfect braced balance but merely went as they could, one after another.

Tadanari stood immobile, his form in contrast immaculate, brought his sword up high, guard at his cheek with his right elbow eye level and his left elbow low. Something in his supreme calm in all the murder and fury that surrounded him gave Musashi check.

Outwards Matashichiro's blood spread, tideburst.

Musashi changed the positions of his swords, raised his longsword high, brought his short low, trying to unsettle him as he had other members of the school. Tadanari's eyes switched effortlessly between the blades.

Range, then. He of shorter sword, shorter arms; take him at length.

The ethereal moment, after all this, all things balanced, souls and bodies tremulous in the burning world.

And that was that, and Musashi went: led as though to stab with the shortsword, but this a feint only, the real attack the long arcing down from above.

Tadanari moved his body to the side, dodged the short, brought his sword to meet the long and turned its path around him. As Musashi's sword descended he slid his own blade along it, stepping in, aiming a thrust at Musashi's vulnerable stomach, and Tadanari's composure broke as he screamed the cry of striking, voice raw and honest and terrifying.

That thing for which Musashi had no name but knew lay within guided him, turned his body for him. Torso swivelled, writhed, and Tadanari's blade did not pierce his belly and lance up into his heart but rather slid along his flank, slicing a path across the side of his ribs. Immense immediate pain, colours flaring in his eyes, and thus dizzied the guard of Tadanari's sword meeting his sternum almost knocked him from his feet.

Staggered, Musashi, hissed, but did not fall. Feet found purchase, and how close they were then, he and Tadanari, locked brow to brow, sword edge entwined with flesh. But a moment only this embrace, less than half a heartbeat. Tadanari snarled at seeing him still upright, and tried to saw the blade further into his chest.

This fresh movement brought fresh pain and fresh anger, and Musashi roared and thrashed his elbow across, knocking the sword free of flesh and spinning Tadanari. He lurched around in the opposite direction and found himself to the samurai's side, and there, now his chance – *it was won, it was won!* – and he hammered his shortsword down across Tadanari's exposed back from the blade of the man's left shoulder to his right hip.

It split the silk of his tea-coloured jacket, it split the cord with which he had bound his sleeves back, but most of all it split his flesh, and at the blow's end Musashi found his shortsword falling from his grasp. The blade rattled to the ground, the hemp it landed upon now entirely sodden crimson.

Tadanari stumbled away, fell to his knees, put his hands out to stop himself falling further, remained there on all fours. Musashi clutched his own wound with his empty left hand, felt the path of blood upon his palm, his wrist. Yet there was no pain – the pain had vanished. He looked down at his foe and the throes of victory started to heave within him. He waited to watch Tadanari collapse, waited to watch him die.

'You killed her,' he found himself saying over and over. 'You killed her.'

From Tadanari's mouth came a long shuddering sigh. Musashi watched his arms, saw the quivering in his elbows, longed to see them yield and falter. And yet somehow Tadanari began instead the torturous process of picking himself up. He led with his shoulders, his cleaved shoulders, forced one leg then the other beneath himself, and then somehow he was standing upright once more, sword still in his hand and hate still in his eyes.

Musashi stared, and Tadanari lunged.

Second hand upon his longsword now, and, as he lurched to block, the simple agony of motion made Musashi cry out. He met Tadanari's sword with the flat of the blade, their swords locked, and the two of them all but collapsed against each other. Guard against guard, knuckles against knuckles. Tadanari twisted, brought an elbow up that met Musashi on the side of his head, knocked him back.

On the fire raged.

Wild swipe of Musashi's sword, and Tadanari stepped around it. From overhead the samurai's sword responded, his motion erratic but fast enough. Musashi could not dodge, had to catch it again on the flat of his sword, found the blow drove him to one knee. All things seeping from his rent side, all strength, all confidence, all ability.

Whatever he had left he put into whirling his sword around, still caught beneath Tadanari's, not a snarl but rather a cry of utter effort escaping him. The motion of the blade made Tadanari stumble, and now the point of Musashi's sword was facing towards him. Musashi thrust and Tadanari somehow pushed it down and the stab of it raked between his legs. The curved edge found the inside of Tadanari's thigh, and Musashi forced the entire length of the blade at him, felt the sword sink deep up into the crevice of the pelvis, and fresh blood flowed and Tadanari collapsed on top of him.

It was dead weight; he was slain now, definitely. Musashi tipped the samurai off him, stumbled backwards, found himself up on his feet once more. Precarious his stance, the lights in his eyes now definitely born of exhaustion, yet he looked down upon Tadanari where he had fallen.

And again, Tadanari moved.

He pushed himself up onto his knees. Blood gushed visible from his thigh and yet Tadanari didn't seem to feel it. What the samurai did was sink the point of his longsword into the wood of the pedestal beneath them and then haul himself up it. Upright, Tadanari swayed upon his feet, looked Musashi in the eye and spoke:

'Die,' he said, no tone in his voice but ultimate emotion. 'Die.'

His jacket was hanging about him now unbound, flapping around the contortions of his arms like the sails of an arson-struck ship. No steadiness in him, no support from his wounded leg, the onslaught like a pendulum, body swinging back and forth with each strike. All technique gone, the pair of them beyond it, no more than men with sharp metal.

Came the blow from the left, and Musashi stepped to the right. His riposte a wild overhead slash, which Tadanari batted aside. Musashi came in close, tried to barge Tadanari over but found the samurai evading, sliding corpselike around him, and on he staggered overbalanced, his stumbling foot kicked Matashichiro's head away into the sand.

The agony of even turning back to face him; the wound at

Musashi's ribs was now a throbbing void that was consuming the entire left side of his body. Tadanari seemed to be trying to speak, his lips moving but no sound emerging, just a stream of breath, of spit. Great swipes of their swords, and then the blades met, rolled, turned into the ground. A barge with the shoulder, Musashi repulsed Tadanari, sent him stumbling backwards. The samurai was slow to raise his sword, slow to raise his guard, his arms were exposed and Musashi saw the chance, all but leapt forward.

He could not stop himself from falling to his knees as he brought his sword down and hacked through Tadanari's arm beneath the elbow.

Tadanari's hand remained clutching his sword for an instant, before his arm pulled free in remnant motion, separated, and the grip of the palm loosened. The samurai did not scream. Instead he looked down at his arms as though he were confused why his sword was no longer responding correctly, saw his hand upon the floor and gazed at it as though it had never been a part of his own body. But something gave within him; his shoulders slumped and he dropped the longsword from his remaining hand.

For a long moment he stood there bereft, firelit and mutilated. Musashi looked up at him from his knees and wondered whether the samurai would die thusly on his feet, perhaps just harden into some horrendous statue, remain in the world as a totem to endurance.

And then Tadanari stirred and came again, furious life yet in him.

Galled, exhausted, Musashi, too stupefied to move. Tadanari put a sandaled foot down upon Musashi's longsword where it rested upon the floor and hooked it away, tearing it from Musashi's fingers. Then he was on Musashi like a beast, clawing with his surviving hand, kicking him, knees and elbows, gouts of blood flying from his stump and all Musashi could do was recoil, try to squirm free from the samurai's grasp.

He found himself on his hands and his knees, and Tadanari did not relent, sank his nails into his throat from behind, bent and down and started biting at his jugular, at his ear, teeth sinking into the lobe of it, into anything, and the noise he was making – this hiss, this moan – uttered direct into Musashi's ear.

There were no words in it, but the communication of it was perfect: Musashi understood then just how truly he was hated.

No swords now, the very last remnants of strength within him. Musashi fought to regain his feet, Tadanari still reaching over his shoulders, and then he hooked his hands beneath the samurai's legs. Up he took him, bearing Tadanari on his back, the samurai still biting at him, still making the same terrible noise, and what Musashi did was carry him and run.

No sprint but a jerking gait. He headed for the edge of the pedestal, clutching Tadanari's legs tight to him. Musashi leapt and kicked his own legs out straight ahead of him, turned Tadanari beneath him in their brief flight. The pair of them did not soar, flew no graceful arc, but instead went outwards and downwards, landed upon the foremost boulder set into the sand and its cresting ridge of obsidian that seemed to glisten in the firelight.

The impact was such that it knocked the wind from Musashi, but it knocked the spine from Tadanari.

Musashi tumbled free, fell to earth, felt soft sand upon his face. He lay there for a long moment simply breathing. The sand was soft, delightful. It would be so pleasant, so right, just to sink into it. But he fought the urge, rolled onto his back, looked up and saw Tadanari.

The samurai was splayed convex over the surface of the boulder above. He could not move himself from it. He was broken, dying now definitely, irreversible, and his inverted eyes glared down at Musashi. Musashi looked up into them.

Imminent death only deepened what had been there, added coldness to it.

Eventually he was still.

After some time Musashi forced himself to sit up, the effort enormous. He looked down at his side, saw the wound all dirty with sand, and the sand all dirty with blood. There was no pain, no feeling any more. He managed to shuffle himself over to rest his back against a boulder opposite that which Tadanari lay upon. There he sat with his head lolling back, looked up at the sky. The stars were stolen by the glow of fire, and the moon it was not crimson.

He willed it to be so, tried to breathe, found the blockage of his nose painful, and suddenly insulting, unbearable. He had to breathe, he deserved to breathe. Both hands he raised to his face and he braced himself, pinched the bridge of his shattered nose and pulled it upwards, crunching outwards, righting it, righting, white . . .

Aware now. Some time must have passed; the building closest, the clerical building within which he had ambushed, killed, that so long ago, that was now on fire, flames even through the roof of it, or what was left of the roof. Musashi watched it burn.

Motion.

Languid, dark on dark.

Across the wooden walkway, foot after ponderous foot came the land turtle. Unhurried, unpanicked, it escaped the blaze with perfect calmness, made its way to the pedestal where the headless body of Matashichiro lay. There it stopped, cast its black eyes out across the garden.

It looked at Musashi.

Musashi looked at it.

Perhaps it was instinct, or perhaps the creature remembered; slowly, the land turtle sank to its belly and withdrew its limbs and its head into its shell.

Chapter Thirty-eight

A time of wandering, free of any notion of anything other than existing.

How Musashi soared or felt as if he were soaring, and he deserved to soar, he knew. A great thing that he had done, a victory. Of all the places that he had the potential of visiting here so liberated, he knew that he wanted to go to the temple of Amaterasu, to Dorinbo. He knew that he could face him now, face the monk with pride and tell him that he had proven himself.

But neither Dorinbo nor the temple appeared. What coalesced instead, out of the long haze of colour and heat, was the form of Munisai, his father who was not his father, there in the armour that Musashi had cleaned so often as a child. Loathsome. Beautiful. Munisai's face beneath the elegant copper crest of the helmet, moustached and close, so close it consumed, enveloped.

'You killed them all,' he said, and there was a tone in his voice that Musashi had never heard from the man's fleshly throat. 'You killed them all.'

* * *

Anchored now.

Other voices. Actual voices. The fire was gone. So too the darkness, the blue of coming dawn above. Vile stink of smoke. Tadanari's corpse still there sprawled upon the rock. The wound still there upon Musashi's side.

'Is there anything left?' someone was saying, a man, distant, unaware of Musashi. 'Can you believe this?'

'Why were we prevented from action?' said another man. 'We had enough men to chain buckets to the canal. Why did they make us pull the surrounding buildings down instead?'

'Got here quicker than us too, though their garrison's the other side of the city.'

'Bastard Edo interlopers—'

'Guard your tongue, they're just outside still.'

Nothing for a while, save for the crunching of debris beneath feet. Then a yelp of sorts, part shock, part disgust, quickly swallowed.

'What?'

'More.'

'Bodies?'

'Nnn.'

'Yoshioka?'

'I cannot tell. The fire has claimed them all.'

'It must be them. Perished, all of them perished. Can you believe this?'

The other man had no answer. Musashi found strength in his legs, pushed himself up the boulder he lay against, sat himself on top of it with his feet still in the sand. He was filthy, blood and ash and sand caked across his arms, his clothes no more than rags now. His throat hurt, his lips were dry. He longed for water, even for the feel of sweat.

Around him he saw nought but ruins of the school left, obelisks of scorched foundation beams jutting through piles of roofing tiles stacked and blackened like the slopes of volcanoes. Even the greenery of the garden had been eradicated. Musashi looked at the sandbed around him, grateful for his little pocket of protection.

He counted thirteen boulders.

Two men appeared then. Young, hale, cropped hair. Over plain jerkins they wore cloth jackets patterned with red and blue hexagons, emblazoned with the name of the ward of Imadegawa on their back; volunteer fire guards from amongst the local residents, picking through the ruins. They almost missed Musashi sitting upon his rock, he all but obfuscated in the like colour and tone around him, gaped in shock when they saw that something lived here still.

Musashi grinned at them, and even that was a struggle.

'I did it,' he said to them. 'I've done it. I beat them. Do you see now?'

'Here!' one of them screamed. 'Here!'

Other fire guards heeded his cry, emerged and gathered to stare at Musashi. All he did was grin back. They took in his joy, and then they took in the great swathe of destruction all around them, saw Tadanari, saw what was left of Matashichiro upon the pedestal.

'You killed them,' said one.

'Yes.'

'All of them.'

'Yes. For you, for all of you.'

'Why?'

'To show you.'

His voice was rasping. He could feel every word in the

wound on his ribs. More of the firemen were still coming, faces blackened with soot and smoke. They stared, and hesitantly they found their tongues:

'How many men dead by your blade?' said one.

'I don't know.'

'Even the boy,' said another. 'The youngest Yoshioka.'

'Not me,' said Musashi, and nodded at Tadanari's corpse. 'That was him. That was Kozei.'

'Child killer,' said someone else.

'He was no child: he was thirteen,' said Musashi, trying to see who had spoken. 'Do you know what I did at thirteen?'

'Was it you who set the fire too?'

'No. That was them. I didn't . . . I fought them only with my swords. The fire, that was them.'

'You mean to suggest they burnt their own school?'

'Yes. To kill me. They wanted to kill me. Or it was an accident, or they . . .'

'The Yoshioka? The most dignified men in the city turned to arson?'

'Lies – look how proud you are. You set the flame.'

'Child killer.'

'They challenged me. They chose to fight me. And I won. For you.'

'My grandfather helped raise that dojo hall.'

'My grandfather tiled it.'

'What if the entire city had caught alight? Would you still have cause to smile then?'

'The little boy, look at him, there's his head in the sand.'

The fire guards had lost their hesitancy now, the voices growing in number and in volume. Musashi stopped trying to answer, simply looked between their faces.

He thought of vessels, and of cups.

He rose to his feet, and his motion silenced them. They thought him lethal still, though he was barely able to walk, the effort of each step immense. He forced himself forward. The men stepped out of his path, watched him as he fumbled for his swords where they had fallen. Gore was scabbed upon them both. Still filthy, he slid them into their scabbards and then headed for the courtyard, away from here, away from them.

The men followed after him, keeping their distance, stepping in time to his feeble pace.

'Butcher,' said someone.

'Arsonist.'

Through the ruins of the compound they went, past corpses, some burnt, some spared incineration and draped in the colour of tea still. Blood had dried ugly like the shadows of vines upon the paving stones.

'Child killer.'

'Demon.'

Through the courtyard and the bodies there, the braziers all burnt out, filled now with white ash. The gate was gone, no sign of it all, burnt entirely or pulled down and dragged away. The street outside was frantic with dozens of men, teams carrying hooked ropes, ladders, mallets, saws, implements of all sorts. They looked exhausted, their desperate work having been to create the isolating space around what had been the Yoshioka compound now.

Not all of them wore the bright jackets of the fire guard. Not all of them were lowerborn: Musashi saw a multitude of Tokugawa samurai in their dark livery and their topknots scattered throughout the crowd, either helping with the labour itself or directing it. Nearby a helmeted officer stood conferring with a subordinate, this samurai having of all things an unstrung longbow resting across his shoulders.

One of the fire guards ran up to the officer as soon as he saw him.

'Sir samurai,' he said, bowing and then pointing at Musashi, 'it's him that did it. We found him in there. He killed the Yoshioka. He set the fire. He's an arsonist. Take him!'

'He's a child killer!' said another.

'Murderer!'

The clamour began now, now that there were other armed men here to protect them, and the firemen soon were shouting their disgust, and the other lowerborn in the street took up the cry. Musashi stood in the centre of them, felt it all pass through him.

'That's him. That's Miyamoto,' said the samurai with the longbow.

The officer gave a gesture with his chin and a third samurai came forward. He bore a tool of suppression, a wide and blunted prong upon a spear shaft. The samurai lowered it and Musashi had no energy to try to fight the man, to even go for his swords. He just watched it coming, watched as the samurai thrust it forward.

The pain of the steel meeting the wound on his chest was such that Musashi was senseless before his back met the earth.

Musashi awoke in a familiar cell in the Tokugawa garrison. How long he had spent there he did not know. He slept, and how good it was to sleep again, uncaring of the heat or the worry. He got the impression that days were passing, and that perhaps the sleep was not always of his own volition, and this he had no quarrel with.

He found the straw beneath him replaced with proper bedding at some point, a thick mat and a pillow filled with dried beans. Men came in often to see him, old men with firm hands who looked down on him with concern. A different man each time, changing the dressing upon his wounds – Musashi was several torpid times surprised anew to find himself bound in bandages, his body washed of all filth and blood – and as these men worked Musashi remembered looking down between their ministrations and seeing his bared chest rent, a white gummy fluid there in the chasm of the wound, and feeling a mild and distant nausea.

But it passed, it all passed, and soon the sleep became less deep, the throbbing and itching upon his ribs relented, and then he awoke to the sound of drums.

They were distant, many of them pounding out different beats converging together, a mess of pulses. Musashi lay listening to them, needing some time before he could distinguish them from his heartbeat. Eventually he decided to sit up. When the dizziness passed he looked down to find himself naked save for the bandages wrapped around his chest. The mat beneath him was damp with sweat, stank of it. Soaked through, ruined.

There was a basin of water and a cup nearby. He drank, and then ate one of a couple of satsumas that lay within a bowl. The taste of the fruit was so sharp it hurt his tongue, but he devoured it all the same.

The door of the wooden cage was open, he saw. Outside he found a pile of fresh clothes, and both his swords in their scabbards.

On the drums played. The sound of them was fully revealed to him when he found his way out into the courtyard. The halls of the garrison had been all but empty, and those men that were there had taken no interest in him. On he had shuffled until he had emerged here. Ahead, standing beneath the frame of the gate and looking out into the street, Musashi saw Goemon.

Beyond the captain there was vivid motion: bright clothes, fans twirling in unison, the brilliant gold leaf upon a shrine being hoisted up on shoulders. The Regent's festival was well under way and the parading would not stop until the sun went down. The noise of it, all the different chants, all the different drumbeats, the rattling of chimes and bells, the cheers, the joy, it checked Musashi for a moment, he the recent inhabitant of a world of numbed senses. He stood, took it in, took in the feel of sunlight, the way his new clothes felt, the cloth of the dark trousers and jacket tough yet woven finely.

It all felt good.

He gathered his strength that he might walk across the intervening space without stumbling, then forced his way towards Goemon. As he crossed the yard he recognized the obsidian ridged boulder across which Tadanari had died. A name had been carved into it: Kiyomori Onodera. Sombre characters and this perhaps a capstone for a crypt.

The captain did not turn at Musashi's coming. In one hand he held a paper windmill, a toy made of folded brightly coloured paper pinned to a length of dowel. He showed it happily to Musashi when he drew alongside.

'Do you see this?' he said. 'A child who lives just up the street made it for me.'

He seemed truly delighted with it. Musashi said nothing, put a hand out onto the beams of the gateway for support.

The wood there was new, set bright against the old beneath it, felt coarse and recently planed to the touch. The pair of them watched the parade pass slowly before them, a large shrine advancing, borne aloft by at least forty men, they seesawing it back and forth between them.

'*Hwaja!*' went the men on the left as they raised their end.

'*Hoja!*' went the men on the right, and on and on it went back and forth.

'Wonderful, isn't it,' said Goemon, 'when so much planning comes together?'

'Isn't it just,' said Musashi.

'How heals your wound?'

'Haven't looked at it. Doesn't hurt.'

'Your nose is crooked now.'

Musashi grunted, sucked air through it to prove it functioned still.

'You should know that you were very near death. Most of the doctors who tended upon you said you would perish.'

'I suppose I owe you for their payment?'

'No.'

'Why would that be?'

'My most noble Lord is benevolent. He appreciates bravery, and admires martial feats.'

'Of course.'

'And quite a feat it was. How many men did you fell, exactly?'

'I don't know. More than twenty. Perhaps.'

'So casually, he speaks of his great victory.'

Musashi turned his eyes to the captain, looked at him blackly for a moment. There were many things he could have said to him on the subject of victory, but instead he looked back to the parade, spoke with cold mirth: 'So rigidly you speak in the Kyoto tongue.'

'It grows natural.'

'Am I to be charged with arson?'

'You already have been.'

'Yet I walk free of my gaol unchallenged.'

'You misunderstand – the Shogunate of my most noble Lord lays no accusation against you,' said Goemon. 'It is the city itself that has declared you guilty. There is no doubt in them whatsoever. They, however, possess no gaol, save for their scorn.'

'And the one they themselves live in.'

'Perhaps, perhaps,' said Goemon. 'What is a city but its people?'

The comment was oblique and Musashi did not understand Goemon's apparent enjoyment of saying it. 'Am I free to go, then?' he said.

'Yes. I thought today best. No one will notice your departure, not with all this occurring. There will be no outcry, no disturbance. No one will demand me for your head. Though some of them may soon realize you are gone, in time they will forget, and Kyoto will be as Kyoto ought.'

The shrine had moved on, and now men bearing taiko drums between them on a yoke were cavorting, swinging each other around and around, all but flipping over, banging out their beat synchronous and unfailing. Their clothes were bright and garish, white zigzags over citric yellow, heads bound in twisted lengths of rope, arms bare save for tasselled bands.

'If they demanded my head of you,' said Musashi, 'would you give it?'

'It would be injustice. The Yoshioka challenged you. You have committed no crime.'

'Suppose, then, I said I did set a fire in the school. Suppose I confessed. Would you believe that it was my hand that caused the blaze?'

He was looking very closely now at Goemon. The samurai did not turn his face. His eyes appeared to narrow, but lost none of their mirth.

'I could see why people might think it arson,' said Musashi. 'The fire rose quickly. The incident, the fight was not long. A matter of minutes from first to last. And yet by the end of it buildings at either end of the school were ablaze. As though it had not spread from one point outwards.'

'The destruction was entire,' said Goemon.

'I recall that there were lights in the air that night. I thought them exhaustion, tricks of the eye. But those lights that lie within the eye, they rise upwards on an erratic path, or have no path at all. Thinking back now, the lights there in the school, they each followed the same direction, unwavering. A downwards arc. Like the path of arrows.'

The crowd was clapping along. The beat was relentless. Only the two of them remained immune to it. Goemon's expression did not alter.

'Was I even supposed to survive in this scheme of yours?' Musashi asked.

Not a flicker upon the captain's face.

'And what of Ameku?'

'Ameku?'

'The blind woman in the slums,' said Musashi. 'I was told that she was dead by the hands of the Yoshioka, saw blood. And yet, Kozei . . . all of them, all of the Yoshioka there, never once tried to taunt me about it. They hated me. Utterly. But not one mention of her.'

'Was she a lover of yours?'

'What does that matter?' said Musashi. 'She was innocent. She was blind.'

'Indeed.'

'Is she truly dead?' said Musashi. 'Did you kill her?'

'Do you believe that I would have her killed?' said Goemon, and his face grew serious, turned to face Musashi.

'Did you kill her, for the sake of an illusion?'

'Whatever I say is irrelevant here,' said Goemon. 'You will believe as you believe. And if you believe that I had her killed, I have returned both your swords to your side, and there are far fewer than twenty of my men here.'

He held Musashi's eyes, stood up to the challenge of them. Dignity in his indignation, a proper samurai face. If it was an act, it was flawless. Musashi relented. Goemon smiled once more.

'Thank you for your faith,' he said. 'It was an agent of mine that spoke to you, smashed her loom. Pig's blood, I do believe he used. The blind woman is well. She is headed for Edo now. The little girl too. The Nishijin guild are opening a branch there, looking for hundreds to work their looms. She carries with her a sincere recommendation from the Shogunate that she be hired.'

'And she just went?' said Musashi, and immediately he thought to himself, *Of course she would go*.

The captain saw the change in him: 'If you like, I could arrange for you to meet her there.'

Musashi thought about it.

'No,' he said eventually.

And that was all he would say. He prepared to let go of the beam of the gate, gathered his strength that he might not show weakness before the captain. He was interrupted, however, by sudden barking from behind him.

Musashi clung on to the frame, turned to look back. Across the yard was a small wooden side gate, a yard within the yard, and it was rattling in its own frame as a dog on the other side of it attacked it savagely. Barking and barking, the sound of frantic scratching, and the creature would not relent. Goemon left Musashi and went over to the gate and unhooked the latch.

A little mangy mongrel pushed its way out through Goemon's legs, squeezed its lithe body through the sliver of the opening, so desperate for its victory that it could not wait for it to open fully. The dog's hide was rotten and it was missing an ear. It ran a few paces out, looked around, scratched at the earth . . .

And then immediately it went back to where it had come from.

Goemon sighed in fond amusement. He closed the door and reset the latch, and returned to Musashi's side. 'I give it all it needs in there. Food. Water. Shade. But still it has to struggle to escape.' The captain settled to lean on the frame opposite Musashi. 'That is the nature of dogs, though, is it not?' he said. 'They are creatures of complete immediacy. Each and every moment, a dog feels as separate and infinite. What it feels then it feels fully. A dog that howls in loneliness has been alone for ever and will always be alone . . . Until it is not.'

Passing before the pair of them on the street a troupe of women danced, women and girls, elaborate wooden crowns on their heads, paper fans twirling in their hands.

'Dogs are like this in all things,' said Goemon. 'Unending love – ended. Boundless rage – evaporated. Or that dog – it fights and it fights and it scratches up against the gate with all its heart, white-eyed and slavering at its boards, even though it hasn't even the slightest conception of what may lie on the other side. All it knows is that it stands, and that this must not be. And then the gate is opened and it gets there, and . . .

'I suppose there's something to admire in that. The totality of it. Honesty, you might call it, or some form of it. But ultimately?' said the captain, and he looked out across the festival, across the street, across the city, across it all. 'This is a dishonest world.'

Goemon turned his eyes to Musashi. Musashi looked back. At his topknots. At his livery. At his swords.

He felt no hatred.

The swordsman sucked in a breath, let go of the gate of the garrison of the Tokugawa. He was done there. He forced himself to stride, headed for the street.

'Miyamoto,' Goemon called after him.

He turned. The captain was holding out a folded sheaf of paper towards him.

'Papers of travel. My most noble Lord is erecting checkpoints upon the roads. These will see you through upon his authority.'

Musashi thought of ignoring him, of walking away, but what would one more empty gesture atop of all the others achieve? He reached out to take them, and as his fingers closed upon them Goemon held on for a moment:

'You should not be dispirited,' the captain said. 'In truth, you did enact change here: you took Kyoto from the Yoshioka, and awarded it to us.'

He grinned, and Musashi could not tell if the smile was mocking or whether it was simply joyous. The captain released the papers. Musashi slipped them into the breast of his kimono. Without another word he turned and stepped onto the streets, slid amongst the crowd and did not look back.

Goemon watched Musashi go, the back of his head visible above the crowd, and the captain could not remove the smile upon his face. The parade, the festival went on before him, and he saw the crowds, saw the faces of all the people of Kyoto, old and young and men and women, all together here, all in order.

He remembered the paper windmill in his hand, looked at the bright blue spokes unmoving. He suddenly wanted to see it in motion, raised the toy above his head, above the crowd, sought the deserved wind that would come to caress the sweat from his body. Up he stared, saw the shade of the paper matched the cloudless sky exact, and wondered if this was perhaps a sign, if this thing he held somehow was actually a totem of nature perfectly attuned, if it was not summoning now, and he stared and stared, certain it was imminent . . .

Of course it remained still. There was no breeze, weeks of the summer left yet. But that was fine, that was more than fine, for Goemon Inoue no longer needed mercy. He could bear the heat now. He had learnt to bear it.

He spun the spokes with his finger and smiled as if he were back in Mutsu.

Epilogue

Kyoto, golden Kyoto.

See it thrive, see its beauty, its streets now swept, its buildings cleaned and polished and arrayed in streamers, frail gay paper hung from the web-scoured eaves made of wood enamelled by time. See the people as they dance, teams of women, scores of them with their fans ever moving, rotating, they sweating and smiling and ever diligent to follow the exact steps their grandmothers danced. See the men with the shrines upon their shoulders, or see them up balancing upon the beams of the yokes themselves, riding the shaking of those below like mariners in a storm, the glimmering and impassive faces of Buddhas and Shinto wisps staring outwards beyond them. See the drums in their multitude, hear them.

The right hand beats the rhythm: *bom, a-bom, a-bombombom.*

The left hand beats the urgency: *atta-ta-tatta, ta-tatta, tatata-atta-ta-tatta.*

The girls all go: *Sore! Sore! Sore sore sore sore sore!*

And they were flawless in their rhythm, all of them together, but it was not his rhythm, Musashi knew now.

The narrow streets were crowded. He made his way along squeezing between the back of the crowd and the walls of buildings. Those that turned to him turned only when he brushed up against them, and dismissed him just as quickly, captivated by the spectacle of the festival. On he passed unnoticed.

Victory a barren word in his mouth. He had overcome, had triumphed, had passed what he had thought the great trial of his conviction, and yet it was no trial at all. Even the simple thrill of its accomplishment had been denied him; that great rush of wellbeing that made his soul sing usurped by exhaustion and pain.

He thought of Ameku, of her words.

The wooden jaws of the costumes of tigers and dragons snapped and flapped and chased each other, chased their tails, the legs of the men hidden beneath the serpentine silk body moving regimented and insect-like. A great gong was struck as people cried out the name of the Regent, he seven years dead, and as the peal of it scintillated into nothing its reverberation within himself revealed to Musashi his hollowness.

What had been certain he now realized to be vapour. His sky for the past years now benighted unto nothingness. He felt betrayal and then failure that at the age of twenty the meaning of existence yet eluded him.

And yet there was no anger.

Not at himself, not at Goemon, not at the world. It had gone. The thing that had driven him since Sekigahara had turned to smoke and fled him in the ruins of the Yoshioka compound. Bled out into the sand, perhaps. He wondered what was left inside of him in the wake of this great sublimation.

What was left before him to achieve?

Through the penumbrae of pagodas and the seething sides of crowds he forced his way onwards. The crowd around him only seemed to grow, slowing his progress with its whims. He found himself pinned up against the balustrade of a canal, looked down into it, remembered plummeting into one. The water was shallow, shadow-patterns of the surface rippling over the cobblestones.

How effortlessly it all flowed.

At his side, as always, were his swords. Unyielding and tangible. He looked at them, and he knew that he could not return home yet. That he could not yet look his uncle in the eye. But of the swords, the long and the short? He knew their extent, and they his. However dubious or minuscule the worth of what it was he had achieved, he had achieved it because of the blades. These the things with which he had spoken the keenest.

Worthy of trust. Of dedication.

Musashi forced his way along to the nearest set of stone stairs and descended into the bed of the canal. The water was cool upon his calves. He revelled in the space free of the press of people, breathed it in, felt his lungs brush up against the wound at his side. The water tugged at his trousers, pulled the wide folds of them downstream. Musashi watched their billowing, saw the direction of the gentle current. The canal would lead to a river, and the river would lead away.

He followed.

On he went, left Kyoto behind him. That which was venerated remained venerated and that which was burnt remained burnt. Over his shoulder all the temples and pagodas and palaces, so many great and towering constructs of man. The vast bronze shells of century-blackened sanctified bells that tolled impermanence in dolorous swells. Coils of incense curling before ten thousand aureate idols and icons, rising in ephemeral arcane patterns that would never be again and yet in the method and reason of their creation exist for ever unchanging.

Not far from him, yet the distance unknown and unbridgeable, a long and slender boat set out upon the river heading for Osaka and the docks there, all aboard bound ultimately for Edo; a bald head in a salt-lined casket, and a young girl's smile offered upwards as a whalebone comb parts her hair, a smile unseen but felt and known.

Over the noise of unfelt festival rhythms that pulse upon the surfaces of great vats of soy sauce and sake and set rings to destroying rings, a dog is barking.

It is a mongrel of a mangy tan hide, with but a single ear remaining, and the sole obsession of this dog is the gate that bars it inside. The dog scratches furiously at it, black eyes rimmed white. The gate is iron and oak. It will not yield. But the dog is up against it, fighting it, barking and barking and barking.

This is the nature of dogs.

Before the man lies nothing now. Musashi's eyes only forward, only at the world that lies ahead wide and empty. He as one with the course of the water, flowing onwards, ever onwards, and then he is gone.

つづく

'The world is as it is. Blind rebellion against it solves nothing.'

First precept of *Dokkodo* (*The Way of Walking Alone*)

Musashi Miyamoto, 1645

Acknowledgements

Thanks and gratitude to the following:

John Drake, for providing information about gunpowder and arquebuses of the era.

Shitsuo Tanaka, for showing me around her home, Mount Hiei.

Adam Mackie, for telling me the difference between a gyaku ude-gatame and an omoplata/omniplatter, even if it was subsequently cut out of the novel.

Takumi Otomo, for her beautiful calligraphy.

And lastly,

Ayako Sato, for everything.